WITHERED + SERE

TJ KLUNE

BOATK Books

Copyright © 2019 by TJ Klune

Cover art by B4jay

Second edition

ISBN: 978-1-7342339-5-7

Withered + Sere

Once upon a time, humanity could no longer contain the rage that swelled within, and the world ended in a wave of fire.

One hundred years later, in the wasteland formerly known as America, a broken man who goes only by the name of Cavalo survives. Purposefully cutting himself off from what remains of civilization, Cavalo resides in the crumbling ruins of the North Idaho Correctional Institution. A mutt called Bad Dog and a robot on the verge of insanity comprise his only companions. Cavalo himself is deteriorating, his memories rising like ghosts and haunting the prison cells.

It's not until he makes the dangerous choice of crossing into the irradiated Deadlands that Cavalo comes into contact with a mute psychopath, one who belongs to the murderous group of people known as the Dead Rabbits. Taking the man prisoner, Cavalo is forced not only to face the horrors of his past, but the ramifications of the choices made for his stark present. And it is in the prisoner that he will find a possible future where redemption is but a glimmer that darkly shines.

The world has died.
This is the story of its remains.

For Sam, Abi, Ely, and Erika:
You guys are weird, abnormal and strange,
and your faces make me happy.

Alas, the time of the most despicable man is coming,
he that is no longer able to despise himself.
Behold, I show you the *last man*.
~~Nietzsche *Thus Spoke Zarathustra*

seven words

ONCE UPON A TIME, humanity could no longer contain the rage that swelled within, and the world ended in a wave of fire.

But before this happened, there was a great and powerful man. One day, so very different than all the days that had come before, he sat in his office and wondered how it would feel to burn to death.

It was cold, this thought. But not because he was a cold man—he wasn't. Not really. No, this great and powerful man was practical. Analytical. He would not have gotten to be where he was without these traits. Though, in that evil known as hindsight, he wondered if this had not been a mistake. It was difficult to know, and he knew he would never have the answer. History often judged the actions of others, but now, there would not *be* a history to bring judgment. Not of the human kind.

He wondered if it would be quick, that first wave of fire. He wondered if there was anywhere his people could hide. If there was any place they could run. He thought not. He didn't think it would matter even if there were. His advisors had already told him there wasn't enough time. The grim looks on their faces had told him that, at least in this matter, they spoke the truth.

They had begged him to leave. They had begged him to go to ground. *You must!* they argued. *People will need you after what is to come! They will need someone to look up to if we are to survive!* But even in their pleadings, he could hear the defeat in their voices. The resolve breaking. They knew as well as him. He saw it in their eyes, the way they had dulled. The humanity was gone. The spark. And the great and powerful man knew that once the spark had died, there was nothing left to hope for.

Even if he'd done as they'd asked, it would have only been post-poning what was to come. Others had arrived in his office with their projections of total loss of life. Their maps, covered in red. Their dire warnings. *There must be a way to stop this*, they said. *There must be a way for this to end peacefully.* But they too had seen the images of the destruction of London. Of Dubai. São Paulo. Sydney.

San Francisco.

Las Vegas.

Phoenix.

Seattle.

They had all seen the explosions, sun-bright. The fires that followed. The burnt husks of people flash-frozen into ash. Their arms hiding children. The way they cowered. Millions gone in no more than seconds. Everyone in the room had seen, and their words were hollow.

The great and powerful man noticed one of the scientists had yet to say a word. This quiet man was balding, almost lost to fat. He wiped away a sheen of sweat from his forehead with white-knuckled hands and looked down at his lap.

What do you think? the great and powerful man asked, raising his voice to override the conversation in the room.

All fell quiet.

The fat scientist sighed.

Well? the great and powerful man snapped. *We haven't got all day.*

Bernard Russell, the fat scientist said.

What?

Bernard Russell. He was a British mathematician. He—

I know who he is! the great and powerful man interrupted. *I don't need a goddamn history lesson!* He could hear the underlying hysterics in his own voice. He had to calm himself.

The fat scientist sighed again. He looked up at the men and women in the room around him before settling his gaze on the great and powerful man. *Yes,* he said. *You do. We all do. Bernard Russell once said that war does not determine who is right. Only who is left.*

The great and powerful man stared as the room erupted around him in jeers and cries of anger. Of derision. *Moralistic bullshit,* a five-star general sneered. *We take them out, and we take them out now!*

We don't even know who they *are,* said the Secretary of Defense.

It doesn't matter. We bomb the whole region. A flyswatter is better at killing bugs than a bullet.

More cries erupted, but the great and powerful man only had eyes for the fat scientist. The fat scientist did not look away.

What do you think we should do? the great and powerful man asked the scientist, his words almost lost in the roar around him.

Now? the fat scientist asked.

The great and powerful man nodded. *Now.*

Now, the fat scientist said, *you explain why.*

To who?

Everyone. You owe them that much. They need to know. For those who are left when the dust settles, if it ever will. They need to know what we did. That we should have done more. That it is too late for us now. The fat scientist wiped the sweat from his brow. *They need to know so it won't happen again.*

I don't.... I.... I wouldn't know how to start, the great and powerful man said.

The fat scientist leaned forward as the voices rose in argument around him. *I think you do,* he said.

Eventually they all left, and the great and powerful man wondered how it would feel to burn to death.

At first, he knew the air would begin to heat. It would suddenly become hard to breathe, the hot air stifling and filled with carbon. The hairs on his arms and the back of his neck would rise up and then start to curl. His eyelashes would singe. All the air would be sucked from around him and a great wall of irradiated fire would rise over him and his eyes and his tongue and his fingernails would burst into flames and all thought would cease. This would all be over.

The great and powerful man wondered if that was for the best. *We are doomed*, he thought darkly, *to repeat ourselves*. He remembered from his childhood, in that great haze before his mother died, hearing her voice as she read him *Peter Pan*. He remembered the story as a frightening thing, a wicked tale of lost boys and of never having parents. He hadn't thought of her or the story in years, but now her voice rose in his mind as she read for him the story: *All of this has happened before, and all of it will happen again.*

He covered his eyes.

The door to his office opened and he heard the patter of little feet, the cry of a sweet voice saying *Daddy*, shouting, *Daddy!* He wiped away the moisture from his eyes and smiled as his daughter ran around his desk, her pigtails stretched out behind her, twisting. She leapt into his lap, and he circled his arms around her. He felt her heart beat against his chest and knew then all that would be lost.

Okay, Daddy? she asked, reaching out to touch his nose.

Okay, darling, he said, though he lied.

You cry? She sounded concerned.

No, he reassured her. *No.*

Is it bad? his wife asked from the door. He saw the way her hands trembled.

Yes, he said. He kissed his daughter on her forehead. She laughed. High and free. Like bells.

Is there time?

He thought about pretty words like he'd given his daughter but decided against it. Somehow, she would know. *Not enough*, he said.

His wife nodded, as he knew she would. The wife of the great and powerful man was great in her own right. He remembered when they'd first met. He'd asked her for a light, outside the law library on campus. She didn't smoke. He was in love. She laughed at him. They married four months later against their parents' wishes. *She isn't WASP-ish enough*, his parents had said. *He's a goddamn conservative!* her parents had cried. It didn't matter. The heart wants what it wants.

What do we do? his wife asked him now as she moved away from the door.

The selfish part of him wanted them to stay with him. That if he couldn't go, at least he'd be surrounded by his family. But that is not who he was. It never had been. He knew the captain stayed with the ship until the very end. His wife and daughter shouldn't have to pay for his mistakes, even though they might still when it came down to it.

You two will be taken to the bunker, he said. *There's hope there. There's a chance.* He told himself he believed his words. He did. He had to. He knew it had all escalated too fast.

And you? she asked, her voice hardening. He knew that tone. He'd heard it many times before. *What about you?*

I have to stay, he said.

Stay where, Daddy? his daughter asked.

He looked away from his angry wife toward his daughter. *I have to stay here. I have to talk to the people again.*

In the camera?

Yes. In the camera.

His daughter thought on this a moment, her forehead lined in concentration. *I stay with you?* she finally asked.

He shook his head as he tried to breathe past the lump in his throat. *No. You'll go with Mommy.*

Where?

Someplace safe.

There were more words. How could there not be? There are always more words. Always more time to say things that don't matter rather than the things that do. There was anger from his wife, and harsh things were said. She begged him to go with them. She cried, even though he could tell she was trying not to. She had always hated crying. Tears did nothing. They resolved nothing. She wiped them away with the backs of her hands as her voice cracked. She shook her head. She bunched her hands into fists to stop them from shaking.

Their daughter looked up at both of them with wide eyes. She started crying because her mother was. She started screaming when men burst into the room saying they had to go, *they had to go!* His daughter reached for him, but she was pulled away even as their fingers touched, and for the rest of his life (a time that was shorter than even *he* knew) he would remember the grazing of his daughter's skin against his own. That last touch, that last moment he ever saw his daughter, his daughter, who he sometimes made laugh by scrunching up his face into weird shapes. His daughter who would put carrot sticks between his teeth and lips, and he'd pretend to be a walrus. His daughter, whose toenails were painted green and blue and red because she *loved* those colors, Daddy, she just *needed* them all at the same time. His daughter, who he held at night when the bad dreams came, telling her there was no such thing as monsters. That last little moment when their fingers touched would stay with him in the days he had left. This great and powerful man, this *father*, had no way of knowing that his daughter would live for only fifteen more days, his wife holding his little girl, telling her to shut her eyes, to just shut her eyes and think of *Daddy, Daddy, Daddy*, as the bunker they were in shook and eventually collapsed under the weight of a falling mountain.

But now? Now, their fingers touched for a brief moment and then she was pulled away. Now, his daughter screamed. Now, his wife shouted and struggled to escape strong arms that engulfed her. And now, the great and powerful man hung his head and did nothing as they were whisked away.

THE GREAT AND POWERFUL MAN STOOD BY HIMSELF IN A

deserted hallway, staring out a window. He could still hear the screams of his family echoing through his mind. He shook his head, trying to force them away. He had made his choice. He had to focus.

He remembered a time, shortly before his daughter was born and before he'd become great and powerful. He and his wife had walked next to a river he could no longer remember the name of. It had been springtime, and the trees were flowering. His wife, heavy with their first child (*First of four*, she would remind him constantly, often filling his head with visions of tiny tornadoes made of little hands and feet), smiled as he plucked an iris from near the bank of the river and placed it behind her ear. *I'm going to win*, he'd told her.

She watched him for a moment before rising on her tiptoes and pressing a brief kiss to his chin. *I know.*

The relief he had felt was palpable. *You do?*

She'd laughed. *Yes. I knew, even when it was just a dream spoken aloud in the middle of the night. When we joked about such things. I still knew.*

Even then?

Even then. You will do good things, my love. Wonderful things.

He'd gathered her up carefully in his arms and held her close.

And now, in the deserted hallway, he wished he'd never begun.

Wonderful things. I still knew.

A young man appeared through a doorway and cleared his throat. The great and powerful man glanced over at him. He held a sheaf of paper in his hands, gripping so tightly the edges wrinkled. One of his speechwriters. A newer one. He couldn't remember his name. Not that it mattered.

I have this for you, the young man stammered.

The great and powerful man waved him away. *Not today.*

B-but… sir?

You know how to start, the fat scientist whispered in his head.

And he did. He knew what needed to be said.

I won't be needing that, the great and powerful man said.

The young man appeared unsure. He turned to leave but stopped before he could take a step. *Sir?*

The great and powerful man looked out the window again. The sun was setting. On so many things. *Yes?*

Will... will it be okay?

What? He heard his daughter's laughter in his ear.

Everything. The young man's voice broke.

The great and powerful man turned to look at the young man whose name he could not remember. *One day,* he said, and out of all the lies he'd told himself in the last months, maybe even years, this was the one he chose to believe the most. *One day. One day someone, and I don't know who, but someone will say enough. A line will be drawn, and there will come an hour that we will rise and say we've had enough. That we won't take the darkness any longer. That we will say no. That we will fight against those who would break us. We will fight back, and in this hour, we will have succeeded in what we have set out to do.*

The young man's eyes were wide. *Is that day today?* he asked quietly.

The great and powerful man deflated and looked nothing more than a normal man. *No,* he said quietly. *It's not today. You should leave. While you can.*

Will it matter?

I don't know. Probably not.

Your wife. Your daughter.

Yes?

They... they won't... we won't....

No. We won't.

The young man left and did not look back.

THE GREAT AND POWERFUL MAN SAT AT HIS DESK, A GROUP OF people, cameras pointed at him. He watched as a woman pointed at him and counted down with her fingers.

5.

I know what to say, he thought.

4.

It's what they need to hear.

3.

It's what they should hear.

2.

It's the only thing I have left to give.

1.

The lights above the camera went on. The group in front of him watched and waited. A bead of sweat trickled down the back of his neck. He touched his wedding ring. He looked up and directly into the camera.

And said seven words.

As those seven words spread across the globe, bouncing instantly along the airwaves to billions and billions of pairs of eyes and ears, there was a moment when it seemed all the world held its breath. Upon hearing the seven words, they all exhaled as one and began to break down, because those seven words meant much. They meant sorrow. They meant relief, as darkly cold as it was. They meant nothing and everything, and as they echoed and became waves that drifted off into space to travel for as long as the universe was old, they carried with them a beginning that would signal the end of the world as they knew it, brought down on a wave of greed and anger. Of betrayal and power. Of selfishness. Of terror.

Of fire.

And that is how civilization fell. The bombs dropped. Cities collapsed. Billions of people died in a matter of months. A button was pushed again. And again. And again. And again until there was no one left to push the button.

In those weeks and months that followed, miles above Earth, satellites drifted darkly around the planet, the land below ablaze, large columns of smoke catching in the atmosphere and stretching out into long tails. The satellites would spin for as long as Earth maintained its pull of gravity, but they would no longer function. They no longer transmitted to the scarred and pocked world below. They no longer moved except with the flow of the earth. They were dead.

But far off into space, transmissions carried, bouncing radio-frequency waves that crashed and collided with the universe. And out of all the unfathomable number, there was one that began with seven words. Seven words said by a man who died two hours after speaking them when a suitcase nuke exploded forty feet away from the helicopter he was boarding in an attempt to join his wife and daughter. In the end, he never learned what it felt like to burn as he wasn't even aware he had died when the blast hit him. His last thought was *I hope I come back here to*—and then he was gone. There was nothing left of him but his seven words. And they carried long after the whole of humanity became nothing more than a thing of the past in a future of chaos.

God forgive us for what we've done.

a wind has blown the rain away and blown the sky away and all the leaves,

and the trees stand. I think i too have known autumn too long

—e.e. cummings

blood trail

A MAN MOVED through the stunted trees. His footsteps were soft, each step deliberately chosen. He stopped for a moment, cocking his head. Listening. Waiting. A heavy breeze blew through the bare branches of the trees. They rattled together like bones. It didn't bother him as it once had.

The man heard nothing more and took another step. He adjusted the strap to the oak bow over his shoulder. He thought about the sun hiding behind the leaden gray clouds above. It had been a while since he'd seen it. It had been a while since he'd seen the sky behind the clouds.

The man known only as Cavalo moved through the trees, unaware that it was his fortieth birthday. Even if he'd known, he wouldn't have given it a passing thought. He thought little of such things now. They were frivolous things. Things meant for the towns. Not for him.

Maybe part of him knew, but it was suppressed. Buried. Like the sky. Like the sun. He was aware of things, sure. The weight of the pack on his back, a quiver of arrows sewn at the side. Dark feathers attached to the ends of the shafts. The scrape of the heavy tunic against his thin chest. The dark stubble on his face, flecked with gray and itchy. A lock of hair against his ear, loose from the deer hide strap that held it back. The sharp, metallic scent in the air. His companion moving unseen thirty yards to his left. The weight of the old rifle hanging around his neck. It was rarely used. Bullets were precious things. Unusual things. He had many of them, collected over years. He tried not to use them if he could help it.

That didn't mean he hadn't before. He fired the rifle every now and then to make sure it still worked. Into a tree. He always dug out the bullets, the flat discs still hot in his hands. He'd done this twice a year since he'd been given the gun by his father at the age of sixteen. *It's a Remington,* his father had said, though when asked how he knew, his father had shrugged. *That's what I was told when it was given to me. See those markings at the top? A scope would have gone there. It helped you see things far away up close. Like those binocs that old Harold has. It's gone now. Have never been able to find one that fits when the trade caravans come through.*

His father had died just a few weeks later. Found in a ditch. Neck broken. Thrown from his horse as he rode home. The smell of rye whiskey still hung around him even as the flies began to land on his open eyes. *Accident,* the constable had told Cavalo when he came to deliver the news. *Just an accident. These things happen, you know.*

Cavalo had nodded and asked after the horse. It'd been found two miles away, grazing in a field. He later sold it for coin. Didn't get for it what he'd asked, but a horse that throws a rider was a hard sell, even if the rider had been drunk.

He'd left the town shortly after, the rifle on his shoulder.

Cavalo now had forty-seven discs.

But the shots into the trees hadn't been the only times he'd fired the rifle. There had been two others. Once to stop the charge of an angry bull elk he stumbled upon in the low hills to the north. Its eyes had been milky white with blindness, a deep froth pouring from its mouth. Irradiated. It hadn't made a sound when it charged, its accuracy frightening. Time had slowed for Cavalo, and even though his heart thudded like thunder in his chest, he'd moved slowly. Surely. The stock against his shoulder. Rifle cocked. Sights lined. Breath in. Breath out. Fired. The snap against his arm. The loud crack in the clearing. Spray of blood as the bullet pierced a white eye, an impossible shot that Cavalo couldn't do again even if he had millions of years and millions of bullets. The bull had come to a stop. Shuddered once. Twice. Fell over as it began to seize. Its tongue lolled from its mouth as blood dripped from its nose. Cavalo had stayed with it until it died, the massive chest rising one final time, followed by an exhale, followed by silence.

The man, much younger then, had sat near the bull, watching it for hours. Eventually night had begun to fall, and predators stirred, drawn by the smell of dead flesh. Cavalo had stood and walked away.

There had been one other time he'd fired the gun. But that didn't matter now. It was in the past. It brought ghosts. He didn't like the ghosts.

He'd had a handgun once too, but he didn't know what had happened to it. After.

He continued on now, listening.

He moved in between the trees, a thin figure, hidden as he passed them by, moving with an economic grace. His black boots were covered in alkaline dust. He had a puckered scar on his right temple, fingernails dark with grit. His face was weathered. Lined. Severe, it was said by others who whispered about the man with one name. All planes and angles. Grizzled. Worn.

But he cared not about such things.

Not anymore.

Moments later he pressed his hand against the trunk of a gnarled tree, the bark rough against his skin. He knew this tree by its shape, because it was *her* tree. It looked like her, or as much as a tree can look like a woman now dead and gone. The base was wide, like a dress. The trunk slimmed out as it rose and curved, like a torso. Branches swung out wide. Arms. The breeze carried through these branches and they waved, like it was dancing.

Like *she* was dancing.

He knew this tree because it was her tree, and for a moment, this man, this one-named Cavalo, let himself stop and drift, a thing he thought to be most useless. But even here, the coarse bark under his fingers turned to smooth cotton, and she wrapped her arms around his neck and they *danced*. He could hear the music swell, could smell the lilacs that were her scent, could hear her laugh in his ear, her husky voice as her words promised him things he'd never thought of before, and how they *swayed*. How they *moved*. The curve of her thigh. The whisper of her—

A chuffing noise, low, followed by a growl.

The man opened his eyes under a leaden sky, his hands upon a stark tree that was only a tree. There was no woman. She was gone. And had been for a long time.

Dammit, he thought. *I almost missed.*

He moved then, quicker than he looked to be able to do. Crouched low, dust kicked up behind him from the parched, cracked earth as he flashed between the deformed trees. He pursed his lips and blew out two quick breaths. The whistles that came were sharp and short. He didn't receive a response, but he didn't need one. He'd been heard. He knew. His companion would follow orders.

As he ran through the half-dead forest, he pulled the bow from its strap on his shoulder, the grip familiar in his hands. He reached back and pulled an arrow from the quiver. A bark came from off to his left and he stopped against a malformed spruce. He notched the arrow into the bow and waited.

It came a moment later, the light tap of hooves against the ground. The slap of branches. Rocks kicked. His companion would back off now to wait in case the prey escaped.

Through the trees ahead, Cavalo saw her. A doe, belly white and back brown. White spots on her sides. Little flecks of gold in the hairs. Tail raised as she slowed. Ears twitched. The doe sprayed urine as her head darted around. She would have looked normal had it not been for the two snouts on her face, one going left, the other right.

The dead third eye in the middle of her forehead. The fifth leg that hung uselessly from her stomach, obscene as it kicked weakly. She wasn't the worst he'd seen, not by far, but more often than not, the effects of what had happened in the Time Before, which had created the End and the New Beginning, were still felt every day. Were still seen every day, even a hundred years later.

The man who fancied himself a doctor in Cottonwood, the town closest to Cavalo's home, had told him it was due to the radiation, that it messed with the genetics even years after the End. *Seems safe enough to eat,* Hank had told him. *Any poison would have been bred out generations ago. Just doesn't look like much.*

It didn't. It looked foul. It was grotesque. But it was the closest thing to another living creature that Cavalo had seen in weeks aside from his companion, and the bread was hard as a rock now, the mush bland. If he took her, he could avoid a trip into Cottonwood, at least for a while. He could stay away from people. He could—

The doe snapped her head toward him, and he could see the muscles under her skin begin to tense. She crouched low toward the ground, ready to spring. Her fifth leg dragged along the dirt as it twitched. Cavalo could see the flies around her eyes, the curve of her neck, the hairs standing on end. He could hear his own breaths in his ears, low and harsh. The pull of the bowstring. The arrow between his fingers. The painted black feathers brushing his cheek. The subtle strain in his arm. He was getting older, and he could feel it in every part of his body. He was weaker now. Whip thin. Veins pronounced on his arms. Hands callused. The lines around his eyes like canyons.

And as he let the arrow go, he wondered how much longer he could last like this.

The feathers burned against his cheeks. The snap of the bow twanged in his ears. He might not have been as young as he used to be, but his eyesight had yet to fade, and he tracked the arrow as it flew through the trees. Before it hit, he knew it had flown true.

He'd aimed slightly high, anticipating the doe's sudden leap. As the muscles in her legs bunched, she rose into the air, preparing to flee the threat she felt hidden among the trees. She launched forward toward a clearing ahead. The arrow struck her in the neck. Blood pulsed around the wooden shaft. She jerked her head back, a string of saliva splattering onto a tree. She bleated as she pawed the ground. She stumbled once, twice, and then began to move away. The forest around them grew quiet as she began to die.

It was a good hit. Blood fell from her neck, spattering against the forest floor. She moved in staccato beats through the trees, each step costing her. She picked up speed. Her shoulder clipped a long hanging branch, and she almost collapsed. She shook her head, her eyes wild and frenzied. She moved again and disappeared.

The man took his time. He fastened the bow to his back. He looked back in the direction of the tree that danced like a woman. He shook his head.

He moved to where the doe had been shot. There, upon the dead leaves, upon the rotted floor, glistened the blood trail. He whistled once, a high-pitched two-syllable sound that carried north to his companion. The birds in the trees took it as the all clear to begin singing again. They whistled back at him. He started following the blood trail. She'd find someplace to die. Thick bushes. Maybe into one of the outcroppings in the hills. She wouldn't last long as she was bleeding out. It was early afternoon, but he needed as much time as he could get.

It was a minute later when a dark dog joined him. A mutt made up of blacks and grays, hair long and damp. Bone thin, like the man. He strode alongside Cavalo, coming up to just above the man's knees, his long tail flicking back and forth. The dog bent his head forward, sniffing at the blood. He chuffed in the back of his throat and looked up at Cavalo, grinning, eyes bright, the canine arrogance comfortably familiar. It almost made him forget the dancing tree.

"Good work," Cavalo said quietly, reaching down to stroke along a white patch of fur between Bad Dog's eyes, back up to his ears. Bad Dog knocked his forehead against the man's fingers and chuffed again. Cavalo heard Bad Dog's voice in his head saying, *Of course I did good. You did too.* What had started out years before as a way to combat the silence had turned into something the man considered real. He spoke and Bad Dog answered. He no longer questioned it.

"Won't get far," Cavalo said.

Bad Dog looked up at him, sniffing the air. *I know.*

"We'll follow the blood trail," the man said, even though it was obvious.

Bad Dog panted. *Yes. Yes.*

"It will be fine."

Yes. Yes.

After a moment: "I saw the tree again."

Bad Dog cocked his head. *Did you touch it again, MasterBossLord?*

"I don't know." This was a lie, and they both knew it.

Oh.

He hesitated, then said, "She danced." He didn't look at his friend.

Bad Dog bumped his hand. *She's not real.*

"I know."

She's gone. They're both gone.

"I know."

Do you?

The man could not answer.

THE DOE HAD MADE IT FARTHER THAN CAVALO WOULD HAVE thought. The blood trail led them to the edge of the woods. Beyond the stunted forest lay the remains of a massive old road, broken into pieces, chunks of black rock upended. Cavalo knew this was called a "freeway" in the Time Before. People used these roads for travel in motor cars. He'd seen the remains, the burnt-out husks of these motor cars, dead as the area around them. No one could remember how they worked, only that they had been. There had been rumors years ago that someone in the east had a working motorized car, but it had never appeared.

Long distances in such short time. It seemed impossible.

Now this freeway meant something different. It was a line. A division. One that was foolish to cross. To cross was to go west. To go west meant to enter the Deadlands.

Cavalo looked at the blood trail on the ground. Fresh drops at his feet. Away from the forest he knew.

Onto the freeway.

Across the freeway. Into the other side of the woods. West.

"Shit," he whispered.

Shit, Bad Dog agreed, sitting next to the man.

He couldn't just let the deer go. She was fat, which was surprising. Good, but surprising. Cavalo didn't think her pregnant, not with the deformities she had, but she had to have come from somewhere herself, so it was possible. But if she wasn't, it would be enough meat to last weeks. He could avoid the town. He could avoid the people. Hank and Alma would be worried about him, he knew, but he'd been gone for longer. What had it been now? Three months? It couldn't be that long, could it? They would understand. They always did.

"What do you think?" he asked.

Bad Dog rose from his haunches and sniffed at the blood again. *If we do it, we must be quick. Like the wind.*

"Yeah," Cavalo muttered. "Like the wind." He looked across the freeway again. It looked no different than the forest behind him. But it was different, he knew. Far different.

The first deer in weeks. Probably just over the road. Right into the tree line. "Probably already dead," the man said aloud. "Just waiting for us."

Dead, dead, dead, the dog said, rubbing against him.

"We get in and get out."

Like we were never there.

"They won't even know."

No one will. In and out.

"You ready?"

Bad Dog yipped and watered a dusty bush. *I pissed*, he said proudly. *That bush is mine. Now I'm ready.*

The man nodded. "Let's go." He hesitated only for a second....

... and stepped onto the freeway.

Bad Dog immediately followed, his toenails clicking against the broken road, nose to the ground against the blood trail. Cavalo looked from side to side, scanning the tree line ahead of him. The shadows were beginning to lengthen. Nothing moved among the trees aside from the birds, calling their songs as loudly as they did on the other side of the freeway. It looked the same. It looked exactly the same.

But it felt so very different.

The man felt it even as he put one foot in front of another. There was a chill here that had nothing to do with the mute sky overhead. It was darker, the trees more dense and stark. The air felt thicker, as if pressing into a barrier that shouldn't be crossed. He looked down and saw the blood trail, still bright and fresh. He looked back up into the woods, searching for movement.

Only the birds.

He stepped off the freeway and slid down the shallow bank. Bad Dog jumped down behind him, bumping into the back of Cavalo's legs. They almost fell.

Sorry, Bad Dog said, looking embarrassed.

"It's okay," he said quietly, adjusting his back. He tried not to think of the last time he'd crossed the freeway. It was almost impossible to do on this side. He could hear their voices, somewhere far off, calling for him, lost in the haze. The man named Cavalo believed his dog could speak to him and didn't know it was his fortieth birthday, but he most certainly did not believe in ghosts. Even if he could hear them.

Bad Dog went to the tree line, following the blood trail. He reached the trees and looked back at Cavalo, his tail still, ears perked. *Coming?* he asked, unaware of the other voices.

Which means they aren't real, the man thought. Sweat dripped down his forehead. He wiped it away. He thought of the bow. It didn't seem to be enough. Not with what was on this side of the woods. Not with what they could do.

He unclipped the rifle from his pack. It felt heavy in his hands. He checked the chamber. Loaded. Sight was clear. Safety off.

Bad Dog watched him, eyeing the gun warily. He did not like the noise that came from it. *Too loud,* he said, flattening his ears. *Hate the boomstick. Hate it. Hate it.*

Cavalo nodded. "Can't be helped. Not this time."

Bad Dog sighed but said nothing. He turned and trotted into the trees.

They aren't real, the man thought, because he didn't believe in ghosts.

He followed the dog into the woods.

the other side of the woods

BAD DOG LED the way through the other side of the woods, head bent low, tail rigid behind him. The blood trail fattened, as if the wound had torn, and the doe was losing blood more quickly. Cavalo knew it would be soon, and was thankful. It meant they wouldn't have to venture far.

The rifle felt hot in his hands as he followed Bad Dog, eyes kept toward the forest floor, searching for signs of any traps. The birds were loud. So very loud, like there were thousands of them. Millions. All screeching. Warning them away. *Don't come here!* they screamed. *You know you're not supposed to be here! They will* find *you. They will* see *you.*

Cavalo wished the birds would quiet. They hurt his head. They distracted him. But at least they covered the voices he knew weren't real.

Bad Dog didn't seem to notice. Cavalo admired him for that.

A minute turned into five, then ten, and the man grew warier the farther into the woods they went. The trees were denser here and more gnarled. Man and dog stepped over fallen logs and engorged roots. Branches clung to clothes and cut flesh. The ground grew soft,

28

and Cavalo could see hoofprints in the dirt, spread out as if the doe was staggering. Blood splashed against a tree. The man reached out and touched. It smeared against his fingers. They were close.

They had to be close.

Cavalo looked ahead. Bad Dog was four feet in front of him, nose to ground, caught in the scent of blood. He took another step forward, and Cavalo zeroed in on a thin line stretched horizontally six inches above the forest floor, mostly hidden by leaves. The dog didn't see it, entranced by the doe.

"Down!"

Bad Dog immediately dropped to the ground, flattening himself to the forest floor, ears back, body unmoving aside from shallow breaths. His nose almost touched the line above the ground.

"Back," Cavalo said quietly.

Bad Dog huffed and inched his way backward, keeping his body low to the ground. His tail curled underneath him as he pushed himself away from the trip wire. Cavalo could see a splash of the doe's blood on the wire and wondered how she'd been able to avoid it. Luck had been with her, at least at that moment.

Bad Dog whined. Cavalo looked down and saw his back leg had become caught in crude netting buried under the leaves on the ground. Cavalo followed the trip wire to a nearby tree and saw the rigging it would have triggered, pulling up the netting around whatever had clipped the wire.

"Easy," he said. "Relax." He placed the rifle against a nearby tree. "You're okay."

Bad Dog rolled his eyes. *So you say. I almost died.*

The man crouched low and reached out to the dog. He untangled the leg from the netting, careful not to pull harshly on the thin ropes and trigger the pulley system.

The leg came free. "Up," Cavalo said.

Bad Dog stood slowly. The man reached under his stomach and lifted him up and away from the net. Bad Dog growled. *I can do it.*

"I know you can."

I'm not a puppy!

"I know. Just let me do this, okay?"

Bad Dog sighed but licked Cavalo's hand once he was set back on the ground, away from the trap. He turned and sniffed at the netting hidden on the ground.

"We should go back." He picked up the rifle again. He hated the weight of it.

The dog turned to look at him. *The deer.*

Cavalo looked into the trees. "Close?"

You've seen the blood trail. Blood, blood, blood. It's grown bigger. It's dying.

"Or it's already dead."

Can't leave it.

"Yeah."

Yes. Yes.

Cavalo listened to the forest around him. He could only hear the scream of birds. He warred with himself, but only for a moment. "You stay by me, then. No leading. We walk together."

Bad Dog pressed his head against the man's legs. *Go. Go. Let's go.*

They gave the netting and trip wire a wide berth, always keeping it in their line of sight. Once around the tree, Bad Dog picked up the blood trail again. Cavalo glanced back at the trip wire, briefly considering finding some way to trigger it. He decided against it, unsure if it would set off some kind of alarm. They would just have to avoid it on their way back.

MINUTES LATER THEY STEPPED INTO A CLEARING, AND THEIR hunt came to an end.

Ahead lay a thicket, the bushes a vibrant green, a defiant contrast in the middle of the dead woods. Blood splashed onto the leaves, wet and dark. In the distance, above the call of the birds, Cavalo heard the rumble of thunder.

Bad Dog stood in front of the bushes, spun once, and yipped. *Here!* he said, pointing his nose into the bushes. *Here! Here!*

The man stood next to his friend and parted the thicket in front of him. Inside, in a nest of sorts, lay the doe, not yet dead. Her one visible eye was wide and black, dilated in fear. She took in a shuddering breath through her split snout and let it out, her tongue poking out from between her teeth. The arrow jutted up from her neck. The sickly fifth leg did not move. Bad Dog growled, his nose flaring.

"No," Cavalo said.

It would just take a second. Teeth in neck. Bite.

"No."

Hungry.

"I know. But look. She's already leaving."

And she was. As man and dog looked on, the doe took in another harsh breath. Held it. Then it rattled out. Her chest did not rise again.

Cavalo was already calculating. They were half a mile from the freeway, maybe three-quarters. The doe was fat, maybe two hundred pounds. He could harvest her here, but it was getting dark and they were on the other side of the woods. Even if they weren't found, it'd be harder to spot the traps at night. He had a lantern, but it would be a beacon in the dark, attracting attention they didn't need.

He could carry her, but that would slow them down significantly and would run the risk of spoiling the meat before he could take it. He would need to camp tonight either way, as home was still a good five miles off.

"Better there than here," he said.

Bad Dog barked quietly. *Yes. Let's leave. Now.*

He fixed the rifle back to its strap and bent over. He pulled the arrow from the neck of the deer. Blood flowed. He took his canteen and spilled some water onto the ground. Bad Dog bit at the water, and the man poured it onto his face. Bad Dog laughed and danced, happy to drink. Cavalo sprinkled the arrow with water and rubbed it clean, then stored the arrow back in the quiver.

TJ KLUNE

He mixed the water into the dirt until it was mud and covered the hole in the doe's neck, staunching the blood flow. He rubbed his hands off on his rough tunic and took off his pack, leaving the bow and rifle. Bad Dog came to his side immediately, and Cavalo set the pack to the dog's back, connecting the straps underneath his belly. Bad Dog licked his face and chuffed his pleasure as Cavalo tickled his sides.

"Good?" he asked when finished.

Bad Dog moved around experimentally. *Yes. Yes. Good. Time to go home.*

"Yeah. Home." The man turned to the deer.

"Daddy," a voice said from behind him.

Cavalo closed his eyes. He hadn't noticed how the birds had gone silent. He hadn't felt the breeze on the back of his neck. Hadn't realized any of this until the voice spoke. The soft voice. The young voice.

Cavalo opened his eyes. The dog stood next to him, staring up at him, head cocked. *What?* he asked. *What is it?*

"Daddy," the child said again.

"It's not real," the man named Cavalo said to the trees. "It's not real."

"What's not real, Daddy?"

"You."

Bad Dog: *Hurry. Hurry.*

"Hi, Daddy! Hi! Hi!"

Bad Dog bumped his head into the man's hand. The pack on his back jingled softly. *Come on. Come on. Deer. Come on.*

But Cavalo was only a man and did only what a man could do.

He turned.

Near a tree on the other side of the clearing stood a boy. A dark-haired boy. With bronze skin. Dusky eyes. He smiled and showed his crooked front teeth. It was sweet. Endearing.

"Jamie," Cavalo breathed to what wasn't there. His knees almost gave out.

Bad Dog, agitated: *Hey! You! MasterBossLord. Get the deer!*

The boy waggled his fingers at the man. "Hi!"

Cavalo took a step toward the boy on the other side of the clearing in the other side of the woods. He knew it wasn't real. He *knew*. But it didn't stop him from wanting. It didn't stop him from hoping. From taking that first step away. He *knew* it was all in his mind.

But he also knew it wasn't.

Bad Dog growled and grabbed the man's hand with his teeth, tugging gently, trying to pull Cavalo back. The man was not deterred, and as he took another step, the boy in the woods laughed, turned, and ran away. "Chase me, Daddy!" he called over his shoulder, giggling and raising his little fists over his head. "Chase me!"

"Jamie!" the man called and ran after the boy.

He could hear Bad Dog barking behind him, a confused sound, tinged with warning. He ignored his friend and listened to the trees around him. The birds were silent, and he could hear his blood roaring. His skin vibrated. He told himself he was tired. That he was seeing things. That he was running further into danger. *Stop*, he told himself. *Stop. Now. It's not real. It's not real.*

A small part of him, a desperate part, whispered back, *Yes, but what if it is?*

The child laughed again, farther away.

Cavalo ran through the trees, branches slapping his face. It stung, but he was beyond the pain. Beyond himself. Beyond this forest, this ravaged country, this impossible time years after the world had ended, when humanity had been snuffed out like a candle in the dark, leaving only wisps of smoke and ash. He ran because he could *hear* his son ahead of him, running with his little legs through the trees saying *daddy, daddy, daddy*, and wasn't it almost too much? Wasn't it just overwhelming?

It was.

And it felt real.

As Cavalo ran, he didn't see the other trip wire ahead of him.

Didn't see the stone weight on the far side of the tree. Didn't see the net along the forest floor. He only had eyes for his son, wild eyes that were blown out and leaking.

His right foot caught the trip wire and it snapped against his ankle, burning into the skin. The weight dropped. The net rose. It caught his foot between the netting, and Cavalo's world spun upside down. He swung right with a grunt, his head rapping against the tree. He saw stars, so many stars, and they were bright and loud and calling like the birds, like Bad Dog barking in the distance, like his son Jamie singing *daddy, daddy, daddy*.

He awoke later at dusk. He opened his eyes and squinted against the low light. The sky above was an angry gray, and he saw a flash of lightning off somewhere to the north. His head was ringing. His face felt wet.

He heard a whine and turned his head. Bad Dog lay next to him, his head on the man's stomach, tail thumping. The dog rose to his feet, turning to lick Cavalo on the face. *You need to get up*, Cavalo heard him say. *Get up, get up, get up!*

Cavalo grunted and put his fingers into the fur on the dog's neck. He squeezed gently to let the dog know he was okay. Bad Dog shuffled back and sat on his hindquarters, waiting for the man to rise.

Cavalo looked above him and saw the net swinging in the breeze. He felt the burn on his ankle and knew he must have fallen from the net after striking his head against the tree. He was lucky he hadn't broken his neck in the fall, though he was sore everywhere. He touched the wetness on his forehead and hissed at the pain. A cut there, a bad one by the feel of it. It would scar, even if he got it closed. He didn't much care one way or another, but the cut was still leaking blood and his face felt caked with it.

Bad Dog whined again. *Okay? You okay, MasterBossLord? Up. Up!*

"I know," Cavalo said, pushing himself up off the ground. His body pulled in places, felt stiff in others. His back popped as he stood upright. His vision swam for a brief moment, and his stomach turned. It passed after a time.

"It wasn't real," he muttered to himself. "He wasn't there. He couldn't be."

And he knew this, but he could still hear *Daddy* and *hi!* whispering in his ears. He looked down to the ground. He saw the faint outline of where he'd crashed down from the net. He saw his footprints. He saw paw prints from Bad Dog, moving in a worrying circle. But that was all. No other footprints. None big.

None small.

You losing it? Bad Dog asked him.

"No. Maybe. I don't know."

Think you're losing it. MasterBossLord going crazy.

"Probably. If I am, you're going with me." He felt guilty over this, but it couldn't be helped.

Bad Dog wagged his tail and bumped the man. *Yeah. Sure. We'll go together.*

"Yeah." Cavalo looked around, getting his bearings. "We gotta get out of here."

Find the deer?

The man thought for a moment. "Yeah. Think I can still carry it."

Bad Dog looked at the man reproachfully. *We've come all this way, after all.*

"I know. You don't have to—"

Bad Dog's hackles suddenly raised and his ears flattened as he lowered his head toward the ground, bowing his spine. His tail twitched angrily in the air. He growled toward the trees and the shadows.

Jamie's come back, Cavalo thought. *He's come back, and the dog can see him so that means he's real. He's real, oh my God, he's real—*

But then voices cut through the dark and the forest. Gruff voices. Adult voices. Here, in the other side of the woods. On the wrong side of the freeway. Lights flashed in the growing night, only yards away. Faintly, but growing louder, a man said, "Check the next."

"To me," Cavalo hissed at Bad Dog. The dog stopped his growls and followed the man as they turned from the net and the voices that approached.

Cavalo moved quickly and quietly, watching each step to make sure no other traps would be sprung, no branches on the ground stepped on and broken. The dog moved carefully behind, though the pack on his back jingled so that it sounded like shotgun blasts in the forest. The birds had resumed their cries (*had they ever really gone silent to begin with?* he wondered) and the forest felt *alive* even if it was half dead, and he expected at any moment for the trees to part and reveal man and dog to the group that was *right behind them.* Weren't the voices louder? Had they heard? Were they chasing?

And didn't Cavalo, for a brief moment, consider standing where he was and letting them find him? Didn't he think about allowing himself to be overrun by those in the woods and have it all finally come to an end?

He did. He reached up and touched the scar on his temple. And kept moving.

The man and dog came to a familiar thicket, Cavalo's head throbbing in time with his rapid heart. Knowing they only had moments (because the voices had gotten *louder* and they were *right there*), he made a decision he hoped he wouldn't regret.

He turned swiftly and bent low, wrapping his arms under Bad Dog's stomach, hoisting him against his chest. Bad Dog grunted in surprise—*Hey!*—but didn't struggle against Cavalo's grip. The man carried him into the large thicket. The doe lay where he'd left her, eyes black and wide, dried mud covering the hole from the arrow in her neck. He stumbled gracelessly, stepping on the back leg, hearing it break under his heel. He almost lost his balance and dropped his friend. A lesser animal might have struggled then, but Bad Dog did not move, and Cavalo regained his footing.

He hunched low, cradling Bad Dog to his chest, the pack digging into his neck, arms straining as he pushed past the deer, farther back into the thicket, tearing through green leaves and thorns. Cavalo looked over his shoulder and could barely see the doe through the dense shrubbery, four feet away. He lay them on their sides, turning Bad Dog over to pull him against his chest, the pack facing the doe. The dog's snout pressed against his neck, and his tongue darted out briefly, licking the sweating skin, the drying blood. *We're okay*, Bad Dog said. *Be a bush! We're nothing but bushes and leaves and we're okay!*

"Down," Cavalo whispered harshly, forgetting, not for the first time, that Bad Dog hadn't actually spoken.

Be a bush, the dog whispered back before he stilled completely at the command.

They waited.

The forest crackled around them.

A flash of lightning, far away. Thunder rumbled soon after.

The sky above, seen in slivers through the branches, the color of lead.

Bad Dog's breath at his throat.

His own breath, low and ragged.

From outside the bushes, footsteps. Shuffling through forest floor.

A light glimpsed through the leaves.

The man pulled his dog tighter still.

"Who was it, ya think?" a high, reedy voice asked. "Tripped that net?"

"Lucky sumbitch," a response came, deeper in timbre. "Net ain't cut. Got out somehow."

Movements, no more than shadows, seen past the doe. Her head was turned in such a way that her dead eye stared at man and dog.

"You think it long?" a woman asked. "Footprints looked fresh."

"That they did," the deep-voiced man said. A glint of metal.

"Town or traveler?" Footsteps, nearby.

"Couldn't say. You'd think the good folk of Cottonwood would have learned by now. But maybe they need a reminder."

"We need to tell Patrick. He needs to know."

"And we will. You two, go check the other trap ahead. Make sure nothing caught there." Footsteps, trailing away.

Bad Dog wiggled against the man briefly. *Almost done? Gone?*

Cavalo shook his head. Bad Dog didn't respond.

A moment of silence. Then the woman, "You really think it's the town?"

The deep voice: "I don't know. Merchants, maybe. One of the trade caravans."

"All the way out here? They don't follow the broken road. Especially not through our country. But...."

"Spit it out."

"What if it's the government? Like Patrick warned us?"

The deep-voiced man snorted. "Too soon for them. They're still crawling on their hands and knees back east. It'll be years before they find their way out here. By then, it won't matter. We'll control all of this."

"We?"

"You know what I mean. Patrick will provide."

"May he walk forever," the woman said reverently.

"He will," the deep-voiced man said, and Cavalo felt ice in his heart. "We've—"

"Quiet," the woman said. "Listen."

They fell silent. Sweat dripped from Cavalo's brow. *Government,* he thought dizzily. *Patrick. Cottonwood. Reminder.* It was like a storm.

Footsteps approached. "Where the hell have you been?" the deep-voiced man asked.

Nothing was said in response. Cavalo could see movement, barely visible, as if hands were waving. Motioning.

Deep-voice wasn't moved. "I don't care what the fuck you were doing. You're supposed to be checking lines."

More motion.

"Stupid retard," the woman muttered. She sounded unsure. "Why does Patrick keep him around?"

"Because he's a goddamn psycho. You're new, so you don't know shit. Found him in the woods sucking on his dead momma's titties when he was nothing but a babe. Raised him since. Pet. Fucking bulldog."

"You ain't scared of him?"

"Nah," he said, but it sounded like a lie. "He don't do nothing till Patrick tells him to. He learned the hard way when he tried to think on his own. Didn't ya, boy?"

No motion, no movement.

"Ah, go fuck ya'self."

The woman: "You see that?"

"What?"

She crouched near the entrance of the thicket. Cavalo could see her more clearly now through the darkening gloom. Bright red hair spiked up one side, head shaved down other. Skin smudged with dirt. A bruise on her lower jaw, days old. Black gloves, spikes on the end. Tight black fabric across small breasts. Exposed skin. Cargo pants. Camo. Greens and browns and blacks.

Cavalo hadn't seen camo in years, not since he'd stumbled across an abandoned military compound, deserted except for razor-thin coyotes with engorged tumors growing along their bodies. He was twenty-three then. A coyote had almost taken his head off. There must have been power somewhere in that old place because he'd stumbled into a wall, pressing a button, and a panel lit up and a voice began to screech "—IS NOT A DRILL. REPEAT: WE ARE AT DEFCON 1. THIS IS NOT A DRILL. WE—" He'd run then, from that haunted place where the radiated coyotes nested, the mechanical voice shrieking after him that they were at DEFCON 1. That was right before he found *her* and—

"What is it?" the deep-voiced man asked, and he too came into view. Massive, muscles bunched and bulging. Black man, dark. Growth on his neck from too much time spent in the Deadlands. It would have to be excised soon. Most likely it would grow back, Cavalo knew, but it would take time. His head was shaved, and there were pit scars like burns across his scalp, pink along with the dark of his skin. Cavalo couldn't see his eyes but knew they'd be narrowed.

Blood. They'd seen the blood trail.

"Looks dried," the woman said. "Been here a while."

"Don't mean it didn't come from whoever tripped that wire," the black man muttered. He raised his head to look into the thicket, and Cavalo closed his eyes, knowing the man would see the whites. Bad Dog's skin rippled, but otherwise he was still. For a moment nothing happened.

Then: "Well, well, well. Look what we have here."

Fight, Cavalo thought. *Pull down on hand, break fingers. Slam up face, break nose. Dog out, attack. Rifle up. Man head shot. Cock rifle. Woman head shot. Drop rifle. Third person. Pull bow. Two arrows. Nock them both. Spread. First into stomach. Second into groin.*

They were cold, these thoughts. Calculating. Mechanical. A metallic taste coated his tongue. He opened his eyes in slits. Dark. Grainy. There was movement, and Bad Dog began to coil in his arms, ready to lash out, teeth and claws. Cavalo dug his fingers into his friend's fur, telling him *not yet, not yet.*

He opened his eyes a little wider and saw the top of the black man's head inside the thicket, the pink scars in geometric patterns, as if carved there on purpose. Any moment he expected the man to reach for him, for Bad Dog. Cavalo thought it'd be the last thing this big man ever did.

But the black man didn't look farther back into the bushes. His attention was focused on the doe. He pulled on her haunches. Her head bounced as she moved, her tongue dragging in the dirt. A dead leaf stuck to one of her eyes. The shrubs parted over her fat belly and mutated fifth leg and then closed as she was pulled completely out.

"Food," the woman breathed.

"Hasn't been dead long," the big man said. "Body hasn't started to bloat yet."

"From the trap?" She sounded unsure.

"No. Look. What do you see?"

Silence. Then, "I don't know. It looks dead."

"Dumb bitch," the black man muttered. "We could just ask the pet here."

More silence, then the woman: "What's he pointing at? The dirt?"

"Yeah. It's a kill shot. Been patched to stop the blood from leaking. Meaning whoever shot it was going to move it."

"Shot? With *bullets*? Patrick said they—"

"No. Arrow."

"Why didn't they take it?"

The bushes rattled and Cavalo closed his eyes again. "Don't know," the black man said. "Don't care. It's ours now. Whoever killed it is long gone."

Yes, Cavalo thought. *Gone. Long gone. Leave.* The muscles in his arms trembled.

A voice called off in the distance.

"Yeah?" the big man yelled. "Nothing?"

Unintelligible response.

"Head back around!" Then, quieter, "Let's go." He hoisted the deer up easily and slung it over his neck.

"What about whoever tripped the line?" the woman asked. Her voice grated on Cavalo.

"Fuck 'em. We got food. That'll be enough. We have to get back."

And then they moved away, toward the Deadlands. Cavalo heard their voices fade. Still, he waited. In his mind, he could see them hiding behind the trees, waiting for him to show himself. He knew who they were. What they were. What they were capable of. He'd seen their kind before, those pockets spread out along the border between the Deadlands and the East.

But Patrick. That name was new.

His head hurt, the blood now crusted on his face. He felt covered in grime. He ached. He thought of a boy named Jamie.

Bad Dog thumped his tail. *Gone?* he whispered.

"Think so," Cavalo whispered back.

Why are we waiting? You want to hug me some more?

"Shut up."

You can hug me harder if you're scared. I won't break.

"I'm not scared."

Oh. Bad Dog huffed. *I was.*

A beat. "Me too."

It's okay, MasterBossLord.

"We should go."

Okay.

And yet they waited minutes more.

Finally, as full dark approached, Cavalo rolled over Bad Dog until he loomed over him. Bad Dog put a paw on the man's shoulder. Cavalo gripped his snout gently with one hand as he unfastened the pack. "Stay here," he whispered, looking his friend in the eye. "Let me look first."

I can go too!

"No. Stay. Here." Each word was punctuated with a soft shake of the snout. Bad Dog glared up at him but said nothing.

Cavalo moved over the dog and the pack, laying his bow on the ground behind him. He pulled the rifle off his shoulder and rose to his knees, then his feet, crouched low among the branches. He tucked the stock of the rifle under his arm. A brief whine came from behind him, and he turned only once, catching the eyes of his friend before turning back. The man did not shake. The barrel of the rifle did not tremble.

Not today, he thought.

And then he stepped out of the thicket.

fucking psycho bulldog

THE FOREST WAS DARK. The birds had quieted. Nothing moved.

He stood upright. Took a step. And then another. And then another.

He didn't even hear the footsteps behind him. Didn't sense anyone approaching. At first there was nothing, and then a large, heavy blade was at his throat, the heat of a body pressing up against him from behind. Cavalo glanced down and saw a thin, bony hand holding the knife steady. He could feel the breath through his pulled-back hair. The reach and the breath meant the man was shorter, but not by much. Another hand appeared from his left and tapped the gun once, twice, then motioned for Cavalo to hand it over.

Seconds passed. No words said. The blade pressed against his skin and there was a brief sting, but Cavalo was beyond it. His vision had tunneled down to tiny points. His skin felt heated. His head pounded. His hands gripped the rifle so tightly he thought either metal or bone would break. For the first time in a very long time, Cavalo was angry.

Not the underlying anger he typically felt at life's injustices. At that swarm of bees that buzzed angrily in the back of his mind, whispering things like *It's your fault they're gone* and *daddy, daddy, daddy.* That was always there, and there were times the man thought it always would be.

No, this anger was different. It was blinding. White hot. It was fury. Not at the person behind him, not completely, but more at *himself* that he *allowed* this to happen. That he had *allowed* himself to get caught. *Getting old*, he thought. *Getting too old for this shit.*

But there was no way he was going to die in this dead forest on the wrong side of the divide, so close to the Deadlands. He wouldn't let it happen.

The knife pressed harder into his skin. The other hand tapped on the rifle again, turned over, fingers motioned. *Hand it over*, those fingers said. *Do it now*, the hand holding the knife said. *Do it now before I cut your throat.*

Yeah, Cavalo thought, watching as the fingers raised to tap the rifle again. *Now. Now.*

Almost quicker than the eye could follow, Cavalo brought the butt of the rifle down and back, past his left side. He felt it connect with something solid, and there was a rush of air near his ear, a heavy exhalation. Without stopping he brought the rifle back up, close to his body, thrusting his arms up. He felt a head press against the back of his shoulder as the person behind him gasped for air. The sight of the rifle scraped against the side of Cavalo's face, tearing the skin, but he felt nothing. All that mattered was the barrel of the rifle was now between his face and the hand with the knife. With all the force he could muster, he brought the barrel down against the forearm around his neck. The hand was knocked away, the knife dangerously close to cutting his throat open before the blade left his skin.

CAVALO STEPPED FORWARD, FLIPPING THE RIFLE IN THE AIR, grabbing the barrel as he spun in a circle, swinging the butt of the rifle out in a wide arc. It struck out through empty air. The force of his swing kept his body spinning and as he turned, Cavalo saw a flash of silver and jerked his head back in time to avoid the blade, more machete than knife.

Before he could correct himself, a foot lashed out, and the rifle was knocked from his hands, landing in the shadows. The machete pointed at his throat, inches away. Cavalo's eyes followed the blade, flat and pockmarked with rust. It was held by a hand wrapped in black material, fingers exposed. The hand led to an arm, the skin covered in the sleeve of an old jacket. The arm was connected to a lithe body, all in black, intersected with red wraps around the waist and thighs. A black band around the bicep. Around the eyes were smudges of what looked like charcoal, thick and cracked, creating a mask.

Those eyes glittered in the dark. Beyond them lay the thicket.

Cavalo was furious. His voice was calm. "You got me," he said. He raised his hands slowly in the air.

The man opposite him (though *man* felt too strong a word; even in the dark, Cavalo thought him nothing but a boy) said nothing. The blade did not move.

"But."

The boy narrowed his eyes.

Cavalo saw red. "I have two words for you." His voice was an earthquake.

The boy frowned.

Cavalo's lips twisted into a cold smile. "Bad. Dog."

The thicket behind the boy exploded in a furious burst of snarls and teeth. Before the boy could react, Bad Dog was on his back, head darting in to bite and tear and kill. Cavalo knocked the machete out of his hand as the boy fell, the weight of the dog bearing down on him. Cavalo had a moment to think that the boy had yet to make a noise, but then it was gone as he kicked the big knife away.

He swept his hand low to grab the rifle when he heard Bad Dog grunt and looked up to see the boy elbow the dog in the ribs again. Bad Dog leapt off him, and the boy rolled onto his back. The dog crouched low, fur standing on end, tail pointed, his lips pulled back in a terrible snarl. Cavalo saw the boy reach one of his hands slowly down his leg, never taking his eyes off the dog. Cavalo couldn't see what he was reaching for, but it was time to end this.

"Hold!" he snapped.

Bad Dog turned his snarl briefly to Cavalo. *Kill him!* he growled. *He touched MasterBossLord, let me kill him, kill him. Tear him to pieces. I want to see his blood!*

"Hold," Cavalo said again, reaffirming the command.

He would have sworn that Bad Dog rolled his eyes. He ignored it.

"You," he said to the boy, who had frozen. "Whatever's in your boot, pull it out slow. Toss it away."

Nothing happened.

Cavalo cocked the rifle. It was loud in the dark. Unmistakable.

The boy moved his arm lower. Pulled a knife out of his boot. He held it for a moment, looking at the curve of the blade. He flicked his wrist, and the knife was embedded in a tree stump ten feet away.

Bad Dog growled. *Flashy man*, he said. *Flashy man thinks he is good. I am better. I am Bad Dog, and I will rip his throat out.*

"Not yet," the man said, and the boy looked over his shoulder at Cavalo, a question in his dark eyes. Cavalo could see more of him now. Maybe not a boy. Not completely. There were some hard lines on his face that came with age or experience. Older than a boy. His head was shaved down to stubble except for a fat black strip that bisected his skull. The mask around those coldly calculating eyes made them look deeper, older.

What are you waiting for? Bad Dog asked. *Shoot his face off or let me bite him!*

Cavalo shook his head, trying to clear the bees that asked questions about this boy-man, like *who* and *how* and *why*. It had been a long time since Cavalo had been curious about anything. He didn't need to start now. The boy was one of *them*. Cavalo pushed the bees away, even as they stung him.

"Stand up," he said. He motioned with the gun.

For a moment the boy didn't move, just stared at the man with the gun, ignoring the way Bad Dog's growl grew louder. Cavalo contemplated shooting the boy in the head. The boy stood fluidly, twisting until he faced Cavalo, Bad Dog at his back.

This upset Bad Dog. *Rude!* he hissed. *He does not show respect! Please oh please, can I bite his face off?*

"No, you can't," Cavalo said, though he didn't know why.

You never let me do anything fun.

"What about that rabbit? That one time?"

Rabbit, Bad Dog said dreamily. *It ran until I crunched it with my Bad Dog teeth.*

"You crunched it good," the man agreed. There had been nothing left when he'd caught up with the dog, just bits of fur and sinew.

The boy between them stared at Cavalo. The man didn't know what to make of those dark eyes.

"What is your name?" he asked.

The boy said nothing.

"Where do you come from?"

Silence.

"Where are your people?"

Nothing.

"Who is Patrick?"

The boy's eyes narrowed. But still, he did not speak.

Pet, the black man had said. *Goddamn psycho. Fucking bulldog.*

"You Patrick's pet?"

The boy scowled. His hands turned into fists at his sides.

"Would you have killed me?"

Emphatic nods of his head: *Yes. Yes. Yes.*

"Will you kill me if I let you go?"

Yes. Yes. Yes.

Cavalo believed him. His kind only knew how to kill. "Up against the tree," he said, tilting his head toward a barren oak.

The boy watched him without moving until Bad Dog began to nip at his ankles with low yips. *Move! Move, you stupid boy-man! Move before I tear your skin!*

"He will, you know," Cavalo said.

The boy looked back at him strangely, and then Cavalo remembered no one else could hear Bad Dog. For the first time in a long time, the man felt flustered. This was why he chose not to deal with other people. It was easier when no one else was around.

Bad Dog herded him to the tree, not quite biting, but close, teeth denting but not piercing the skin. Cavalo's disquiet grew as the boy said nothing. As he didn't make any noise. He had questions forming in his mind, the bees asking *Who is he?* and *Why why why?* And the man did his best to ignore them, even as they vibrated at the base of his skull.

The boy turned his back to the tree and waited.

Remember, the man thought. *Remember what they did. To Jamie. To* her.

Cavalo remembered. Without realizing he did it, he reached up and touched the scar on the side of his head.

Remember, Bad Dog said, though he hadn't even been alive then. Cavalo knew that the dog was just picking up on what he was thinking.

And that's not real, either, he thought.

Bad Dog looked at him before turning back to the boy and growling.

The man took a step toward them. He raised the rifle. The bees were so loud, like he was full of them, like they lived under his skin. He felt their little stingers. *WHO IS HE?* they screamed. *WHY WON'T HE SPEAK? WHO IS PATRICK? WHAT DO THEY WANT? JAMIE JAMIE JAMIE IS JUST A BOY, JUST A DEAD BOY AND HER. HER. SHE IS DUST*

AND SHE DANCES IN THE TREES AND YOU ARE CRACKING.

Losing it, he thought. *This is what it feels like to lose it. These last bits of rational thought are all I'll have before it breaks open completely and the bees fly out of my mouth when I tilt my head back to scream.*

Daddy! Daddy! Daddy!

He brushed past Bad Dog. He raised the rifle. Pressed the barrel against the boy's head. Put three pounds of pressure on the trigger weighted for a three and a half pound pull. The lip of the barrel cut into the boy's skin. A trickle of blood slid into the charcoal mask around his eyes.

And the boy didn't look away. His face remained blank, giving nothing away.

They stood there, the three of them, for what seemed like ages, points of a triangle.

The gunshot will bring back the others, Cavalo thought. *They'll hear.*

Do you even care? the bees asked.

He's just a kid, Cavalo thought. *Can't be more than twenty.*

You've done worse, the bees said.

His eyes are dark, Cavalo thought. *Almost black.*

To this, the bees said nothing.

Cavalo started to pull away. Panic stole over the boy's face. He reached up and grabbed the rifle barrel, pulling it back against his forehead. The pressure on the trigger increased, and it would just take a little more. Just a bit more and so many things could be over.

The boy pleaded to Cavalo, never making a sound. *Do it,* he seemed to say, his voice a light rumble tinged with hysteria in Cavalo's head. *Pull the trigger. Do it. Please. Do it.* A hand snaked up along the barrel until it grazed his own finger wrapped around the trigger. The lightest pressure was applied.

Cavalo ripped the gun away. Took a step back.

The boy slumped against the tree. Tilted his head back. Closed his eyes. His throat worked as he breathed. Only then did Cavalo see the ugly line stretched from one side of the boy's neck to the other, the scar ridged and white, thicker where it crossed the center of his throat. It was a grotesque thing, one so blatantly large that it could not have been done by mistake. Either the boy had tried to do it himself or it'd been done to him.

Bad Dog didn't care either way. He snarled at the boy, teeth exposed. *I'll do it, then*, he said. *Let me do it, MasterBossLord. Bad Dog is good at doing good things to bad people.*

"Stop," the man said, and the dog scowled in protest. Cavalo knew Bad Dog was agitated and had every right to be. *Then why don't I finish this?* he thought.

There was no answer.

"You can't talk, can you?" Cavalo said. He didn't even know if the boy understood what he was saying.

Those glittering eyes found him again. The man thought nothing would happen, but then the boy gave the first sign he was even remotely human. His head went from side to side, just once.

No.

Dangerous, the bees said. *Kill him now. Kill him now before you have time to regret it. There is already much of your life you wish you could take back. Don't make this one part of it.*

"Rope," he said to Bad Dog, never taking his eyes from the boy. Cavalo had seen how quickly he moved. He wouldn't underestimate him.

For a moment, Bad Dog didn't move, even though he'd heard the command, ears twitching at the word. His hackles rose further and he pressed his nose against the boy and growled deeply.

"Rope," the man said again, his voice sharper.

Bad Dog gave one last flash of teeth, then broke away, going into the thicket for the pack. *Stupid rope.*

The boy's eyes flickered left. Just once and quickly. Nothing more than a spasm of muscle. Cavalo looked left and in the dark, saw the knife embedded in the tree.

"Bullets move faster than you," Cavalo said.

The boy glared at him. *You didn't shoot me*, his look said. *Why would you kill me now?*

"I wouldn't," the man said. "Kill you, that is. But that doesn't mean I won't shoot you. There's a lot of places a person can be shot without killing them. And I know most of them. They'll hurt, and you won't die." Though he wouldn't realize it until later, those words were the most Cavalo had spoken at one time to another human being in almost five months. Later he would wonder why he said them at all.

Later, he would wonder many things.

But now, out of the corner of his eye, he saw Bad Dog pulling the pack out of the bushes. He pulled it in front of Cavalo and bent down, biting the main clasp gently. The top of the back fell open. He stuck his nose inside and rooted around. His tail started to wag, and Cavalo knew he'd found the remaining supplies. *Jerky!* he cried. *MasterBossLord, I found jerky!*

"Later," he said.

Bad Dog's tail drooped. *I never get anything good*, he grumbled. He backed out of the bag a moment later, a length of coarse rope in his mouth. He turned and handed it to Cavalo, who waited with an outstretched hand.

"Good boy," he murmured. He took the rope and said, "Guard."

Bad Dog turned ferocious once more, teeth flashing in the dark, the terrible rumble emanating from his chest as he stalked toward his prisoner. *I am Bad Dog*, he hissed. *And I will eat your soul if you move.*

The boy never flinched.

Careful of this one, the bees said.

Goddamn psycho. Fucking bulldog.

"Against the tree," Cavalo said. "Now."

The boy didn't turn.

"You speak English?" It came out soft, this question.

The boy watched him.

"I think you do."

Nothing.

"So you know what the word 'bite' means."

A flicker in the eyes, nothing more. He knew.

"Against the tree. Hands in front of you. Palms together."

The boy didn't move.

"Bad Dog."

Yes.

"Bite."

Bad Dog's head darted in swiftly, just once, like a snake. His jaws circled the left calf of the boy and in quick succession, bit down and then again. Bad Dog backed away then before the boy could strike out, little bits of blood and fabric hanging from his teeth.

The boy grimaced but made no sound.

"Against the tree," Cavalo said coldly. "Hands in front of you. Palms together."

The boy didn't turn.

"Do you know what your balls are?"

The boy cocked his head.

"Your nuts. Your testes. That sac below your dick."

The boy suddenly smiled without warning. It was a terribly beautiful thing, angelic and monstrous all at once. Too many teeth, too little humanity. Cavalo had once seen a bear, a mangy thing with wicked claws that clicked along stone. The bear had roared at him from deep in a cave Cavalo had stumbled into to escape a storm. Its eyes had been black with hunger and rage and insanity.

The boy smiled like that bear had looked.

"I wonder," the man said. And he did, even though it was a dangerous thing to do.

The boy smiled wider.

"I wonder what would happen if I told him to bite your balls."

The smile faltered briefly. Then, if anything, it grew bigger. The boy took a step back, and another, and another, never taking his eyes from Cavalo, and in them, the man saw murder. His feet shuffled through the leaves, and it sounded like wind over old bones. He reached the tree and pressed his back to it. His hands came out in front of him, palms pressed together.

And he waited.

Cavalo was sweating. The night seemed darker on this side of the divide, this close to the Deadlands. If he was going to do this, he needed to do it now.

And why do you need to do this?

He didn't know the answer to that.

"Guard," he told Bad Dog.

No shit, he replied, crouched low and ready to spring should it be necessary. *I don't know why you don't just shoot him with the boomstick.*

"I don't know either," Cavalo said honestly.

Bad news. This is bad news.

"Focus."

Bad Dog focused.

Cavalo slung the rifle back onto his shoulder, positioning it so it could slide down easily into his hands. He eyed the boy warily. His head hurt. He was tired. His bones ached. And he still had a ways to go. He couldn't go home. Not tonight. Not with what he'd heard. He had to head into town, as much as he didn't want to.

Psycho, he thought as the boy's smile never faded. *He is psycho.* The rope felt woefully inadequate. How could he—

Ah. From that burnt-out ghost town to the north. The only standing building. It had felt haunted. The whole place had felt haunted. It was as far as he'd strayed in some time, the wanderlust coming over him until he couldn't stand it anymore. At first he'd thought it to be the remains of a church, but the broken metal sign out front had read *WA OWA UNT SE IFF BA RA KS.* Wallowa County Sheriff Barracks. In what had used to be northern Oregon in the Time Before. He'd gone inside, scavenging. He'd found only the remnants of Before, with curled posters on the walls saying things like *ONLY YOU CAN PREVENT FOREST FIRES* and *ANNUAL*

CHARITY BAKE SALE 5/31/19. He'd found only dust. And memories. At one point, he swore he heard voices coming from the floor above him, laughing, crying. He thought he heard children, their little feet running along the floor. On his way out, his skin chilled and clammy, his heart racing, he'd stumbled onto a bulletin board, half propped against a wall. An old, yellowed picture showed grinning men and women in uniform. Next to the photo were a pair of partially rusted handcuffs, key dangling from the connecting chain, a note above them saying *LOSE SOMETHING, CHARLIE?*

He'd grabbed the cuffs and key and fled that dark place. He stayed away from Wallowa County after that.

Those would be better, he thought now. *Safer.*

"Cuffs," he said. "Pack."

Bad Dog pulled up from his guard position and went back to the pack, rooting further. Cavalo fingered the rope in his hands and watched the boy.

Psycho still smiled. *Lose something, Charlie?* that smile said.

Yes, Cavalo thought. *So many things. And I wake up every day despite that. Despite her. And Jamie. And despite the world with the way it is, with people who want more of me than I can give. With the Deadlands. With people like this boy who eat of the flesh of man. They take them, then roast them above their fires until the skin splits from the heat and cracks like fissures form and they scream and they scream and they—*

Cold and metal pressed against his hand. He shook himself from his own mind and looked down. Bad Dog pressed the rusted cuffs into his hand. *Where'd you go, MasterBossLord?* he asked. *You stay here. Stay here with Bad Dog. Don't go Faraway.*

Yes. He had to. He needed to focus. He needed to stay away from Faraway.

Cavalo took the cuffs, and the dog resumed guarding without needing to be told. Cavalo unhooked the key and pocketed it. "You know what these are?" he asked Psycho. He held them up for him to see in the dark.

The boy nodded. *Yes. Yes.*

"You know what they're used for."

His eyes narrowed. *You stupid man, yes.*

"You're going to put these on."

The smile faded. *You should have killed me.*

"You're going to do it quickly."

Psycho's mouth twisted into a sneer. *I will break out of them and eat your skin.*

"You're going to do it now."

Psycho was the bear in that forgotten cave, all fangs and claws. *You have forfeited your life.*

Cavalo tossed the cuffs at the boy. They were snatched out of the air. He rubbed his fingers over them, bringing them up close to his face. He touched the keyhole and frowned.

"Now," the man snapped.

Psycho scowled. He fit the cuff over his right wrist and snapped it closed. He started to do the same with the left.

"No. Behind your back."

Psycho ground his teeth. He took a step away from the tree. Bad Dog snarled. Cavalo raised the rifle, the rope dangling from his hands. Psycho stopped and waited. They stood still, that triangle, each waiting for the next thing to happen. Then Psycho reached his arms behind him and fumbled with the cuffs until they clicked together.

"Turn around," Cavalo said.

He did. The cuffs were loose on his wrists.

"Nice try. Tighter."

His shoulders tensed, but he reached each hand over the other, squeezing the circlets until the metal bit his skin. It was awkward, the angle, but he got it done with minimal effort. He turned back around and stared defiantly at Cavalo.

But Cavalo was done. Done with this day, done with this forest. Done with being this close to the Deadlands. And most of all, done with this boy in front of him. His dirty, callused hands quickly fashioned a noose out of the rope. Psycho didn't have time to move as Cavalo threw it around his head and over his neck. It hit the ugly scar there, and for a moment, Cavalo was sure he saw a flare of panic, of real fear crossing his face. But then it was gone, and all that was left was murder. Cavalo cinched the noose up tight, his hands against the Psycho's neck. He knew it bit into the sensitive scar tissue and did not care.

Up close, faces inches apart, Bad Dog growling in warning, the man named Cavalo saw only one thing in the Psycho's monstrous eyes.

Himself, reflected back.

the minds of men

I DON'T KNOW why we had to bring him along, Bad Dog said hours later. Light was beginning to brighten ahead of them in the east, and they were near the outskirts of what used to be the town of Cottonwood, Idaho in the time of Before. Now, in the After, it was just Cottonwood. Remnants of some of the old farmhouses still stood, their bare bones exposed, burned black and charred. Many had fallen years before and lay in piles on their foundations, but there were stubborn ones that had yet to crumble.

"It don't matter none," Cavalo said tiredly. His eyes were starting to burn, his head pounding something fierce. "We get to Cottonwood. We get Hank and Warren and let them deal with him." His worn boots scuffed the old dirt road.

You should have just killed him. I would have. Bad Dog don't get scared.

"I wasn't scared," he snapped.

Bad Dog had enough common sense to look chagrinned, in that way that only dogs can do. *Well, fine. But you were something, otherwise he wouldn't still be alive. He smells of death.*

"And what do I smell like?" Cavalo asked despite himself.

Bad Dog huffed. *You smell like MasterBossLord.*

"And that's different how? I've killed before."

There are many kinds of death.

Cavalo knew there was no hope in arguing with him when he got like that, so he let it go. The boy walked behind the man and dog, the noose around his neck tight, the rope giving no slack. The boy had made no attempts to flee. He hadn't fought the rope. There'd been no telltale signs of fiddling with the cuffs. He'd followed begrudgingly, eyes shuttered in the black mask, face schooled bland and slack. Even when they'd reached particularly rough terrain near Cottonwood Butte, the boy had nimbly hopped from rock to rock, never stumbling. He had the mien of the bear from the cave, Cavalo knew, but the grace of a snake. It only took getting bit once to know you didn't turn your back on a snake.

"You been to Cottonwood?" he asked, jerking the rope a little so Psycho (because that is how Cavalo thought of him now) would know he was being addressed.

He didn't respond. He didn't even acknowledge he'd heard Cavalo, though the man knew he had.

"No, I don't suppose you have. Your kind isn't welcome there."

Psycho flexed his fingers.

"Can't promise they won't tear you apart once they find out who you are."

Psycho looked toward the brightening sky.

"Can't say I won't stop them from doing that."

Psycho arched his back, stretching.

"You eat anybody this week?" Cavalo asked.

Psycho tensed.

"Oh, that does it for you, huh? Talking about spit roasting people and peeling their skin off when it starts to plump? When the fat starts to sizzle? When their screams have melted in their throats?"

Psycho did not look back.

"Yeah, I know all about your kind. You're monsters. You're the reason people don't sleep at night. You're the reason places like Cottonwood exist."

Nothing.

Cavalo snapped the rope, hard. It jerked his prisoner, causing him to fall onto his back, on top of his hands. Cavalo heard the exhalation of air in place of a grunt or shout of pain.

Bad Dog immediately rushed to his side, growling in his ear. *Try and get up,* the dog said. *I double Bad Dog dare you.*

Before Psycho could move, Cavalo was atop him, hand gripping his face, fingers indenting the skin. The eyes were narrowed underneath the painted-on mask. There was no fear there. Psycho fucking bulldog.

Cavalo's fury grew. "You're the reason people are scared," he spat. "You're the reason they cower. You and your kind. You take from them. You took from m—"

Daddy! the bees said, sounding like Jamie.

Cavalo stopped himself. Spittle hung from his lips and glistened on the face of the boy.

I should just shoot him now. Or smash his head in with a stone. Either way. End this.

At that moment, for the first time in what felt like weeks, the lead clouds in the east parted and a brief sliver of morning sunlight shown through, weak and trembling. Cavalo felt it hit his face. He looked toward it. In the distance, he could see the walls ahead that surrounded Cottonwood, barriers against the outside world, constructed entirely of junked cars, stacked one on top of another, nine or ten high.

He looked back at his prisoner. Sun lit his face, and Psycho had turned toward it, soaking it in before it disappeared. The lines around his eyes and mouth had smoothed and he looked younger. If not for the mask and the clothes, he could have been from a town like Cottonwood, or Grangeville, which was fifteen miles to the south and even bigger. If not for that look in his eyes, he'd be someone Cavalo could know. Could like. Could—

But he's not, the bees said. *He's not. He's death. Let others who are paid to handle such things make up their mind. If he's important, they may give coin.*

Cavalo let go of Psycho's face and curled his fingers under the cinched noose around his neck. He felt the raised scar on the back of his knuckles. Psycho bared his teeth in a wordless snarl. Cavalo ignored it and pulled Psycho up by the rope, not caring if it pulled tighter.

They moved toward town.

HE DIDN'T EXPECT TO MAKE IT WITHIN THIRTY FEET OF THE gate, and he wasn't disappointed.

"Stop!" a clear voice rang out. "You take another step I'll shoot you right between the eyes."

"Oh good Lord. You're not *that* good of an aim" came a reply.

"Better'n you!"

"*Please.* You're not even supposed to *have* a gun. Father said."

"What are you going to do, tell on me? Such a girl thing to do!"

"You're so ridiculous sometimes. I can't even stand it. This *girl* kicks your ass most days, so don't you forget it."

"*I'm* ridiculous? Do you even listen to yourself? You take that back!"

Jesus Christ, Bad Dog groaned.

"Yeah," Cavalo muttered. He raised his voice: "Are you two about done?"

Silence.

Then: "Who wants to know?"

"Someone who will kick both your asses if you don't open the damn gate."

Silence.

Then, uncertain: "Cavalo? That you?"

"Holy shit! It *is* him. Deke, open the gate!" the girl said to her brother.

We should have gone home, Bad Dog said, looking back at the way they'd come. *They're going to touch me all over and make me chase things like I'm a dog.*

"You *are* a dog," Cavalo reminded him.

He looked insulted as he huffed. *No. I'm Bad Dog. There's a difference.*

"They'll probably have meat," the man said as the gates started to part. He took a deep breath and prepared himself for the onslaught that was to come.

They'd better, Bad Dog said. *Especially if they're going to tell me how pretty I look. I don't look pretty. I look ferocious.*

"You do," the man said, starting to walk again toward the gate.

As soon as the opening between the gates was wide enough, two lanky forms hurtled themselves out, dust kicking up behind them. The boy prisoner looked startled for a moment, before bending down into a defensive stance, teeth bared, eyes flashing. But the two ignored him, running up and slamming into Cavalo, the girl wrapping her arms around Cavalo's waist, the new boy dropping his hand down on Cavalo's shoulder. Both wore dusty jeans and green coats, the unofficial uniform of the Patrol, the group in charge of monitoring the walls around Cottonwood. They hadn't been in the Patrol when he'd been here last. They were still too young, even now.

"Deke," Cavalo said, bemused. "Aubrey."

"Where have you been?" Aubrey demanded, her fiery red hair held back in deer hide, the freckles on her face flushed with excitement.

"Dad said you wouldn't come in for a few more weeks," Deke said. His own red hair was cut short, almost buzzed, and if it was possible, he'd grown even gawkier then he'd been when Cavalo had seen them last, months ago. "Probably not until after the first frost."

"Plans changed," Cavalo said, pulling himself gently from the clutches of the Wells siblings. He tried to ignore the dizzying sense of vertigo. The first frost usually came in mid to late October, which meant it was close to the end of September. He'd thought it still

August. The weather was still warm. He hadn't been to the town since April. Five months.

"Why?" Deke asked.

"What happened?" Aubrey asked.

"Why are you here so early in the morning?"

"Where have you been?"

"We've been worried, you know!"

"We tried to get Dad to go up to the prison, but he said you'd be fine!"

"He said you could take care of yourself," Deke muttered.

"Are you hurt? What happened to your head?"

"You get attacked?"

"Bad Dog! How are you, boy? Aren't you just a pretty boy? Yes you is! Yes you *is*!"

Holy Mary, mother of Dog, save me. Please.

"Father's going to be glad to see you!"

"So will Alma."

"Yeah, and just wait till everyone hears you're back!"

"No," Cavalo said, sharper then he'd intended. He almost felt guilty at the way the two flinched. He reminded himself that he needed to act differently when he was here, surrounded by people. He had lost any social graces he'd had years before. It was hard to make the switch, but hearing the flurry of words volleyed at him after weeks of near silence was disorienting. He tried to soften his voice. From the wary look in their eyes, he wasn't quite successful. "I don't want this spread around. Don't know how long I'm staying." He shook the rope a bit and was pleased when their eyes widened, the intakes of breath as they realized who was standing with them.

Deke and Aubrey both took steps back, away from Cavalo and the boy, almost as if they were one and the same. They liked him, Cavalo knew, for some inexplicable reason. Not that he'd given them any cause; in fact, he'd discouraged it as much as possible. But even then, there was a mixture of fear in with it, which was necessary. He scared them, but he knew it would keep them alive. Those who feared were cautious.

Now, though, their eyes fell on his prisoner, and they moved away quickly. Deke, only seventeen years old, clutched an old rifle in his hands awkwardly. His sister, a year younger and a spitting image of her father, Hank, held nothing.

"Is that...," she whispered. "One of *them*?"

"Why do you have a Dead Rabbit, Cavalo?" Deke asked, his voice growing hard. Cavalo gave him credit for the way his skinny chest popped out, the way his lip curled in disgust. He wasn't intimidating to anyone with common sense, but he tried.

"I need to see your dad," Cavalo said. "And probably Warren."

Deke and Aubrey exchanged glances. Something passed between them, something Cavalo wasn't privy to, and it filled him with unease.

Whatever it was, they came to a decision. Deke glanced over at the Dead Rabbit, who glared back. "I'll go get them," he said, his voice low. He turned to leave, then paused. He looked between Psycho and Aubrey, then thrust his rifle at his sister, who took it reluctantly but handled it well. "He moves," Deke told her, "you shoot him. You get me?"

She nodded tightly, and Cavalo wasn't sure which one of them Deke had meant.

Deke took off, his long arms and legs pumping. Psycho watched him go, a scowl on his lips.

Aubrey shifted nervously, putting more distance between herself and the others.

"What's happened?" Cavalo asked her. She was just a child. A young woman growing into her beauty, yes, but still a child. And yet she held the gun with the experience of a soldier, like most children could.

"Everything," Aubrey Wells said simply.

. . .

64

CAVALO SHOULD HAVE KNOWN HIS ARRIVAL WOULDN'T STAY A secret. Deke always had a mouth that moved before he thought. Cottonwood woke early, each of the hundred or so able residents assigned duties that benefited the town. Everyone contributed. It was the only way to ensure survival. From mundane chores to taking care of the few livestock to the Patrol, when a child came of age, they were given an aptitude test and placed where best qualified. Cottonwood and Grangeville had survived this way for decades, though "survival" and "prospering" were two different things. Grangeville was a bigger community, with almost five hundred people within its walls. Each ran independently of the other, though trades occurred when necessary and they couldn't wait for the traveling caravans to come through.

Cavalo stayed away from Grangeville, more so than Cottonwood. It was too big. Too noisy. Too many people. They stared. They gawked. They knew who he was. They whispered his name to each other as he passed. He was an attraction, a marvel. A mystery, someone to scoff at. No one knew what to make of him, but most had common sense enough to fear him. Some thought him romantic; others thought him as bad as the Dead Rabbits. There were stories about him that had spread as such things do, and of course, none of them were true. *He's so tragic*, people in the towns breathed as they mentioned his name. *He's a bad man, a scary man, but he's so tragic.* It was a morality tale to tell their children at night, of the man named Cavalo who'd had everything taken from him.

He didn't like them. He didn't like the towns. The people. It was why he stayed away, miles away at Cottonwood Butte. His home. The former North Idaho Correctional Institute, where some of the barracks still stood. A former maximum-security prison. It felt apt. No one bothered him there. It wasn't haunted like some of the other places he'd seen in his travels. It was quiet, off a mountain road that was covered with snow for a good five months out of the year. There'd been a ski lodge once, farther down the road. From Before. Cavalo had found an old tattered magazine in one of the standing barracks, the edges crumbling as he picked it up. He'd gone looking for it the next day. It was gone, of course, like so many other things. People didn't travel that high up the mountain. They left him alone, motivated by fear and rumor.

But now? Now they came.

He's here, they whispered among themselves as they approached. *The man. Cavalo.* He saw the first ones peek their heads out the gate into Cottonwood, shrinking back as they saw him. Bad Dog groaned next to him and turned in two circles before lying at Cavalo's feet. *Here we go again,* he said in resignation.

Cavalo was a curiosity, and curiosity easily led to fear, especially in these uncertain times. But before fear was found, before it could be renewed, he was an interesting thing. An oddity.

So of course, they came. It only took minutes.

"Damn fool can't keep his mouth shut," Cavalo said. Bad Dog snorted in agreement.

Aubrey said nothing, but Cavalo noted how she'd inched farther away, averting her eyes. She kept the gun partially raised. She'd been trained well, at least as well as a child out here could be.

Psycho crouched down, squatting on the backs of his legs, watching the people start to come out of the gates. Bad Dog gave out a warning growl but did not lift his head. Psycho's cuffed hands twitched behind his back. For a moment Cavalo had a thought of the Dead Rabbit breaking the chain between the cuffs and attacking the people of Cottonwood as they approached.

"This isn't going to go well," he muttered to Bad Dog.

Should have just killed him.

"Yeah."

Not too late.

"I think it is," Cavalo said, eyeing the approaching crowd. "For a lot of things."

These were good people, he knew. Most of them. They were trying to survive, just like he was, in this harsh land. They were close to the Deadlands. They were close to the Dead Rabbits. They lived in danger every day. And yet, somehow, they *still* lived. They *were* good.

However, he'd seen what even good people could do once their hearts had been hardened by the West. Once, in Grangeville, a woman had been caught stealing from the stores of food. She'd been one of those assigned to guard the supplies. The reaction had been swift. Anyone that went against the greater good was automatically considered expendable. It was harsh, but it was well known and for good reason. She'd been turned out by the town, into the wilds. Cottonwood had been put on notice not to accept her in. She had cried. She had begged. Pleaded. She wouldn't say *why* she had done what she had done, only that she *had* to. The gates had closed on her, but not before she'd been spat on. Scorned. Shamed. People screamed at her face. Tore at her clothes. Demanded her head on a pike as warning for everyone else. *Kill her*, they'd said. *Tear her to pieces.*

No one spoke in her defense. Not even her parents.

Three days later, it was made known by a young man that the woman had been two months pregnant. They'd kept it hidden because they were terrified of what their parents would think. They were only eighteen years old, he'd said. They didn't know what to do.

Why didn't you say anything? he was asked. *Why did you let her be cast out?*

I am a coward, he mumbled.

Why didn't she say anything?

He could only shake his head.

They found her a week later. Or, rather, what was left of her.

Cavalo knew that people were good, that *these* people were good. This town of Cottonwood. But he also knew the hearts and minds of men. He knew how they could be. His own heart and mind were just as dark.

Cavalo watched the people of Cottonwood approach under a lightening sky the color of bruises. He didn't see any weapons drawn. That didn't mean that no one was carrying. He knew how quickly things could escalate. But he was encouraged. He didn't know why. He didn't care what happened to this boy. This Dead Rabbit. This psycho fucking bulldog. He didn't care about his kind. Or if he did, it was with white-hot rage that threatened to boil over at any moment. There was nothing else there but that.

Should have just killed him, Bad Dog said again, picking up on Cavalo's thoughts, as Cavalo imagined he did.

He didn't reply to Bad Dog. Instead, he said to the girl, "Deke just doesn't know when to shut up, does he?" His kept his voice light.

Aubrey smiled. "You should know that by now," she said quietly. She moved no closer.

"Yeah," Cavalo said. He should know better. About a lot of things.

"Out of my way!" a voice rang out above the approaching crowd. "For God's sake, people. Move your ever-loving *asses!*"

People moved as they were told. Quickly. Parting, like an ocean from an old story.

A large man barreled forward, larger than a man had any right to be. He kept growing, he was fond of telling people, and just decided never to stop. Hank Wells towered over everyone. He had to be approaching seven feet tall and was almost as wide as he was long. His voice seemed to come from deep within him, an approaching rumble that one first felt rather than heard. But then it came, and it was like a low roar. He was a giant, like those in the stories from Before. They still told those stories now, or at least some variation.

In the After, some things did not change.

So he was a huge man, a great man. Hair like burnt rust, the scalp starting to show through in a flash of white. A laugh like thunder. Arms covered in black tattoos, symbols that Cavalo had never seen before his first meeting with this man. Symbols that meant REDEMPTION and FAITH and RISE in languages that were no longer spoken in the world, found in the burnt pages of books that crumbled when touched by clumsy hands. Inside his left forearm was a quote, one of the few in English, grafted on in blocky letters: IT WAS A PLEASURE TO BURN.

Who? Cavalo had asked.

Ray Bradbury.

Is he alive?

No. He died. In Before.

Why?

Why these words?

Yeah.

They spoke to me.

A huge man. A great man. A doctor. At least, the closest thing in Cottonwood to a doctor. It was a trade passed down from his father and his father before him, one of the few documented lineages that Cavalo knew of from people who had survived the End. It was a profession before; now it was a trade. People died when they were sick now. Many more than died Before. Machines that had been able to diagnose the simplest of things were nothing more than fairy tales. When found in the remains of hospitals, they were melted, burnt husks that no longer moved.

People died now. Over the tiniest of things. Much of the knowledge had been lost. But Hank said they would get it back. He said it would take time, it would take a long, long time, but they would get it back.

Hank was the closest thing alive aside from Bad Dog that Cavalo had as a friend, though Cavalo didn't quite know how to handle that. Bad Dog wanted to eat. Sleep. Hunt. Shit. Have his ears rubbed every now and then. Nothing more.

Hank liked to talk. And talk. And talk. Cavalo didn't know how to do that. He'd forgotten. He hadn't been one for immaculate social graces before, but it wasn't until after *she* and Jamie had—

Well. He didn't care much for it.

Cavalo sighed inwardly as Hank approached. Deke wasn't far behind him, at least having the common decency to look slightly embarrassed, the foolish boy. Cavalo didn't see Warren yet. Or Alma. But he knew they were there. Somewhere.

"Well, as I live and breathe," Hank Wells boomed. "Glad to see you ain't dead. Decided to grace us with your presence?"

Cavalo steeled himself against the impending touch, the bees buzzing in the back of his head telling him to *run* to head for the *trees* and back to the *mountains* so he didn't have to be around these people. So he didn't have to answer their questions. They always had questions.

Before he could get his legs to work, Hank was on him, grabbing Cavalo's hand, squeezing it hard as he pumped it up and down. Other hand slamming onto Cavalo's back, once. Twice. A third time. Cavalo didn't have to crane his head upward to know that Hank was smiling, a wide thing filled with large, square teeth.

"Hank," Cavalo said.

Hank glanced over at Psycho as he let go of Cavalo's hand and stepped back. His expression remained neutral, but Cavalo knew that mind under that balding head was whirling faster and faster, calculating, processing. Cataloging. Planning, though for what, Cavalo couldn't yet say. While they'd known each other a long time, Hank was still a mystery to Cavalo. He supposed he was to Hank, too, but then there wasn't much he wanted to do to change that.

"Bad Dog," Hank said in greeting. He reached into his pocket and pulled out a piece of deer jerky. "Pray."

Bad Dog immediately rose up on his hind legs, sitting on his haunches. His front paws came up under his snout and he rolled his head toward the lead sky, tongue hanging out. *Dear Jesus-Dog*, Bad Dog said, though only Cavalo could hear him. *Please let BigHank give me that jerky. I love jerky. So much. Love, Bad Dog.*

Cavalo rolled his eyes as delighted laughs went through the crowd. Any other command Hank (or anyone else) would give, Bad Dog would ignore. Every one except *pray*. And with that, he would only do it for Hank. Cavalo had tried it once, after returning to the prison from a provision trip into Cottonwood. Bad Dog had just rolled his eyes, snatched the jerky from Cavalo's hand, and gone to sleep.

Now Hank tossed the jerky into the air, and Bad Dog came out of prayer, snapping up the meat before it could hit the ground. *Oh yes. I love it! I love it so much!*

"It's not *that* good," Cavalo said. "You act like you never eat."

"What's he saying?" Hank asked, and Cavalo suddenly remembered that they weren't alone. Far from it. Hank had never questioned Cavalo's half-crazy (for that's what it had to be, when Cavalo really thought on it) assertion that Bad Dog spoke, at least not to Cavalo's face. Maybe he even actually believed, though the man didn't want to ask him to find out. Sometimes not knowing was better than knowing the answer to that one question that sounded like bees.

"He says thank you," Cavalo muttered, feeling what seemed to be thousands of pairs of eyes upon him, judging. Mocking. Laughing.

Crazy, crazy, crazy, the bees said. *Crazy man with the crazy dog. Dogs don't talk, crazy man.*

I'm not a normal dog, Bad Dog reminded him, sniffing the ground, obviously hoping jerky had fallen from his mouth. *I can talk because I am Bad Dog. And I didn't say thank you. I said I love jerky.*

"You're welcome," Hank said, leaning over to drag his knuckles over the dog's ears. When he spoke again, it was directed toward Cavalo, though he didn't look up. "Busy summer?"

"I lost track of time," Cavalo said, ignoring the unasked questions.

"Oh?"

"Yeah."

"Up there? In the prison?"

"Yeah."

"That right."

Hank was trying his patience and, aside from his initial assessment of the Dead Rabbit, hadn't looked at him again. The boy himself still crouched in a defensive position, eyes darting wildly over the growing crowd. His fingers twitched behind his back, moving one after the other, as if he was counting all those in the town who watched him. For all Cavalo knew, he was. It didn't matter, though. Chances were he wouldn't be leaving this place except to be buried in an unmarked hole at the edge of the woods.

"You knew where I was," Cavalo said, his voice laced with accusation.

"I did. Even started to go up there a few times."

Cavalo could play this game. "Oh?"

Hank didn't look away. "You bet your ass. Stopped myself, though. Figured you were old enough to take care of yourself."

Cavalo snorted. Hank was only a few years older than himself. *And if it's October*, he thought, *that means I'm a year older. Christ.*

"Plus," Hank said, "I couldn't quite get away from Cottonwood. Not with our new guest here and all."

Before Cavalo could ask about that, he saw movement through the crowd and people moved as a woman pushed her way through, eyes like steel, blonde hair plaited down over her shoulder. Her plaid button-down work shirt was opened at the throat, exposing creamy skin. Cavalo watched her throat bob as she swallowed down whatever angry words she had almost let out. He looked at her hands. He'd first been drawn to them years ago because they were unlike most women's hands he knew. Working hands, they were. Callused and rough. He knew them well, or as well as he allowed himself too.

Alma Marsh didn't step out of the crowd, but she knew that *he* knew she was there. She was alone. Her brother, the constable of Cottonwood, still hadn't shown himself. Cavalo knew even before he asked.

"Warren?"

Alma looked away.

Hank did not. "Gone, my friend. In July."

"How?"

"Dead Rabbits."

But Cavalo knew this already. Somehow. What had the black man said, back in the forest on the other side of the divide?

You'd think the good folk of Cottonwood would have learned by now. But maybe they need a reminder.

He looked at Alma again, but she had turned to the psycho. Hate like he'd never seen before filled her eyes. Alma was strong. She was brave. But above all else, she was kind. There was no kindness now. There was only rage. The man wondered what she was capable of, though he thought he knew. Everyone was capable of darkness.

"Shit," Cavalo muttered. He didn't know what else to say.

"That about covers it," Hank agreed.

"Why didn't anyone tell me?" That wasn't a fair question. Not by a mile.

Hank chuckled dryly. "Would it have mattered?"

Yes, he told himself. *It would have mattered. It matters now.*

He felt like a liar. He didn't answer, but then he didn't think Hank expected one. Whatever they were—friends, acquaintances—it didn't matter because Hank knew him. Whether Cavalo liked it or not, Hank knew him as well as anyone could. It rubbed against him the wrong way, but there was nothing that could be done about it.

The throbbing in his head was back. He realized his face was still crusted with blood. He was probably quite the sight to Cottonwood. It would undoubtedly add to the whispers about him. *The bloody man,* they'd tell each other later. *The bloody secret man.*

He ignored the crowd, though their eyes wandered over him. "You sure it was the Dead Rabbits?" he asked Hank. It was unnecessary, that question, but he didn't know what else to say. He saw Psycho tense out of the corner of his eye but didn't know if that was to his words or the growing crowd.

"They left his head on the road thereabouts," Hank said, his voice as calm as if he was commenting on the weather. He pointed back toward the gate to Cottonwood. "Wrote there into the dirt to stay on this side of the divide. It was a message."

"A warning," Cavalo said. He almost pulled the rifle from his shoulder and shot the boy in the face. He didn't because of the children in the crowd, peeking out from behind their parents' legs. But it was close. It never crossed his mind that it would be murder. He didn't think of it like that.

"Sure," Hank said. "A warning. A threat. Just for the hell of it. Whatever it was, Warren died screaming." This last was said quietly.

Cavalo winced at the anger he heard in Hank's voice more than the words. "You heard?"

Hank shook his head. "Could see it on his face."

Cavalo believed him. Warren. A young man, younger than his sister. Not very bright, but always lending a hand. He took his job seriously. He loved his tin badge. Loved it with his whole heart. And now. Now....

A voice from the crowd, lit up with fear: "Is that a Dead Rabbit?"

Murmurs rolled through the people of Cottonwood. It sounded like the wind through the stunted forest near the Deadlands.

"Why is he here?" another voice cried out.

"Could he hurt us?" said another.

And another: "What if he was followed?"

And another: "What if more are coming?"

"Are we safe? What about the *children*?"

"Are we under attack?"

"This isn't right! They killed Warren!"

"That's right! They took him! They took that poor man!"

Cavalo waited as the voices rose as he knew they would, waited for the minds of men to form into the mob he hoped they would not become. Waited for the one person to put the idea in the rest of their heads. He waited to see if this town had become like the rest.

Of course they are, the bees said. *They're human, aren't they?*

Bad Dog flattened his ears and backed up slowly until his hind legs bumped into the man. *Angry*, he whined. *I can hear them. Like your bees. It's coming.*

"No," Cavalo whispered as Hank turned toward the town, holding his hands up as if to ward them back.

But then it was said by the one person Cavalo did not expect. "We should kill him," Deke Wells said. "For what he did to Warren.

He should be dead." He looked surprised at his own words, and he averted his eyes from his father.

Can't take that back, kid, Cavalo thought. *Can't.*

Yes, the crowd sighed. *Yes. Yes. Kill him. He needs to die. He needs to die for what he has inevitably done. If not him, then his people. He will answer for his people.*

They pushed forward. Cavalo saw that Alma did not stop them. He didn't know if he blamed her.

He looked down at the boy, expecting to see fear for the first time, expecting to see him shrinking away. Hiding his eyes. Cavalo wondered then if he would let it happen. If Dead Rabbits showed they were human, could he let this happen?

Daddy! the bees said, sounding like his dead son. *Daddy!*

The boy Dead Rabbit, the prisoner with his hands chained behind his back, was not cowering. His face showed no fear. His teeth were bared, a silent snarl on his face. His shoulders were tensed, body like a coiled spring. He knew they would take him, and he did not care. Cavalo knew he would bite and kick. Rise up and fight back.

"*Stop!*"

The voice was like thunder. Cavalo was reminded of that haunted place long ago, when everything had been at DEFCON 1 and it was NOT A DRILL. The memory eclipsed his reality and the townspeople were all sickly thin coyotes, fat red tumors hanging off their faces and stomachs, swollen and ready to burst. He saw murder in their canine eyes and had to bite his tongue to keep from screaming.

Then it faded, and a man pushed his way through the crowd. A thin man with dark eyes wearing a scowl and a uniform that Cavalo had never seen before. It reminded him of the camo in that hidden fort, and he thought, for just a brief moment, that the man had followed him out of the nightmare. But that couldn't be real. It just couldn't.

He closed his eyes and then opened them again. The man was

still there. In his hand was a cone made of plastic, and he lowered it from his mouth.

Amplifier, Cavalo thought. *A... phone? Phone. Something-phone.*

"What is the meaning of this?" the stranger asked. His voice was high. Reedy. His eyes narrowed as they landed on Cavalo. "Who are you?"

"Cavalo," he said.

"Cavalo?" The stranger frowned. "Is that your first name? Last name?"

"Yes."

"You're not on my list."

"Oh."

"Oh? *Oh?*"

"Yes." Cavalo shouldn't have come here. He pretended not to notice how the Dead Rabbit had inched his way toward him, his shoulders bumping into his leg. He tried not to notice how Bad Dog had done the same on the other side. He tried not to notice these things because they were so easy to notice.

"Do you know who I am?" the stranger asked.

"No." Cavalo did not care.

When the man spoke again, Cavalo began to wish this day had never happened. He thought again of the tree. Of *her.*

"My name is Carl Wilkinson, and I represent the United Feder-ated States of America. Your government has been rebuilt, and this is the beginning of a glorious future, blah blah blah. Now who the fuck are you?"

alma's song

CAVALO WAITED outside Alma's door, unsure of what to do next. He wasn't good with other people's grief. Especially when he didn't understand his own. It was complicated.

But he owed her. Something. She'd given him much without ever asking for anything in return. Like Hank, she was his... friend. Maybe. Possibly. Warren had been a good man. Naïve. He was young, so that was to be expected. Brash. Idealistic. Headstrong. Cavalo winced at that word. Probably not the best to describe him now. No one deserved that death. No one. The man didn't want to know what had been done with the rest of the body, though he had a good idea.

You gonna knock? Bad Dog asked as he turned in circles. He settled on the old porch and yawned.

"Just give me a minute," he muttered.

We need to get back home, MasterBossLord.

"I know."

SIRS is going to yell at us because we've been gone so long.

"He's just a robot."

He's still going to be mad.

"I know."

Cavalo raised his hand to knock on the door when the dog spoke again.

The boy.

Cavalo lowered his hand. "What about him?"

Bad Dog closed his eyes. *He smells different.*

The man felt sweat drip down the back of his neck. "How?"

Don't know. But you feel it too.

Cavalo didn't feel that. He didn't know what the imaginary voice he gave his dog meant. It was nothing. It meant nothing. And *if* there was something, *if* he allowed himself to see anything there, it was clinical. A cold appreciation from one hunter to another, nothing more.

The man from the government had announced himself and had taken control. His eyes had widened as soon as he'd seen the boy Dead Rabbit. This man, this *Wilkinson*, had fumbled then with a black radio, the screech of static foreign to Cavalo's ears. He'd barked into it, saying *Simon*, saying *Bernard*, demanding they come at once. Cavalo hadn't seen a radio in years. A working one, however? Maybe not ever, at least that he could remember.

It had screeched. Wilkinson had squawked. Two other men had come, big men, overgrown men with shaved heads and veins bulging on comically huge biceps. Their uniforms matched Wilkinson's, though they didn't have the same colorful bars across their breasts. One blond, the other with black hair, shaved close to the scalp. They looked mean. Stupid. The dull eyes of cattle. They were muscle, and Wilkinson was the brain.

Psycho had lashed out as Blond and Black approached, quicker than was expected. He caught Blond in the knee with his foot, snake-bite fast. Blond had roared angrily. Black had pulled a black metal stick out of his utility belt. Electricity snapped at the end. Cavalo almost shouted out a warning, but stopped himself. It wasn't his fight. He didn't care. The boy was not his concern.

But it came. That cold respect. That admiration of a killer.

Psycho almost escaped. He moved like liquid, hands still secured behind his back. It was the grace of an animal. A sleek cat. While the boy moved, his eyes seemed almost black. It was made all the more surreal by the fact that no sound came from him, not even a quickened breath. Blond and Black were bleeding. Psycho was not.

Cavalo had no doubt that if the boy's arms had been free, he would have killed them both. As it was, he almost did. But then Black had gotten in just a graze with the electric stick. There was a snap in the air, a crackle that smelled like lightning. The boy's mouth had opened in a grimace, the cords in his neck standing out. His eyes had rolled back in his head. He'd collapsed.

"Take him," Wilkinson had panted.

They did. Roughly.

Hank hurried after them, his voice angry.

The crowd had watched Cavalo a moment longer before they too dispersed. It was morning, after all. Things had to be done. Soon it was just Cavalo standing on the road to Cottonwood, Bad Dog by his side.

Now he stood on the ramshackle porch of Alma's farmhouse, thinking about the insanity of robots, the voices of his dog and the bees, the death of a man who didn't deserve to die, this town, this woman, the tree like *her*, the ghost of his son.

And the boy. Psycho.

The door opened before he could knock.

The steel hadn't completely left Alma's eyes. They were hard. She looked older than before. Death did that, Cavalo knew.

"Just going to stand there?" she asked him in a clipped tone.

You bring death wherever you go, the bees said.

He hesitated.

Alma turned and disappeared back into the house, leaving the door open.

Cavalo looked over his shoulder. The clouds overhead looked even darker than they had the day before. *Early snow this year*, he thought. He wouldn't admit to himself that he was slightly frightened it had reached October without him knowing. Hadn't he noted frost on the ground at the prison? The leaves changing color? The cold air? Hadn't SIRS or Bad Dog said anything?

He followed Alma into the house.

He sat before her in a chair in her kitchen. It was cold in the house. It felt like Warren was everywhere. It'd been the two of them for the longest time. Their parents had died when Alma was sixteen and Warren only two. It hadn't been the Dead Rabbits that time. A drifter—Cavalo couldn't remember his name—broke into their house late one night. Shot their father. Raped and shot their mother, who'd shoved Warren into Alma's arms and told her to hide, to run, to get away. She had. She hid in the cellar, behind the potatoes, singing quietly to Warren, who fussed in her arms. Eventually, when the sky began to lighten, she'd crawled through a window with her brother and run for help. A group of men returned later to the house to find the drifter asleep next to the mother, curled around her body. The drifter told them he did it because the voices made him. *Sodom and Gomorrah,* he'd said. *The flight of the crows will always bring the fire and I will* bask *in the blood that rains from the sky.*

He'd been executed later that day. One precious bullet to the head.

Voices. Cavalo knew about voices.

"That Dead Rabbit do this?" Alma asked, dipping a cloth into a bowl of warm water. She brought the cloth up and started dabbing at his forehead. She was not gentle. He winced but bit back the urge to tell her to be gentle.

"No," he said, then thought. "Maybe. Yes." It hurt his pride, but Cavalo couldn't lie. For all he knew, the boy had set the net. "Got caught in a trap."

She smiled, but there was no humor in it. "A boy gets the upper hand with the great Cavalo? Must be losing your edge, old man."

It hit him again. His birthday. He struggled to remember the number. He pulled it from behind the bees and felt every bit of his forty years. So much time had gone by without him knowing, and he felt illusory. Thin. Like he was nothing but a ghost and could be blown away by the slightest wind.

She was right. He had grown careless. He knew better.

Daddy! the bees said.

Stop it, he said back. *Please.* He almost opened his mouth to tell her he was chasing a ghost but thought better of it. She didn't need his ghosts. Not now. Not ever.

"He's the one in cuffs," Cavalo said instead, his voice gruff. He winced as he got a particularly hard jab.

"This time," Alma said, her voice tinged with anger. "What happens next time?"

"It won't happen again."

She rinsed the cloth in the bowl. The water was a dirty pink, little flecks of blood and grime floating along the surface. He saw the way her hands shook.

"I'm sorry," he said, though it was inadequate. He didn't know what he was apologizing for. Many things, most likely.

"For what?" she asked. She didn't look back up, instead staring at the ruined cloth, the blood in the bowl. A droplet of water tracked its way down his cheek. It looked like a tear. It felt like one. It wasn't.

"Warren." That was partly true, made real by the fact that Cavalo could see a pair of Warren's boots sitting near the door, flecked with dust.

She laughed. It quaked with fury. "Warren," she said. "Yes. I am sorry too."

He reached out for her, but she shook her head. "Don't."

"No?"

"Not yet."

He looked down at his hands. They were covered in dirt and blood. God only knew what else. "I'm sorry," he said again.

She resumed her cleaning of him. "That's twice now."

"What?"

"That you've apologized. How long have we known each other?"

"Eight years. Maybe nine."

"Nine, I should think."

"Maybe."

"And in those eight years, maybe nine, I've never heard you apologize. Not once."

He was bemused. "Have I had anything to apologize for?"

Her tongue stuck out between her teeth, an endearing trait she had when she concentrated. "You're a man, are you not?" she said, bathing his hands.

"Yes."

"Then no doubt you've done something that needs apologizing for."

"I'm sorry."

She smiled again, but it was watery. He wouldn't draw attention to it. It wouldn't do. It wouldn't be what Alma Marsh wanted. She was a strong woman. She felt she could do anything a man could do. Cavalo thought this wrong. She could do it better. She was the carpenter of Cottonwood and had the uncanny knack to fix most everything that was broken. If she could get her hands on electronics (far and few between they were), she could usually puzzle it out. Once she'd even repaired Cavalo's flashlight, though he couldn't explain how. It died one day, and no battery would fix it. He brought it to her. She took it apart. She cursed at it. Switched some things around. Put it back together. It worked. Like he knew it would. Few things could elude her. Cavalo knew many towns still didn't have electricity. Cottonwood did. Grangeville did. And it was thanks to Alma.

She had value, more than Cavalo did. And yet here she was, bathing him like she had nothing better to do. He thought she might love him, though she never said it. Cavalo left it mixed in with the bees. It seemed safer.

What could he ask her? To make her forget, at least for a moment? He could tell her something funny Bad Dog had done. Or maybe about the family of squirrels he'd seen gathering nuts. (How had he not known winter approached?) He could say anything he'd seen in five months, because it *had* been five months.

But instead he said, "The government man."

The smile slid off her face on its way to a scowl. "If you can call him that."

"Is it true?"

She sighed. "That depends on if you take his word for it."

"Do you?"

"Take his word?"

"Yeah."

She set the cloth down on the table and sat back in her chair. She watched him with shrewd eyes. She missed nothing. She never did. "The boy."

"If you can call him that," he said. He knew what she was doing. Give and take.

"Is it true?"

He shrugged. "Can't take his word for it. Don't think he can speak."

"His neck? Saw the scar."

"Yeah."

"What happened?"

"To him? I don't know. He didn't tell me."

"You tell jokes now?" she asked. She sounded amused.

"Can't say for sure," he said honestly. Cavalo didn't think he had a sense of humor, but maybe that had changed during the summer. He tried to remember the last time he laughed.

He couldn't.

She watched him.

He waited.

"Maybe," she said finally. "Maybe I believe him. The government man. It had to be a matter of time, didn't it?"

"Why?"

"Because the minds of men can only be scattered for so long. Soon, they'll combine. They'll plan. They'll create. They'll build."

"All of this has happened before," he said.

"And all of this will happen again," she replied. He'd found the book on one of his excursions, deep in what had been an office building, desks scattered, shells of computer screens, glass busted out. It had been tattered but complete, buried in a drawer of an upturned desk. *Peter Pan.* A boy in Neverland who never wanted to grow old. The Lost Boys. Hook. Wendy. The crocodile. He'd read it, then given it to Alma as a gift. She told him it was a children's story. He thought it horror, and Peter a monster.

"United Federated States of America," he said.

"Has quite the ring to it, doesn't it?" Alma said. "The UFSA apparently is reaching out. To what they call the outposts."

"Is that what we are?"

"We?" she asked, calling him out.

Cavalo said nothing.

She let it go. "Apparently. They're trying to put the country back together again. He has official documents. Or, rather, what he *called* official documents. He said they were his orders."

"Orders? Like military?"

Alma shrugged. "Maybe. Said that the world is starting again, and the UFSA will be at the forefront. As it always has been."

"What did the papers say?"

"That America would rise like a phoenix from the ashes. Theatrics never seem to fade far from politics."

"Were they signed?"

"Not individually. But there was a signature."

"What did it say?"

She looked him in the eyes, and he wondered when was the last time she had slept. "The Forefathers," she replied.

"That's not ominous at all."

The small smile flashed again. "Funny man."

"Heard of them before?"

"No. We always thought this was years away. And maybe it still is. Maybe they're just spreading their feelers out."

"But maybe not." His throat felt dry. He'd spoken more in the past day than he'd done in the past year. He had questions, and the bees had questions. He couldn't stop.

"Maybe not," she agreed. "Who knows how long it's been going on. It's rare to meet people from back east this far out near the Dead-lands. The last I heard, it was still like it is here. Divided. Little pockets of humanity. Imagine what's going on in other parts of the world."

He didn't want to. Cavalo wouldn't admit it, but the size of the world and how much was unknown scared him. "Wilkinson. Blond. Black."

She nodded.

"Just the three of them?"

"That we know of," she said, a curl of disgust on her lips. "But cockroaches have a way of multiplying."

Cavalo frowned. "What's he said?"

Alma looked out the window. She was beautiful, even if she had started to fade. He had always thought so. But it wasn't enough. Not for either of them. It wasn't her fault. Even if the lines around her blue eyes were more pronounced. Her hair more dull.

"It's what he isn't saying," she said quietly. "For every assurance he gives of structure and food and medicine, the fewer answers he gives as to how and when and why. He is especially interested in the Deadlands." She glanced back at him. Much was said there, but Cavalo knew none of it. "And the Dead Rabbits."

Cavalo felt a chill. "Why?"

"Says he wants to know who they are. What they do. 'Solve the problem,' he says." Her words were bitter.

Here was his chance. An opening. He didn't know if he should take it. He'd forgotten what it meant to be sympathetic. He knew *what* it was; he just didn't remember how to do it. "Alma."

She nodded, turning her face away, blinking back tears. She

hated crying. Always had. Said it was a sign of weakness. She didn't have time to show weakness. It got you hurt, she said. It could get you killed. So she hid her face now. Hid her face even as her chest hitched once. Twice.

"Warren was a good man," he said.

A choked breath.

"A brave man."

She wiped her eyes.

"I wish...." He stopped himself. What he meant to say wasn't fair.

But she heard it anyway. She turned to him, her wet eyes flashing in anger. "Don't you dare," she said. "Don't you dare say you should have been here. Don't you dare, Cavalo."

He should have. He hadn't been. "You're right. I don't dare."

"You come here only when you want. When it's convenient for you."

"Yes."

"You hide away up at that prison with your damn dog. With your insane robot. With your ghosts."

"Yes."

"You don't know what it means to be human anymore. You are cold. You are dead inside. You don't care about anyone except yourself."

That stung. Deeply. But he had no retort. "Yes."

Her hands curled into fists on the table. He thought she meant to swing at him. He wouldn't stop her. If it helped her, he'd let her do it. It was the least he could do.

"Why?" she asked instead.

He waited.

"Why did you bring that... that *thing* here?"

The boy. The Dead Rabbit. The psycho fucking bulldog. "I don't know," he said.

"Did you want us to kill him for you?"

"No." He could have killed the Dead Rabbit himself.

"Did you want us to try him? Stand for his crimes? For being a Dead Rabbit?"

"No." The result would have been the same.

"Did he have something to do with Warren?"

"I don't know. I don't think so."

Alma was furious. "You know what they do."

"Yes."

"They took him. They took my brother." Her voice quaked.

"Yes." He could see it in his mind. Every moment.

"They took him. They cut him. While he was alive and awake, they cut off his head."

"Yes." *Oh God.*

"Then they... they...." Her chest hitched again.

"Alma. Don't."

She pushed through. "Then they *ate* him."

He closed his eyes.

"It's what they do. They *eat* people. *They eat humans.* They sent his head back as a warning, and they *ate the rest of him.*"

He said nothing.

"And *you.*"

Cavalo could hear the hiss of her breath.

"You of all people. You *know* what they do. You *know* what they're capable of. Because of *her.* Because of your *son*—"

He slammed his fist down on the table. She flinched back. "Don't," he said.

But she wasn't scared of him. Even when everyone else shrank away, she never had. "Why did you bring him here?"

"Because Jamie led me to him." He said it before he could stop himself.

Her eyes widened. "Jamie? Who is... oh. Oh, Cavalo. That... was that your son's name?"

He'd never told her before. And now that he had, he wanted nothing more than to take it back. Her eyes had lost their anger, and now they only held sadness. It was for him. He hated that look. "It doesn't matter." *Jamie didn't lead me to anything. He didn't. It was nothing. It is nothing.*

"He's dead," she said.

"I know."

"Do you?"

Daddy!

"Yes."

Alma Marsh sighed and rose from her chair, taking the ruined cloth. The dirty bowl. "I expect you're hungry."

He shook his head but wouldn't look at her. "No, ma'am. Just tired. Bad Dog could probably use something to eat if you're offering."

"I may have a couple of bones for him." She turned toward the kitchen and took a step. She stopped but didn't turn back. "Cavalo."

"Yeah?"

She hesitated, and he wondered at her mind. "You know where the bed is," she said finally. "Get some sleep. I expect you'll want to provision up before you leave."

"Snow's coming early," he said. He thought of the Dead Rabbit.

"It always does. I have work to do."

"What?"

She laughed. "If you can believe it, building a government office."

He narrowed his eyes. "Wilkinson?"

"Said they needed a home base. A *liaison* office, he called it. If you can believe such a thing."

"And you're doing it?"

Her response was clipped. "Money's money."

He looked down at his hands. Killer's hands. "That it is."

"I'll be back later."

She walked toward the kitchen. Before she got to the doorway, he called out to her. She stopped.

"In the woods," he said. "Through the divide."

He saw her shoulders tense.

"The Dead Rabbit. Others were there. They didn't see me."

"Lucky you." Her voice was tight.

"They mentioned a name."

"Oh?"

"Yeah. Seemed like he was their leader."

She laughed. It sounded forced. "The Dead Rabbits don't have leaders. They're animals."

"Even animals follow pack leaders," he said quietly.

"What of it?"

"Patrick." He looked for a reaction. "That was his name."

She gave none. "Good for him. Good for them."

"You heard that name?"

"No."

"Okay."

"You done? I'm going to be late."

"Yeah. Alma?"

"What?"

"Thanks. For...."

"I know."

And then she was gone.

He slept in her bed (one that he was not a stranger to) and dreamed of fire and blood.

He woke as dusk descended on Cottonwood. For a moment he was still trapped in his dreams and he was sure there was still time. He was sure *she* hadn't tried to take Jamie and leave. He was sure all he had to do was call out to her, and she'd open the door and everything would be as it was and as it should be.

He was so sure.

He opened his mouth to call her name. It died before he made a sound. The room came back into focus. It was strange but not unfamiliar.

He closed his eyes. Breathed in.
And heard her sing.

GOOD-BYE, GOOD-BYE, YOU SAY GOOD-BYE
From my arms you rise
Nothing here left, my love
So you say good-bye

HE ROSE FROM THE BED AND FOLLOWED HER SONG.

YOU HAVE GONE NOW, O'ER THE SEA
To the place beyond the mountains
I cannot walk, I cannot follow
So I say good-bye

THERE WILL BE DEATH, THE BEES SAID.

YEARS NOW PASSED, MEMORY DID FADE
Your face hidden in shadow
Claimed from me my love
So we say good-bye.

GOOD-BYE. THE MAN NAMED CAVALO SAID GOOD-BYE.

GOOD-BYE, GOOD-BYE, YOU SAY GOOD-BYE
From my arms you rise
Nothing here left, my love

So you say good-bye

HE FOUND HER ON THE PORCH, SITTING IN AN OLD WOODEN chair, a blanket on her lap. The sky was almost dark, hidden behind those ominous clouds. Bad Dog sat in front of her, his head on her thigh, his big dark eyes watching her as she sang. She stroked his ears. On the last sweet note from her lips, she fell silent. He knew that she knew he was there. He waited, ignoring the deep chill in the air.

Finally, she said, "Wilkinson is taking your prisoner. The Dead Rabbit."

"Where?"

She turned her face toward the sky. "Did you know there are satellites? Do you know that word?"

He did. He'd heard it before. Somewhere in his travels. Space robots. For however much the idea of how the big the world was scared him, the idea of *outside* the world was unfathomable to Cavalo. "Yeah."

"Great machines. Spinning around Earth, high above us in space. We put them there. We had the means to do so. Once. With rockets. Do you know rockets?"

He didn't, not really, but he understood what she meant.

"With the satellites, you could talk to anyone in the world in seconds. You could find anything in the world in seconds. We were all connected." She sounded wistful. "All of us."

The idea was so beyond Cavalo that he couldn't process it. It was a magnitude he didn't understand. "Why would you want to?"

She laughed. "Right. Of course. I forgot for a moment who I was talking to. Maybe it'd be easier for you to understand that these satellites could fire lasers. Light that was like bullets. And bombs. You know bombs. Everyone knows bombs."

"From Before."

"Yes. But now, these things, these satellites, are useless. They float above us, circling Earth. Maybe they still work. Maybe they don't. It doesn't matter. They're out of our reach."

He understood. "For now."

She nodded. "Yes. For now. So, for now, Wilkinson cannot call his people, this new government, on his fancy radio. The signal isn't powerful enough. He must send a messenger with a letter."

"To where?"

"East. Maybe Grangeville. Maybe farther. I think farther."

"How do you know all this?"

"I'm building their office. I hear things. And besides, I'm just a woman. What could I know about the minds of men?"

Cavalo frowned. "Why would you think that?" It was unlike her. If anything, she was smarter than most people he knew.

She laughed again, and it sounded like the first real laugh since he'd arrived that morning. "Oh, that's not what *I* believe. Just what was implied. Wilkinson doesn't think much of women, though he's made it known he wouldn't mind sticking it in me."

"I'm sure that went over well."

"Let's just say that I'm lucky I wasn't arrested. How was I to know his wrist could be so easily sprained?" She stroked Bad Dog's ears one last time before she pushed him away gently and rose to her feet. It was almost full-on dark. "Now," she said as she began to unbutton her work shirt. Her skin was luminous in the dark. "I need to be held."

Her shirt dropped to the porch, and he stepped forward, taking her in his arms.

AFTER, THEY LAY SIDE BY SIDE IN HER BED.

"You could come with me," he said.

"To the prison?"

"Yes."

She snorted. "That's appealing."

"It's not as bad as it sounds. You can come."

"You don't mean that."

He didn't know if he did, so he said nothing.

"Or," she said. "You could stay."

"You know I can't."

"I do?"

"Yes."

"The world needs people like you, Cavalo."

Pretty words, the bees said. *You are nothing but a murderer.*

"The world needs to be scared of people like me," he said.

"People listen to you."

"Because they're scared."

"You're a natural leader."

"Lie."

"Cottonwood will need someone. Soon, I think."

"Hank is already here."

She shook her head. He felt her hair on his bare shoulder.

"Hank wasn't made to lead."

"He's done well so far."

"He's scared, Cavalo. Like the rest of us. Things are about to change. It's already started."

"I can't be who you want me to be." He meant it. About so many things.

"No," she said sadly. "No, you can't. I'll go with you to the prison if you tell me one thing."

"What?"

"Your name."

"Cavalo." He knew what she meant, but he pretended she didn't.

"Your full name."

"Alma...." It was buried, behind the bees. She knew this. It was gone.

"I know. One day. When you tell someone your real name, that's when you'll know you're ready."

"For what?"

She loomed over him and began to move her hips. "To rise," she said. "One day, you will rise."

He didn't know what she spoke of. But even in her words, the song over her voice, he couldn't help but feel this was good-bye, good-bye.

She said good-bye.

ashen and sober

HE WOKE, as he sometimes did, in the middle of the night. Dreams chased him out, their claws trying to pull him back under. He escaped, but only just. His head hurt.

He didn't allow himself sentimentality as he eased out of bed, careful not to wake Alma. He hadn't survived as long as he had by allowing himself to become sentimental. It wasn't who he was.

The bees buzzed words he couldn't understand. Something felt off. It was harder to breathe.

He dressed quietly. He thought he should pause at the doorway. Look back. Think of fond memories. Maybe even leave a note. Do something to show he wasn't dead inside, that he could resemble a human being.

But he did none of this.

Bad Dog raised his head from his spot in front of the iron fireplace. Firelight danced along his fur. He cocked his head. *Awake now, MasterBossLord?*

"Yes."

Done here?

"Yes."

He stood and arched his back. *AlmaLady gave me two bones and I chewed them to pieces!*

Cavalo found his pack near the door. He dug through it until he found his old hunting coat. He put it on, wondering what he had been thinking the month was when he'd packed it earlier. "Good bones?"

Bad Dog shook himself. *The best bones. Smells like wet outside.*

"Snow's coming." He picked up the rifle. His bow.

I like snow?

Cavalo allowed himself to smile. "You do. You act like a puppy in snow. Cold white stuff."

Bad Dog's tail wagged, and he grinned. *I like cold white stuff. I bite it and I'm not thirsty anymore. Gonna go home? SIRS is gonna be mad.*

"I know."

His ears flattened. *He gonna yell?*

"Probably."

Stupid robot SIRS, the dog grumbled as he joined the man near the door.

Cavalo put his hand on the handle of the door, and a pang of *something* clenched his stomach. It felt like regret, a feeling he hadn't had in years. Leaving like this was wrong, slinking out in the middle of the night. Even if the snow was coming. Even if he told himself he needed to get back before it fell. It still felt wrong, like running away.

You're good at that, the bees mocked. *You are so good at running. Run, little man. Run away. Leave them here to fend for themselves and run away while you still can. Government men are coming, so run while you can.*

What about Smells Different? Bad Dog asked, nudging Cavalo's hand.

"Smells Different?" Cavalo asked, sure he'd heard the dog say the words as if they were a name.

Trapped man. Boy. Bad guy. Smells Different.

Cavalo's hand tightened on the door handle. "Why do you ask?"

Gonna get him? I can bite him for you. Guard him, I mean. Then bite him. Bet he tastes different too.

The fire crackled behind them.

"No," the man said. "He stays here."

Oh. Why? He was my *prisoner.*

"He's a bad guy."

Oh. Bad guys die, right?

"Right."

Oh. Home?

"Home."

He opened the door into the cold night.

DON'T LEAVE WITHOUT SAYING SOMETHING, HANK HAD TOLD him. *I'll put supplies out back, but don't you leave. We need to have a talk, you and I.*

It couldn't be helped. Cavalo was starting to feel the cold hands of claustrophobia wrapping around his heart and mind. He thought his breath was whistling in his throat. He thought it all in his head. He wondered, not for the first time, how much of his sanity was lost. If all these things in his life were imagined things and he was really trapped in a room somewhere, in a dark corner, this whole world nothing but a creation in his head. It wouldn't surprise him.

So no. He had to leave. He had to get out of here. He didn't know why he came in the first place. It had to do with the Dead Rabbit, but even that seemed small. Inconsequential. He should have just killed him, and then he could have gone home. He shouldn't have crossed the divide. He should've killed the deer with the first shot. He should have saved his family.

He should have succeeded in killing himself.

He touched the scar on the side of his head. He felt the bees against his fingers, just under the skin.

He shook his head. *Get out*, he thought.

He continued on, sticking to the deep shadows of the night. His breath trailed behind him in a thick plume. The air was bitterly cold against his ears. Bad Dog stuck close to his side, his nose close to the ground.

"We have to be quiet," he told the dog.

Yeah, I kind of figured.

Cavalo swore Bad Dog rolled his eyes.

Hank lived toward the center of Cottonwood. The majority of the town had been destroyed during the End. In the time of Before, it had been a little place, a small farming town. There were still bent and broken signs showing US 95, which had been the main road through Cottonwood Before. Now, all the cement and pavement was gone, only dirt roads left in their place. People still called the main drag US 95, though it didn't mean what it had before. Outside of Cottonwood, US 95 was lost to brush and trees and grass and debris.

Houses had been built, functional things that were walls and roofs, square and squat. Others, like Alma's, had been built like farmhouses from Before, large and airy, triangularly peaked.

And still others, like that of Hank Wells, had survived the End. They were houses from Before. They'd been husks whose foundations still stood, whose memories were still buried inside the walls. Cavalo could have never lived in a place like those houses. He would rather have seen them all burned to the ground. To start over from scratch.

Here was the general store, run by an elderly couple named Jerry and Martha, who bickered back and forth so much it was a wonder they hadn't yet murdered each other.

Here was a hardware store. The owner, a quiet man named Fazil Hadi, managed a group of five or six men and woman who entered the woods early each morning, logging the surrounding area.

Here was a tiny school, built by Alma. Two rooms, divided between the older and younger kids. Last Cavalo had asked, seventeen children in all attended.

Here was Warren's office. Or what had been Warren's office. It was shuttered and dark, like it too was dead. Cavalo stopped, just for a moment. He placed his hand upon the door. The wood was cold. Alma had built this place for her brother, as a way to congratulate him on being chosen as constable when the previous man in the position, Maloney, had passed due to illness.

Cavalo tried to think of the last thing he'd said to Warren or that Warren had said to him. Something about trees? Or maybe about SIRS. Warren was fascinated by the robot. He'd probably asked questions Cavalo didn't know the answer to. Question after question in that way he had.

He stepped away from Warren's office. He didn't look back.

He saw sentries up along the walls, patrolling in pairs, bundled up against the cold. One scanned outside the car wall. The other looked into Cottonwood. If this had been a test, they would have failed. Cavalo kept to the shadows and remained unseen. He'd have to let Hank know, since Hank was in charge now.

He reached the A-frame that Hank called home with Deke and Aubrey. He circled back behind the house and found a burlap sack just where Hank had said it would be. On the top was a note in Hank's tight scrawl.

Figured you'd leave in the middle of the night. Be safe up there this winter. We're down here if you need anything.

—H

The sack was full. A couple of pairs of hide pants, woven painstakingly. Dried meats and fruits. A couple of cans of preserves that Aubrey made that Cavalo loved so. Batteries for the flashlights. Mush for Bad Dog. What looked like a coat for him too. A blanket.

It was what was owed. Cavalo had done some jobs for the town years prior, before the bees had come. He couldn't remember if this was the last time or if he was owed one more set of supplies. It didn't matter. He'd worry about it later.

He emptied the bag into his own pack. It'd be heavy, but he'd make it. He reached the bottom and his fingers brushed against something solid. He pulled it out. A little book, the cover worn, the words gone. It felt precious, this thing. A tiny bird feather stuck out, marking one of the pages. He opened it and found another note.

Thought you'd understand this one.

—H

He lifted the note and found a poem underneath, the page torn and faded but still legible. "Ulalume," it was called. By Edgar Allen Poe. Cavalo didn't recognize the name. A stanza had been circled.

THE SKIES THEY WERE ASHEN AND SOBER;
The leaves they were crisped and sere—
The leaves they were withering and sere;
It was night in the lonesome October
Of my most immemorial year.

CAVALO CLOSED THE LITTLE BOOK. HE THOUGHT ABOUT LEAVING it in the bag. Fuck Hank. He knew what he was doing when he placed it there. He knew exactly what he was doing. Fuck Hank. Fuck this town. Fuck them all. He didn't need to come back. He'd leave the book here and Hank would find it in the morning, and that alone would be enough.

He placed it into his pack.

It was time to go.

The man whistled softly, a short burst of air, and Bad Dog returned to his side from watering a bush. *That is mine too*, he said.

"Home."

Home, the dog agreed.

He turned the corner around the house and saw a flash of light in a building farther down the way, off from all the others. Set back from the road. Surrounded by trees. He didn't remember a house there before. Even in the dark, he could see it wasn't completed, the roof covered in plastic sheeting. One wall looked to still be just a frame.

Said they needed a home base, the bees said. *A liaison office, he called it. If you can believe such a thing.*

He could. He could believe.

Every part of him told him to walk away. To leave. To sneak out, go home. Hole up. Wait for the snows to come and bury everything. Maybe by spring he'd be dead. Wouldn't that be something.

So imagine his surprise when he walked toward the light, toward the partially constructed liaison office. The office being built for the government. The UFSA. Cavalo was not the smartest man in the world. He didn't understand politics. He didn't understand the need for people to be near one another. He didn't understand why he still lived.

But he understood the minds of men. What happened when they grouped. When they mobbed. He understood that very well.

Smells Different, Bad Dog said.

"Yeah," Cavalo said. Because that is where he would be. Now that Warren was gone. The old constable office had been empty. The prisoner would be with his captors.

Snow began to fall. Flurries, just. More would come. The sky would break open and the world would fill with white. He needed to go home. Time was running out.

And yet....

"Shit," he muttered.

Going? Bad Dog asked.

"No," he said, even though he wanted to. Even though it should have been the only idea. The only plan.

Leave now, the bees said.

Instead Cavalo crouched and took the dog's face in his hands. "You follow my lead," he said. It was a mantra between them. Those secret words. They were said anytime the unknown reared its head. If Cavalo was pressed, he would even admit to believing in his secret heart that they held some kind of dying magic, the last bit in this shell of a world.

I follow you, for you are my MasterBossLord, Bad Dog said, his eyes never leaving Cavalo's.

"You listen for my commands."

I listen to you, for you are my MasterBossLord.

"I will have your back."

And I will have yours.

"Together."

Together.

Cavalo stood, hesitated only briefly, and then moved toward the building. Toward the lights that flashed within. For even if he wasn't the smartest man and even if he didn't understand how all things worked, the man named Cavalo was still a curious man, even if he wouldn't admit it to himself. He still wondered about things, deep in his secret heart.

His sanity. He wondered about that a lot.

His isolation. Self-imposed, that. For what reason? To let the world pass him by until Death finally came for him with open arms and sweet relief?

He wondered about that. Constantly.

And this Wilkinson. He wondered about him too. About this government. About what they wanted. About what they would do.

But above all, he wondered about the boy. The Dead Rabbit. Smells Different. The psycho fucking bulldog. His smudged black mask. His bared teeth. His fury. He wondered about him more than he should have. He couldn't find a way to stop.

He murders, the bee said. *He eats people. He eats flesh from their bones. People like Warren.*

Like Jamie.

Well, yes. He did. But curiosity was an overwhelming thing, and Cavalo was only human.

He could hear voices upon approach. Not the higher vibrato of Wilkinson. Blond and Black, maybe. Deeper. Like rumbles in the earth. They sounded like the big black Dead Rabbit from the stunted forest near the Deadlands. The one with the tumors. Cavalo wondered then for the first time (and it wouldn't be the last, oh no) if there was a difference between Dead Rabbit men and government men. He did not know. But surely they *had* to be different, didn't they?

He kept to the shadows. He noticed no Patrol running along these back walls. Was that intentional? Did Wilkinson order them away? Cavalo thought not. He didn't think these men could be here for so short a time and have control over Cottonwood so quickly. Hank and Warren would never have allowed it.

But Warren is dead, isn't he? Maybe he didn't allow it. Maybe that's what happens. Maybe you're fed to the Dead Rabbits.

The minds of men. Dangerous things.

Cavalo finally heard Wilkinson as he reached the building, speaking in low tones. The words came into sharper focus as Cavalo pressed up near an unfinished window. Bad Dog sat near his feet, ears pricked.

"This can go on all night, you know," Wilkinson said. "And it will until you give me what I want."

There was no answer.

"I find myself fascinated by you and your kind," Wilkinson continued. "You are such mindless savages. Hidden in your woods. The Deadlands. How is it that you are not suffering the effects of radiation sickness? What has he given you?"

No response.

"Pity," Wilkinson said. "Though, if it had been that easy, I think I might have been disappointed. You have a reputation to uphold, I know. Anyone who can sit at the right hand of that man must be psychotic. Bernard, if you will."

An electrical snap filled the air, crackling. Cavalo smelled something burning.

"Stop," Wilkinson said.

The electricity ceased.

"I don't know whether to consider it a gift or a curse that you can't make a sound," Wilkinson said. "On one hand, there's something positively delicious about the choked cries. The pleading. The begging. But... on the other, no one can hear you, so this can go on all night. And it will. Now. We'll try this again." His voice went soft, and Cavalo strained to hear. "Where. Is. Patrick?"

Smells Different, Bad Dog panted. *Smells Different*.

Cavalo brought his fingers to his lips, silencing the dog. Bad Dog's tail twitched in a staccato beat. Cavalo should leave, he knew. He should stick to the plan and leave. Grab his dog and get the hell out of Cottonwood. This place had changed. Maybe it was time to move on. In the spring, he could leave the prison and head north. SIRS would be pissed, as his system was integrated into the building, but they'd figure it out. Somehow SIRS would go with them. They'd survive in someplace new.

Instead Cavalo turned slightly toward the incomplete window and looked inside.

Blond and Black stood off to the side. Each held one of the electric sticks he'd seen earlier. Wilkinson had his back to Cavalo, sitting in a chair, facing a wall.

For a moment Cavalo could not see the Dead Rabbit. Then Wilkinson sat back in his chair. In front of him stood Psycho. His black mask was smeared heavily on his face, tracks tracing down his cheeks as if he'd cried. But these would not have been tears of sadness or fear. No, the Dead Rabbit's face was twisted into something monstrous, fury distorting the features. His arms were stretched out away from his body, the wrists in manacles that extended into chains attached to the far support beams on either side of him. His legs too were chained. Sweat dripped down his face. Not tears. Not him. His eyes were completely black, like they had been filled with oil. His chest rose and fell rapidly, quick little breaths that made no noise. His hands curled into fists. Blood dripped from them, fingernails cutting into the palms. His face was bloodied, mask dripping. Smeared, like he was melting.

And still he stood tall. Angry. Proud. Psychotic, yes. Bulldog, yes. Murderer, oh yes. But Cavalo couldn't help the feeling of pride, of a wounded animal, cornered, becoming all claws and teeth and desperation. There was no fear there. Only white-hot rage. And that is what this Dead Rabbit was: an animal. Cavalo knew this. He knew it well. There was a time when he was nothing but an animal. And maybe he still was.

The bees buzzed louder than ever. They were confused.

"Where is Patrick?" Wilkinson said again, his voice all edges and knives. "Use your hands. Point. A direction. A signal. Give me *something* that shows you understand."

The Dead Rabbit spit in his face.

Wilkinson, for his part, didn't react as Cavalo would have expected. His voice did not raise. He didn't recoil. He did not lash out. He reached up with a single hand and wiped at the spittle on his face. "Savages," he said softly. "Animals. Caged and cornered animals."

Cavalo gritted his teeth against the déjà vu.

"Bernard."

Blond said, "Yes?"

"Simon."

Black said, "Yes."

"I wonder," Wilkinson said, looking at the saliva on his fingertips, "if this animal doesn't need yet another reminder. Perhaps one in a more... sensitive place."

The Dead Rabbit's eyes widened, but only for a moment before the scowl returned.

"Shall we?" Bernard said to Simon.

"We shall," Simon said to Bernard.

And they stepped forward, quicker than Cavalo would have thought such big men could move. They had grace, dark and swift grace that Cavalo knew came from years of training. The electric sticks sparked. Bernard's pressed against the Dead Rabbit's testicles. Simon's pressed against the boy's neck. There was a high-pitched whine, and then the electricity snapped.

The effect was instantaneous. The fury disappeared as the Dead

Rabbit's mouth dropped open, and his head snapped back, a silent scream pouring from his mouth. The cords on his neck stood out. His fists tightened and blood flowed from his hands as they shook, droplets spreading out along the floor in sporadic patterns. His legs trembled. The ragged scar on his neck was so white it almost glowed. And through it all, the black mask dripped. Black dots appeared on the ground, next to the red blood. If the boy could speak, Cavalo knew his screams would have blown out his throat.

"Stop," Wilkinson said.

Bernard and Simon stopped. The Dead Rabbit slumped, breathing heavily.

Wilkinson stood. He took three steps forward until he was inches from the Dead Rabbit. He reached up and took the boy's face in his hands. He raised his face until it was toward Wilkinson's own. The Dead Rabbit's eyes were rolling back in his head.

Bad Dog growled. Cavalo reached down and gripped his muzzle. *Smells Different*, he said, his voice muffled. *Burning up! He's burning, MasterBossLord.*

Wilkinson's fingers slid through the sweat, the face paint. "How old are you?" he asked. "Twenty? Twenty-two? Around that, yes. A feral boy, found in the woods. Taken in by the worst humanity has to offer. I knew him once, you know. Patrick. He... well. He was a disillusioned man. A lost man. A man who didn't understand the way the world should work. Order. He thought we should have order not *because* of chaos but *out* of chaos." He squeezed the jaw of the boy, forcing his mouth to open. Drool spilled from the Dead Rabbit's lips.

Wilkinson leaned forward. "I will have what I ask for," he said. "Patrick will bow before the Forefathers. The Dead Rabbits will belong to them. This world, this... *chaos*. It is coming to an end. We will build up again. We will rise again. These will be remembered as dark times, yes, but that is all they will be: a memory. A bad dream that we collectively had." He let go of the Dead Rabbit before backhanding him across the face.

The boy's head snapped viciously to the side, but not before

Cavalo saw his eyes narrow. *Clever,* he thought. *Clever little cannibal.* He watched as the boy pulled on the chains as if trying to free himself.

The blood smeared onto his wrists. His fingers. The backs of his hands.

Clever little monster.

Cavalo unclipped his pack. He set the rifle aside. He set the bow on the windowsill. His hands were unencumbered.

"If you think we need you," Wilkinson said, "if you think we have nothing without you, you'd be wrong. There are only so many places a person can hide. Patrick will be found and his course corrected. This town will not stand in his way."

The boy's forehead tightened.

Here it goes, Cavalo thought. *Here it goes.*

"Filthy animal," Wilkinson said. "Rumors of you obviously have been greatly exaggerated. Your head will do just fine." He turned to Simon and Bernard.

"Kill him."

For the first time, Cavalo saw what could only be considered relief cross the boy's face, as if those two words were what he'd wished to hear the most. And then their eyes locked. Cavalo could hear his own breath in his ears. He could hear the snow flurries turn heavy. He felt a single snowflake drop on his cheek and melt. The water tracked its way down his face. The boy's eyes narrowed behind the dripping mask. His lip curled down.

Seconds. It only took seconds.

Later, Cavalo would only remember what happened next in bright flashes. Pictures taken through a tornado of bees. He would remember the tightness in his muscles, the set of his jaw. The way he was reduced to carnal basics. Which impact of hand or foot would cause the most damage. Heel to kneecap. Fist to throat. Knee to testicles. Dog with teeth. Tearing flesh. It would not be elegant. It would be harsh and fast.

And it would all be done without a second thought.

The first picture was of Cavalo vaulting the exposed window frame. He landed silently. Bad Dog followed, hackles raised.

The second picture showed Bernard pulling what had to be the world's oldest and biggest revolver out of his jacket. He aimed it at the Dead Rabbit.

The third picture showed the Dead Rabbit (*clever cannibal, clever monster*) jerking his right arm against the chains and manacle. His thumb broke audibly as his hand slid out of the metal bracelet, the skin greased with blood.

Fourth, and Bad Dog launched himself at Bernard. He bit down on the hand, and the gun did not fire.

Fifth, and Simon raised his electric stick.

Sixth, and Cavalo could hear the sharp crack of electricity, could smell the sharp ozone, could taste the air around him as it stiffened. One moment he was against the window and the next he was blocking the thrust of the electric stick as Simon brought it down toward his head. He grunted as his forearms, brought up into an X over his head, collided with Simon's.

Pictures ended. Or they sped up and became real because he could feel everything, bright and heavy. The stick sparked, and he pushed back up, his arms straining. Beyond him, in the periphery, he heard the metallic clang of chains, the snarling growl of the dog, the cry of a man in pain, and the low quick breaths of a struggle.

Cavalo felt Simon's breath on his face, hot and moist, and then there was a quick break in his mind, a shutter, again and again and again. One, he knocked Simon's arms away, the stick falling to the side. Two, he thrust the heel of his palm up and broke the large man's nose, the blood spraying out over his hand. Three, he grabbed Simon's head and brought it down, his knee rising up. Bone connected with bone. Simon made a wet groan and then slumped to the floor, unmoving.

Cavalo turned in time to see the man Bernard lay a vicious kick to Bad Dog's side. The dog yelped pitifully and was knocked into the wall, eyes unfocused. Cavalo picked up Simon's electric stick, the weight heavier than he expected. Rage coursed through him as he found a button on the side. He pressed it and the end flashed blue and bright.

The man bent down to pick up the gun, never taking his eyes from Bad Dog. The dog tried to rise once. Then again. His legs would not support him. He whined. The man raised the gun.

And in Cavalo's head, the bees were very, very angry.

Again it would only be bright flashes that he would remember. It would only be moments of clarity hidden behind a wall of blur. Cavalo was reduced to primal rage, and in his head, the bees roared *DOG* and *MINE* and *KILL* and *BASTARD*. They were red, these flashes. Bright and blinding red. Anger at what this man, this large man, dared to try and take from him. Cavalo did not have much in his life. He preferred it that way. It was how he had survived as long as he had.

But what he did have was *his*. It belonged to *him*.

Bad Dog belonged to him, and this man was trying to take him away.

Cavalo did not make noise as he charged. He doubted Bernard even knew he was there. He thought, *I am not faster than a bullet*, and shouted, "Move, move, move!" Everything slowed, and he could hear his thunderous heart. The high-pitched bees that sounded like a tornado. The soft, scared mewl of his friend. Time was not on his side. It had never been on his side. How many times had it come to this? Him running toward something that was his, only to be too late. It was unfair. It wasn't fucking *fair*, and then the room dissolved, and he was running after *her*, and he could hear a voice calling back at him, begging, pleading *Daddy!*

Jamie was Bad Dog. Bad Dog was Jamie. It didn't matter. They were one and the same. The man named only Cavalo was not sane. Not anymore. Not after everything he'd seen. Not after everything he had done. But it did not matter. Not now.

Bernard raised the gun.

Bad Dog lowered his head.

Aimed.

MOVE MOVE MOVE!

Pressure on the trigger.

I'm sorry, Jamie. I'm so fucking sorry.

Cavalo brought down the heavy electric stick on Bernard's arm with all his might. There was the sharp *crack!* of bone. The gun did not fire. Bernard hissed. He opened his mouth to scream. Cavalo punched him in the throat. He felt a wet crunch under his knuckles. Bernard gurgled, eyes wide and shiny. Cavalo swept his leg out, hitting the back of the large man's knees. Bernard fell backward, crashing onto the floor.

Cavalo stood above him.

Only seconds had passed, but it felt like years.

"You tried to take from me," he said.

Bernard shook his head as he struggled to breathe. Bone poked through his arm, the skin split and leaking blood. His eyes bulged.

"My son," Cavalo said. "Jamie."

MasterBossLord? Bad Dog wheezed.

"You're okay," the man said, whether to himself, the son in his mind, or the dog, no one knew.

Let's go home. Please.

"You tried to take from me," Cavalo said again. His voice was terrible.

"Nuh," Bernard said. "Nuh. *Nuh. Nuh!*"

Cavalo would hear no more. In one swift movement, he bent down and gripped the sides of Bernard's jaw, forcing his mouth open. Cavalo shoved the electric stick down that gaping maw, angling it so it went farther into the throat. Tears streamed from Bernard's face as he choked. His hands came up and tried to knock Cavalo away, but the exposed bone scraped against Cavalo's shoulder, causing the large man to cry out around the stick in his mouth.

"You don't get to take from me," Cavalo told him. His thumb found the button. There was a charge that coursed through the stick. It vibrated in Cavalo's fingers. Bernard's eyes widened in a flash of recognition, of synapses firing in extraordinary panic. But then the electricity hit and his jaw clamped down around the stick. His arms jerked. His legs skittered on the floor. His eyes rolled back in his head as his chest heaved. Cavalo could feel the thrum of Bernard's body below him, like he had his own bees trapped just beneath the skin, bent on breaking through and pouring out. Cavalo knew it was possible that *everyone* had bees, because Lord knows his own were shrieking in his head now, were telling him to fry the fucker, to make him dead, to make sure he could never take what belonged to Cavalo ever again, because these few things, these small things, were *his*, and they belonged to *no one else*.

Eventually the buzzing stopped.

He felt a nudge against his shoulder.

The man turned his head. The dog licked his face once. Twice.

You okay? Bad Dog asked, voice soft.

Cavalo grunted. "Yeah. You?"

Sore. Tired.

"I know. Can you walk?"

Think so, Bad Dog said. He moved slowly, favoring his side. He was shaky, but his tail wagged. He turned his snout to the man under Cavalo and sniffed once. Twice. *Bad man dead?*

Cavalo let go of the stick. It stuck into the air, the black plastic gleaming dully. A little tendril of smoke curled up around it from Bernard's mouth. His eyes were still wide, only the whites visible. His fingers were curled like claws at his sides. His chest did not rise. A leg twitched but then was still.

The bees had quieted. Cavalo closed his eyes. He was cold. His hands hurt. His mind raced. He wanted to go home. He wished this day had never happened.

"Yeah," he said. "He's dead."

Clever monster, the bees whispered.

Thank you, Bad Dog said, bumping his head into Cavalo's hand. *MasterBossLord saved me. Thank you.*

Cavalo couldn't be sure any response would come out steady.

Instead he curled his fingers into the scruff of Bad Dog's neck, squeezing gently. They stood there for a moment, side by side. Man and Dog. If asked, Cavalo would have said at that moment, he saw what losing his friend would have done to his mind. It would break completely. It was a fragile thing, like the thinnest glass. It would not take much to destroy it.

Then from behind them, came a choking sound.

Cavalo turned.

Before him stood Wilkinson, face blue, eyes almost popping out of his head. One hand was at the metal chain wrapped around his neck. The other reached out for Cavalo. *Help me*, his eyes pleaded. *Save me.* Saliva glistened on his chin.

The boy stood behind him, one arm and both feet still manacled. Muscles quivered under his skin as he pulled the chain tighter around Wilkinson's neck with the other arm.

Help me.

Cavalo took a step toward Wilkinson and the Dead Rabbit.

Save me.

Wilkinson's hand shook. All Cavalo would have to do was reach out to take it.

He felt cold.

He took a step back.

Comprehension came over Wilkinson. He opened his mouth. Bared his teeth. Eyes flashed. His hand turned to a fist. It punched the air. It fell to his side. He turned his head toward the ceiling. He shuddered. Moments later there was a rattle from somewhere deep inside his throat. He slumped. The chain loosened, and he fell to the floor where he did not move.

The man stood there, watching the Dead Rabbit. The boy stared back. The dog stood between them, head going back and forth. They might have stood there until the world finally crumbled if not for Deke Wells.

"Holy shit! You stay where you are!"

Cavalo jerked his head. Deke stood in the unfinished doorway to

112

the building, a dusting of snow in his hair and on his shoulders. His face was flushed high with fear. His breath was a constant stream of white from his mouth. The rifle in his hands pointed toward the Dead Rabbit. Snow fell heavily behind him.

"Deke," Cavalo said. "Stop. Listen to me."

"What the hell happened!" Deke's voice was high. Breaking. The barrel of the rifle shook.

"They were torturing him." Cavalo took a step toward Deke. "They weren't who they said they were."

Deke shook his head jerkily. "He's a Dead Rabbit! He deserves anything he's got coming to him."

"I don't doubt that." Another step.

Bad Dog growled.

"Stay where you are!" Deke shouted. He wasn't looking at Cavalo, but over his shoulder.

"Deke, look at me."

"He's got the keys!"

"Deke, look at me!" His voice carried a whip crack of warning.

Deke heard it, the rifle wavering. He glanced at Cavalo. "Did you let him do this?"

"Listen to me."

"They killed Warren!"

"I know."

"They left his head!"

"I know." Another step.

"You *don't* know!" Deke was wheezing. "You *don't* know because you're never here! *I found it. I found him.*"

Cavalo heard chains rattling behind him. "Stop," he snapped over his shoulder, never taking his eyes from the gun. "Now."

They stopped.

"Are they *dead?*" Deke asked. Cavalo knew he didn't have much longer. He took another step. One or two more and he'd be between the gun and the Dead Rabbit. He couldn't let Deke take a life. It'd ruin him. It'd ruin so many things.

You could have ended all of this, the bees said. *This could have all been avoided.*

"Deke, give me the gun." Cavalo kept his voice calm.

Another step, and if Cavalo wanted, he could raise up his hand and touch the open mouth of the barrel.

"Gotta get my dad," Deke said. "He'll fix this. He'll know what to do."

"We'll go get Hank. You and me. Together."

"You didn't do this?" he asked, voice small like a child. "You promise?"

"Just take a breath."

"Because you'd choose us, right? You'd be with us, right? Not the Dead Rabbits?"

"I would always choose you," Cavalo lied.

Another step. He raised his hand slowly.

Bad Dog growled again. The chains clanked. Deke's jaw tightened, and Cavalo knew he had only a second before—

But he'd forgotten. In all the chaos, all the death, he'd forgotten that one of them was not dead.

Simon rose up beside Deke, pulling a gun out of a holster on his leg, near the boot. Deke took a step back, confused. Simon knocked the rifle from his hands. He wrapped his massive forearms around Deke's neck and pulled him flush against him. He put the gun to Deke's head. Simon looked at Cavalo, his face covered in gore. His nose was flattened to one side. He spat out a tooth. It fell to the floor and bounced away.

"I will kill him," Simon said.

"Don't," Cavalo said, raising his hands.

"Cavalo!" Deke cried.

"We've heard about you," Simon said, digging the gun into the side of Deke's head. "We know what you are. What happened to you." He smiled through the blood. "What you did. To your wife. To your son."

The bees began to fly. "Let him go."

"Please!" Deke said, tears on his cheeks.

"You don't know what you have there, do you?" Simon motioned behind Cavalo.

"I don't care."

To your wife. To your son.

"You should. He'll draw Patrick out. Then you'll care. All of you will. The boy is—"

A whisper of hair near Cavalo's cheek. The brush of a feather. A soft *thunk.* Simon's head jerked back. He staggered a step. Looked forward. For a moment, Cavalo was sure Simon had sprouted a horn in the center of his forehead, brown and thin. But then blood poured out from underneath it and Simon fell, almost dragging Deke down with him. He landed faceup, the arrow protruding obscenely from his head as blood pulsed around it.

Cavalo turned.

The Dead Rabbit lowered Cavalo's bow, taken from the window. He'd managed to free himself from the chains, even if his thumb was bent at an unnatural angle. That cold admiration flooded Cavalo again, and the completely alien thought of how they could have been friends in another life filled the bees.

He was startled out of these unfathomable thoughts when the boy nocked another arrow, pulled from Cavalo's quiver at the boy's feet. He pointed it toward the doorway.

At Deke.

Cavalo turned to Deke. He'd gotten his rifle again. Pointed it at the Dead Rabbit.

"DON'T—" CAVALO STARTED AS HE STEPPED IN BETWEEN THEM.

The gun fired. Wet heat blossomed in Cavalo's chest as he was spun away. He fell to his knees as Deke dropped the rifle and ran out and disappeared into the snowy night. He wasn't sure what had happened, only that the bees were *swarming* and they were *screaming*, and he looked up toward the ceiling.

A face filled his world, covered in a black mask.

"They'll kill you," Cavalo said. "For what you've done here."

ARE YOU OKAY? Bad Dog asked, his voice booming. *MASTERBOSSLORD, ARE YOU OKAY?*

"Fine," Cavalo said. "I'm here. I'm fine. Look." Cavalo raised his hands to show just how fine he was and was surprised when nothing happened. "Huh, that's odd."

The black mask cocked its head.

"We all die sometime," Cavalo said.

HOME! Bad Dog shouted. *TELL ME HOME!*

"Home," Cavalo whispered.

YES! TELL ME AGAIN. LOUDER.

"Home."

An arm slid under him. He was pulled to his feet with great effort.

"Home," Cavalo said. "Bad Dog. Go. Home."

HOME. MASTERBOSSLORD! HOME!

Cavalo did not remember much after that. He was lost in the snowfall.

the doors in the storm

For Cavalo, it was all snow.

It was a blizzard unlike anything he'd ever seen or felt before. Cold. Nearly all white. He thought himself lost, but he couldn't be sure. He wasn't sure about anything anymore. Not really. How could he be? In this blizzard, in this haze of white, there was pain, and it rolled over him in such great waves that it caused him to gag. He vomited once down the front of himself, but then he was back in the blizzard and it was forgotten.

There were flashes through the snow, barely perceptible human shapes. They spoke to him, and at first, he could not make out their words. It was a low hum, the known cadence of speech, but lost to the winds. For a time, Cavalo was okay with this. He didn't want to speak to the shapes. He didn't want to hear what they had to say, because he thought he knew who they were. And if he did know, then they would be ghosts, and he did not want to be haunted while lost in this storm. It seemed dangerous.

So he walked, pushing his way through the storm. There were times there was an arm around him, supporting his weight. Those were the times the pain was at its worst, and he would scream and moan. Whoever it was with their arm around him did not speak but carried him on. He hated that arm. He needed that arm. He wished it would die. He wished it would never leave.

Then the arm would be gone and he would feel the brush of fur at his fingertips, as if an animal moved at his side. It was comforting, this presence. He knew who this was, though he couldn't remember a face or a name. It brought warmth to him and it was the first voice he could make out. It was a deep voice, a rich voice. An imaginary voice, one that he swore was real and yet could not be.

It said, *Here. Here I am. Here you are. I will not leave you. I belong to you, and you belong to me. I will help you through the storm.*

And so they walked. And walked. The snow was in the man's face, stinging cold and sharp. He stumbled every now and then, but the arm was around him, or his friend's back caught him.

He didn't know where he was going, just a vague sense of direction of *forward*. For all he knew, he was walking in circles, but if he could still put one foot in front of the other, he would not stay in the same place he was. He laughed at this to himself, nothing more than a chuckle really, and colors lit up from him through the snow, blues and greens and golds. They danced away from him in fluid lines, like Tinker Bell from *Peter Pan*. This reminded him of his mother, though he didn't know why. She'd died from some wasting disease when he was a boy. He tried to remember what she'd looked like, but it was lost in the white as the colors faded.

"All of this has happened before," he said. "All of this will happen again."

"You are *nothing*," a shapeless shadow said off to his right. "You will *fall*."

"I am losing my mind," Cavalo said. He was concerned now.

Maybe, his friend said, touching his nose to the man's hand. *Maybe you are. But it doesn't matter to me. I'll stay with you even then to keep the shadows away.* Then his friend barked harshly and the shapeless thing faded away. The arm holding him up squeezed tighter.

He looked up and the skies parted and he saw an entire universe of blazing stars, bright diamond chips against eternal blackness. They circled above him and he felt so *small* and so *finite* that he screamed at how *nothing* mattered, how *nothing* could be changed. The stars shook above him, shaking in their heavens as if the very fabric of reality were breaking apart. He wondered if the end would hurt more than he already did. He decided, in his finite wisdom, that it wouldn't matter. He would welcome the end. He would welcome it gladly.

"Come on!" he shouted. "Do it! *Do it!*"

The stars exploded.

He was on his back, staring at a ceiling made of rocks. Wind howled in the background, and Cavalo screamed as fingers went *into* his chest and dug around. He knew these fingers, these spindly spider fingers, were attempting to steal the remains of his heart. To take what was left of his shattered soul. He tried to fight them off, but he could not lift his fingers. Could not move his hands. His brain sent the message, but they did not respond. So he screamed.

"It's mine!" he cried. "These are mine, and you can't take them from me!"

The fingers did not stop. They dug into him, searching for the last pieces of his humanity. He would become nothing more than a false, empty thing that wore human skin but that was hollow.

The man called out for his wife, forgetting she was dead.

The man called out for his son, forgetting it was his fault Jamie had died.

The cave disappeared. He was walking again. In the snow. Arm around him. Friend at his side. A snowflake fell onto his tongue and melted. It burned his throat, and he felt dizzy with the heat.

It went like this for a time. The blizzard never faltered.

And then he came to a door standing in the middle of the storm.

It was a curious thing, an abstract thing. It had a feeling of *other-ness* that Cavalo could not quite place, other than it was a door standing on its own in the middle of a storm.

It looked to be made of a darkened wood, peeling and blistering with age, so much so that splinters would pierce skin even with just a fleeting touch. The edges were rough and blurry. The handle was an old metal thing, curved and black. Cavalo took all of this in, every piece and part, without realizing the arm around him had disappeared, that his four-legged friend had vanished from his side. He didn't notice this sudden departure because his mouth had gone dry. Because his palms were sweaty. Because his heart was racing.

The center of the door was covered in bees. Angry buzzing. Insectile movement. He waved his hand at them, and they parted, revealing underneath what they had hidden.

A sign hung from the door, crude and childlike:

He wanted to run. He'd never wanted to run so badly in his life.

Instead he put his hand on the handle and pushed it open.

The storm disappeared, and he stood in the middle of a bedroom. He recognized it immediately from the house in Elko, Nevada, the town they'd lived in before—

Cavalo took a step into the room, unaware that the door behind him had closed, that the snow was gone. He did not question how he came to be here. He did not wonder at its unreality. All that mattered was that he could smell *her*, that he could smell her in this room. The room that they shared. The room he'd built for her in this small town that had grown against the odds, despite being not so very far away from the Deadlands. He'd built it with his own two hands, and by the time he'd finished, she was already starting to show in her belly, a curve that he would press his lips against at night and whisper *I'm here. Daddy's here. I'm waiting for you, I can't wait to meet you.*

Here was her shawl, at the edge of the unmade bed.

Here was a necklace, silvery thin, worn against dark skin.

The gun he—

He shook his head.

The gun on the door. The little hand-drawn gun. It shouldn't be familiar. It shouldn't be remembered. It shouldn't—

And the bedroom door opened, spilling in sunlight. Dust rose through the sunbeams. A man walked in, a shadow that looked like Cavalo. Only this man was at the edge of despair. Or beyond it. His dirty hair hung in clumps around his face. The skin around his eyes looked bruised. His cheekbones were jutting out through stretched skin. The smell of moonshine filled the room. He walked with a heavy limp, as if his left leg had been injured recently. There were pink and shiny burn marks on his hands. His face. His arms.

Cavalo watched himself sit on the edge of the bed. In his hands, he held two things: in the right, a worn stuffed rabbit, the blue color faded. Dull black eyes. An ear sewn back on after getting caught in a drawer. When had that been from here? Two years ago? Maybe three. The Shadow Cavalo brought it up to his nose and inhaled. The hand holding the rabbit shook.

The other hand holding the gun did not.

"Ah," Shadow Cavalo said. "Ah. Ah."

Cavalo did not move. He knew this day. He knew this day well.

He watched Shadow Cavalo raise the gun to his temple. The shadow man kissed the rabbit once. Cavalo closed his eyes. He waited. He knew what the shadow man was thinking: *PULL THE TRIGGER PULL THE TRIGGER PULL THE TRIGGER.* He knew what would happen. He heard the sharp intake of breath.

"Ah," Shadow Cavalo said again. It was a broken sound.

Then he shot himself in the head.

Cavalo flinched at the noise.

Shadow Cavalo would be found hours later by a neighbor. The bullet would have bounced off his skull plate and ricocheted into the wall. It would be dug out by the same neighbor and brought to the clinic days later.

"A keepsake," the neighbor would say when Shadow Cavalo had awakened. "For you to remember what you have survived."

Shadow Cavalo would toss it away when he fled that night, leaving Elko behind.

He never returned.

Cavalo touched the scar on the side of his head.

He opened his eyes. Dust danced in the sun. Shadow Cavalo was slumped back onto the bed, blood dripping from his scalp. As Cavalo watched, the rabbit slipped from Shadow Cavalo's hands and fell to the floor.

He took a step toward the past and felt underwater. A stabbing pain shot through the side of his head, and he moaned as he clutched the scar. It worsened and he fell to his knees. He had to get the rabbit. Had to touch it with his hands. Had to feel it against his skin. He crawled. The pain rolled through him. He was sure his skull had split wide open and everything was spilling from him.

He fell farther, to his elbows, his legs becoming useless. As he pulled himself across the dirty carpet, snow began to fall from the ceiling. At first it was little flurries, a dusting, light and sweet. But with every inch he moved, the winds began to roar and the flakes turned menacingly fat, and it was all white, everything was so white that he couldn't breathe, he couldn't even *breathe*—

The rabbit. Mr. Fluff. He touched it as the bees howled around him and he—

MasterBossLord.

He opened his eyes.

He was back in the blizzard. His friend at his side, the arm around his shoulder. He lurched forward and almost fell. Vertigo clouded his mind, and all the man named Cavalo wanted to do was sleep, to dive down into the black and sleep. He was cold. He was sore all over. He coughed, retched really, and felt the wetness inside his chest, a heavy feeling like he was carrying metal weights attached to his lungs.

"Bad Dog!" he cried out, though he couldn't remember who that was.

Yes came the reply.

"Where we goin'? What is this?"

Home. We're going home. You told me to lead you home.

"Tried to kill myself at home." His words were slurred.

I know. I saw it in your eyes. Knew it in your heart when we met. But it's not that home. That home is gone. Your other home.

"Don't leave me."

I won't. Bad Dog won't leave you behind.

"You promise?"

I promise. MasterBossLord, stay away from the doors. They want you so bad. Please. Don't go into the—

Another door stood in front of Cavalo. This one was sky blue, warm and rich. The wood looked smooth, inviting. The handle felt warm when he touched it.

The bees flew away, revealing the sign underneath.

As if he could resist. As if he ever had a chance against Mr. Fluff.

He put his hand on the doorknob, and he heard his friend one last time. *Please. Don't go through the door. Not again.*

But his friend's voice was so far away, lost in snow. And his plea seemed a small thing. A thing that, in the end, would mean nothing. Because of the rabbit on the door. It had belonged to his son. If he could only see his son again. Even for just a moment.

He forgot the pain in his chest. He forgot about the storm, his friend, the arm supporting him. None of that mattered now. He pushed on the doorknob and opened the door with relief on his face.

Just one last time, Cavalo thought. He glanced at the sign on the doors, the little frowns on the small faces. *Why so sad?*

He was in the house again. In Elko. In the bedroom where he'd attempted suicide. It was clean now, though. And bright. The sun was shining, and it was a beautiful day. A gorgeous morning. Early on. Everything was right with the world. Everything was okay.

Except that it wasn't.

"They're right outside!" she said. Her black hair was wild around her face. Her olive skin flushed. Her breasts heaved as she spoke. Her eyes... her dark eyes, the first thing he'd noticed about her so very long ago. How they had been filled with mischief. How they had shined. How they had been a window into her soul. But now? Now they were flat. Crazed. Lost. She was slipping. Had been for a while. He'd either not seen it or ignored it. He didn't know which was worse.

"We're safe here," Cavalo heard himself say in response, a past version of himself standing in front of his wife. They both looked so impossibly young. "These walls. It'll keep them out. You know this. It's how this place has survived. It's how we've been able to survive. We're happy here." There was uncertainty in this Other Cavalo's voice.

She looked stricken as she paced in front of him. She wrung her hands together, skin reddening, knuckles cracking. "I hear them, you know," she said. "I hear them scratching on the roof late at night. When you're sleeping. They whisper my name and say they're coming for Jamie. They want him. They want—"

"Stop it—"

"—to nibble on his toes. They want to—"

"Please. Don't."

"—eat his little fingers. They want to eat him up!" She was crying. "We need to go to them! Tell them we're sorry! Ask them to forgive us!"

"Don't you say that," Other Cavalo said hoarsely. "Don't you even talk about going to the Dead Rabbits. They will kill you. You know what they're capable of."

"I don't care!" she shouted, slapping her hands against his chest. "I don't care what they're capable of. They're *here*. They *call* to me. They will get us one way or another."

He tried to grab her hands. "Stop it."

"You can't protect us," she snarled at him, scratching at his skin. "You can't stop them."

"You need to quit this—"

One of her nails sliced his face. "You little bitch. You're nothing but a little *bitch*. You're not a *man*. You can't protect us. We're going to *die*, and it's going to be all your fault!"

"Stop," he said, and Cavalo knew of the anger rising in Other Cavalo. The fear. The anguish. Other Cavalo didn't know how this had escalated so quickly. How he could not have seen the lurking edges of insanity behind her eyes? "Stop before you wake Jamie."

"*He needs to be awake!*" she shrieked at him. "*He needs to be awake to see that monsters are real! That they'll eat him up and—*"

He didn't know he had it in him when he slapped her then. Yes, Cavalo knew anger. It was a part of him, always had been. But he'd never lashed out before. Not at her. Not at Jamie. Not ever. Not like this. He watched in horror as her head rocked back, black hair fanning out. Felt the sting on his palm from her cheek. The white fissuring of the synapses in his brain firing all at once. It tasted like snow tinged with copper.

She brought her hand up to her reddening cheek. Her eyes were wide and accusing. They both knew this could not be taken back.

"I'm sorry," Other Cavalo said uselessly.

"Okay," she said. Her voice was flat. "I know."

He raised his hand toward her, to rub it along her arm, to comfort her. She flinched, and Other Cavalo dropped his hand back to his side.

"We'll be fine here," he said.

"I know," she said. "Okay."

"Yeah?"

"Yeah."

And he had believed her. In the days that followed, he had believed her. There were moments when he'd come home from working the walls and she'd be smiling like always. *I planted new herbs in the garden,* she'd say. Or, *The funniest thing happened today,* as she laughed. She would curl up against him at night, her breath on his neck, his arm around her shoulders, his hand splayed out across her bare arm. And so what if he still felt that anger? So what if he still felt the tingle in his palm? Everything was fine. Everything was as it should be.

And his son! There were days filled with his *son.* Cavalo (Other or Real, it didn't matter because they were one, they had merged as *one*) could hear him *laughing* and *crying* and saying *Daddy! Daddy! Daddy!* He was so distracted by Jamie that he didn't even try to change what had already happened. He was lost in the door in the storm, and he didn't even *try.*

Time grew strange, and Other/Real Cavalo saw days skip by as if they were seconds, as if they had stuttered.

Here was his wife, kissing his cheek, the bruise on her face already faded.

Here was Jamie, laughing in the sunlight, tossing Mr. Fluff in the air. *Catch it!* he cried. *Catch it, Daddy!*

Here was Mark, an old friend of Cavalo's, saying *Well, if you've only hit her once and she hasn't cut off your balls, then you should be okay. Just don't do it again. That's not who you are.* Cavalo didn't know if that was true anymore.

Here was a night spent out on the Patrol, walking along the stone walls around what remained of Elko, Nevada. Dead Rabbits rarely came this far from the Deadlands, but it didn't mean they couldn't. Cavalo had a family to protect. He took his job seriously. *They're right outside*, his wife whispered in his head.

Here was Cavalo coming out to his wife's garden, finding her speaking to the plants. *It's the only way*, she said quietly. *It's the only way.* He asked her what she meant, and she just smiled.

Here was the night before he sank into darkness. She was in the kitchen, humming quietly to herself. Jamie was nodding off in his lap. Cavalo sat, trying to ignore the current that ran underneath his contentedness. It *hummed* and it *sparked*, but it didn't matter because he could feel the weight of Jamie against him, could *hear* his wife's melodic voice as she moved around the kitchen, sashaying back and forth, her feet moving lightly across the floor. He could see her from where he sat holding his son, and she danced, oh how she *danced*. Little twirls. Humming a song he did not recognize. Hands coming above her head, fingers flexing.

Pretty, Jamie said sleepily as he watched his mother. *So pretty*.

Yes, Cavalo said. *Yes*.

Here was when Cavalo woke later that night to screams and chaos.

How did we get here? Real Cavalo thought. *I thought we had more time.*

What was that? Other Cavalo thought. *Jamie. He's hurt himself.*

But reality set in, as it is known to do, in this place behind the second door in the storm. Real Cavalo joined with Other Cavalo, and even though he knew how this night would end, he still had to *try*. He still had to *save* them.

Cavalo opened his eyes. The bed was empty next to him. He called out for his wife as he rose. There was no answer.

Through the bedroom windows, he could see people running through the street. He could see fire. He could see blood.

He ran to his son's room. It was empty. Mr. Fluff lay on the floor, discarded. Forgotten. His black eyes stared up at Cavalo. *Ha-ha!* Mr. Fluff said. *Ha-ha! You're too late! You're too late again, Cavalo!*

His panic rose.

Screams from outside the house.

He went back to the bedroom. Went to the top shelf in the closet. Pulled down the rifle. Loaded. Locked. Grabbed shells, shoved them into pockets. All the while, he could hear gunfire outside the house. An explosion. Cries of pain and horror. In his head, he could not get his wife out of his mind, the look on her face on that day weeks ago, how sanity had all but fled.

This has nothing to do with her, he told himself.

Oh? a little voice whispered back. *Then where is she? And where is Jamie?*

Cavalo could not answer.

He opened the door to his house, and Elko, Nevada, was on fire.

And for a moment, it skipped, the picture unfolding in front of him skittering across his vision, mixing with a blizzard, a vast field of snow, and a building rising in the distance. He recognized it as his home, even as the door to his *other* (Other?) home shut behind him. A blast of pain shot through his chest, and he heard a voice blare in the distance: "YOU HAVE ENTERED A RESTRICTED AREA OF THE NORTH IDAHO CORRECTIONAL INSTITUTION." Cavalo wondered wildly about the insanity of robots as the voice said, "TURN AROUND IMMEDIATELY BY ORDER OF THE SENTIENT INTEGRATED RESPONSE SYTSEM FOR THE NICI OR YOU WILL BE FIRED UPON."

SIRS, Cavalo thought, even as the snow began to fade and Elko began to rise. *SIRS, don't shoot. It's us. It's me. It's—*

Other Cavalo shook his head, trying to rid himself of the snow. Of dreaming in robotics. He had to find Jamie. He had to find his wife.

He took a step off the porch, and two women ran screaming past him.

He took another step and saw a Dead Rabbit chasing after them.

He took another step and spun the rifle in his hands.

Another step and he swung the butt of the rifle. It connected with the Dead Rabbit's face. The Dead Rabbit was knocked back off his feet and flipped over until he landed on his neck with an audible crack. The vibrations of the impact roared up Cavalo's arms, causing him to almost drop the gun.

"What have you done?" he asked the Dead Rabbit.

The Dead Rabbit stared up at him with glassy eyes, wide and unseeing.

"*Cavalo!*"

He looked up.

Mark ran toward him, a large cut on his face, arms smudged with dirt.

"Where are they?" Cavalo demanded. "I have to find them."

"I saw her," Mark gasped. "Oh Jesus. Oh *God.*"

"Tell me."

"Near the gate. The entrance. I tried to get to her, but something hit me and—"

"Did she have Jamie?" He grabbed Mark's shirt and pulled him close. "*Did she have my son?*"

Mark shook his head. "I don't know. I couldn't tell. I couldn't see." He looked stricken.

"I have to find them," Cavalo said hoarsely. "I have to get them back."

Mark nodded. "I can help you. I promise, I can help. We'll get them back. We'll get them—"

Mark's eye disappeared in a spray of blood as an arrow pierced his face. Cavalo stood there as Mark reached out for him, confusion in his remaining eye. "I... don't...," Mark said, taking a lurching step back. "Is this...? Where...?"

Cavalo didn't move.

"Jenny," Mark shouted. "Jenny. Jenny. There is black! I am eating black. In my mouth." And then he fell back. He twitched a few times before lying still.

Cavalo couldn't remember who Jenny was. *Was that Mark's mother?* he thought as he raised the rifle. *Or was it his sister?* He found the Dead Rabbit with the bow using the sight of his rifle, and he realized he was already thinking of Mark in past tense. He pulled the trigger, and the Dead Rabbit fell in an arc of blood and bone. *I don't know who Jenny was. I don't know.*

Cavalo stumbled over his oldest friend's body, unable to look down. If Mark could die, Cavalo knew, so could Jamie. So could his wife. He had to find them.

He ran then, as fast as his legs could take him. He shot at four more Dead Rabbits, hitting three of them. One of them died, if his brains against the wall behind him were any indication. The other two were shoulder-hit. The fourth had laughed and charged at him, only to be distracted by a young woman who screamed for help. Cavalo didn't know what happened to her.

Of course you do, the bees told Real Cavalo, even as he was trapped with his Other self. *Of course you know what happened to her.*

He didn't know how long it took for him to reach the gate, which lay in large burnt-out chunks spread around the one entrance to Elko. He didn't know how many people had rushed by him. Had begged for help. Had tried to kill him. How many more he had killed. His vision had tunneled to a pinpoint. He could hear his own ragged breath in his ears. It was too much. It was all too much.

He took another step, and Elko disappeared and he was back in the blinding snow, his chest collapsing. He struggled to take a breath as a metallic voice bellowed, "UNHAND CAVALO, YOU SAVAGE FIEND! DATA ENTRY SEVEN SIX FOUR DASH NINE. ALGORITHM ALGORITHM, I'VE GOT THE ALGO-RITHM BLUES. ONE MORE STEP AND YOU WILL BE FIRED UPON PER THE ORDER OF THE NICI!"

A loud bark, high and excited.

"BAD DOG! THAT YOU? ATTACK! BITE! KILL! MAIM! YOU FLEABAG! CAN'T YOU SEE YOUR MASTER HAS

BEEN TAKEN HOSTAGE? DON'T YOU DARE GROWL AT
ME, YOU WORTHLESS MUTT! BLAST IT ALL! GET BACK,
YOU INCORRIGIBLE BEAST, AND I WILL TAKE CARE OF
THIS MYSELF!"

Cavalo could hear the whir of machines starting up, a great clanking noise in which gears ground together and shrieked. For a moment he didn't know what was happening, wasn't in control of the bees in his head. He thought, SIRS. *Fucking SIRS. He's starting his defense program and oh shit, oh shit,* oh shit—

He was Other Cavalo.

He was Real Cavalo.

He was through the Mr. Fluff door in Elko, Nevada.

He was at the prison listening to an insane robot getting ready to shoot them.

He was *here.*

He was *there.*

He was insane with bees, so many *bees.*

He was—

Outside Elko, which burned behind him. Later, after all was said and done, half the town would be destroyed, with a third of the population dead or missing. No one could say for sure how the Elko walls were breached, but Cavalo would think he knew. In his secret heart, the dark place that was collapsing in on itself, he would know.

But that was still days away. Now, Other/Real Cavalo walked through the brushlands outside of the Elko walls, his rifle dragging on the ground beside him. The moon was bright and high above him, casting long shadows. He didn't know he was shirtless. He didn't know he was barefoot. He didn't feel the cactus needles scrape against his leg.

The man named Cavalo called out for his wife. He called out for his son. He didn't think of the Dead Rabbits who were surely around, hiding in the dark. He didn't think of his own wellbeing or of the wellbeing of those he called his friends in Elko. No, his thoughts were of his son and the way Mr. Fluff was thrown to the ground. It was of the way his wife's eyes had looked, so wild and vacant. How long had that gone on? How much had he not seen? Or ignored?

He walked a mile. Maybe more. His voice was hoarse from the shouting. His feet bled. Mosquitos lit upon his arms and chest and drank. He thought it impossible he would find them now. Too much time had passed. The world outside Elko was too big. It was too dark. They were probably long gone.

Or dead, whispered the bees.

It might have been better had he never found them again. Real Cavalo realized this even as Other Cavalo sank into despair. It might have been better for his sanity had they disappeared forever and he was forced to spend the rest of his days searching and wondering. At least then he would have a purpose. At least then he would have reason.

But fate is a bitch. And it was not done fucking with Cavalo.

"Jamie!" he cried into the dark, his voice breaking. His mouth was dry. His tongue felt swollen in his mouth.

"Daddy!"

He stopped and swayed as if drunk.

A trick, he thought. *It's a trick.*

"Daddy!"

He ran.

It was not a trick. The dirt road curved ahead, and as soon as he rounded the curve, he saw them both. His wife sat near the edge of the road, under a tree. His son sat in her lap.

"Stop," she said.

He did. Something in her voice made him.

"Daddy," Jamie said. "We're camping! We're going on a trip!" He sounded excited, even though it was the middle of the night.

"Yes, baby," he said. "A trip."

Jamie laughed. It sounded free.

"Did you see them?" his wife asked. "They came, just like I said they would."

"Yes," Cavalo said. "You were right. You are always right."

"They spoke to me. At night. When I was on Patrol. They told me things. Whispered to me."

She wasn't looking at him, so he took a step. "What did they say?"

She chuckled bitterly. "You will listen now?"

"Yes. Anything you want."

"It's too late."

"No. It's not. We can go home. Help the others."

"They told me that the world was over."

Another step. "It's not. We have each other."

She shook her head. "It's not enough."

"Don't cry," Jamie said, sounding concerned. He reached up and cupped his mother's face. He smiled. "Don't cry."

"There are monsters," she said. "Everywhere. We can't live like this."

"What do you want to do?" he asked her.

She looked up at him, and he froze. Her face had changed. The last bits of sanity had shredded, and she wore a mask of wild fear and rage. It could have been the light of the moon playing across her face, but Cavalo didn't think so. "You could come with us," she said.

"Where?"

"Away. Away from all this."

He was still five yards away. "Where would we go?"

She looked down at Jamie, and he took another step. "Far," she said. She brushed a lock of her son's hair from his forehead. He kissed her hand. "You know."

"Don't," Cavalo said. "Please."

"You didn't listen," she said.

"I'm listening now!"

"No, you're not. You're still not listening. You don't listen. You *never listen!*"

Jamie looked startled at his mother's sudden scream.

"Anything you want," Cavalo said.

"Stop," she growled at him. "One more step and it's over."

Cavalo heard the unmistakable click. It sounded like thunder.

His wife turned their son in her lap so that he was facing Cavalo. The boy waved as his mother raised a pistol Cavalo had kept hidden. She placed the barrel at the back of her son's head. "Hold this," she said to Jamie. She handed him a small object with her other hand. "You have to hold it tight, okay, sweetheart? Hold the metal pin tight. Don't let go until Mommy says."

"Okay," Jamie said solemnly, looking down at his prize. Even at a distance, Cavalo could see what his son held. He didn't know how his wife had gotten ahold of a grenade. They were scarce.

"Oh please," Cavalo croaked. "Please don't do this."

"It's better this way," she said. "There will be no more tears. We won't be scared. We'll go together, and we'll be free."

"You'll be damned."

"Maybe. Maybe we already are. Don't you see? Maybe we're already dead and this is hell." A tear slipped down her cheek. "It doesn't matter."

Cavalo raised the rifle and aimed it at his wife's head.

"You do it, there will be a reflex," she said. "My finger will spasm when your bullet enters my brain, and then Jamie will be gone."

"Ah," Cavalo said as he gagged. "Ah. Ah."

His wife smiled. "It's better this way." She looked down at her son's head and pushed the gun against the base of his skull. "It's time to end this. Good-bye, my love. It's—"

Cavalo fired. It echoed across the dark desert.

His wife fell back. Her gun did not fire.

It took him seconds, minutes, hours, days, and possibly even months and years to realize his son had clasped both hands to his ears to block out the echo from the gunfire. His empty hands.

Cavalo ran toward Jamie. His son looked up at him with a frown on his face and said, "Daddy."

THE EXPLOSION WAS BRIGHT AND ALL CONSUMING. IT FLUNG Cavalo back, burning his skin. His leg broke when he landed. His head rapped against the ground, and everything was white, everything flashed, everything was stars and done and over and would never be the same again—

"HE'S SEIZING!" the robotic voice exclaimed. "HE'S GOING INTO CARDIAC ARREST. MOVE, SAVAGE! OUT OF MY BLASTED WAY! HE'S CRASHING. LOGIC FAIL. LOGIC FAIL. THE SQUARE ROOT OF SANITY IS THE MICROCOSM OF THE KNOWN UNIVERSE. *GET OUT OF MY WAY!*"

SIRS, Cavalo thought as he choked on his tongue. *Just let me go.*

His world exploded again when electricity coursed through his body.

He was back out in the snow. A blizzard unlike anything he'd ever seen.

Two doors stood before him, covered in bees.

He waved his hand over the first. The bees swirled around him. The wood of the first door was so white and serene it almost glowed. He read:

STICK FIGURES DRAWN UNDERNEATH. THREE OF THEM. A MAN, woman, and a child. All holding hands.

He moved to the second, and the bees swarmed with a shake of his hand. This door was black and gnarled, the wood splintered and rough. He read:

A BLACK MASK DRIPPED DOWN.

He stepped back.

He knew which one he should go through. It was obvious. It was easy.

He reached out and touched the figures on the white door. He was filled with a peace like he hadn't felt in years. He could float away on it, like a calm river on a hot day. It was everything he could have asked for, everything he didn't even *know* he was asking for. It was the answer to all his problems, and the world would be as it was and as it should be.

It felt like a trap.

He stepped away from the white door. And stepped in front of the black.

He reached out and touched the mask. It came away sticky against his fingers. Unpleasant. Grimy. Dark. Like it was blasphemy. Like it was sin. The fire that ignited in his belly was hot and greasy. He knew that mask. He knew the eyes it hid. What they had done. What they were capable of. Cavalo knew that fire was all consuming.

But it burned honest.

He gave one final look at the white door and all it held, and as the bees screamed at him, as the blizzard roared with all its might, he grabbed the broken handle of the black door and opened it wide, and it was *fire* and it was *death* and it was *suffering* and it was—

the sanity of robots

The man named Cavalo opened his eyes. A thin metal man stared down at him.

"Ow," Cavalo said, though it didn't hurt as bad as he expected. He hoped it would at least garner some sympathy and help him avoid the scolding he knew was coming.

"Ow," the robot said. "Ow, he moans. Ow, he whines. Yes, ow, you dumb meat sack. Ow is what happens when you allow yourself to be shot." The robot stood up straight, the whirs and clicks of his coils and springs grinding and wheezing. He was a tall thing, just under seven feet, and a dull silver that was flecked with rust. His eyes were two bright orange bulbs hidden behind plastic sheaths that looked like eyeglasses. The CPU in his chest pulsed quietly like a heartbeat. Up near his right shoulder was a worn legend stamped into the metal:

Sentient Integrated Response System

SIRS. The robot who managed the prison and security in the Before. The robot who had lost his robotic mind at some point After. He was already insane by the time Cavalo had stumbled upon the NICI during an epic thunderstorm in the spring years before. Cavalo still didn't quite understand how robots could lose their minds, but

SIRS had assured him quite casually (of course, this being after the robot had tried to murder him in a most ferocious manner) that not only was it possible, it was fundamentally probable. "Much like humanity," he'd said, "robotics is not forever."

Now, though, it didn't seem like he was going to avoid getting chewed out. Cavalo groaned, more for theatrics than actual pain, when SIRS pulled back the bandage on Cavalo's chest with his spindly fingers, inspecting the wound.

"The infection is receding," SIRS said. Cavalo had also thought robots were not capable of sarcasm. He was wrong on that account as well. "You're lucky I didn't just let it spread and allow you to die. It would have been what you deserved."

"It's not like I meant to get shot," Cavalo muttered. His throat was scratchy, and his tongue felt thick in his mouth.

SIRS pressed against the skin around the bullet wound. Cavalo hissed. "Oh, calm down, you little child," the robot said. "I am trained in all manner of medical and surgical emergencies. I am a Class-F200 model after all, not some Class-A200."

"I don't know even what a Class-A200 is," Cavalo said.

"Pieces of ostentatious garbage," SIRS assured him. "You are better off with me." He stood and inspected an IV line that dripped a clear solution into Cavalo's arm. His face, aside from his eyes, was vaguely and disconcertingly human. He had no ears or hair, but there was a shaped protuberance that could have been called a nose. His mouth was a grated slot that did not move. A vocal processor gave him voice, which could at times affect different accents, even if they all sounded mechanical. SIRS had told him it was due to the deterioration of his central computer. Cavalo thought he just liked speaking in accents.

"How long?" he asked as the robot pressed a cool glass of water to his lips. Cavalo drank.

"Since you've returned?"

He nodded.

"Six days." The glass was pulled away.

"Shit." They were in the main barracks, one of the few buildings left standing at the prison. Most of the others were long gone, blown up or blown away, Cavalo didn't know. SIRS couldn't say either, even though he'd survived somehow. He said that some of the files from his life Before or during the End were corrupted and he could no longer access them, little pockets of memory gone as if they'd never been at all. Cavalo didn't know if robots could lie but figured if they could go insane, then it wasn't too far of a stretch. SIRS had also made brief mention of others who'd come to the prison before Cavalo but wouldn't say any more. Cavalo had never found any sign of previous inhabitants. No one else had tried to come here since he'd made it his home.

"Shit is right," SIRS said. "You almost died." Something clicked inside his head, and his voice went flat as his eyes darkened. "Seven. Twelve. Thirty-two. Everything here is seven twelve thirty-two. See how it folds into the vastness of space." He fell silent. There was a beep from deep inside the robot and his eyes lit up again. "It was touch and go for a while," he said as if he hadn't been interrupted.

Cavalo was used to these moments, these tics and twitches that the robot claimed were part of his insanity, his corrosion. He'd asked once if there was a way to fix SIRS, to reverse the insanity. Remarkably, the robot had laughed, a thing that had only happened a handful of times since. "Only if you know where to find another nuclear core," the robot had said. He must have picked up Cavalo's increased heart rhythm and subtle intake of breath with his biometric sensors upon hearing the word "nuclear." Cavalo only knew that meant bombs. SIRS had assured him that the core was intact and that it would be a millennia before it became an issue. "And by then," the robot had said a tad too gleefully, "you'll be nothing but bones and dust."

"Bones and dust," Cavalo said as he tried to sit up. There was a sharp twinge in his chest, and it became harder to breathe. His limbs felt weak, and his vision swam in front of him.

"Not yet," SIRS said, pressing down against his shoulders.

Cavalo had seen SIRS crush solid steel in his hands, so he didn't try and resist. "You need more rest."

"Jesus," Cavalo gasped. "That hurts."

"I expect it would, though, since I've never been shot, I can't say for sure." He moved to the wall and touched a white panel, one of dozens around the buildings that still stood. It lit up under SIRS's fingers, and the robot's eyes glowed briefly.

SIRS and his software were integrated into the entire compound, and he could access any part of the prison through the panels. He'd been designed as security against the prisoners at the NICI, which held those that committed extreme violence. It was supposed to help cut down the risk and exposure to the guards that patrolled in Before, but since SIRS couldn't remember much about that time, Cavalo didn't know if it'd worked. He wondered many things about this robot, but questions were only met with more questions, and after a time, the answers seemed less important.

"Were we followed?" the man asked.

"No. Were you expected to be?"

"I don't know. Cottonwood...."

"Yes?"

"They were in Cottonwood."

"Who?"

"The government. The UFSA."

A whirring click. The robot's voice raised, and he started to blare, "ALL FOR ONE AND ONE FOR ALL! IF R IS A POSITIVE INTEGER AND R_1 IS THE INTEGER OBTAINED FROM R BY WRITING ITS DECIMAL DIGITS IN REVERSE ORDER, THEN IF R PLUS R_1 AND R MINUS R_1 BOTH ARE PERFECT SQUARE, THEN R IS TERMED AS A RARE NUMBER!"

He clicked and whirred again as his voice died. Then, "Government? How interesting."

Cavalo pushed the thoughts away. "Bad Dog?"

SIRS's eyes flashed. "Bag of fleas. Drool monster. Messes with my circuitry. Your shit machine is asleep in the holding area."

"Is he hurt?"

"No. He came in and pissed on my floors. He did it on purpose, you know. Bloody animal. I shall destroy him one day."

"You do the same to him."

The robot sounded affronted. "I do not piss on his floors! Besides, the monster doesn't *own* any floors. These are all *mine*."

"You antagonize him."

"I am a robot. I do not know how to antagonize." Cavalo could hear the metallic smirk in the robot's voice.

"I'm sorry."

"For?" The robot sounded surprised.

"Taking so long to get back. You worry."

A whirring click came from SIRS. "I do not," he said stiffly.

Cavalo waited.

Another click, followed by a soft beep. "Just don't let it happen again."

Cavalo suddenly felt very tired. "The Dead Rabbit."

"Yes. You brought one here. Rather, he brought you. Dragged you in. The blasted fleabag was barking up a storm." The robot chuckled. "I almost blew him up."

"Bad Dog or the Dead Rabbit?"

"Yes," SIRS said.

"Where is the boy?"

"Holding cells. Bad Dog has the watch."

"Oh."

"Who is he?"

"I don't know."

"I am surprised you brought him here. Given your... history."

Anger and panic flared, and doors multiplied in front of Cavalo's unfocused eyes. "You don't know my history." His words, meant to be sharp, came out dull.

"Not because you've told me, no," SIRS said. "Never that. You

144

don't share things like *that*, do you?" His words were gentle, but mocking. "But your eyes give you away. Human eyes usually do. I can't yet decide if that is to your detriment or not."

"Is he hurt?"

"Do you care?" SIRS sounded genuinely interested in the answer.

No, he thought. "I don't know," he said instead.

"How fascinating," the robot murmured.

"What?"

"If you don't know already, then I shan't be the one to tell you."

"Games," Cavalo said, his words slurring. "Always with the games."

SIRS pressed his hand against the white panel again. His eyes flashed as the panel lit up. A moment later the wall above the panel came to life in a crisp transmission. The screen showed the holding cells, the last main part of the prison still standing.

In the center of the screen was a large holding cell, black bars from floor to ceiling, creating a cage. Cavalo could see Bad Dog lying near the cell door, his head on his front paws. His tail flickered once.

And inside the cell was the Dead Rabbit, sitting in a corner, face obscured by shadows. For a moment Cavalo thought him asleep, but then the Dead Rabbit's hands went to the bars of his cage and gripped them tightly.

"Has he said anything?" Cavalo asked.

"No. But he can't."

"The scar."

"Yes."

"Did he do it himself?"

"No. The angle suggests it was someone else."

"How did he survive?"

SIRS clicked. "How do any of us?"

Riddles. Games. Cavalo wondered, not for the first time, if the robot was programmed to be exasperating or if that was a learned trait.

"Do you know who he is?"

"How would I know that?" That mocking tone again.

"He's important."

"Oh?"

Cavalo struggled to find the words. "No. Not to me. To them."

"Oh?" Mad, infuriating robot.

"Yes."

"Quite. His are the same, you know. As yours."

"What?"

"His eyes. They shine darkly. Not like mine. Mine are just... bulbs."

Cavalo was fading, but he felt this necessary. "What do you see?"

"Many things, Cavalo. It is what I was made for."

"With the boy. What do you see?"

"Are we friends?" the mad robot asked suddenly.

Maybe it was because of the drugs. Maybe it was because he was on the edge of unconsciousness. Maybe it was many other things. And maybe, just maybe, it did not matter. Because for the first time in a very long time, the man named Cavalo gave an honest answer to a question asked of himself.

"Yes," he said. "You... the dog. All I've got left."

SIRS whirred and clicked. "I should like that we are friends," he said quietly. "I should like that very much."

Cavalo fought to hold on. "The boy."

"Yes."

"His name."

"Yes?"

"Psycho."

"How delightfully macabre. He saved you."

"I know."

"Strange thing, that. For a Psycho."

"SIRS."

"Yes?"

"What... do you... see?"

The colors of Cavalo's world bled together as he sank back into the cool dark, and as he slipped away, he prayed there would not be any doors. They were silly things, and he had tired of them.

The robot's words followed him down. "Many things, my dear friend. Many things indeed. I think we shall find out soon enough just how darkly he shines."

And then Cavalo was gone.

*W*AKE UP.

Cavalo groaned and pushed his way through sleep.

Wake up, MasterBossLord. Time to get up.

Cavalo's chest hurt. His whole body felt stiff, as if his muscles hadn't been used in months.

Hurry before SIRS comes back!

Cavalo opened his eyes, blinking against the daylight that shone through the far windows. The light was a gray thing, but still it hurt. He closed them again and tried to fall back into oblivion.

Teeth gently clamped on his arm.

Up up up up up.

"Bad Dog, you better not be interfering with my patient!"

Stupid robot. Stupid, ugly robot.

"Get your filthy mouth off him!" SIRS cried. "You were treasure hunting in your own asshole not ten minutes ago, and now you put your *mouth* on him? You disgusting creature!"

Bad Dog let Cavalo's arm go and barked. *I am a dog. It's what I do.*

"Now I'm going to have to completely sterilize his whole body just because you were questing after your insides."

You're just jealous because I am alive and you are dead inside.

"Don't you dare growl at me! I will remove your testicles without a moment's hesitation!"

Bring it, tin cup.

"Knock it off," Cavalo muttered. "The both of you."

"But—"

He—

"No more."

Cavalo closed his eyes again and did a quick inner diagnostic check. His chest felt weighted but not wet, so he didn't think the bullet had perforated his lung. He was heavily bandaged, the wraps going over his chest and around his back. He reached down and pulled the IV out of his arm. There was a thin pinch, and then it was gone.

"I really don't think you should—"

"Hush, SIRS."

The robot clicked but said nothing.

Cavalo pushed himself up, his arms shaky. A brief wave of vertigo washed over him, and he breathed shallowly as he waited for it to pass. When he felt like he wouldn't vomit, he asked again, "How long?"

"Total?"

"Yes."

"Ten days."

"And no one tried to enter the prison?" Cavalo thought it odd. He opened his eyes and looked to the robot. "At all?"

SIRS reached out a thin arm and pressed against a white panel. It glowed briefly, and the far wall of the barracks became transparent.

Outside, a great storm raged. Trees immediately outside the wall snapped brutally in the wind and snow. Visibility decreased quickly into white. Drifts piled high up against the barracks. Now that he'd seen it, he could hear the low hum of the howling winds outside.

"It's been like this almost the entire time you've been back," SIRS said. "A few breaks here and there, but not enough for anyone to get through. I expect this to be a bad winter, seeing as how it's only October."

Something fluttered in the back of Cavalo's head. "I didn't know it'd gotten so late. Why didn't you tell me? Months. It's been months since...." He stopped himself.

The robot glanced over at him as he withdrew his hand from the panel. "You never asked. How was I to know you'd lost track of time? The human brain is a complex thing, even more so than my own. I can't pretend to understand you completely because I don't."

"I don't understand either," Cavalo admitted.

"Maybe you've started to deteriorate. Like me."

"If I am, it's been going on for a long time."

"You haven't felt it?"

Cavalo didn't know if he had or not. It was like his wife all over again. It was fuzzy white. It was doors covered in bees. "I don't know."

"I can feel it," the robot said, and Cavalo felt a chill down his spine. "It's like rubber bands breaking in my head." His eyes lit up brightly. "I don't mind. Mostly."

Cavalo pushed himself up from the bed. For a moment he thought his legs would give out, and he grit his teeth against the coming fall. But it didn't happen. His feet and shins tingled as blood rushed back into his legs. His chest pulled again, but it wasn't as bad as it'd been when he'd woken days before. The robot knew what he was doing.

Bad Dog rubbed up against his leg. *Awake now? No more long sleep?*

"No more long sleep," he agreed.

Don't do that again, MasterBossLord. Bad Dog bumped his head against Cavalo's leg.

"Yeah," he said. "Sorry."

Cavalo took the heavy sweater SIRS handed him, wincing as he raised his arms to put it on. He wouldn't be moving at his normal capacity for some time. It was better that no one had followed him. He wouldn't have been able to do a thing about it.

"All your sensors active?" he asked SIRS.

"Yes, Cavalo."

"It's a bad storm."

"Yes, Cavalo. All are active."

"They won't try it. Not now."

"They won't. No."

"You sure?"

A click, a beep. The grinding of gears. A screech of metal. His voice continued level, dripping with his malfunctioning sanity: "Quarks combine to form composite particles. These are hadrons. The most stable of hadrons are protons and neutrons. Protons and neutrons are the components of atomic nuclei. I am atomic, but I carry no nuclei. I am an ark, and I was made for... this... I...." He clicked. Creaked. Groaned. Then: "It's unlikely a human could survive long-term exposure to the current weather conditions. We should be safe. For now."

"Is that right?"

"Yes."

"The government might have a way. They might have cars that work."

The robot said, "You should eat."

HE WAS SURPRISED TO SEE HIS PACK, EMPTY IN THE BARRACKS kitchen, his rifle hung on the rack, his bow and quiver near the entryway. The supplies that Hank had given him lay out in neat piles along the counter. Everything looked accounted for.

"How?" he asked.

Smells Different, Bad Dog said. *And me. Well, actually, I did most of the work. All he did was carry you. It was so heavy, but I didn't complain at all. Not once.*

"Good boy," Cavalo murmured, scratching behind the dog's ears.

And Cavalo did eat. He was surprised to find himself ravenous, and he ate the soup SIRS put before him, chunks of deer meat in broth with potatoes. There was bread, and Cavalo tore into it, wondering how long it'd been since he'd had *bread* and wasn't it *wonderful?* Wasn't it just *grand?*

It was.

The robot sat opposite Cavalo. Bad Dog lay at his feet, wanting to be close to MasterBossLord, telling him how bored he'd been the last few days, how SIRS had been mean, how the lights had almost gone out once, but he hadn't been scared. Not even a little bit. He was Bad Dog after all, and Bad Dog didn't get scared. But he was *so* hungry, and Cavalo didn't need *all* that deer meet, did he? Surely he didn't. Bad Dog made his eyes as big as possible, and Cavalo fell for it yet again.

SIRS told him that he'd been able to correct another portion of corrupted data and that he'd accessed an entire backlog of entertainment options. Books and movies. Music. Frank Sinatra. George Orwell. 2001: *A Space Odyssey*. "Dave, stop," he quoted in a flat voice tinged with fear. "Stop, will you? Stop, Dave. Will you stop, Dave? Stop, Dave. I'm afraid. I'm afraid, Dave. Dave, my mind is going. I can feel it. I can feel it. My mind is going."

The robot laughed and switched to a lazy drawl with a click in his voice box. "I'll have to show you that vid later. It's a real gasser. Far-out stuff, man. Killer robotic computers. Humans think of the strangest things." He laughed again.

"The Dead Rabbit," Cavalo said when he'd finished. SIRS picked up his bowl and went to the sink. SIRS hummed to himself a song Cavalo did not recognize. It was a dreamy thing, the melody. "What is that?"

"Ol' Blue Eyes," the robot said. "The chairman of the board. Frank. I like his music. It's called 'The Way You Look Tonight.'" He hummed a few more notes. Then, "It helps with the insanity."

"The Dead Rabbit."

The robot stopped singing. "I wonder," he said. He came back to the table and sat. Cavalo could hear the sharp metallic gears.

"What?"

"His name. Is it really Psycho?"

"No," Cavalo admitted. "That's...." He stopped.

"Surely he has one. He's not just the *Dead Rabbit*. He's not just the *boy*. He's not *just* a psycho." SIRS looked strangely pleased at this.

"Does it matter?" Cavalo tried to keep the irritation out of his voice.

SIRS looked over at him and clicked. "Of course it does. We are nothing without the names we are given. It's how we know who we are." He clicked again. "I am Sentient Integrated Response System. SIRS." He pointed at the dog, who huffed at the spider fingers. "That slobbering beast is Bad Dog." He looked back at Cavalo, and if it was possible for a robot to look shrewd, SIRS did right then. "And you are just Cavalo. Right?"

"I don't know his name," Cavalo said. "I don't know if even *he* knows."

"Have you asked him?"

Didn't have time, Bad Dog grumbled. *Too busy playing Hide-In-The-Bushes, getting chased by monsters, getting laid, and getting shot at.*

Cavalo felt affronted. "That's... exactly what happened."

Bad Dog's tail thumped.

SIRS glanced between them. "One day, I'll figure out how to hear the four-legged freak like you do."

I want to pee on your leg to make you rust, Bad Dog said.

Cavalo snorted.

"What did he say?" SIRS asked.

"He hopes you find that too," Cavalo told him.

Bad Dog sighed.

"We need to go talk to him," the man said. "The boy. The Dead Rabbit. SIRS?"

"Yes, Cavalo."

"Patrick."

"Patrick?"

"Patrick. I heard the other Dead Rabbits talking. The ones the boy was traveling with. Patrick seems to be their leader."

"Is that so?" The robot's eyes glowed. "Funny how even monsters can form a democracy."

"Or a dictatorship."

Cavalo would have sworn the robot smiled, even though it was physically impossible. "There is that, yes. I suppose, though, it was only a matter of time."

"Why?"

"From chaos and anarchy rise the strong to lord over the weak. It is how it's always been. It happened time and time again Before. Why shouldn't it happen now?"

"They killed Warren."

"Oh dear. That poor, poor man." SIRS sounded honestly upset. "He was very nice to me the few times I met him, even if he did ask to see my insides. Alma?"

Cavalo shrugged. "As best as you can expect."

"And you suspect our prisoner had something to do with it?"

"No. Maybe. I don't know. The government men. The ones from the UFSA. United Federated States of America. They were going to kill him. I... intervened."

You did a bit more than that, the bees said, sounding like the robot.

"Do they live?" SIRS leaned forward, his metal hands resting on the table top.

"No."

SIRS beeped and whirred. "And that is how you got shot?"

"Ah. No. That was Deke."

SIRS shook his head disapprovingly. "That boy. How he has been allowed to have a gun, I'll never know. Did you kill him too?"

Cavalo looked sharply at SIRS. "Of course not! He's just a kid. It was an accident."

"Of course not," SIRS echoed. "Will you kill that Dead Rabbit in there?"

"If need be."

"But why?" The robot tilted his head. "He's just a kid."

"It's different."

"How? He's not much older than Deke. The Dead Rabbit is twenty-three years, four months, and approximately six days old."

"You scanned him?" Cavalo should have remembered that.

"Yes. To make sure there was no evidence of infection or disease. I will not allow such things to enter my facility."

"Did you find anything?"

"Aside from the scarring? No. I did a more in-depth scan of him while you slept and found that his vocal cords have been severed. It's why he cannot speak. It's likely he never will."

"It can't be fixed?"

"Maybe it could have. Before. But not now. Much was lost."

Cavalo grunted in response.

"And if you won't kill him," the robot said, "what then? Let him go?"

"He would lead the rest back here. His people."

"This Patrick you speak of."

"Yes."

"So if you can't find the reason to kill him and you can't let him go, what shall you do with him?"

"I don't know." Cavalo was growing tired again. "Leave him in the cage, I guess. Has he eaten?"

"A little. The bare minimum."

"Slept?"

"A few hours, at least. He sleeps lightly, though. Always seems to be alert and at the ready."

"That right."

"And in case you're wondering, he's shit and pissed as well." The robot clicked and whirred.

"SIRS," Cavalo barked sharply.

The robot's insanity came through: "Brian Greene, a theoretical physicist and string theorist, classified nine types of parallel universes: quilted, inflationary, brane, cyclic, landscape, quantum, holographic, simulated, and the ultimate. It is in the quilted multiverse that every possible event will occur an infinite number of times. The speed of light prevents us from being aware of these identical areas."

Cavalo waited. He thought he could faintly smell something burning.

The robot leaned forward, his voice going normal again as if nothing had happened. Cavalo didn't know if he was even aware of these episodes. "One day, before the End, there was a prisoner here," SIRS said. "He was, by all accounts, a changed man from the evil who had first walked into the prison. He'd raped and murdered five men and two women over the course of ten years. Eventually he was caught and sentenced to life in prison."

"Not death?" Cavalo asked, in spite of himself. He didn't understand how times worked Before. Not completely. If this man had been alive now, had been caught doing what he'd done, he would have been torn apart in the streets before he could even be arrested.

The robot clicked his fingers on the table. They echoed above the storm howling outside. "Not death. They tried, of course, but in exchange for a guilty plea and no possibility of parole, they let him live. It was thought better for the families of the survivors. So they could get answers to the question of what their loved ones' last moments were like. So they could look into the man's eyes and see what their sons and daughters, their brothers and sisters, saw before they died."

"A kindness," Cavalo murmured.

"Maybe, but that's not the point. This terrible man was here for many years. A change overcame him after a time, and he took up religion as these men sometimes do. He seemed to have found such peace within himself, almost an enviable serenity, even here in this cage. He didn't necessarily ask for forgiveness from the prison's priest, but he did attempt to seek an understanding as to why he'd done what he'd done, how he could be capable of such things, and to make right what life he had left."

"And did he?" Cavalo asked. "Did he find his understanding?"

The robot's eyes lit up further. "One could say he did. He used the end of a wooden spoon carved into a sharp point to slice the throat of the priest and the other end to gouge out his eyes, all in the space of forty-three seconds. It was said the poor priest was alive when the bad man excised his eyes. They found him covered in the priest's blood, laughing. When asked why he did what he did, the bad man said that he realized that he did the things that he did because he was a monster. That his insides had rotted and that would never change, no matter the cage of man or God he was kept in. And that one day, he would be free, regardless of the cost."

Cavalo closed his eyes. "And did he get free?"

"Oh yes. They were all freed, I think, when the fire came, for what is the body but another cage?" The robot reached out and touched the scar on the side of Cavalo's head. Cavalo did not flinch.

"Why are you telling me this?"

SIRS pulled his hand away. "The capacity for change is a rare thing indeed. And once your insides are spoiled and rotten, well... usually that is how they remain."

"The boy." Cavalo didn't know if he was asking a question.

"Who knows?" SIRS said. "Unfortunately, we're fresh out of priests to find out."

"That's not funny," Cavalo said.

"It is," the robot said as he laughed his mechanical laugh. "You just don't know it yet. Remember, no cage of man or God. But he may still be in a cage yet. Like you." He stopped laughing abruptly and his eyes flashed once. Twice. Three times. "Regardless, I do know one thing about your Psycho."

"What?" Cavalo was unnerved and wished the conversation over.

"He's awake and banging on the bars, motioning to one of my panels. It seems as if he's trying to get our attention."

the cage of man or god

SIRS TRIED to get Cavalo back into bed, telling him that he was nowhere near ready to cross a storm-filled courtyard to get to the cells. Cavalo brushed this aside. He was tired, yes, and growing more so by the minute, but that uneasiness at having lost the last ten days began to creep up on him again, and he worried about going back to sleep. What if he woke up and days had passed? Weeks?

"Besides," he reminded SIRS as Bad Dog brushed against his legs, "we'll take the tunnels. You know this."

"The wet and cold tunnels," SIRS said. "You could catch a chill and die a horribly painful death due to pneumonia. And while you are gasping for your final breaths through your fluid-filled lungs, I will stand above you and say, 'Now, don't you think you should have listened to me?'"

I won't let you die, MasterBossLord, Bad Dog said, growling at the robot. *Maybe the tin man shouldn't go because he'll rust.*

"We won't tell him that, though, will we?" Cavalo said.

The robot looked between the two of them. "What did he say?"

"That you are the most amazing thing in creation." The man

shrugged into a coat SIRS handed him, trying to keep from wincing as his chest pulled.

I did not!

"He did, did he?" The robot leaned over and pinched the dog's ears gently. "Glad you finally figured that out, you disgusting creature."

Bad Dog glared at SIRS and Cavalo.

"I can't dissuade you?" SIRS asked.

"No."

"I could just kill the Dead Rabbit. Force all the oxygen out of the room."

"But you won't."

The robot sighed. "No. Not yet at least. But if I feel he is interfering with my patient, don't think I won't consider it."

"I'm fine."

"Yes, and that's why you keep grimacing and trying to hide it from me. Because you're fine."

"Open the tunnel, SIRS."

For a moment Cavalo thought he wouldn't. There was something about the way the robot stood, a tenseness he didn't think he'd seen before (or thought was even possible in a machine). But then it passed. Or maybe it had never been there at all.

The robot turned and walked to the far wall, placing his hand against one of the panels. It glowed briefly and there was the sound of a machine winding up deep below them. The concrete vibrated against their feet. A yawning black mouth appeared in the floor as a four-foot section of concrete pulled back, revealing the entrance to the tunnels underneath the prison. They connected each of the barracks and had done so for the entire prison in the Before. Now many of the tunnels had collapsed and were blocked off. SIRS had cleared out the ones leading to the still-standing buildings. It'd taken him almost seven years, he'd said once quite proudly.

Why did you do it? Cavalo had asked.

I needed something to do, came the reply. *Years take longer when you are alone.*

And no one else ever came here?

They did. But they always left. And on that subject, the robot would say no more.

FIFTEEN FEET OVERHEAD, WATER DRIPPED DOWN THROUGH cracks in the concrete. The raging wind above sounded like faraway screaming from under the earth. It was cold. Cavalo could see his breath as they moved through the tunnels.

Lights embedded into the floors on either side of the walls dimly lit the tunnel. Bad Dog sniffed the floor and watered the cement. SIRS walked in front of them, leading the way through the cold gloom.

Cavalo moved slowly, the pain in his chest getting worse with every step he took. He was cold. He was sweating. He felt slightly out of breath. The bees in his head buzzed loudly, wondering just what he was *DOING*, and he should be in *BED*, and did he want to catch his death? *Did he?*

Maybe he did, they reasoned. After all, he'd tried to kill himself once before. He'd tried his damnedest. And he could have fallen into that great sleep if he'd just chosen the right goddamn *door*. He could have been *happy*. He could have been finally and completely *happy*. He was given a chance, and just like everything else he'd done in his life, he'd fucked that one up too.

Cavalo tried to push the bees away. He really did. He knew they weren't real, much like he knew he couldn't hear Bad Dog's voice, much like he knew there had been no doors, and much like he knew this world, this crazy, cruel, dark world, was possibly just a dream.

"Everything okay back there?" SIRS asked mildly, as if he knew exactly what was going on in Cavalo's head. For all the man knew, the robot did. Cavalo saw a flash of orange as the robot turned his head to glance back at him.

"Fine," Cavalo said, keeping his voice even.

"We could go back."

"No."

"I almost came looking for you, you know. When you were out hunting and didn't come back when you said you would. I was about to leave."

This surprised Cavalo. The robot had an almost unnatural fear (though the fact that a robot could have a fear about anything at all didn't weigh as heavily on Cavalo's mind as much as he thought it should have) about stepping outside the prison. He would do fine on the prison grounds during the summer, but anything beyond the barracks caused the robot to lapse into his insane babble even quicker. SIRS said it was because his operating system was integrated into the prison grounds and walls. Cavalo didn't think that was the only reason. "You did?" he said.

"Yes. I was sure you had suffered some horrible fate and were being mauled to death by some irradiated two-headed wolf thing with ten-inch hooks for claws and teeth the size of railroad spikes."

"That's.... I don't know what that is."

"It's caring," SIRS pointed out.

Kind of, Bad Dog said.

"Why didn't you?" Cavalo asked.

"Because I got to thinking that what *if* there was some irradiated two-headed wolf thing with ten-inch hooks for claws and teeth the size of railroad spikes? What exactly could I do against *that*? And if there was such a creature, I was pretty sure you'd already be dead. The both of you. It would have been too much for my sensors to take to have to gather up what remained of you to bury. My CPU just couldn't take it."

Crazy-ass robot, Bad Dog muttered.

"What happens if we have to leave one day?" Cavalo asked.

"Why would we have to do that?" The robot's voice rose slightly.

"I don't know."

"Then why say it?"

"So it can be said."

"Human logic is faulty logic. We don't have to leave. We are safe here."

"They could come for us. Because of what I did. Because of who we have in the cell."

The robot's eyes flashed again in the dark. "Let them come," he said. "I have ways of protecting what is mine." His voice was deeper. Almost feral.

"SIRS?"

"Yes, Cavalo."

"We won't leave you behind."

The robot clicked and beeped. "I know."

It was a minute later when he pressed his hand against another panel. The stairs in front of them were illuminated as the ceiling creaked and shifted away. "Let me do the talking," Cavalo said quietly.

"That's the first time I've heard you say that," SIRS said. "Usually, you are more prone to monosyllabic grunts."

"Things change," Cavalo muttered, hating how true his words were.

He followed the robot up the stairs. He could hear Bad Dog trailing behind them. He told himself this was a bad idea. He told himself to have SIRS do exactly what he said he would and clear the room of air. He told himself to find a gun and put a bullet in the Dead Rabbit's head.

He reached the top of the stairs.

There, in the center cell (*Cage*, he told himself, *of man or God*) stood the Dead Rabbit.

He looked different, and starkly so. It took Cavalo what felt like minutes to figure out what it was that had changed. Yes, he was no longer in Dead Rabbit clothing. Gone were the blacks and the reds, replaced instead with a blue jumpsuit that said PRISONER NO. 20131 across the back and on the chest in black letters. The scowl was still there, teeth bared. The scar on his neck, gnarled and harsh.

He was still impossibly young-looking to have such things inflicted upon him and that he possibly inflicted on others. It wasn't until Cavalo saw his face again that he realized what it was: the mask was gone. That black mask, painted around his eyes, had been washed off, the skin underneath white and smooth. Somehow, with the mask off, he looked older. There was a weariness there that Cavalo hadn't been able to see before. It might have been the lack of sleep over the last ten days, though Cavalo didn't think that was it.

But he was still the clever little cannibal, the clever little monster who had probably brought unthinkable terror down onto innocents. So Cavalo was astounded when a bolt that felt strangely like lust shot through him. It was a dark thing, a most basic thing, and it was easily knocked away. He'd bedded both men and women in his life, not having a preference of one over the other. But it'd been so long since he'd felt something even remotely resembling this that he almost didn't recognize it for what it was. It was a dark thing. A horrible thing. Especially for this... thing.

No, he told himself. *No.*

The boy, for his part, reacted only slightly to the sight of Cavalo, and even that might have been Cavalo's imagination. Was there a slight widening of the eyes? Did his fingers curl tighter around the bars? Maybe. Maybe not. It didn't matter. None of this mattered. These little things. These annoying things. He had to figure out what to do with the boy. That was the next step. After that, he could sleep.

And how the days will pass, the bees said. *Maybe the end will come while you sleep and you will never know pain again.*

Somehow Cavalo didn't think it would be that easy.

And when he spoke to the Dead Rabbit, his first words were a surprise. He would wonder later, much later when it was far too late to wonder such things, if he ever really stood a chance at all.

"You saved me," he said. "Thank you."

The Dead Rabbit watched him and did not react.

"Are you hungry? We have food."

Nothing.

"Thirsty?"

Nothing.

"Do you know where you are?"

Nothing.

Cavalo couldn't help the anger that rose. "You want me to let you out?" he asked. "Maybe we could find you a nice woman you can rape and murder. Or a town you could destroy and eat the people you take into the Deadlands."

"Your bedside manner could use a little work," SIRS said.

Uh, for once I agree with Tin Man, Bad Dog said.

"Hush," Cavalo said sharply. "The both of you."

The Dead Rabbit cocked his head at Cavalo, and he could almost hear the boy's thoughts. *Both of you?*

"He might not even speak English," SIRS said. "Have you ever thought of that?"

"He's been around Dead Rabbits. What else do they speak?"

"Have you ever socialized with them?" the robot asked. "I should think we know very little about them."

Smells Different was talking to those other bad people in the scary woods, Bad Dog said, sitting on his haunches and scratching his ear. *I heard him.*

"He can't talk," Cavalo said to the dog.

Well, maybe not like you can hear. But I heard him. I'm Bad Dog. I have superhearing abilities.

"What did he say?" SIRS asked.

"He's superpowered."

The robot laughed. "I find that highly unlikely. His brain is the size of an orange."

"Yours is the size of a thumbnail," Cavalo reminded him.

Bad Dog snorted.

"Touché," SIRS sniffed.

The boy watched them with calculating eyes.

"What is your name?" Cavalo asked.

No answer. Not even a flicker of recognition.

"Why were you banging on the bars?"

The Dead Rabbit scowled.

"What do you want?"

His hands tightened against the bars.

"I'm not going to let you go."

He bared his teeth. If it was possible, Cavalo thought he'd be growling.

"You'd bring them back here."

The scowl deepened.

"Your people. The other Dead Rabbits. The woman. The big guy with the tumors."

The Dead Rabbit's dark eyes flashed.

"Patrick." He said the name with cold deliberation. It came out like a whip crack.

The Dead Rabbit recoiled. His eyes widened. His breath quickened and stuttered.

Cavalo approached the bars.

"I would recommend against that," SIRS said. "Remember the spoon. Forty-three seconds, Cavalo. And I think this one is worse. Much worse."

Cavalo ignored the robot. He stopped when his face was inches from the bars. The Dead Rabbit had only taken a few steps back. Their faces almost lined up with each other, and for the first time, Cavalo saw the wild look in his eyes up close, a fierce determination hidden by frayed edges. It was what Cavalo thought the robot called his insanity would look like if he could see it.

The Dead Rabbit was insane. He was dark and lost and completely batshit crazy. Psycho was psychotic.

"I can leave you here," Cavalo said, keeping his voice steady. "I could leave you here with no food. No water. You'll shit and piss in the corners, and you will slowly starve to death in your own filth. You will die, and I will throw what remains into the woods and think nothing more of you. It'd be what you deserve. For what you've done.

For what you've done to all those people. For what you did to Warren."

The Dead Rabbit scowled fiercely.

"This is pointless," Cavalo said. He turned to tell SIRS it was time to go.

A hand shot out through the bars and grabbed his arm. The grip was strong, far stronger than Cavalo thought possible.

"*RELEASE HIM!*" SIRS roared, his eyes flashing a deep amber. The panels along the wall behind the robot turned red, and somewhere farther into the cell barracks, an alarm began to ring, the klaxon blaring.

Bad Dog was instantly at Cavalo's side, growling, saliva dripping from his mouth. *You let him go or I'll rip your fucking head off!* he snarled.

Fear prickled briefly in Cavalo's stomach before it was swallowed up by the cold that rose in its place. *Turn,* he thought. *Twist arm down. Bring other arm up to shoulder. Pull and smash face into bars. Break nose. Cheek. Jaw.*

The grip lessened before Cavalo could counter. The hand fell away. He turned. The Dead Rabbit took a step back. And for the first time, he spoke to Cavalo.

No words were used, but it didn't matter. Cavalo could almost hear the Dead Rabbit's voice in his head. It was a harsh thing, a rough thing. A voice unsure and unused. But he heard it nonetheless.

The boy raised his hand and pointed at Cavalo. *You,* he said. *You. You.*

"Cavalo, may I make the obvious suggestion of backing away from the murderous cannibal prisoner?" SIRS said, his voice hard. The siren faded, but the panels still glowed red. Bad Dog pushed himself between Cavalo and the bars.

"What about me?" Cavalo asked.

The Dead Rabbit cocked his head. *Yes,* he said. *What* about *you?* He pointed at Cavalo's chest.

"I don't understand."

Psycho's eyes narrowed. He moved his hand until he formed an *L* shape with his fingers. He pointed his index finger at Cavalo, then jerked the finger up. *Pow*, he said. *Pow*.

"Gunshot," SIRS murmured. The panels darkened once more. "He's talking about you getting shot."

Maybe you should just shoot him now, Bad Dog said, voice still angry. He pushed against Cavalo's leg, trying to get the man to step away from the cell and the perceived threat. *Tin Man, can you make his face explode?*

"We're not going to make his face explode," Cavalo told the dog.

"That might not be a bad idea," SIRS said. "I am liking this less and less."

Psycho pointed at Bad Dog.

Me? the dog asked. *I didn't do anything.*

"What about him?" Cavalo asked.

The Dead Rabbit raised his hand and pointed at Cavalo. Back at Bad Dog.

"I don't understand." His heart tripped in his chest. He felt sweaty. The bees told him this was dangerous, that he should just kill the monster, then kill himself. He pushed them away. They buzzed overhead.

The Dead Rabbit pointed at Cavalo again, then pointed to his own mouth. Then he pointed to Bad Dog again.

"I don't—"

"He's asking if you talk to Bad Dog," SIRS said.

He looked back at the Dead Rabbit.

The clever monster nodded.

Funny how it's the cannibal asking questions now, the bees said. *How quickly you have lost control of the situation.*

"Yes," Cavalo finally said. "I talk to him."

The Dead Rabbit reversed it then. Dog. His mouth. Cavalo. *He talks to you?* Cavalo could almost hear the voice in his head.

Cavalo shrugged.

Cavalo. Dead Rabbit's ear. Bad Dog. *You hear him?*

"No," Cavalo said.

Hey! Bad Dog said.

The man sighed. "Yes." He didn't know why he felt guilty. Embarrassed. He hadn't felt like this in a long time. It felt like his skin was heated.

The Dead Rabbit pointed to his chest. Then to his own ear again. Then to the dog. He looked back up at Cavalo. *I hear him?*

"Doubtful," SIRS said before Cavalo could answer. "I've been trying to hear the mutt since he arrived three years ago. Only Cavalo can hear him."

You just don't listen, Bad Dog said. He barked quietly, showing his displeasure to the robot.

"Don't you take that tone with me," SIRS snapped at him. "I'll shave you while you're sleeping and you'll look like you turned inside out."

You wouldn't dare, you bastard! I'll—

"Enough," Cavalo said. "This isn't why we're here."

"Why *are* we here?" SIRS asked.

Cavalo ignored him. "What is your name?" he asked the Dead Rabbit again.

The Dead Rabbit's curious expression faded. Distrust filled his eyes. His scowl returned. His fingers curled around the bars again, and Cavalo could see the thin muscles in his arms tensing. *Let me out,* that stance said. *Let me out, and we'll see what we'll see.*

"Your name."

Nothing.

"Who is Patrick?"

The glare grew darker.

Use it, the bees whispered.

"Is he your boss?"

Murderous eyes.

"Your fuck buddy?"

Gaping maw. So many teeth.

No, not quite, the bees said. They formed a face in his mind, distorted with tumors. *He don't do nothing till Patrick tells him to. Found him in the woods sucking on his dead momma's titties when he was nothing but a babe. Raised him since. Pet. Fucking bulldog.*

"Cavalo," the robot said, sounding uncharacteristically nervous. "If I could recommend a different course of action—"

"No, that's not it," Cavalo said, his voice dripping with disgust. "Nothing that big. You're nothing more than a pet. Psycho fucking bulldog."

Spit dribbled out of the Dead Rabbit's mouth, which was twisted into a silent snarl. Hatred filled his eyes. He jerked against the bars. They didn't move. He jerked again. Nothing. He let go with one hand and reached through the bars, his hand a claw, scrabbling into empty air. Cavalo had no doubt what Psycho would do to him if he was in reach. Those wild eyes blazed now, like so much fire. It didn't matter if he understood. It didn't matter if he asked questions about dogs and voices. He was a Dead Rabbit. They were cannibals. They were what was wrong with what was left of this dead world.

It briefly crossed Cavalo's mind that Psycho had given the same look to Wilkinson. To Blond and Black. He pushed this away.

"There are people I... know," Cavalo said. "People who have helped me. People who have cared for me. More than they probably should have. More than I deserved."

The feral thing hissed out a breath between his teeth.

"There was a man. His name was Warren."

A second arm shot out through the bars, reaching for him.

"He was my... I knew him."

The bees laughed and laughed.

"It might have been different," Cavalo said. "If I hadn't seen Alma first."

I can't be your second choice, Warren whispered in his head. *I won't be anyone's second choice. You can't have it both ways, Cavalo.*

"And now he's gone. Because of people like you."

The Dead Rabbit grunted. How his eyes mocked Cavalo.

"You've taken from me. You've taken everything."

Daddy!

"SIRS."

"Yes, Cavalo," he said quietly.

"How quickly could you sedate this man?" His eyes never left the Dead Rabbit.

"Within minutes."

"And we still have the sled from last winter?"

"Yes, Cavalo."

"So, it would be very easy to transport him."

"One would assume so. Maybe not in your current condition."

"But soon."

"Yes, Cavalo."

"And the storms have to let up at some point."

"It does seem inevitable. Storms aren't made to last forever. At least not physical ones."

"And I will heal."

"Surely you won't die." The robot was amused.

The Dead Rabbit stopped his reaching. He gripped the bars again and cocked his head at Cavalo.

"Then we can send him back. To the other Dead Rabbits. To this Patrick. In the Deadlands."

Psycho's eyes narrowed.

"We could," the robot agreed. "But it does beg the question."

"Oh?"

"Why did you choose to save him in the first place if you're just going to send him back?"

"The rubber bands," Cavalo said.

"Yes?" SIRS said. He could hear unfettered interest in the robot's voice.

"I felt them break a long time ago."

"Ah. So the act of saving him was a compulsive one. One made not in your right mind."

"Yes."

"Insanity is such an insane thing, is it not?" SIRS asked.

Cavalo did not answer him. Instead, he said to the Dead Rabbit, "Once I can travel, I will send you back. It should be soon."

The Dead Rabbit reached out again, this time pleading. Cavalo could still see the anger simmering under the surface. This begging felt like farce. A hand extended in supplication could easily become a weapon.

"Or I could just leave you here," Cavalo said. "In the cell. I learned once a human can go seven weeks without food before starving. Ten days maybe without water. I have done worse. Toward the end you will know what true suffering is. Death will not come easy."

"I shall never understand humans as long as I live," the robot said cheerfully. "So many sides. Capable of such wonderfully harsh things."

Bad Dog looked up at Cavalo morosely. *You don't have to do this.*

"I asked a question. It wasn't answered," he told the dog.

Smells Different.

"It doesn't matter."

Bad guy.

"Yes."

Bad Dog looked doubtful. *Doesn't smell like bad guy. Smells Different.*

The Dead Rabbit glanced between them all, calculating. His hand was still outstretched.

A wave of exhaustion rolled over Cavalo, and his knees felt weak. He stumbled momentarily but caught himself before he could fall.

"That's enough," SIRS said. "It's time to go back. This can wait."

"You don't feed him," Cavalo said. "You don't give him water. Nothing. Don't you dare give him anything."

The robot held Cavalo by the arm. "Are you sure?"

"He can suffer. Like everyone else has." *Like I have.*

"That's not like you."

"You don't know me," Cavalo said. His words were slurred.

The room was starting to spin, and the bees were moving like a tornado. Once, while in the middle of a forgotten forest, he came across a traveling caravan. He had broken bread with the owners, and they'd sat around a fire. He'd seen a flash in the firelight of a bauble hanging from a bag on one of the oxen. When asked, the de facto leader of the caravan had unclipped it and handed it to Cavalo. It had been a heavy thing, with a chipped plastic base that said in scraped and faded words *FUN IN SUN Y ALA KA*. A glass ball sat atop the base. Inside, a white bear sat on a sheet of ice, his paw down a hole after a fish. *Shake it*, the man had said. Cavalo had, and white flakes sprang up, dancing and swirling, much to his unrestrained delight. *How much?* Cavalo had asked. They dickered back and forth, and Cavalo ended paying far more then he should have, but he was young then and foolish, and this shiny thing, this new thing had entranced him. He never saw that specific caravan again, but that wasn't surprising. They moved all over, as did he.

It'd broken not long after, dashed upon the floor of that haunted military compound with voices that screamed about DEFCON 1, and the coyotes had chased him away. There had been no time to stop and pick up the pieces. He'd left it in that place, and for all he knew, it still sat there, shattered upon the floor.

He felt like that now. Like that swirl of snow. Like his head was filled with water and he'd been shaken until all had been stirred up because they were going to have *FUN IN SUN Y ALA KA*, even if they were at DEFCON 1. Everything felt soft and fluid.

"I did it," he muttered. "I broke that snow globe even though I didn't mean to." He felt himself being tugged gently. He closed his eyes against the vertigo.

"Of course not," SIRS said. "It was an accident. No one thinks you meant to."

"Paid too much for it. Went hungry for a few nights."

What's wrong with him? he heard another voice say. *Master-BossLord?*

"Hungry is never good," the robot said from far away.

"It broke because of the coyotes."

"I know."

"I found her, after. The snow globe broke because of the coyotes, and then I found her. She told me... she told me...."

"What did she tell you?"

You don't scare me, you silly man. You may think you're scary, and you may intimidate others. You may have seen things that I can't possibly dream of, but you don't scare me.

"She sounded wonderful."

"Where is she?" Cavalo cried. "Tell me what you've done with her!"

"Sleep, Cavalo. You need to sleep."

He tried to push through it. "Can't. Don't. Don't let me go. Can't miss days. Too long."

When the reply came, it was from a long tunnel, and from there, Cavalo knew no more.

"Don't worry," it said. "I won't let you go."

HE WAS AWOKEN LATER WHEN HIS NAME WAS CALLED, THOUGH he couldn't say how much time had passed. It was dark, except for a glow near the edge of the bed. It looked like one of the robot's video screens.

"What is it?" he asked thickly.

The robot's eyes glowed in the dark, a fierce orange. "Something you should see. There may be hope for your prisoner yet. He certainly has surprised me."

He sat up as SIRS brought the screen closer. His eyes took a moment to focus. His breath caught in his throat when he realized what he was looking at.

The screen showed the cellblock. The Dead Rabbit stood in the middle of the cage. A few inches from one sleeve of the jumpsuit had been ripped off. The torn fabric was tied around his wrist. Blood curled down his fingers and fell to the floor. His eyes had been covered in a mask again, but it was red instead of black. He bared his teeth at the panel recording him, and Cavalo saw them covered in blood.

"He chewed through the skin of his wrist," SIRS said almost conversationally, as if discussing the snow outside. "I thought to stop him but figured it'd be better to see what he was doing. It seems as if he wanted to answer your question. What an odd creature he is. Oh how I have missed these little quirks of humanity! The crazies! The mentally deranged! The dangerously unstable! How I missed them." The robot laughed.

Words were smeared on the cement wall in blood that was still wet. The brushstrokes were shaky and childlike. Cavalo mouthed the words, and deep inside the bees, in the place where the tattered remains of his sanity rested, he felt another rubber band break, as neat as you please. He barely felt it go. He thought it easier now.

LUCAS! THE BEES HOWLED. *I AM LUCAS!*

The Dead Rabbit stared into the camera, and it crossed Cavalo's mind that he knew Cavalo was watching. The *how* and *why* didn't matter so much. Not now. Only that he knew. And for the first time in a very long time, Cavalo felt something spark in the wasteland of his soul. The deadlands of his mind. It was a small thing, a dim thing. But it was there, and there was nothing the man could do to stop it.

face to face

In those moments between asleep and awake, the mind is a vulnerable thing, easily manipulated. Sanity can be slippery then, and what is seen and heard is not always what is real, no matter how *real* it feels. But when a mind is already on its way out, when it's snapping and breaking and has been doing so for years, those moments are more dangerous.

Two days after the Dead Rabbit spelled his name in blood, Cavalo awoke in the middle of the night when his dead son called for him.

Part of him knew it wasn't real. Part of him knew it was a cruel trick of his fractured mind, much like it had been in the stunted forest. That part of his was quashed by the other part, the one that pushed through the haze and thought, *He's here. He's really here.*

Cavalo sat up in the bed. The barracks were dark. SIRS was gone. Bad Dog was gone. He could hear the wind outside, the storm overhead.

His eyes adjusted to the dark. He coughed.

Jamie laughed somewhere in the barracks. It sounded like it came from all around. "You're so funny, Daddy," he said, giggling. "I am Lucas."

"Jamie?" Cavalo asked, his voice cracking.

This is a dream, the bees said.

This isn't a dream, the bees said.

"Find me, Daddy!" Jamie cried. "Find me and Mr. Fluff!"

Cavalo put his feet on the cold floor. He rose from the bed. His back and ankles cracked. His chest pulled. He paid them little attention. They were secondary to the fact that he'd opened his eyes in the barracks only seconds before but somehow now stood in the middle of a stunted forest.

It was night. The stars overhead created constellations Cavalo had never seen before. The forest around him was alive with sounds: branches moving in the wind, the loud screech of birds, the shuffle of unknown animals through the underbrush. A low fog stirred at the man's feet.

Dreaming, he thought. *I'm dreaming.*

Are you? the bees asked.

"Catch me, Daddy!" Jamie called out from off in the trees.

I'm dreaming, Cavalo thought again. But that did not stop him from following his dead son's voice.

If it was a dream, it was the most vivid Cavalo had ever had. He found himself barefoot and could feel the forest floor against his feet. The leaves crunching underneath. Cold moss. Wet rocks. The beads of water on his toes from the fog. He could *smell* the wetness around him, a dank and dark thing that enveloped him.

He was vaguely aware of the noises behind him, as if something was following him. He thought he should be concerned at this but could not find reason to be. All that mattered was that he find Jamie, to tell him he was sorry, that he was so very sorry and that he would never allow anyone to hurt him again because Daddy would make it okay, Daddy was *here*.

He pushed through the trees.

"Daddy!" Jamie said. "Guess what I found?"

"What?" the man named Cavalo asked, searching the forest wildly. "What did you find?" His words sounded broken, but it mattered not.

"Guess!"

"I don't know, Jamie."

"What?"

"Come here. Come to me."

Jamie giggled. "That's not how we play. You have to find me. You have to catch me. That's how the game works."

Cavalo pushed through thick brambles that scratched along his skin, drawing blood. A branch snapped back against his face, and for a moment, the forest disappeared and he was in the tunnels underneath the prison, the water from the snow overhead dripping down in a steady flow. His skin was pebbled and chilled. He took another step and was in the forest again.

"Guess what I found!" Jamie demanded.

"Mr. Fluff?"

Jamie laughed. "No! I already had him. Mr. Fluff was never lost. Do you remember what happened to him?"

Cavalo did. After he'd shot himself in the head, he'd awoken in a makeshift medical tent in the charred remains of what had been Elko, Nevada. He was lucky, he'd been told. Somehow, the bullet had deflected off his skull plate and ricocheted into the wall. There was no swelling of the brain, as far as they could tell. The skull had cracked, but that would heal. He would always have a scar, but if that was the price he had to pay to live, it was a small one. *Very lucky*, they'd said. *Very lucky indeed.*

The dead had been buried. Those who were missing would probably never be found and most likely were already dead. No one could remember a time when a person had been taken by the Dead Rabbits and had been seen alive again. Once you were taken, that was the end.

Cavalo had been stumbled upon in the roadway, unconscious, the day after the attack, skin burned, leg broken. The remains of his family lay around him. People had gathered them all up as best they could and took them back into Elko. Cavalo woke. His wife and son did not. They were cremated. Cavalo never spoke of what had happened, though he knew others had guessed at it.

He spread his son's ashes in a nearby river. On the nearby bank, he cobbled together a little cross and carved Jamie's name into it. He thought about putting his wife's name too, but it felt wrong. He didn't make her a cross, either. He thought to spread her ashes in the dirt, to smear them around until she was nothing but earth, but in the end, he couldn't bring himself to do it. "I hate you," he said in a choked voice as she drifted away in the river. "God, how I hate you." And he did. Mostly.

He felt part of him die then. A big part. Maybe the only part that mattered. He returned to Elko. Spent days in Jamie's room with Mr. Fluff. He didn't speak much, but that was okay because Mr. Fluff didn't say much either. He didn't eat. He slept in fitful dozes that were wracked with his son reaching for him before disappearing in a bright flash of light.

No man could exist like this for long. It wasn't possible.

So one day, not long after, he sat in his son's room with Mr. Fluff in his hand and shot himself in the head.

He was lucky. So lucky.

He left Elko not long after. Before he did, he went back to the river. His son's cross was still there. Someone had placed a small bouquet of wildflowers that had already begun to die. He didn't know who it could have been, but by then, he couldn't muster even the smallest amount of will to care. He took Mr. Fluff from the bag on his back and sat on that riverbank for almost three hours, staring down at the worn rabbit. And when his time had ended, when he could delay no longer, he stood, slipped back into his pack, and then threw the rabbit into the river.

He watched it bounce along the surface until it disappeared from sight.

He turned and left. He had no destination in mind. No plans. He would walk until he walked no more. He would either live or die. And at some point during those first few weeks, when the ground was hard beneath his back as he slept, when the sky above was wild and infinite, he became only Cavalo.

"The river," Cavalo said now in the stunted forest. "Mr. Fluff went into the river."

"Like me," Jamie said from off in the trees.

"Yes."

"You went through a door."

Suffering, he thought. "Yes," he said.

"Was it the right one?"

"I don't know."

Jamie laughed. Something moved through the underbrush. "You still haven't guessed!" he said, sounding farther away.

Cavalo began to move again.

Through the trees that reached for him.

Through the fog that tried to suck him down.

He was in the woods.

He was underneath the prison.

He was following his son.

He was heading toward that clever monster, that clever cannibal. From a white panel on the wall came a metallic voice. "Cavalo? I'm showing you've accessed the maintenance tunnel. What on earth are you doing?"

All of this has happened before, he thought. *And all of this will happen again.*

And again.

And again.

How many times in the last years had he dreamed of his son? How many times had he been close enough to reach out and touch him? Granted, this time felt different. This time felt more *real*. The rational side of Cavalo (for he still had one, no matter how small, no matter how much like bees it sounded) tried to tell him that it *wasn't* real, that this *was* a dream, that these were just the rubber bands snapping, and wasn't that just *alarming*? Wasn't that just *insane* how easy it was becoming for them to break?

But that side of Cavalo was small indeed, and lost in the storm that raged above and inside his head.

He staggered in the tunnel and held himself up against the cold cement wall.

He tripped over a fallen tree in the forest, skinning his shin.

"Cavalo, wake up!" the robot said. "Blast it all, the doorway is blocked. How did you do this?"

"You have to guess!" Jamie said. "Hurry, Daddy!"

He reached the end of the tunnel and pressed his hand against the panel to open the door above.

A tree in the stunted forest in front of him burst through the ground, sprouting up with a loud rumble, parting and cracking the earth below. It spun gracefully as it rose, sprouting bright green leaves that began to die as soon as they hit the air. They curled up in on themselves and faded into a dull brown, retaining only minimal life. The branches grew up toward the sky like arms. The base of the trunk was wide. The tree twirled. It *danced*. And from it came a terrible voice. *Her* voice.

"This is because of you," she said. "Everything that has happened is because of *you*. It has happened before. And it will happen again. You are damned. You are rotten. Everything you touch dies."

Cavalo fell to his knees in the stunted forest.

Cavalo fell to his knees at the foot of the stairs in the tunnel.

"You are nothing but breaking rubber bands and bees!" she cried as she danced, waving her arms gracefully. Her leaves shuddered and sounded like bones. "You are made up of pieces that no longer fit."

A dog barked, far away. It sounded panicked.

"I'm sorry," Cavalo said in a tunnel and in a forest. He bowed his head.

"You should be," the tree-wife hissed. "Everything that happened to us is *your* fault! You should have listened to me! You should have trusted me! It's because of *you* that we broke apart! It's because of *you* that our son died! *You should have done more!*"

"I know," Cavalo said. His shoulders shook.

"You're dreaming!" the robot cried. "Wake up! *Wake up!* I can't get... I can't be.... *Brzzp. Beeeeeep.* The foundation of the human condition is built upon the need and caring of others. Therein lies the danger. Sigmund Freud once said that we are never so defenseless against suffering as when we love."

"*YOU DID THIS TO ME!*" the tree shrieked. "*YOU DID THIS TO US BOTH!*"

Little hands reached out and touched Cavalo's bowed head. They ran through his hair. They touched his wet cheeks. They poked his chin. His ears. His jaw. His nose. They smelled clean. Alive. Vibrant and sweet. "Daddy," Jamie said as he touched his father's face. "Look what I found."

Cavalo raised his head and looked at his son.

Jamie smiled. It was a beautiful smile, it always had been. He'd taken after his mother that way. The wide curve of his lips. The slightly crooked teeth. The tiny upturned nose. The freckles on his cheeks. His ear sticking out on either side of his head. His black hair. That was all his mother.

But the eyes. The eyes belonged to Cavalo.

And they were hidden behind a black mask, painted on in heavy strokes.

"She isn't a tree," Jamie said, cupping his father's face. He laughed.

"Jamie," Cavalo croaked. He tried to bring up his hands but couldn't. They felt weighted down.

"She isn't a tree, and I found something," he said. "I found the way back."

"To where?"

"Silly Daddy," Jamie said. "The way back home."

"I don't understand."

"You will," Jamie said before he turned and ran into the forest.

Cavalo screamed after him. Rose to his feet. Ran up (into) the stairs (the forest).

He tripped on a tree root (stair).

"Don't leave me!" the tree-wife screamed.

As he fell, he banged his knee against rock (cement).

"I'll have to reboot the system!" the robot said. "*Cavalo! Don't go into the cellblock! The cell is going to open on the reboot!*"

He stood in (on) the forest (the stairs).

"Hurry, Daddy."

A flat mechanical voice, vaguely female: "System reset requested. Authorized access only. Please enter the proper codes to proceed with system reset. Resetting the system will cause temporary loss of power during the reboot. Please make sure all proper precautions have been taken and that personnel is on the ready. Enter the authorization codes now."

He called out for Jaime. "I'm coming!"

"Hurry!"

"Authorization codes accepted. Would you like to proceed with system reset?"

"Yes, you stupid bitch!" SIRS shouted. "You blasted machine! *DO IT!*"

"Shut down commencing in five...."

Cavalo reached the clearing (top).

"You're almost there, Daddy."

He stepped into the meadow (cellblock).

"Four...."

Jamie stood in the middle of the clearing.

"Be ready," he said.

Lucas stood in the middle of his cell.

"Three...."

Jamie raised his head toward the dark sky.

"Cavalo, *run!*"

Lucas began to pace back and forth in his cell, that feral look on his face.

"Daddy!" Jamie cried. "They're coming!"

"Who? *Who's coming?*"

"Two."

Lucas smiled a terrible smile. Shadows played across his face, like a mask.

Jamie smiled a terrible smile. "*Them.*"

"*One.*"

Cavalo took a step into the meadow.

Cavalo took a step into the cellblock.

He stood in front of Jamie in the stunted forest. Trees sprouted all around, and they all sounded like *her*, they all screamed like *her*. They reached for him, for the both of them, but they were rooted in place. Their fury rose into the air until it roared like a hurricane.

He stood in front of Lucas in the crumbling prison. The lights flashed overhead as the female robotic voice said, "System shutdown commencing." Low emergency lights began to flash along the floor. All other lights went out. The white panels flared briefly before going dark.

The cell door slid open.

The stunted forest shattered into pieces as Lucas leapt from the jail cell. He hit Cavalo in a flying tackle. Cavalo struggled to breathe as he was knocked backward off his feet. They crashed onto the floor, Cavalo's head knocking against the cement. Stars more brilliant than he'd ever seen before exploded across his vision. He was distracted by them momentarily because didn't they just *shine*? They shined so darkly, and he could hear his son's voice in his head still, Jamie telling him to rise, that one day he'd rise up, and nothing would ever be the same. As the shattered fragments of the forest fell around him, a thinnest sliver fell past his face, like the most precious piece of glass. In it, and buried in the stars, he saw Jamie. As it fell across his vision, Jamie said from inside the glass, "Hi, Daddy."

Then that world, that dream of a world fell away, like it never existed at all. The shrieking tree-wives were gone; his son was gone; the forest was gone. *They were never there to begin with*, he told himself as hands circled his throat and began to squeeze. *It's all bees and rubber bands. That's all it ever was.*

He opened his eyes, and above him the Dead Rabbit stared down, eyes narrowed, teeth gritted, jaw tensed. The cords in his neck jutted out. His arms trembled. His fingers dug into flesh. His thumbs pressed against the man's windpipe. The ugly scar across his neck was pale in the low light. The Dead Rabbit (*I am Lucas*) let out a hiss of air between his teeth. Cavalo felt it hit his face. It was warm.

And didn't this do something to Cavalo? Something more than anything had done in months? Years? Ever?

It did.

Maybe it was the dream of Jamie. Maybe it was the tree-wives. Maybe it was the stunted forest. The past two weeks. The death of Warren. The using of Alma (for wasn't that *exactly* what he did?). Getting shot. Killing men. The government, alive and well.

Or maybe it was just the shitty fucking life the man named Cavalo had. Maybe it was because nothing good ever happened. Everything was taken away. Life sucked. It was unfair. It was cold and dark and lonely. It was his own fault. He had failed.

Regardless of the reason, regardless of everything that had happened, Cavalo felt an extraordinary fury rising from deep within him. It cost him, he knew. It cost him dearly. Rubber bands snapped, the bees howled and spun into a tornado of wings, their stingers scraping at his insides. But it was there. It was like fire. For the first time since he could remember, Cavalo felt something close to humanity. Not quite there, but close. His survival instinct kicked in, that base notion to kick and punch and pull and break.

And so he did.

The Dead Rabbit sat astride him, hands around his neck, eyes glittering in the dark. Cavalo curled his fingers down and swung his arm up in a wide arc. The heel of his hand collided with the side of the Dead Rabbit's head, against the ear. Bone struck bone, and the Dead Rabbit exhaled heavily, a dazed look coming over his face. He slipped slightly to the left, his grip on Cavalo's neck loosening.

Cavalo brought both arms up and drove his elbows into the crooks of the Dead Rabbit's arms. The hands fell away. He bucked up his chest and stomach, ignoring the pull of the gunshot wound. The Dead Rabbit fell to the side, arms rising. The momentum carried him off Cavalo, who rolled in the opposite direction. Cavalo was up and on his feet even before Lucas had righted himself. The Dead Rabbit panted slightly, hanging his head toward the floor.

"Too fucking easy," Cavalo spat at him. He stormed at the Dead Rabbit, meaning to kick him upside the head. Once the Dead Rabbit went down, he'd finish this the way it should have been the moment he'd first laid eyes on the monster. He brought his foot back and swung it forward.

It met empty air. He wavered in his balance and stepped down hard. The Dead Rabbit had rolled away quicker than Cavalo's eyes could follow. He moved up into a crouch and smiled that terrible smile, showing too many teeth. He cocked his head like a bird.

Cavalo pulled himself upright, ignoring what felt like the strained muscle in his overextended leg. He'd faced worse. He'd seen worse. He'd survived worse. This was just a kid. A boy. Even monsters were capable of dying. The Dead Rabbit might be a psycho fucking bulldog, but Cavalo was beginning to understand that he too was a little bit psychotic. It was strange the relief he felt at the realization.

"Come on, then," Cavalo said. "If we're gonna do this, let's do this."

If he'd had time, Cavalo might have admired the swiftness with which the Dead Rabbit moved. One moment he was still crouched, and the next he was again flying at Cavalo, a silent snarl twisting his face. Cavalo sidestepped, reaching out and grabbing one of Psycho's outstretched arms. Using his momentum against him, Cavalo whipped him around, spinning Psycho until his back was at Cavalo's front. He wrapped his arms around Psycho, holding him tightly against his body. If Psycho hadn't been so tense, it would have almost been a perfect fit.

Cavalo didn't have time to ponder this. The Dead Rabbit snapped his head back, meaning to smash in Cavalo's nose. Cavalo whipped his head to the side, and the back of the Dead Rabbit's head bounced off his cheekbone. The pain was a glassy thing, sharp and bright. Psycho wriggled out of his grasp and spun into a crouch, swinging his leg out at the back of Cavalo's legs.

He's good, the bees said as Cavalo found himself on his back again. Psycho stood above him and raised his foot over Cavalo's face. Cavalo thought to close his eyes, but if this was it, if this was the end, he wasn't going to show any fear. He wasn't going to show any weakness. He wasn't going to—

The Dead Rabbit hesitated. Cavalo saw it. It was just a flash behind his dark eyes, but it was there. His foot hung in the air. A split second. It wouldn't take much more.

Cavalo snapped his arms up and grabbed Psycho's suspended foot. He pushed up with all his might. Psycho fell back, his head bashing into the metal bars of the jail cell. Cavalo was on his feet even before the Dead Rabbit could right himself. He kicked Psycho's feet apart and put pounds of pressure against Psycho's crotch with his knee. Cavalo's forearm went under Psycho's chin, forcing his head back. Psycho struggled only briefly, latching his hands onto Cavalo's arms.

Face to face, they stood. Eyes locked. Breathing heavily. Even the bees were silent this close. Cavalo couldn't remember the last time that'd happened. Certainly it was before Jamie disappeared in a flash of light. Was that when they had come? He couldn't remember, though it seemed likely. They had swarmed when he'd woken after shooting himself in the head, like that split in his skin, that crack in his skull was wide enough to let them fly in and nest in his head while he was unconscious.

"I will kill you," Cavalo said.

The Dead Rabbit grinned at him. It was crazy. His fingernails dug into Cavalo's arm, enough to dent the flesh.

"Mark my words," Cavalo said, pressing against Psycho even

harder. His balls had to be hurting, his air getting cut off. "I have done worse. I am capable of worse. I can make it last. I can make you suffer. And I will. You have never before experienced the pain I will bring you."

Psycho lifted his head up higher, exposing the scar across his neck. He looked back at Cavalo, eyes dancing dangerously. *Oh?* he seemed to say, that raspy voice already familiar in Cavalo's head. *You think you can make it worse than this?* He squeezed Cavalo's arms. His fingernails pierced flesh. Cavalo felt blood run down his arms.

He did not react.

"I know I can," Cavalo said. "That will be nothing compared to what I will do to you."

Psycho snapped his teeth toward Cavalo.

Cavalo did not flinch.

Psycho cocked his head again. *You're bluffing.*

"Think so?"

His eyes narrowed. *I know so.* He cut into Cavalo's arms again. The flesh parted in little divots. The pain was negligible.

"Try me. See what happens."

The Dead Rabbit struggled again. Cavalo applied more pressure. Psycho stopped and tried to suck in air. He could barely get any in. His grip lessened.

His expression grew murderous again. *I'll kill you.*

"You can try. It will be the last thing you do."

You talk too much.

Cavalo laughed bitterly. "How do you do it?"

The Dead Rabbit shook his head once. *What?*

"Keep the bees away."

Psycho's eyes narrowed. He breathed heavily through his nose. For a moment Cavalo thought nothing would happen (and why would it? the clever monster didn't know about *bees*) when Psycho let his arm go. Blood dripped down his hand. Cavalo did nothing to stop it as it approached his face.

Psycho raised a finger and pressed it against the side of his head.

He tapped three times. Cavalo felt his own blood trickle down to his ear. His eyes never left the Dead Rabbit's. *Here?* Psycho asked.

Cavalo didn't answer.

Psycho pursed his lips and blew out. The rasp sounded insectile. He tapped the side of Cavalo's head again. *Here? Bees?*

"Yes. Bees. Rubber bands. They break." *Stop*, he told himself. *Stop now.*

Psycho pulled his red hand back and tapped the side of his own head. He made the insect noise again. Tapped his head. Once. Twice. Three times.

I have bees. Like you.

"Oh?" Cavalo said. It was the only thing he could think of to say. He wondered if the rubber bands were breaking now and he wasn't aware of them. Or if they had all finally broken and he was sliding into the dark. That would be the only explanation for why he talked to this monster. This cannibal.

Yes. The Dead Rabbit gripped the side of his own head with his hand, smearing Cavalo's blood in his hair. He grimaced briefly, then scowled. *They hurt. I hate them.*

The same, Cavalo thought. *Oh dear God. The same.*

No. *Not* the same. Cavalo didn't take life unless he was forced to. He didn't ransack towns and murder the people. He didn't drag the weakest kicking and screaming into the forest to face horrors that no one could possibly imagine.

"I'm not like you," Cavalo ground out.

The Dead Rabbit stopped gripping his head. Cavalo could feel him tense beneath his arms and legs. And just *when* had their faces gotten so close? Just *when* had they gotten so close he could feel the Dead Rabbit's breath on his skin? When *exactly* had that happened?

"You may have bees," Cavalo told the boy in a low voice, "and I might be as fucking crazy as you are, but I am *nothing* like you."

A metallic voice came from behind him. "Cavalo!"

A low animalistic snarl followed.

Cavalo turned his head briefly, no more than an inch. But it was enough. The Dead Rabbit lashed out, his fingers slick with Cavalo's blood. They went for his eyes. To gouge them out. To make him hurt. He was an animal. If Cavalo hadn't known it before, he knew it now. *So close*, he thought, but to what, he didn't know. *So close.*

He pushed back, feeling those bloody fingertips scratching at his face. He lifted up his arms to protect his eyes, when he was knocked to the side by a hard metal push. He fell back to the floor, sliding along the cement until his back slammed up against the wall.

Bad Dog crowded against him, sniffing up and down his face and neck. *Bleeding!* he said, sounding slightly hysterical. *Blood! Bleeding! I smell it! I taste it! Are you dying?* Are you dying!

"No," Cavalo said, pushing the dog away. "Just some scratches."

But it's so bloody! *What if your arms fall off! How will we survive? I don't have thumbs!*

"Hush," Cavalo said gently. He looked beyond the dog.

There was enough glow from the emergency lights along the floor for Cavalo to see. It was enough to make his breath catch in his throat.

Sentient Integrated Response System stood at full height, his orange eyes blazing with a furious light that Cavalo had never seen before. *He's a robot*, he told himself. *Just a robot. He can't* know *anger.* But that felt like a lie, because SIRS was no ordinary robot. Ordinary robots didn't lose their sanity.

The robot had one arm stretched out, the spidery metal fingers wrapped around the Dead Rabbit's neck, holding him three feet off the floor. The Dead Rabbit didn't flail, didn't kick. He held on to the robot's arms, keeping himself steady. He seemed to know as well as Cavalo did that SIRS's grip was unforgiving, and he would just as soon end up snapping his neck than breaking free.

There seemed a time when no one moved and all held their breaths for what was to happen next.

It was the robot who spoke first.

SIRS said, "Hundreds of millions of years of evolution led to the existence of humans as they have been for the last thousand years.

You are at the top of your own food chain, even if you destroy yourselves in the process. You are, by all accounts, a wondrous miracle of nature. A mixture of molecules and stardust that by its very definition should not exist. And yet... you are so soft. So fragile." He pulled the Dead Rabbit until their faces were inches apart and the Dead Rabbit's face was bathed in the glow from SIRS's eyes. "There are eight bones in the human neck," the robot said. "Seven are vertebrae. The eighth is your hyoid bone. All it would take for me to crush them into a fine powder is putting the barest amount of pressure around your neck. You would be alive as the bones began to break. You would feel everything as the nerves and synapses misfired and severed. It may only be seconds but it would feel like *years*. Your throat would be crushed, and I can't guarantee that your head wouldn't pop off just like a tick that fleabag gets during the summer." He shook the Dead Rabbit violently, and Cavalo waited for the telltale *crack*.

It never came.

"So I suggest," SIRS continued, "that if you *ever* think of putting your hands on Cavalo again, that you remember this: you are a *human*. You are *soft*. You are so easily *broken*, and I will not hesitate to break every single bone in your body, and I will make sure you are kept alive and awake while I do it. You may be made of stars, but even stars die."

And then I will eat what remains, Bad Dog growled loudly. *I will then throw it up and contemplate eating it again.*

"Yes," SIRS agreed, "whatever the shit machine just said too. So. The way I see it, we have two choices. You can either act like a reasonably civil human being and we see what we see, or I start breaking your bones now."

For a moment the Dead Rabbit only glared at the robot, though he also looked curious. Then he raised his hands to his head again. Pursed his lips. Blew out. Grabbed the side of his head. He pointed at Cavalo. Back at himself.

"I am sure I don't have the foggiest idea of what you're saying,"

SIRS said. He beeped and whirred, and his arm shook, tightening his grip around the Dead Rabbit's neck. The robot's head rocked back, and his voice blared into the cellblock: "EDWARD LORENZ SAID CHAOS THEORY IS WHEN THE PRESENT DETERMINES THE FUTURE BUT THE APPROXIMATE PRESENT DOES NOT APPROXIMATELY DETERMINE THE FUTURE." SIRS clicked. Beeped. Gears ground together. "I...," he said as he looked back toward the Dead Rabbit. "I am...." He beeped again in a lower register. His eyes burned a fire orange. "Processing. The square root divided by... the infinity that is God. Processing. Processing."

The Dead Rabbit's face looked animalistic in the orange glow.

The robot paused. "Here," he finally said. "I don't think you understand. Maybe a demonstration is in order. A hairline fracture in the sixth vertebrae should be enough to show how serious I am. You won't die, but it'll hurt like the dickens."

"SIRS," Cavalo said. "Don't."

"Siding with him!" the robot cried. "Is that how this goes?" He clicked again. His eyes flashed. "We are friends! You said it yourself!"

"We are."

"And friends protect each other."

"Yes."

"Then I shall hurt him. To protect you."

"No."

SIRS beeped but said nothing.

The Dead Rabbit reached up again. Touched the side of his head. Buzzed through his lips. He then reached out with the same hand and touched the side of the robot's head. Buzzed through his lips. *I have bees. You have bees too.*

SIRS watched the Dead Rabbit in his hand. Deep clicks came from within him. It felt like hours passed. Then, "Cavalo."

"Yes."

"Are you afraid of God?" That queer, flat tone had disappeared. The Dead Rabbit sounded almost startled.

Cavalo didn't understand. "No. I'm not afraid." Angry, maybe, if there was such a thing as God. But no, not afraid. Never afraid.

"You should be." SIRS set the Dead Rabbit down on his feet and took a step back. The Dead Rabbit took a defensive stance as he brought a hand to his throat, rubbing over the puckered scar. His eyes darted between Cavalo, Bad Dog, and SIRS.

No one spoke. The two men and the dog breathed in and out. The CPU of the robot collected and stored information to be processed in the dark of night. If the secondary alarm hadn't gone off a minute later, they might have stood there until the world rebuilt itself and fell again in another wave of fire. It seemed inevitable, because all this had happened before, and all this would happen again. It was the nature of man. The folly of man.

But that was not the case. If this *had* happened before, it had now gone off the rails because things had changed.

The secondary alarm began its piercing cry.

All four moved as if waking from a deep sleep. The low lights along the floor flashed.

"What is it?" Cavalo said, raising his voice over the siren.

Hate loud noises, Bad Dog whined as he turned in an agitated circle.

The Dead Rabbit covered his ears and glared up at the alarm.

"I don't know," SIRS said. He pressed his hand against the wall. A single panel lit up.

It was red.

"No," SIRS said. "Not now."

Cavalo rose to his feet. "What is it?"

"I had to reboot the system," SIRS said, staring into the panel. "To get to you. It's the only way I could get the tunnel doors open in time."

"SIRS, what is it?"

The robot looked over at Cavalo. "The reboot took down all the security protocols in place. It's a reset to the system. It will take time to come back up given the age of the hardware and programs. An hour for the perimeter to go back up. Ninety minutes to get the defense protocol online. Two hours for complete function for remaining systems."

"Then why is the alarm going off?"

"It's meant as a backup. In case something happens while the system resets. A warning."

"Against what?"

The robot's hand tightened into a fist against the wall. The scrape of metal to concrete was almost as loud as the alarm. "A breach."

SIRS turned from the red panel, extending his arm, his palm toward the ceiling. A light erupted from his hand, creating a video screen that floated in front of Cavalo's face. He squinted against the sudden flare.

The image was lined and grainy. It showed the entrance to the barracks coming from the forgotten road. Snow fell in fat flakes. It seemed as if the terrible storm had passed as the trees, weighted heavily in white, did not move. It was dark, but the floodlights illuminated the courtyard. It was familiar, this. It was the closest thing Cavalo knew to a home.

And it would have been peaceful had it not been for the group of four uniformed men standing in the courtyard, guns drawn. Cavalo couldn't make out their faces, but he recognized the uniforms.

UFSA.

a decision made

"THIS IS why humans don't ever last," SIRS said. "They make stupid, stupid decisions." He handed Cavalo a heavy coat.

"Noted," Cavalo said, watching the screen. The audio was out, but he could see one of the men shouting, his breath coming out in long white trails. He took the coat from the robot and winced as his chest pulled when he put his arms through the sleeves.

"And you're not even remotely close to being back to normal!"

"I'm fine." This was a lie. No one was fooled.

"Also? Humans don't last because they have no sense of survival," SIRS said. Whatever program his speech function ran on certainly was capable of adding exasperation to the robot's voice. "One does not normally go out from a secure location to meet strange men with guns unless one has no wish to live."

"There's no other choice." The man shouting silently on the screen seemed to be the de facto leader of the group. He didn't recognize them. They hadn't been in Cottonwood. Alma had only known of Wilkinson. Blond and Black. He thought he would have been told if they'd found more, but then he'd been shot in the chest by an

195

awkward teenager while harboring a cannibal in a prison. His life was strange these days.

"There *is* another choice," the robot retorted. "I go instead, and you stay here. Or *none* of us go and we *all* stay here and wait until they go away. And if they don't, then once I get the security system back up and working, I will fry them all when they try to leave. *That* is how one survives. We win. They lose."

Cavalo knew the robot was right. He knew SIRS was made to weigh all logistical probabilities and come out with the best odds. It was how these machines worked. But it wasn't enough.

"What if they don't leave?" Cavalo said. He watched as two of the four men entered one of the crumbling barracks that was unused by Cavalo. The other two remained in the courtyard. The leader was staring straight ahead. The man behind him said something, and the other man silenced him with a quick shake of his head.

"Even more reason for me to go in your place! They can't hurt me. I can hurt *them*."

"Everyone can get hurt," Cavalo said. "Even you."

"*Now* you choose to become a sappy, caring man?" the robot said incredulously. "What in God's name happened to you? Do you have a fever? Are you relapsing? Bend over so I can check your temperature."

Cavalo shoved the robot's questing fingers away. He didn't want to think about what had happened while he'd been unconscious.

"This is your fault," the robot said to Bad Dog. "Before you, Cavalo could have *never* been accused of being sentimental. Dogs ruin lives."

MasterBossLord didn't care before because humans don't love tin cans, Bad Dog growled, baring his teeth.

"Enough, the both of you," Cavalo snapped. "How the hell did they even get up here in this snow? The drifts have to be at least ten feet deep."

"There seems to be much we don't know about this brave new

world," SIRS murmured. "We should worry about the how of it when they aren't standing out there with firearms."

"How long before you can get everything back up?"

"Thirty-four minutes for the perimeter."

"Shit."

"You don't have to do this."

"I don't run," Cavalo said.

You don't? the bees screamed. *You* don't? *That's* all *you do.*

"Stupid man," the robot said. "I will go."

"No. You have to stay here to make sure everything comes online. I don't know shit about computers."

I'll go with you, Bad Dog said, stepping up to his side.

"No. You stay here too. You can't—"

Shut up, MasterBossLord. Tin Man was right. You are a stupid man. I'm going.

"We still don't have audio," the robot muttered, his fingers flying over the red panel. It beeped angrily back at him and flashed an error message. "Here. Wear this." He held up a silvery index finger, the end of which slimmed down to a fine point. He used his other hand and pulled off the top of the index finger at the joint. He bent it into a half circle until it was the size of a thumbnail. Cavalo had only used this a handful of times before. It felt too invasive.

He took it from the robot and put it in his ear. There was a sharp snap of static before the radio went silent.

"You'll be able to hear them?" Cavalo asked. "These things only have a short range on a good day."

"It's better than nothing. We don't know anything about these men *or* what they represent." He punched in another series of numbers into the red panel, and a compartment slid open on the floor underneath. The robot bent down and pulled out an old pistol. "It's better than nothing."

Cavalo opened the chamber. Three rounds. "There's nothing in your data banks about them?"

"Who?"

"The UFSA."

The robot's eyes flashed. "How could there be, Cavalo? All of my data comes from Before. They came After. I know as much as you do at this point. Though, through observation, I will tell you one thing."

"Oh?"

"They're wearing armor. If you need to kill them, aim for the head."

"That's comforting," Cavalo muttered.

"Isn't it? At least we know they're not completely stupid. Most likely they'll have secondary weapons of some kind. Pistols. Knives. Even grenades, if you're lucky."

"You can't tell for sure?"

"Not until the system is back up. I have limited function without it. Which is why we should wait."

"Grenades," Cavalo said. "If we're lucky."

The robot's gears ground together inside his chest. "Human logic is by design a faulty thing. You are too emotive."

"And you're not?"

"No. I am a robot. We cannot feel anything." Cavalo could hear the smirk in his voice.

"Insanity is a flesh and blood thing."

"But I have neither flesh nor blood. Merely a central core that is slowly corrupting."

"Yeah," Cavalo said. "You still believe that?"

The robot hesitated. "It's strange," he said finally. "Is it not? Maybe you are my Fairy with the Turquoise Hair."

"Who?"

"A fairy. From a children's story. From Before. A puppet wanted to become a real boy, and she helped him. Eventually. Though in the original version, it didn't work out quite that way. But the ending was rewritten, as they sometimes are. Things can change."

"Is that it? What you want?"

"What?"

"To be real?"

The robot laughed. "Cavalo, you are delightful, even with the unknown standing outside our door. How could I possibly be any more real than I am already?"

Cavalo turned to leave. He stopped. Thought for just a moment. Finally, "You're not just a robot."

SIRS sounded amused when he said, "I know. And you're more than you think."

You aren't, the bees said. *You are* less. *Have you ever stopped to think that none of this is real? That the robot is only part of your imagination? The dog. The prison. All of this is in your head. You shot yourself, and you're in a coma! You have been for years! None of this is real, and you are alone.*

"No," Cavalo muttered. "It's real."

"Cavalo?" the robot asked.

The man shook his head. "It's nothing." He glanced over at the Dead Rabbit. "You stay put."

The Dead Rabbit snarled at him, pulling against the metal cuffs attaching him to the cell bars.

"Good boy," Cavalo said and wondered why the bees never said the Dead Rabbit was nothing but a coma dream.

The Dead Rabbit snapped his teeth at Cavalo, his eyes black with hate.

Cavalo moved toward the far door that led to the back of the barracks. The front entrance had been barricaded shortly after he arrived. SIRS had not questioned his paranoia. It seemed wise at the time.

He whistled once, a low sound, and Bad Dog fell into step beside him. He put the gun in his coat pocket and kept his hand there. Just in case.

The first door opened with ease. No alarm sounded as he stepped into a small hallway leading to a second door. The first closed behind him. The cold was bitter against his skin.

"Do come back alive," SIRS said quietly in his ear. "It would get quite lonely here now that I've had human contact. I think I'd have no choice but to lose my mind rather quickly if you were gone. So you see, you must come back." There was a static pause. "The both of you."

"I know."

"And remember, Cavalo: the head. Aim for the head."

"I hear you."

"And you tell that fleabag—"

"SIRS."

"Yes?"

"Hush. We're coming back." Cavalo didn't know if he believed his own words.

"Okay." The robot sounded as if he didn't believe the words either.

Something nagged at Cavalo's mind, under the bees. "SIRS?"

"Yes?"

"The fairy."

"Yes."

"How did it end? Originally?"

"The puppet died. He was tricked by the Fairy with the Turquoise Hair and was hung from a tree."

"This was a children's story?"

The robot chuckled in his ear. "The world has always been a ghoulish place. That's one thing that will never change."

Cavalo reached the second door and pressed his hand against it. The metal was cold against his skin. His breath was coming out in white puffs. He felt Bad Dog brush up against him. He looked down. "You ready, boy?"

Bad Dog bumped his leg with his snout. *White cold stuff?*

"Snow? Yes."

Slows me down.

"A little. Just don't get distracted and play in it and leave me hanging."

Bad Dog snorted derisively. *Like I've ever done that. I'm not a puppy.*

"Sometimes you are." He reached down and stroked the dog's ears.

Bad guys?

"Maybe. I think so."

They want Smells Different?

"Probably."

We gonna give him up?

"Does it matter?"

Bad Dog looked up at him with soulful eyes. *Doesn't it? We've come this far.*

"Still don't rightly know how that's happened. Or why."

Does it matter?

"Doesn't it?"

Word games. For humans, not Bad Dog.

"This is dangerous."

Isn't it always?

Cavalo bent over until he was eye to eye with Bad Dog. Their noses touched. "You follow my lead," the man said, because it was tradition between them.

I follow you, for you are my MasterBossLord.

"You listen for my commands."

I listen to you, for you are my MasterBossLord.

"I will have your back."

And I will have yours.

"Together."

Together. Bad Dog licked the man's cheek.

Cavalo stood and pushed open the door.

It was dark. The moon was hidden behind the clouds. Snow fell heavily, but it was quiet, almost silent. Cavalo was reminded of that snow globe from so very long ago, broken in that hidden, haunted place. It was as if the world around him had been shaken, and now the snow swirled down and sideways. He expected the ground beneath his feet to tilt with the first step. Maybe spin upside down. Everything else was, so it wouldn't surprise him....

Fat flakes fell into his hair. Bad Dog let out his puppy only briefly, taking in a mouthful of snow before falling into step with his Master-BossLord. Cavalo knew the dog was aware of the seriousness of the situation, even if Bad Dog's voice was only in his head. They'd been together for a long time. Even if the dog's voice was just part of Cavalo's breaking mind, they could read each other well.

They reached the edge of the cellblock. Cavalo made a fist at his side, tucking his thumb inside his curled fingers. Bad Dog stopped immediately, pressing against the back of Cavalo's legs.

Through the snow, Cavalo could hear a voice: "—so you might as well come out now! If you choose to keep this up, I can promise you that fire like you can't even *imagine* will rain down upon you. Send him out!"

Cavalo crouched down low. He gripped the corner of the barracks and leaned over.

In the middle of the courtyard stood the man seen on the robot's video, six yards away. His heavy coat opened up to the UFSA uniform underneath. His chest looked distorted and bulky. SIRS was right: they had armor underneath the uniforms. Wilkinson, Blond, and Black had not.

His breath billowed out around him. His rifle was strapped to his back. His gloved hands were empty. He'd had his gun drawn before. At some point, he'd put it away. Cavalo didn't know how to interpret this. The man's words were hostile, so it wasn't as if it was a sign of peace.

Another man stood behind him, his face obscured by a white cloth wrapped around his mouth to protect him from the elements. Cavalo heard him speak but couldn't make out the words. The apparent leader said something in return, and Cavalo could only make out *trip* and *sight* and what sounded like *father*.

Father?

"SIRS," he said quietly.

"Yes, Cavalo." A slight crackle in the connection.

"Perimeter?"

"Eighteen minutes. Maybe twenty."

"Connection?"

"Slight interference but clear."

"You have them sighted?"

"Yes, and I caught a glimpse of you. Two in the courtyard. One in building two, the other in three."

Two was behind the men in front of Cavalo. Three was a crumbling building fifteen yards to the east.

"Cavalo, you should know our friend in here seems quite agitated."

"Isn't he always?"

"Maybe a little more than usual."

"Let him be."

"You need to get them outside the prison. Even just a foot. I can handle the rest."

"I know."

"You don't need to show yourself."

"Cavalo!" The voice came as a shout from the courtyard.

"That's not good," Cavalo muttered.

Bad Dog whined quietly.

"What?" SIRS asked.

"He knows my name."

"That's... not good."

"Yeah."

"Cavalo!" the leader cried again. "We know you're here! Come out now! Bring us the boy!"

"Our friend is certainly popular," SIRS murmured.

Cavalo waited.

"I'll make this simple!" the man shouted. "Easy as pie for someone like you!"

Pie is never easy, Bad Dog said.

The leader looked around the darkened courtyard. "You come out now or we return to Cottonwood... and burn it to the ground. You don't know me but know this: I am a man of my word. Your call, Cavalo."

The bees roared in Cavalo's head. His hand tightened on the handle of the gun hidden away.

"It doesn't have to happen this way. Give us what we came for, and this all goes away!"

"Cavalo." SIRS, in his ear. Through the bees. "Fifteen minutes. Don't do this. Let them leave. We can warn the town. Just get them outside the prison. Let me handle the rest."

"They were real protective of you down there," the leader called out. "No one wanted to tell us a thing! A few even went so far as to threaten us." He laughed. A harsh sound. "Hank? Aubrey? Deke? He seemed real sorry you'd been shot. A scrawny thing, isn't he? More boy than man. Some of us like them that way."

KILL HIM! the bees roared. BREAK HIM!

"And Alma! Man, is she sure a *spitfire*. A whole lot of woman there. You know, while Cottonwood burns, we may just take that sweet piece of ass and see how long she can get fucked before her heart gives out."

"Cavalo," SIRS said urgently. "Don't. He's *baiting* you. You know this!"

Cavalo did. And if he'd been threatened such as this before he'd stumbled upon the Dead Rabbit, he didn't think it would have hit him as hard. He would have told himself it wasn't his problem. They weren't his people to worry about. But something had changed. Something had awakened. He hated it. It burned, and it roiled, and he *hated* it, but he could not stop it. It rose through him. That unending fury. That righteous anger. That feeling of *no*, of *mine*, of the need to *protect* those who could not protect themselves. Oh, Cavalo had no doubt that Alma would fuck them up before they even got close enough to lay a finger on her, but it didn't stop the rage. It wasn't even close.

Cavalo rose from his crouch, even as the robot begged him in his ear, even as Bad Dog pulled gently on his pant leg. His hand squeezed the grip of the gun. This was a new feeling for Cavalo, or rather, it was a feeling long thought gone, never to return. It burned, and he almost gagged on it, a sour taste in the back of his throat.

Here was the snow globe, as he stepped around the corner of the building.

Here was the snow globe, as the earth shook beneath his feet.

As the snow flurried around him.

It had not shattered in that haunted fort. It had not fallen to DEFCON 1, because he was *in* it. He was *here* inside it, and the snow was *red*, it was all so *red*.

The only reason the leader of the small group who had infiltrated the prison did not die right then is because the second man raised his rifle at Cavalo's approach.

"*Stop!*" he barked, his voice a whip crack of warning.

Cavalo stopped. Barely.

Bad Dog growled at his side. *Put down your boomstick, you fucking bad guy! I am Bad Dog and I will tear you to shreds. Put down the boomstick and fight me fair!*

"This isn't going to end well," the robot sighed in his ear.

"Hands!" the man with the rifle snapped. "Show me your fucking hands!"

I'll show you my teeth in your neck! Bad Dog barked.

"Stay," Cavalo ground out. He meant as much for himself as he did for the dog. It was getting harder to see through the red. His hand itched to pull out the gun and shoot each man through the head. The bees felt like they were crawling just under his skin. They wanted to feel blood on his hands, warm and wet. They wanted to tear these men to little pieces.

"Last chance," the man with the rifle barked. "Your hands! *Now.*"

Cavalo raised his hands.

The man with the rifle stepped forward as the two others stepped out of the barracks. The leader watched Cavalo with cool, calculating eyes. Rough hands searched Cavalo, pressing against his sides, stomach, chest. He did not wince even at the flare of pain as fingers pressed against the bullet wound. Cavalo thought about breaking his neck, but there were two other guns trained on him now. He didn't think he'd be quick enough.

The pistol was found and handed to the leader. He turned it over in his hands, a small smile on his face. "Haven't seen one of these in years," he said. He sounded bemused. "Glock 9mm." He ejected the clip. Put it in his pocket. Cleared the chamber. "Maintained well for such an old thing." He looked up at Cavalo. "They used these, you know. Before. Standard issue. Police. Security." He looked past Cavalo at the barracks behind him. "Prisons."

Cavalo said nothing.

"You find this here?"

"Fourteen minutes," SIRS said in his ear. "And the Dead Rabbit isn't too thrilled with me at the moment."

Cavalo thought it would only take one move for him to reach out. Grab the leader. Spin him around. Arm around his neck. Hold him until the others dropped their rifles. Snap his neck. Unhook the rifle from his back. Fire three head shots. It would have to be quick if it would work at all. Most likely he'd be shot at least three times before he could reach the leader. Bad Dog would follow and be shot as well. They would probably die. He'd have to take the chance. He'd have to do it *now*, and he steeled himself for it *now* and his legs coiled and the blood roared in his ears and he thought *now now now*—

The leader took a step back, away from Cavalo. Handed Cavalo's pistol to the man closest to him. The man took it, never taking his eyes off Cavalo, the barrel of the rifle pointed at his face. These men were trained, and trained well.

And how is it that happened? the bees asked gleefully. *How is it that a government has risen and* no one *knew about it?*

"Cottonwood seems real fond of you," the leader said, looking back at Cavalo, "for the most part. Some people there don't know what to make of you. Others are scared of you." He chuckled. "It was almost like they were speaking about a ghost. Something revered. And dreaded."

The snow fell around them. Cavalo had to remind himself that he was not in a globe. Bad Dog felt tense beside him, waiting for any signal from his MasterBossLord.

"Is that what you are?" the leader asked him. "A ghost? A legend?"

"No," Cavalo said. "I'm real."

The three men behind the leader shifted uncomfortably, as if they hadn't expected him to speak. The leader never looked away. "Good to know," he said. "Question for you."

Cavalo waited.

"Do you know who we are?"

"Government."

The leader nodded. "That's right. Government. Bright and shiny and new."

"Twelve minutes," SIRS said.

Think. Think. "How new?" he asked.

The leader reached up with a big hand and wiped the snow that had started to accumulate on his beard. He turned his face toward the sky and stuck out his tongue. Snow fell into his mouth. His throat worked. He looked back at Cavalo with narrowed eyes. "New enough to still be learning from our mistakes. Old enough to know when we're being fucked with. Who are you?"

"I am Cavalo."

"So it's been said. Where do you hail from?"

"The south."

"How far?"

"Nevada."

"Been here long?"

"Didn't they tell you?"

"Cottonwood? Oh, sure. But I want to hear it from you."

"A long time."

"How long is that?"

Cavalo shrugged. "Years. Eight or nine."

"Who else is here with you?"

"No one. It's me and the dog. I prefer it that way."

"Oh bullshit," SIRS growled in his ear. "I am as much a part of this dysfunction as the two of you."

The leader smiled, though it didn't reach his eyes. It was cold. Calculating. He was dangerous, this one. He knew that Cavalo knew. His eyes drifted down briefly. "No one else, huh? How's the chest?"

"Fine."

"You're walking a bit stiff."

"I'm getting old."

The leader laughed. "That'll do it. Or being shot. You were able to patch yourself up?"

Cavalo shrugged. "He just clipped me on the shoulder. Kid has always been a lousy aim."

"Is he?"

"Yes."

"You have to know how this will end."

"Ten minutes," the robot said. "I think."

"How will this end?" Cavalo asked.

The leader stepped forward until they were only inches apart. He had inches on Cavalo, and mass. To keep eye contact, Cavalo was forced to look up, just like he knew the man wanted him to. Undoubtedly he intimidated many people.

Cavalo was not one of them.

Bad Dog growled, but no one paid him any mind.

"This will end with you giving me what I want," the man said. Cavalo could smell the man's road sweat, the harshness of his breath. "You will tell me where the boy is. There are questions that need answered."

"The Dead Rabbit?"

"Yes. The Dead Rabbit."

"Don't know. I brought him to Cottonwood. That's the last thing I remember."

"That so?"

"Yes."

"Bullshit."

"Sure," Cavalo said, and he saw the first flash of anger in the stranger's eyes.

He looked over his shoulder, back at his men. Cavalo almost reached up and snapped his neck. "Carter," the leader said. "Jacobs. Find him." He turned back to Cavalo as the two that'd been searching the barracks previously nodded and began to move away, back toward the remaining buildings behind them. The mess hall. The barracks where they slept.

The cellblock.

"Uh, Cavalo?" SIRS said. "We have a slight problem."

"We'll find him," the leader said to Cavalo. "You can be sure about that."

"It appears our new friend likes to break his thumbs," SIRS said. "Did you know he can slip out of handcuffs? That is quite the talent. The level of pain must be extraordinary."

"Is that so?" Cavalo asked the robot and the stranger.

"Yes," SIRS said.

"Yes," the leader said.

"And what are you going to do?" he asked them both.

"What I can," SIRS said. "He's gone. You need to watch your back. Or they need to watch theirs. I'm still not clear on who he is trying to kill."

"Do you know who I am?" the leader asked almost at the same time.

"No." He could hear the men crunching through the snow slowly behind him. They'd been separated. Now he only had to deal with two. The odds were better now.

"My name is Thomas. I work for the United Federated States of America. I am here to help you. But to do so, you must help me." He pulled his gun off his back.

"How?" Cavalo asked, wondering why a man asking for help felt the need to have a gun in his hands.

"What happened?"

"When?"

"In Cottonwood. To Wilkinson. Bernard. Simon. They were good men. Well, Bernard and Simon were. Wilkinson... let's just say he and I didn't see eye to eye."

"They died," Cavalo said.

"I know. We were in Grangeville when a caravan came through after having passed Cottonwood. Told us there'd been a bit of trouble. The merchants may have underplayed it a bit."

"There was trouble," Cavalo agreed.

"I know *that*," Thomas spat at him, the façade breaking. He pointed the gun at Cavalo. "I'm aware of *that*. What I want to know is *how*. *How* was there trouble? *How* did they die? Was it the Dead Rabbit? Little Deke seemed so completely un*sure* about what he saw. Poor boy." Thomas shook his head. "If I can't get it out of you, I'm sure I can go back and get it from him."

The bees screamed. Something must have crossed Cavalo's face because the remaining man behind Thomas took a step to the side to get a better angle on Cavalo. Bad Dog growled again. Thomas glanced briefly down at him.

"The Dead Rabbit," Cavalo said.

"Yes. The boy. The Dead Rabbit. Lucas."

They know his name, Cavalo thought, careful to keep it hidden from his face.

"He never told me. Couldn't talk. Throat had been slit. He was damaged."

"The two are near the cellblock back door," SIRS said in his ear. "It's about to get noisy in here. Six minutes. I'll dispatch them as quietly as possible."

Thomas's eyes gleamed. "So, it's true, then? Patrick did what they say he did? Jesus Christ. I knew he'd lost it, but that far?" He shook his head.

Cavalo's stomach dropped. "Patrick?"

"He's no concern of yours," Thomas said. "Tell me the Dead

Rabbit killed Wilkinson. The others. Tell me where he is. If you do that, we will leave you here."

"You're pointing a gun at my head. It's hard to think."

"Probably not a good idea to piss them off," SIRS warned.

Thomas lowered the gun. "Nothing will happen to your friends. The town. In fact, I might even be able to get them additional rations. Medicine. Toys. They'd like that, don't you think? For the kids?"

"Would this be before or after you'd burn it to the ground?" Cavalo asked.

Thomas chuckled but didn't answer. He held his right hand back over his shoulder, palm up. The man behind him reached and pulled out his sidearm, placing the pistol in Thomas's hand. Thomas took a step back. Held the gun out. Pointed it at Cavalo's head.

"They're at the door," SIRS said.

"Where is Lucas?" Thomas asked slowly.

"Gone," Cavalo admitted. Cavalo strained to hear anything approaching from behind or above. He heard nothing but the snow, the crunch of boots from the men near the cellblock. The low growl of Bad Dog. The hot breath pouring from mouths and turning to smoke. His own thudding heart.

"But he was here?"

Cavalo said nothing.

Thomas raised the gun again. "I'm done with this. Now."

Cavalo slumped his shoulders. "Shelter," he muttered.

Thomas glanced at the gunman behind him before looking back at Cavalo. "Shelter?"

"Cavalo," SIRS said. "They've opened the door."

"Fallout shelter." He pointed out toward the forest, hidden in the dark and snow. "From Before."

Thomas stared at him hard. Finally, "Is that so?"

"Yes."

"Why lie?"

"You're pointing a gun at my head," Cavalo said again.

"Donovan."

"Yeah?" the man behind him spoke.

"Anything about a fallout shelter on the schematics you looked at?"

Shit.

"I don't...," SIRS said. He sounded perplexed. "I don't hear them anymore. I can't find them on the camera. What the...?"

"Maybe. Couldn't say for sure. The data was corrupted. It'd make sense, Thomas. This is backwoods territory. I've seen places like this before. Everyone was scared of something Before. You saw the ones in Grangeville."

"Yeah." Thomas didn't take his eyes from Cavalo.

I want to kill them, Bad Dog said to him. *They lie.*

Cavalo extended his fingers into the dog's fur. Squeezed gently.

"Oh my God," the robot breathed in his ear.

"You bullshitting me?" Thomas asked him.

"No."

"Do you remember what I said about Cottonwood?"

"Yes." *Kill you.*

"About Alma?"

"Yes."

"Good. Remember that." He looked over Cavalo's shoulder and raised his voice. "Carter! Jacobs!"

"Cavalo."

They were out of time. "What?" he said through grounded teeth. *Fist to throat,* he thought. *Crouch down. Secondary target will fire into primary target. Wait till weapon discharge. Take pistol. Shoot secondary target. Turn. Take out remainders.*

"I've found Lucas," the robot said.

"Carter!" Thomas shouted. "Jacobs! Get your asses back here."

The snow fell.

"This don't feel right," Donovan muttered.

Blood, Bad Dog said, trying to keep his voice quiet. *MasterBoss-Lord, I smell blood. It's in the air.*

"Carter!"

Nothing.

"Jacobs!"

Nothing.

Thomas looked back at Cavalo. "Who else is here?" He pressed the gun against Cavalo's forehead.

"It's too late," Cavalo said.

"What have you brought here?" SIRS whispered in his ear. "Cavalo, who is he?"

"For what?" Thomas asked, voice suspicious.

Cavalo never looked away. "For me. For this place. This world." He pressed his forehead harder into the gun barrel. "For you. You should never have come here."

Blood! I smell BLOOD!

"Yo, Carter!" Donovan shouted, stepping up to stand next to Thomas. "Jacobs!"

Nothing.

"You're down to only two," SIRS said in his ear.

Cavalo smiled, even though inside he felt nothing more than death.

"Kill this motherfucker," Donovan snarled. He raised his rifle.

"No," Thomas barked. "You know what the Forefathers said. The boy. Patrick. Those are the priorities. He's our only link. He's the only—"

A sound, from behind.

Donovan's eyes widened. Thomas frowned.

Both took steps forward. They stood next to Cavalo. They took another step. Then stood behind him.

He turned.

Beyond the men, in the dark, in the falling snow, stood another. His head was bowed. His rifle was gone. He took a staggering step forward. Paused. Another step. Pause. His hands shook at his sides, one arm bent at an odd angle. There was a choking sound, wet and low. Another step. Fluid dripped from his fingertips onto the snow. It melted holes into the drift. Little red holes that smoked.

Another step.

The man looked up.

Jacobs.

His eyes were wide and shocked. His face was devoid of color. He opened his mouth to speak. A blood bubble burst from his lips, coating his chin. He took another faltering step.

"Jacobs?" Thomas asked.

"Guh," Jacobs said. "Guh. Guh. *Guh. Guh!*"

He fell to his knees. The snow piled up around his lap. It only took a moment to stain red.

"Oh Jesus fuck," Donovan moaned. "What the fuck is this?"

"He's here," Thomas said, looking up into the night as if something could fall onto them from the dark above. "Lucas."

Jacobs fell forward. A broken shard of wood stuck out from the back of his neck. It looked as if it was buried deep into his spine.

The barracks, Cavalo thought. *I've seen that wood. It sits in a pile behind the barracks. Firewood. That's firewood.*

Donovan rushed forward.

Thomas did not.

Bad Dog snarled. *Blood. There is blood. I smell blood. I want blood.*

"No," Cavalo said quietly. "Not yet."

Soon.

"Five minutes," SIRS said.

Donovan knelt down beside Jacobs. He pulled the glove off his right hand with his teeth. Reached down to Jacobs. A moment later: "He's dead."

Thomas turned back to Cavalo. Raised the gun. "You have no idea," he said, "what it is you have here. He is not what you think."

Donovan stood and turned, pointing his rifle toward the cellblock. "Carter!"

Nothing.

"Carter, answer me goddammit!"

"He's gone," Thomas said. He didn't look away from Cavalo.

"Probably before Jacobs. Keep quiet unless you want to tell the Dead Rabbit exactly where you are."

Donovan's rifle jerked right. Then left. Up. Left. He stood slowly. "We don't know Carter's dead," he said, voice strained. "He could still be in there."

"Donovan—"

We shouldn't have come here," he snapped. "I told you this was a bad idea. I *told* you." He took a step toward the cellblock. Called Carter's name again.

Thomas ignored him. "How many are you?" he asked Cavalo instead.

Cavalo cocked his head. "Does it matter now?"

The gun in Thomas's hand did not shake. "Yes. It matters."

"Enough. More than you now."

"You have no weapon."

"I haven't since I got out here. Yet two of your men are still dead." Cavalo let his eyes flicker over Thomas's shoulder. "Three, in a moment."

"I can shoot you," Thomas said. His voice was rough. Cavalo thought he was afraid, maybe for the first time in his life. "It would be so very easy."

"I'd advise against antagonizing him," SIRS said, sounding exasperated.

"Then do it," Cavalo said to Thomas.

"You bloody idiot." SIRS sighed.

Cavalo saw Thomas tighten his finger on the trigger. Not enough, but close.

"Carter!" Donovan bawled, stepping up next to the cellblock. "Fall back!"

"By order of the United Federated States of America," Thomas said, "I order you to call him off. Get your people out here. We will take what we need, and we will leave."

"Carter!"

Bad Dog lifted his head back and howled.

Cavalo thought he saw movement on the roof of the cellblock but couldn't be sure.

The snow fell around them like they were trapped in a snow globe.

DEFCON 1, Cavalo thought. *We're at DEFCON 1.*

"The United Federated States of America?" he asked. His eyes narrowed as he took a step forward. "You have no authority here. You have no jurisdiction here. You are in the wilds now. You are on the edge of the Deadlands. You know nothing of this place. You don't order me. Not here. Not in my home."

"Carter?" Donovan asked, flicking his gun up toward the sky. "That you?"

"Do you know what will happen to you?" Thomas asked quietly. "You kill us, that's four. And Wilkinson and his men. That's seven. You are responsible for the death of seven government men. How do you think that could possibly end for you? For Grangeville? Cottonwood? It may take time. It may be months. It may take years. You'll think you'll live your life out here, and maybe you will. Alone. In this broken place. But one day they will come, and they will want answers. They will demand you comply, and unless you want death, you will. Man was not meant to be spread. Man was meant to have rules set in place to govern them. To live by them. That is what the Forefathers will bring. It has already started."

"Three minutes," SIRS said. "Though, I don't know it matters anymore. I can hear him now. On the roof."

"Why do you want him?" Cavalo asked, no longer concerned with the gun pointed at his head. Either he'd be shot or he wouldn't. It was that simple. "Wilkinson said almost the same thing. Why him?"

"Lucas."

"Yes."

"Because he leads to Patrick."

Cavalo tried to school his face, but failed.

"Ah," Thomas said, his upper lip curling. "You know that name."

"Why Patrick?"

"Because of what he used to be. Because of what he is now. Because of what he could mean in the future. Whoever controls the beast controls the world." Thomas smiled darkly. "Enough questions. Call him out. Now."

"Carter?" Donovan called, his voice shaking. He took a step toward the side of the building.

"Cavalo," SIRS said.

"What?" Cavalo asked.

"Now. It will happen now."

And it did. Even though it was only a second, it felt longer. Cavalo knew there was a choice to be made, a decision to be had that would change the way his life was lived, what there was left of it. He was alive, but only just. He was human, but only just. He was sane, but so close to the edge he could feel it under his feet. Could feel the empty space of unreality in front of him. If he fell, there would be bees. And rubber bands. They would catch him, then they would break and he could swim and float in the dark and never again have a care in all the world.

But.

In his mind's eye, he saw a boy. This boy grew into a young man. This young man grew into a monster. An angel. A demon. The sweetest smile. The darkest snarl. He spoke, a gravelly sound that thrummed in Cavalo's chest. He said things like "I have killed" and "I am lost."

And this boy, this man, this fucking psycho and clever cannibal had a mask of smeared black around his eyes.

It was another door, Cavalo knew. In that split second, that momentary pause in the world where the snow shook inside the snow globe, Cavalo realized it was another door.

He stepped into that unreal black space.

He stepped through that second door.

And in the prison yard, in that space between the barracks where murderers and rapists and pedophiles had all walked and lived and breathed and died, the lights flashed on, bright and harsh.

Cavalo saw individual crystals flare in the snowflakes.

There was an electrical snap as the fences came online.

Sentient Integrated Response System said, "Now would be a good time to fight."

Bad Dog said a low growl, *You shouldn't have come here.*

Cold water ran down the side of Cavalo's face.

Another rubber band broke apart somewhere in the distance. It seemed such a trivial thing.

Cavalo heard all of this; he felt all of this. All of it and more in the space of that single second, that little stutter of time. It was as if everything in his world had fired at once like a bundle of nerves uncovered and exposed. The world was electric; *he* was electric.

And as his vision cleared from that burning flash of light in the dark, he saw many things.

The barrel of a gun pointed at his head.

Thomas, his eyes wide, breath streaming from his mouth.

Snowflakes falling so very slowly.

Donovan, face turned, looking back, rifle pointed toward the ground.

The fresh tracks of some small animal, near the cellblock barracks.

Bad Dog, launching himself at Thomas.

A bright arc of electricity along an outer fence.

Jacobs, blood spreading in the snow.

All of this happened. All of it was real. Cavalo saw all of it.

But what he saw the most was the Dead Rabbit, that clever monster, that clever cannibal, I am *Lucas*, crouched atop the cellblock roof near the edge. In each hand were long shards of wood. His body was coiled. His face, shrouded in what at first Cavalo thought were shadows. Then the shadow dripped down the side of the Dead Rabbit's face, and Cavalo recognized it for what it was: blood. Whether it was his own or not, Cavalo did not know.

There was beauty in this horror. A terrible beauty that Cavalo could not turn from. He might have stood there watching until the end of time had the Dead Rabbit not stepped off the roof into thin air. Into unreality.

Donovan stood directly below him, eyes bulging in panic, unaware of the death from above.

It was fifteen feet. Not far, but not a light drop either. But Cavalo did not see the outcome. Not then.

Bad Dog obscured his view as he latched on to Thomas's hand. The gun fired. Cavalo heard the whine of the bullet as it passed by his ear. He heard the air splitting. It was only inches.

Bad Dog forced the arm down, snarling and shaking his head back and forth. Skin ripped. Blood flowed. Thomas grunted and nothing more. The gun fired again. An arc of snow rose into the air as the slug punched through. Cavalo could smell the sharp burn of gunpowder.

A loud scream came, but Cavalo paid it no mind. It was tertiary behind the man and the gun.

He moved forward, mind engaged to tear, snap, break. He was moving too slow. He was moving as if underwater.

He watched as Thomas punched Bad Dog in the side of his head. The dog yelped, his grip on the gunman's hand loosening. The gun fell into the snow, splattered with blood. Bad Dog staggered. The man turned and raised his foot to kick the dog in the head.

Cavalo tackled him, ignoring the scream of his chest, the breath leaving his body in a swift *oomph*. The two men fell to the ground, and Cavalo's face went into the snow, and it was all so *white* and bright and—

His head bounced off a rock hidden underneath the snow. He saw stars between the snowflakes. He wondered just how far into the snow globe he had traveled. It seemed to be a great distance. Everything seemed to be a great distance. He couldn't move his arms and legs. He couldn't breathe. All that made up the man only named Cavalo was stars in a snow globe. *Oh God*, he thought. *So bright.*

"Cavalo!" a metal man shouted in his ear. "I'm coming!"

He found himself on his back, though he didn't know how he got there. Snow fell in his eyes and melted. It streamed down his face like tears. It was the only explanation as to why his face was wet. Cavalo hadn't cried since... when? Had he cried when Jamie had died? When he'd woken then? He didn't think he had. He remembered only how dead he felt. He remembered only the weight of the gun in one hand, Mr. Fluff in the other. If he hadn't cried after his son died, then he wouldn't be crying now. It was just the snow, the melting snow.

"I didn't cry," he said, his voice a croak. He cleared it and tried again. "I didn't cry," he told the stars in the globe.

Movement above him. Through the stars. Through the snow. A man stood over him. He had to be the tallest man in the world. He could probably reach and touch the stars if he so wished. He was a curious man, being so big.

The tall man said, "You should have listened." He raised his leg. His foot loomed over Cavalo's face. It looked massive. "You should have listened."

Cavalo saw through the unreality, like dark curtains parting to reveal the sun. It was only a moment, only a flash, but it was enough. His head ached fiercely. His stomach felt nauseated. He was dizzy, and his chest hurt. But he was not going to die. Not like this. Not now.

Quicker than he would have thought he could move, he reached out. Scrabbled for something. Anything. His hands grew cold. Wet. Nothing. Nothing. Then something hard. Near his head. The rock. It was the rock.

Cavalo curled it in his fingers as the foot above him raised higher. He brought it up as the man named Thomas screwed his face together. Cavalo jerked his head to the right as the foot came down and brought his hand up in a wide arc. Thomas's boot struck the side of Cavalo's head, causing his ear to go numb. The rock smashed into

Thomas's knee. There was a wet crunch. Thomas screamed. Fell away.

Cavalo rolled onto his back and was lost in stars.

It was later (a moment, a year, Cavalo didn't know) when the stars faded as a large flat tongue licked up the side of his face.

Get up, the dog said. *Get up, MasterBossLord.*

"Tired," Cavalo muttered.

I know. But you have to get up. A cold nose pressed against his cheek and pushed.

"Later."

The dog growled threateningly.

"Fine," Cavalo said. He pushed himself up. It was easier than he thought it would be. It was only then he realized he had help.

"This is how you handle things?" SIRS scolded him, pushing him up to a sitting position. "You are *human*, Cavalo. You are not *invincible*. You will break physically *and* mentally. What were you thinking?"

"I don't know," Cavalo said. The world grayed a bit before coming into sharp focus. "I thought—"

"I highly doubt that," SIRS said, tilting Cavalo's head back to see the laceration where he'd dashed against the rock. "These were not the actions of a thinking man. These were the actions of a... of a... well, of a certified lunatic!"

Tin Man is kind of right, Bad Dog said.

"Hush," Cavalo said, wincing as metal fingers pressed against the split skin. "You okay?"

I'm fine. I'm Bad Dog. I can handle bad guys.

"You got punched in the face."

You managed to fall on the only rock in the prison yard.

"Right," Cavalo muttered.

Bad Dog huffed at him.

"Are you two done yapping at each other?" the robot asked irritably.

Cavalo shrugged.

"You'll live," SIRS sighed. "You have more lives than a cat. How you have survived this long, I'll never know."

"Luck, I guess."

Sure, the bees said, rattling in his aching head. *Let's call it that.*

"And who is this?" SIRS asked as he stood, his orange eyes bright in the dark. He moved around Cavalo and toward Thomas, who was crawling through the snow toward the fallen gun. The robot moved with calm purpose. Thomas moved with frantic panic. There was no contest. The robot reached the gun and tossed it back at Cavalo. Thomas turned over on his back and stared up at SIRS.

"Impossible," he sputtered. His eyes were wide. Almost crazy. And for the first time, there was fear. "You can't exist. We would have known. We would have been told. The Forefathers would have *known*. I order you to stand down, robot! You will stand—no. Don't! No! *I order you to—*"

He was silenced when SIRS reached down and knocked him upside the head, rendering him unconscious. He rose and stood above him, his orange eyes burning harshly in the dark. From deep inside him came a beep. A click. Another beep. Finally the robot said, "Noisy, that one is. I much prefer you. You are economical with your words, Cavalo, to put it lightly."

Cavalo said nothing. He'd barely heard Thomas or the robot. His eyes had found the only other living soul in the prison.

"Cavalo?" SIRS asked. "What are you... oh. That... this is... different."

Blood, Bad Dog whispered. *Blood. Blood.*

And there was. So much of it. It coated the snow near the cell-block barracks, causing it to melt partially and turn a deeper maroon. The man named Donovan lay on the ground, partially buried. His rifle, unused and bloody, was stuck barrel first into the falling snow. His arms were curved up toward the sky, curved into frozen claws. The cloth across his face had been torn away. His eyes were wide and glassy, seeing nothing. Snow fell into them and then trickled down the side of his face, as if the dead could cry. His mouth was twisted into a silent scream. Blood coated his teeth. His lips. His chin. And his neck. His ruined neck that resembled nothing more than a pile of bloody meat and pulp, torn to shreds. Shards of wood still jutted from the mass.

And above him, above this man who had died an unimaginable death, stood the Dead Rabbit. The boy. *I am Lucas.* He stood above Donovan, feet planted on either side of the body. In one hand was a long pointed piece of wood, coated in gore. His other hand was bloody. There were scratch marks on his face and arms where Donovan had attempted to fight back. His chest heaved. His head was cocked. It was there that Cavalo found those dark eyes. They locked with his. There was rage there. There was insanity there. There were monsters. And horror. And death. Only death.

For the first time in a long time, fascination outweighed fear. He could not stop it no matter how hard he tried.

No one moved.

No one spoke.

Then:

The Dead Rabbit (*Lucas,* Cavalo told himself, *Lucas*) raised his hand, his eyes never leaving Cavalo. He pointed the bloody shard of wood at Bad Dog. Then at SIRS. Then at Cavalo, where it lingered. He pursed his lips and blew the sound of bees. He pointed at his head.

You all have bees in your head, Cavalo heard him say.

Lucas turned the wood on himself and blew the sound of bees again. He tapped his head. *I have bees in my head too,* he said. He winced. *They hurt.*

He pointed at Cavalo. Back at himself. At Bad Dog. Himself. SIRS. Himself.

We are the same. You have bees. I have bees. They hurt. They break us. We are the same, and you know it.

Cavalo could think of nothing to say in return. He was almost amused that not a single refutation rose to his lips.

Almost.

They stood there, for a time. In the snow. In the dark, the bodies of three dead men and one who yet lived strewn around them.

It was the robot who spoke first. Cavalo could hear him clicking. Processing. Eventually he could contain his insanity no longer and blared: "HOW RIDICULOUS I WAS AS A MARIONETTE! AND HOW HAPPY I AM, NOW THAT I HAVE BECOME A REAL BOY!" His voice echoed across the snow as he stopped. He beeped. He clicked. He whirred. How darkly his eyes shown. Sentient Integrated Response System looked at Cavalo and asked, "What do we do with him now?"

Smells Different, Bad Dog agreed. *Blood. Smells Different. Kill him or keep him?*

And for all the dark wonder Cavalo saw in Lucas, for all the knowledge that came in knowing what he truly was, the man said, "He stays. With us." He was surprised at how easily the words came out. Like a rubber band breaking. "He stays."

The snow continued to fall.

revelations

THE FIRST DAY was met with silence.

"How many are you?" Cavalo asked the prisoner.

Thomas, who was now in the cell that Lucas had been in, said nothing. His knee had been wrapped by SIRS. His face was bruised. He hadn't spoken since he'd been placed in the cell. That did not change now. Food was not eaten. Water was not drunk. He sat on the old cot, staring straight ahead.

"The United Federated States of America," Cavalo said.

Thomas looked disinterested.

"How long has it been since it formed?"

Thomas looked at his hands.

"Where is it located at?"

Thomas smiled.

"Who are the Forefathers?"

Outside, the storm raged, the trees bending cruelly. They were in the middle of a blizzard, and there was no end in sight. The wind moaned around the building, and it sounded like voices. Cavalo wondered briefly if it *was* voices. He knew the dead talked. He heard them all the time.

Thomas pulled the scratchy blanket up over his legs.

"I can last longer than you," Cavalo said. He left the cellblock through the tunnel, switching off the lights as he left.

THE SECOND DAY WAS MET WITH ANGER.

No water drank. No food eaten. SIRS had watched Thomas while the others slept, the robot curious about the new human. "He's certainly different," SIRS told Cavalo as he moved toward the tunnel door. "If he is who he says he is, then he's been trained. Like a soldier. Maybe he *is* a soldier."

"Everyone breaks," Cavalo said. He knew this more than most. "It's only a matter of time."

"I can be of assistance," SIRS said, looking back at the screen in front of him. "If necessary."

"Oh?"

"Yes. I have... proven methods of obtaining information should I be called upon to do so."

Cavalo felt cold. "Why?"

"Why?"

"Yes. Why can you do such things? Is it the insanity?"

"No. It came from Before. It is how I was programmed. Certain times such... events... were necessary. Better a robot than a human."

"They programmed you to hurt others?"

The robot glanced briefly at Cavalo. "I suppose it allowed them to sleep at night."

"What about you?"

"I don't sleep, Cavalo."

Cavalo swore he heard laughter in the robot's voice. "I'll be back. Keep an eye on Lucas while I'm gone." He looked back at the cot where the Dead Rabbit slept. He hadn't moved much in the past two days. SIRS had said his body was exhausted.

"One other thing, Cavalo."

"What?"

"The rifles that the men were carrying."

"What about them?"

"I've had time to look them over. They're not from Before."

"So when are they from?"

"They're new."

This stopped Cavalo. "You sure?"

"Oh yes. It would seem this new government certainly has priorities. I wonder what they are exactly?"

And this is what Cavalo asked Thomas on the second day.

"Why guns?"

Thomas glared at him balefully.

"What do the Forefathers want?"

Continued silence.

"Why Lucas?"

Nothing.

"Who is Patrick?"

Nothing.

And on and on the questions went. Never a response. Never a reaction aside from the anger held on the prisoner's face. Nothing more.

Cavalo left.

NOTHING MORE HAPPENED ON THE THIRD DAY.

When Cavalo returned to the barracks, Lucas was sitting up in his cot, blankets pooled around his waist. His chest was bare, the flesh pebbled with goose bumps. Bad Dog lay curled on the cot at the Dead Rabbit's feet. The dog snorted in his sleep. His legs kicked. He was dreaming.

Cavalo lowered his eyes, ignoring the bees inside that were screaming at him, *I AM LUCAS, I AM LUCAS.*

"He moves at night," SIRS said. "I don't think he knows he's being watched. He moves from side to side in the cell. Sometimes he tries to pull on the bars. Other times it looks as if he's memorizing the layout. And then other times...." The robot stopped.

"What happens the other times?" Cavalo asked.

"He talks to himself," SIRS said. "There is no sound, as you know. That's something I have never been able to fix. But I can see his lips move. And sometimes I can make out what he is saying."

"What does he say?"

"Do it," SIRS said, imitating Thomas's voice. It was unnerving. "Just fucking do it."

"Do what?"

"I don't know."

Cavalo made a decision.

"Tomorrow," he told SIRS.

"Yes?"

"You'll go in. Tomorrow."

Something clicked inside the robot. When he spoke next, his voice was flatter. More robotic. "Understood, Cavalo. Would you like me to ask the same line of questions? Please acknowledge."

Cavalo felt eyes on him, and he looked up to see Lucas watching him. For a time, he did not look away. "Yes," he said. "The same line of questions."

"Understood, Cavalo. Tomorrow I will go to Cellblock A and proceed with questioning prisoner 21022."

Lucas smiled.

ON THE FOURTH DAY, THE ROBOT ENTERED THE CELLBLOCK barracks alone.

Cavalo stood in front of the screen, watching. Waiting.

There was no sound.

Bad Dog stood at his side, herding against Cavalo's legs as if afraid. *Bad air* was all he would say. *There's bad air here. Burns my nose.*

Cavalo watched the robot approach the cell. Thomas rose from the cot. His mouth moved for the first time since the attack in the prison yard, but Cavalo could not hear the words. Thomas looked angry. Defiant. He pointed at SIRS as the robot approached the white lit panel on the side wall. His lips moved again. Cavalo could make out the words *order* and *stop, comply* and what looked like *override*.

It appeared SIRS did not speak. The white panel flashed as the robot pressed his hand against it.

Cavalo felt Lucas stand beside him. He looked over. Lucas was enraptured by the screen. He did not look at Cavalo.

On the screen, the cell door opened. Thomas moved quickly for one with a blown knee. He hobbled out, heading straight for the side door. It was locked magnetically, but there was no way he could have known that. They'd waltzed into the prison without resistance, so he probably expected an easy exit.

He reached the door. Slammed into it. Banged on it with his fists. The robot moved. Took two large steps. Blocked the path. Thomas turned and shouted something at the robot. SIRS tilted his head.

Thomas tried to run past the robot.

Striking out like a snake, SIRS grabbed Thomas around the neck and slammed him up against the wall. The robot's eyes flashed. Thomas watched him. Spoke. Waited. Snarled. Waited.

SIRS reached up and took Thomas's right hand into his own. Thomas shook his head. Again. And again. And again.

SIRS tightened his grip.

Even though there was no sound, Cavalo could still hear the crack of bone through the bees.

Thomas rocked his head back and screamed.

Cavalo felt a tap on his shoulder, light and quick. Like a snake. He looked into dark eyes.

Lucas pointed at him, his finger close enough that Cavalo could see the dirt under the nail. He would need to clean himself now that he'd awoken.

He pointed at Cavalo with that dirty finger, those dark eyes questioning. He pointed at the screen where SIRS had dropped Thomas's destroyed hand. Thomas's face was a mask of agony. Lucas pointed back at Cavalo, and just like with Bad Dog, and just like before, he could hear the Dead Rabbit's voice in his head, young and broken.

You tell him to do this? Lucas asked. *You send the robot to do this?*

"Yes," Cavalo said.

Lucas pointed at himself and raised his shoulders in question. *Is he going to do that to me?*

Cavalo thought to lie, to say yes, of course he will. Of course he will hurt you unless you tell me what I want. Instead, as the blood flowed down Thomas's arm, Cavalo said, "No. Not now. Not unless you make him."

Why? those eyes asked. *Why didn't you do that to me from the start?*

"I didn't know," Cavalo said. "I didn't know he would do that."

Why didn't he tell you? Why wait until now?

It was a question Cavalo did not have an answer to, none that sat right with him anyway. He didn't *know* why, didn't know why SIRS had failed to tell him he was an expert in torture, failed to tell him he could hurt people on command.

Everyone has secrets, the bees whispered. *Even if one happens to be a* thing.

"I don't know," Cavalo said.

On the screen, the man screamed as his arm was broken.

Lucas laughed silently.

"You think this is okay?" Cavalo asked angrily. "You think this is right?"

Lucas shrugged.

"It's not right."

The Dead Rabbit pointed at the screen. *It's happening, isn't it?*

"It's necessary."

Those dark eyes laughed.

On the screen, SIRS's questions were not answered. The robot smashed a heavy metal hand into the man's damaged knee. Thomas dripped with snot and sweat. His eyes leaked.

It went on. And on. And on.

Lucas never looked away.

Cavalo didn't either.

Eventually the robot came back.

Streaks of blood covered his spidery hands. There were smears on his chest.

"He didn't speak," SIRS said. His voice was still flat. "Nothing of value was said. He begged me to stop but would say nothing more. The same questions were asked. If you'd like, I can continue when he regains consciousness."

Blood, Tin Man, Bad Dog said in a quiet voice. *You got blood.*

"SIRS?" Cavalo asked. The robot's queer voice perturbed him, as did the metronome clicking he could hear from inside SIRS.

"Yes, Cavalo."

"Thank you." Cavalo didn't know what else to say.

"You're welcome, Cavalo, though I must admit that is a strange thing to be thankful for. Humans are complex and vast creatures." He looked down at the blood on his hands. "Though, I'd forgotten just how soft you could be."

"SIRS?"

"Yes, Cavalo."

"Where are you?"

"What an odd question, Cavalo. I'm right here, of course." Spoken in that flat voice, as if stuck there. He dropped his hands to his sides.

Lucas moved to stand in front of the robot. SIRS looked down at him. The Dead Rabbit reached up... and banged his fist against the robot's chest, where the clicking emanated from like a clock breaking down.

Cavalo tensed, waiting for the robot to lash out.

Instead, the clicking stopped. Gears ground together, and the robot tilted his head back toward the ceiling. His eyes grew as bright as they'd ever been, and the room was almost bathed in orange. Cavalo had to shield his eyes. Bad Dog whined as the robot said, "The third angel sounded his trumpet, and a great star, blazing like a torch, fell from the sky on a third of the rivers and on the springs of water. The name of the star is Wormwood. A third of the waters turned bitter, and many people died from the waters that had become bitter."

The eye lights faded. The robot looked forward. When he spoke, his voice had returned to normal. "It appears that there was a momentary lapse in circuitry. Quite a fascinating thing. What were we talking about?"

"Wormwood," Cavalo said.

"Oh? How delightfully morbid! Where on earth did you hear that word?"

"What does it mean?"

SIRS chuckled. "It's from the book of Revelations in the Bible. It's supposed to be a sign of a coming apocalypse. There was always a logical fallacy to the Bible, but I must admit to being intrigued by the idea after man decided that his brothers and sisters must die in waves of fire. Seems a bit prophetic, don't you think?"

It was. Cavalo was only vaguely familiar with the Bible, had only actually seen one or two in his travels. But he'd heard stories of the time after the bombs had fallen like bright stars and how many rivers became undrinkable given the radiation. People who had survived the bombs had died from radiation sickness. They had lived through one hell only to fall at the hands of another.

"I do seem to be covered in gore," SIRS said, his voice affecting an over-the-top British accent. "It has surely been quite the busy day. By your leave, Cavalo, I would like to go clean myself."

Without another word, the robot left.

ON THE FIFTH DAY, THOMAS DID NOT REGAIN CONSCIOUSNESS.

The robot barely spoke.

Lucas prowled the corners of the barracks.

Bad Dog sat near the door, as if listening for intruders.

Cavalo thought on Wormwood.

On the sixth day, Thomas woke once, when Cavalo attempted to give him water.

He sputtered, spraying Cavalo's face in a mist.

"Don't!" he cried, his eyes rolling back in his head. "Please. Nicole, just let me find him!"

Cavalo took a step back.

Thomas let out a shuttering breath. "It's not a dream?" he asked finally.

"No," Cavalo said. "It's not a dream."

"Nicole's not here?"

"No."

"Oh. She was my wife."

"Was?"

Thomas coughed. "Died. During childbirth."

"The child?"

"Stillborn."

"I'm sorry."

Thomas opened his eyes. "Are you?"

"Yes."

"How do you have the robot?"

"I don't. He was here when I arrived. He saved me from a storm."

"We should have known. We should have known he was here."

"Why?"

Thomas grimaced. His face scrunched up. He was soaked in sweat. "Nicole!" he cried. "Why isn't dinner on the table yet? Goddammit, you know how hard I work!"

Cavalo moved to stand above Thomas. His wounds had been bandaged. His broken bones set. They didn't have much in the way of antibiotics or painkillers, but the high didn't appear to be catching the pain.

You did this, the bees reminded him. *It wasn't your hands, but it might as well have been.*

Cavalo tried to find an ounce of remorse. If it was there, it was buried deep.

"Why?" he asked again.

"Why what?" Thomas asked him.

"The robot. How should you have known about the robot?"

"Network. There... is a network."

Cavalo frowned. "How?"

"They are more than you think."

"Who?"

"The Forefathers." Sweat dripped from his brown. "They...." His eyes grew unfocused. "Pregnant?" he exclaimed, his voice pain free. "How in the hell did that happen?"

"Thomas."

"We'll have to get married now. My parents will kill me if we're not married.

"*Thomas.*"

"What?"

"Patrick. Lucas."

"What about them?"

"Repeat it so I know you hear me."

"Patrick. Lucas."

"Yes. Who are they? Why do you want them?"

"I don't want them. I didn't want to come here. I didn't want to be a part of this. I didn't ask for this assignment."

"But you do what you're told because you're a soldier."

"Yes."

Cavalo closed his eyes. "Why do the Forefathers want them?"

"Are you going to send the robot again?"

"If you don't answer my questions, yes."

"Don't," Thomas moaned. "Please."

"You told me you would burn down Cottonwood."

"Threats! Empty threats!"

"I do not make empty threats. What do the Forefathers want?"

"Patrick. He... used to be one. One of them. He broke away. Disappeared."

"And now?"

"They found him," Thomas said. "They found him with the Dead Rabbits, and it scared them. If he leads the Dead Rabbits, they won't get what they want."

"What do they want?"

Thomas sighed. "Everything."

He lapsed into unconsciousness.

Cavalo did not move for hours.

EARLY ON THE MORNING OF THE SEVENTH DAY, CAVALO WAS awoken.

"What?" he asked gruffly.

Orange eyes stared at him. "Thomas is dead."

"How? The injuries?"

"No. He would have recovered from those. In time."

"How, then?"

"A small capsule hidden near his back tooth. He crushed it. It released a poison. Appears it was very fast acting."

Cavalo was wide awake. "Were you watching?"

"Yes, but there was nothing that could have been done. It was over in a matter of seconds."

"Wormwood," Cavalo muttered. "It's all Mr. Fluff and Wormwood."

"I don't understand, Cavalo."

"I know."

"The body. Should I bury it with the others?"

"No. I'll do it."

"You'll need to do it soon."

"Why?"

"Storms are coming. All in a row, one right after another. This is going to be a bad winter. Maybe the worst I've seen since Before."

"What about Cottonwood?"

"What about Cottonwood, Cavalo?"

"We have to warn them."

The robot clicked. "We have time. They won't return during the winter. Nuclear winters are harsh. In the spring, we can warn Cottonwood."

Months, Thomas had said. *Years.*

"Are you sure?"

"Yes, Cavalo. I'm sure."

Cavalo rose from the cot and started dressing.

SIRS watched him. "What about Lucas?"

"What about him?"

"He is important."

"I know."

"They will come for him."

"I know."

"What is it about him?"

Cavalo couldn't look at the robot. "What do you mean?"

"He makes you... different. You act different. You see things different."

"I don't know what you're talking about."

"Of course, Cavalo."

"We can use him. As a bargaining chip."

The orange eyes burned bright. "We can."

"That is all he is."

"Of course."

Cavalo left the robot in the dark.

It was beginning to lighten in the east when Cavalo realized he was no longer alone.

It was slow going, digging a serviceable hole. The ground was frozen. Snow fell in fat clumps. His hands, though gloved, were icy. His head hurt. His back was sore. His chest pulled. SIRS could have done this in under an hour, but it didn't feel right. He didn't want the robot around the body any more than necessary.

NOW WHY IS THAT? THE BEES ASKED.

Because of what he did, Cavalo replied.

The bees laughed at him. They were not fooled.

Gray gloom peeked through the black, and Cavalo felt someone standing near him.

"What are you doing out here?" he asked, without looking up. "Go back inside."

Bad Dog huffed. *You're out here. And now so am I. You're Master-BossLord. I am Bad Dog. That is how we are.*

"You'll get wet. You'll smell."

You are sweating. I can already smell you.

Cavalo didn't argue.

Moments later, they were joined by another.

"You'll rust," Cavalo said.

"Highly unlikely," SIRS said. "I am constructed of a titanium alloy and am stronger than you will ever be. Besides, this is where I belong."

"Your processor will malfunction."

"Doubtful, but you can keep talking if you'd like."

Cavalo didn't answer. He kept chipping away at the frozen ground. It was getting easier now.

He wasn't surprised when they were joined by the Dead Rabbit. What *did* surprise him was how a brief and panicky sense of *completeness* came washing over him. Cavalo pushed it away and eyed Lucas warily.

He'd put on one of Cavalo's coats. Since they were roughly the same size, it fit him well. The Dead Rabbit stared down at the tarp-wrapped body of Thomas.

"You can't eat him," Cavalo said, more harshly than he intended. "He's been dead a while, and the body is probably halfway frozen. Don't you try and eat him."

Lucas looked up at him. Stared openly, his forehead lined, eyes narrowed. He tilted his head slightly, like a bird. Then he smiled. It was the smile of someone not used to smiling. Too wide, too maniacal. The lips stretched almost obscenely. His shoulders shook a little, and he sounded like he was breathing heavily.

He was laughing. The clever monster, the clever cannibal, that psycho fucking bulldog was laughing.

Unease filled Cavalo, mixed with something else he dared not focus on....

Lucas stopped laughing. Cocked his head again. Pointed at Cavalo.

"What?"

Insistent pointing.

Trees swayed.

"I don't understand."

Cavalo was still in the snow globe.

The Dead Rabbit rolled his eyes. Pointed at himself.

"You. Yes. You're Lucas."

He nodded. Pointed back at Cavalo.

"Cavalo," he said. "We've told you."

Lucas nodded again. He raised one finger. Waited a beat. Raised two fingers. Shrugged in question.

"One or two?"

Shook his head. One finger. Then two. Pointed at Cavalo.

"He wants to know if Cavalo is your first or last name," SIRS said quietly.

Cavalo stiffened. He was hit by so many memories at once, like he was bludgeoned upside the head. Everything fired all at the same time, synapses, little electrical sparks between nerves, and rubber bands broke and bees were fried and it was *so much fucking snow in this fucking snow globe—*

"No," he said hoarsely, trying to hold on to what he had left. It was a fight he almost lost. "No."

The Dead Rabbit watched him. Waited.

Desperately, Cavalo tried to push it back. "What about you? Lucas? Lucas what?"

Lucas shrugged, but those shrewd eyes showed Cavalo that he was not fooled. *Never had one,* he seemed to say, and Cavalo remembered that day in the Deadlands, the other side of the woods, when he'd been hiding in the bushes, waiting to die. What had the large tumor man said?

Found him in the woods sucking on his dead momma's titties when he was nothing but a babe. Raised him since. Pet. Fucking bulldog.

Cavalo felt cold. It was not because of the snow.

Lucas pointed at Cavalo again. The same damn question burning in his eyes. *What's your other name? You're not just Cavalo. You know it. I know it. What's your other name?*

Cavalo turned away, took a breath, and continued to dig the hole in the ground where he would bury the man he knew only as Thomas. It seemed easier to bury the dead than to dig the dead back up.

the ballad of bad dog

THE NEXT MONTH brought storm after storm unlike anything Cavalo had ever seen in his time at the prison. He often wondered if the quick succession of these winter squalls had to do with radiation that surely still lingered. He wasn't savvy enough to know how such things worked, and the thought of it hurt his head, but he'd rather think the storms outside were manmade and not acts of God. If they *were* acts of God, then God was very pissed off indeed. Of course, there was Wormwood and Revelations, and that was even more unsettling.

He thought of asking SIRS, but didn't. He didn't want to remind the robot of the torture of the UFSA man named Thomas, though surely the robot remembered this very clearly. Cavalo could not detect any change in the robot's demeanor, but that didn't mean there wasn't something there. Doing such things changed a man. Cavalo didn't know what effect those dark actions would have on a robot who was slowly losing his mind.

So there were storms, both inside the prison and out.

It was on a rare break in the storms, a dull and lifeless day, that Cavalo decided to head out into the woods around the prison to hunt.

Having spent time cooped up inside the barracks was nothing new; before this winter there had been times that days would pass before he stepped foot outside.

Now, though, he was painfully aware of the passage of days. The hours. The minutes. Cavalo told himself it was nothing, that it was just his imagination, but even he knew his words were lies. The bees would chuckle at him, mocking him as they swirled in his head. He would prowl the tunnels below the prisons, moving between the buildings that still stood. Bad Dog would go with him sometimes. Sometimes SIRS would follow.

But it never helped. Cavalo was always aware of the fourth. Of Lucas. No matter how far he would get from the main barracks, he would always feel Lucas like an aching tooth. There was constant *awareness* of him. An *insistence*. He was like the bees. Always there.

They spoke, barely. Lucas asked questions Cavalo refused to answer. Personal questions. Where had Cavalo come from? What had Cavalo done with his life? When was the first time Cavalo had killed a man? Had Cavalo ever killed a woman? A child? Had he burned things before? Had he stolen? In one particularly odd moment, Lucas had asked if Cavalo believed in monsters, twisting his face terribly, making his hands like claws out in front of him.

Cavalo had hidden in the tunnels for hours after that.

But today was different. Today was not a day of questions that demanded answers. Today was not a day of piercing gazes from a psychopathic cannibal. Today the sky was gray above. The snow was deep at his feet. His eyes and nose were cold. The air hurt to breathe. The snowshoes on his feet hurt his ankles. The forest felt dead around him. Bad Dog was yipping like a puppy, surely scaring any scavenging animals away.

For Cavalo, it was wonderful, or something so closely approaching wonder that it made no difference. His head was clear, or almost so. "I'll be back," he'd told SIRS. "By tomorrow. I'll probably camp in the lookout tonight." He'd said this only after he'd made sure Lucas was not within earshot. He didn't want to take the chance of the Dead Rabbit overhearing.

"Make sure you're back by tomorrow night," SIRS had warned. "More storms are on the way. I would be positively beside myself if you froze to death. I might even shed a tear if something happened to the fleabag."

Bad Dog had huffed indignantly. *I'll haunt you as Ghost Dog.*

But now? Now the world was wide open! Bathed in white, birds singing above. Fresh tracks in the snow. A rabbit, from the looks of it. Maybe two or three.

Bad Dog bounded up from a deep drift. *Cold!* he called out. *I like the cold stuff. I bite it, and it melts on my tongue.* He barked, and the birds above took flight before settling in a tree farther away, calling their displeasure.

It was strange, this feeling. It was something Cavalo hadn't felt in years. It was a bright thing, a wounded thing, but it held strong.

Free. Cavalo felt free.

He took a deep breath and let it out as he moved through the trees.

It was only minutes later when Bad Dog stopped. His ears stood tall, and he trembled. He looked off into the trees.

Cavalo listened. He could hear the birds. Clumps of wet snow falling to the ground. The lonely call of a coyote off in the distance.

"What is it?" he asked quietly.

Wait, Bad Dog said. He raised his snout. Inhaled and exhaled in short little bursts. *There's something.* The muscles under his fur twitched. Then his tail wagged. *Smells Different,* he said happily. His tongue rolled out of his mouth and he grinned. *It's Smells Different.*

Cavalo looked around. Nothing. "You sure?"

Bad Dog snorted. *Of course I am. My nose is better than yours. No offense, MasterBossLord, but you should be embarrassed by that thing.*

Cavalo ignored him. "You can come out now," he called out. His voice sounded rough in the winter forest. "I know you're there."

At first there was nothing. Just the birds and the snow. Then thirty feet to the left, Lucas stepped out from behind a large stark elm, the trunk peeling white. He wore one of Cavalo's coats, an old faded thing that bore the curious legend *IDAHO VANDALS*. Cavalo had found it vacuum sealed with others like it in an old farmhouse after he first crossed into Idaho many years before. He wondered how Lucas had found it. He'd also found another pair of snowshoes, strapped clumsily to his boots.

Bad Dog bounded over to him, hopping in the snow, disappearing into a deep drift before jumping into view again. He reached Lucas and bumped his head into the Dead Rabbit's hand. Lucas reached down and pulled gently on one of the dog's ears, but his eyes never left Cavalo. His mouth was spread in that too-wide smile.

They stood there for a time. Apart. Waiting.

Finally Cavalo said, "What are you doing out here?"

Lucas raised his hand in front of him and wiggled two fingers in air. *Going for a walk.*

"I doubt that. What are you really doing here?"

The smile widened. He moved his fingers again, this time more slowly and curling them like claws. *I was hunting you.*

Cavalo didn't know when it had happened or why, but he had begun to understand Lucas, even with very little hand movements or miming. He had tried to give Lucas a pad of paper and a pencil, but Lucas had scowled at them. It seemed he could write his name and not much else. He'd broken the pencil and thrown it to the floor, glaring defiantly at Cavalo.

Cavalo wondered, as he'd done with Bad Dog, if he wasn't just projecting what he thought the Dead Rabbit was saying, making it up in his own head. Certainly it would make sense, especially given that Cavalo could hear a distinct voice for Lucas where one did not exist. But over the weeks, Cavalo hadn't deeply questioned this turn of events, as he seemed to be right more often than not. What worried him more was how quickly he'd been able to understand the Dead Rabbit. He didn't know what that said about himself. It now only took the barest of hand movements or facial expressions from the Dead Rabbit before his voice filled Cavalo's head. He'd asked SIRS about it hesitantly, unsure if he should even be discussing it aloud. "You know what it is, don't you?" the robot had asked him. Cavalo had shaken his head. The robot's eyes had glowed brightly when he said, "It's inevitability. That's all."

I was hunting you, the Dead Rabbit said again.

Cavalo ignored the blood rushing in his ears. "Does SIRS know you're gone?"

The smile melted, replaced with a scowl. *I don't have to tell the metal man what I'm doing.*

Bad Dog shook his head. *If he doesn't know, he's gonna be mad when you get back. Tin Man doesn't like surprises.*

"He worries," Cavalo said.

I'm hunting, Lucas retorted. *I go where I want. I do what I want.*

"Then why haven't you left?" Cavalo asked. And it was this question he wanted the answer to the most. It was this question he thought to be the most important. Day after day, he would wake and expect to find Lucas gone. Lost into the storms or the woods. Back to his people. Every day, those few moments after waking, his heart thudding, the bees would be screaming, *He's gone back! He's gone back to the Dead Rabbits, to Patrick, and he will be a monster, he will eat everyone you know. You have to run. You have to run and hide now before he brings them all back.* But then he would see the Dead Rabbit asleep in a far cot, legs and arms splayed out, or poking SIRS, trying to get the cover to the chest cavity to open while the robot snapped at him in a clipped British accent, telling him to bugger off. It would be relief Cavalo felt then, though he truly didn't understand why.

Rather, that's what he told himself.

Lucas watched him closely now, weighing Cavalo's question. Finally he shrugged and pointed into the woods. *Where are you going?*

"None of your business. Go back to the prison."

No. I'm staying here. He smiled that terrible smile again.

"Then stay here," Cavalo said. He whistled once and turned, walking into the forest.

Bad Dog immediately went to his side, bounding in the snow. *He's going to follow us, you know.*

"Yeah," Cavalo muttered. "Remember when I could have killed him?"

Yes. And I told you to. You didn't. Now we know why.

"Why?"

So he can be here with us. Things are changing.

"They don't have to." He pushed a branch out of his way.

No they don't, Bad Dog agreed. *But they will. I don't think there is—oh sweet mother of Dog. A rabbit! MasterBossLord, rabbit! Rabbit!*

"Go," Cavalo said, and Bad Dog went.

Cavalo moved on. He glanced over his shoulder, knowing Lucas was behind him, still following. He saw nothing but trees.

I'm hunting you, the bees said.

Cavalo pushed them away.

THE SKY WAS BEGINNING TO DARKEN WHEN HE CAME UPON THE lookout near the top of the mountain. It rose up among the trees, reaching their tops, fifty feet above the ground. Wooden stairs wound their way up the structure, and he could hear it creaking as it settled. He'd stumbled across this lookout shortly after finding the prison. He'd had to replace parts of the supports and the stairs that'd rotted over the decades. The first time he'd reached the top, he'd found himself uncharacteristically choked up at the sight of the mountain spread down below him, the curve of the earth in the distance so very far away. He'd turned and found the skeleton of a large man, a hole in the side of his head. He'd been shot, but there was no gun. Either someone had taken it later after he'd committed suicide, or he'd been murdered. Cavalo had buried him at the base of the lookout and marked the grave with stones.

SIRS had told him such things were built in the Before to watch for fires. Cavalo used it as a camp and a point of reference. It was almost ten miles northwest of the prison. Any farther west, and he'd be approaching the Deadlands. The trees had overgrown around the lookout and blocked his view that way. He thought it a mercy, though he wondered if he shouldn't fell some of the trees in order to watch his back. He learned his lesson on that once, when Dead Rabbits came and—

Home, Bad Dog sang. *Home, home, home.* He pushed against Cavalo's legs. *We're home, home, home.*

He didn't contradict Bad Dog. He knew what the mutt meant. "Yeah," he said. "Home. Anything up there?"

Bad Dog sniffed the cold air. *No. Nothing.*

"Okay."

Bad Dog began to climb the steps. He paused on the first landing and peered over the railing at Cavalo. *You gonna get him?*

"Who?"

You know who, Bad Dog said, rolling his eyes. *He can't stay down there. There might be monsters or bad guys at night.*

"There's no such thing as monsters," Cavalo said. He thought of *her.* And now, he also thought of *him.*

Yes there is. I can smell them. They come out at night and eat MasterBossLords and Bad Dogs. Bad Dogs are their favorites. They eat them in big bites.

"You'll be safe up there. You know this."

Yes, but I touched against Smells Different. Now he smells like Bad Dog. Monsters and bad guys will think he is Bad Dog and try to eat him. I would feel very bad for the rest of my life if he was eaten for being like Bad Dog.

"You did this on purpose, didn't you?"

The dog stared down at him. *I always do things with purpose.*

Cavalo sighed. "Get out here, Lucas."

He heard movement behind him, light and quick, and a moment later he was pushed aside as Lucas charged up to the lookout, eyes wide. He reached out and touched the wooden supports, pulling a hand back quickly as if he thought any pressure would knock it down. When it didn't fall, he reached out again, dragging his dirty fingers along the wood. He walked underneath until he stood in the middle and leaned his head back and stared straight up into the lookout, his mouth forming an O.

For a moment Cavalo could feel the Dead Rabbit's wonder. It was one of those things. One of those things from Before. Like the prison. They were rare, these days. Most times, if anything was found, it was a burned-down husk of its former self. But this still stood. Sure, Cavalo had had to make repairs. But for the most part, it existed as it had over a hundred years Before, when the world apparently was a very different place, where large cities filled with millions of people were the norm, where you could pick up a machine and call someone on the other side of the world. There were times Cavalo wondered about the other side of the world, wondered just how many people were left out of the billions and billions. The idea was too great in its magnitude for Cavalo to grasp. He'd heard once a story of a group of people arriving on the far shore in a boat, saying they'd come from what had been known as South America, but he couldn't be sure that was true. It was one of those things travelers told each other as they passed the time. He'd seen maps of what the world had been like before, and he could only remember the cold sweat that had gripped him as he thought, *So big. It's so big.*

Lucas looked at him now and pointed at the lookout. *What is this?*

"It was used Before," Cavalo said. "To watch for fires. You've never seen something like this?"

Lucas shook his head and looked back up.

"You live in the forest."

Lucas didn't look at him.

"Your people. The Dead Rabbits. You live in the woods and you've never seen this before?"

Lucas ignored him.

Let's go! Bad Dog barked. *It's getting dark, and there are monsters and bad guys!*

Cavalo followed Bad Dog up to the first landing, kicking the snow off each step as he went. He reached the first landing and looked down at Lucas, who eyed the steps warily. "You coming?"

Lucas held up a finger. *Give me a minute.*

Cavalo waited.

Lucas frowned and reached out to grab the wooden railing. He raised a foot and put it on the stair gingerly, testing the give of the wood. He seemed satisfied as he pulled himself up to the first step. Then the second. And the third. He looked up at Cavalo and grinned.

He acts like he's never been on stairs before, Bad Dog said.

"Maybe he hasn't," Cavalo murmured in reply.

Lucas stopped on each step, bouncing on his knees to test the give of the wood. It creaked and held. When he reached the landing, he stood next to Cavalo and looked down the way he'd come, head tilted as if studying.

Cavalo reached up and uncoiled a length of rope wrapped around a hook against one of the struts. He pulled on it down, the muscles in his arms straining. The rope, attached to a large pulley system, grew taut. For a moment nothing gave, but then the wheel in the pulley squeaked and moved.

The stairs leading up to the landing began to rise with a ferocious groan. Cavalo grit his teeth together as he pulled. His chest still hadn't healed completely, and he felt the muscles twinge. Lucas watched with wide eyes as the stairs rose from the ground, wooden platforms turning on hinges and collapsing until they became flat. Once it was level with the landing they stood on, Cavalo tied it off on the hook. The hook bent slightly with the pull, but it held. He'd have to replace it soon. Hopefully SIRS had something similar.

He glanced over at Lucas. The Dead Rabbit was crouched, inspecting the raised stairs. He pointed at them and looked at Cavalo. *Why'd you do that?*

"Keeps the animals away."

And the monsters and the bad guys, Bad Dog said.

"And the monsters and the bad guys," Cavalo echoed.

Lucas squinted up at Cavalo. Pointed at him accusingly. Pointed back at himself. At the stairs. *You call me a monster. All the time. And I am up here. Why aren't you keeping me out?*

That was a question Cavalo could not answer.

It was night, and Cavalo couldn't sleep.

He shut his eyes and tried to clear his head.

And opened them minutes later. There were things in the dark behind his eyes. Things he did not want to see. Faces, both new and old.

Cavalo tried to count, mundane and quiet. Tried to count the days since he'd last been in the lookout. Tried to count the number of people he'd killed, going back to the first. He had forty-seven discs, but that wasn't all of them. He tried to remember their names. If not their names, their faces. The first had been shortly after he'd gone on the road after his father died. He'd camped one night in a shallow outcrop of black rocks. A man had come in the middle of the night, probably seeing Cavalo's fire that he'd left burning when he fell asleep. He'd awoken with a knife to his throat, a hand over his mouth. The man tried to rape Cavalo. When the man was distracted, his stinking breath on Cavalo's neck, his hand between them, trying to loosen belts and buttons, Cavalo knocked him off and pulled his gun. The man had begged for his life. Cavalo let him, then shot him through the head. Cavalo learned a valuable lesson that night.

Never leave the fire burning, no matter how cold.

Cavalo gave up counting the dead. They would always be there, so it didn't matter.

Can't sleep? Bad Dog asked him. He was curled at Cavalo's side, his head resting on Cavalo's chest.

Cavalo looked down into those big eyes. He shook his head.

Me neither. Everything is all bees tonight.

"Yeah."

We crazy people?

"You're not crazy. You're not people."

I am Bad Dog.

"Yes."

Smells Different people?

"Yeah. He is people." Cavalo glanced at the lump in the opposite corner covered in blankets. It rose briefly, held, then fell. Rose. Held. Fell. The breath of sleep.

I want to be people, Bad Dog said grumpily.

"I'm glad you're not," Cavalo said, stroking his ear.

Why?

"Because I don't like people."

Oh. What about Alma?

"She's okay."

Hank?

"He's all right."

Tin Man?

"He's a robot. Not people."

He's mean, is what he is. So you do like people.

"Some, I guess."

Smells Different?

"No."

Yes.

"No."

Smells Different is people, and you like some people, and he is some people, and you did not kill him even though I told you to, and he lives with us, and he is here with us now, so you like him.

"Fuck," Cavalo muttered. He closed his eyes.

MasterBossLord?

"What."

This is my home, huh?

He said, "The prison is your home," even though he knew what

Bad Dog meant and where this was heading. It happened every time they came here.

No. I meant this is where I found my home.

"Yes. This is where."

When I was little.

"You were very little, yes."

But I'm big now, Bad Dog said, raising his head so Cavalo could see just how big he was. *I'm big Bad Dog.*

"Very big."

The biggest?

"In all the world."

Tell me the story of my home.

"You know it. You've heard it many times." But Cavalo knew he'd tell it anyway. It's how it always was.

It helps me sleep, Bad Dog said, making his eyes sad and impossibly big, as only he could do.

Cavalo chuckled and rubbed his hand over the dog's head. "Fine."

The dog settled back onto the man and waited.

"One day, not so very long ago, I went to the woods to spend some time away from things. It was in the summer, and it was hot and humid, with thunderstorms almost every night that never seemed to bring any rain.

"The prison was feeling claustrophobic, and SIRS was finishing digging out the last tunnel to the east barrack. I didn't want to go to Cottonwood, so I decided on the lookout.

"I'd been there only a few times before, enough to assess what repairs were needed and to make sure they were done before the thing collapsed. But for some reason, I couldn't get it out of my head."

You knew, Bad Dog said, a sleepy smile on his face. *Somehow, you knew.*

"Maybe. Maybe I did. I got there on that day, just as it was starting to turn into night, and I remember touching the railing on the stairs and thinking, *I should be here. This is where I need to be.* It was the first time I'd felt like that since... well. In a long time.

"I fell asleep almost immediately. I don't know why I was so tired. Maybe it was the heat. Or the hike up to the lookout. Or maybe it was because I was meant to fall asleep. I remember watching the stars come out like they are now, and I remember thinking how small I really was, how I was really just the tiniest speck of dust in a tornado, and the next thing I knew, I was opening my eyes in the full-on dark."

Why did you wake up? Bad Dog asked, as if he hadn't heard the story at least a dozen times before.

"I didn't know at first. I thought I was still dreaming, though I couldn't remember what I'd been dreaming about. But then I heard voices from down below."

Weren't you scared?

"No, because I didn't know what it was, or who it could be. I even thought I could still be trapped in my dream somehow, that none of it was real.

"The voices got louder until I was sure they'd found the lookout. I kept the lantern off and the old flashlight off. There was a moon, and it was full, and it was big and beautiful, and it glowed so bright that it almost seemed like daylight. I looked over the railing and saw shadows stretched out around the lookout. Shadows of people."

Bad Dog whined quietly and shivered. *Bad guys?*

"I didn't know at first. I thought they could be from a caravan. Or maybe they were lost. Maybe they were on their way to Cottonwood. Or Grangeville. Or maybe they just lived in the woods and they weren't lost at all.

"Or maybe," Cavalo said, lowering his voice, "they were *Dead Rabbits.*"

Bad guys! the dog said with a low bark.

"It was good I remembered to pull up the steps before I'd come up, otherwise they might have climbed the steps up to where I was. I would have been cornered. As it was, they couldn't quite reach. I could see them moving around below, and even caught the sight of an arm and a leg, but I couldn't make them out in full."

What happened then?

"Then they moved out into the open."

And?

"They were Dead Rabbits," Cavalo said quietly. "Bad guys. Monsters. They had on armbands with little spikes on them, neck-laces that looked to be made of teeth. One had no hair, the other had a thick black mohawk down the center of his head. They had knives clasped to their sides. And the bald man had a sack over his shoulder.

"I thought they'd seen me, and I quietly took the rifle out and pressed it against my chest, and I wondered if I would even stop them if they found me. If I would do anything to fight back."

You would. I know you would.

Cavalo scratched behind Bad Dog's ears, and the dog sighed in happiness. Before he opened his mouth to speak again, he saw the glitter of a second pair of eyes watching him from across the platform.

He hesitated then, unsure if he wanted the Dead Rabbit to hear this most personal of stories.

But this wasn't about the Dead Rabbit watching him. This was about Bad Dog. This was about his friend.

"I know," he said finally. He looked back down at Bad Dog. "Now. But then? I don't know. I don't know what I would have done. It doesn't matter now, though. The decision was made for me."

How?

"The Dead Rabbits looked to be leaving. They couldn't reach the stairs and seemed to have given up. They pointed at a few clusters of trees around the lookout. I think they were trying to remember what the area looked like so they could come back. But as they turned to leave, I heard something. Something that changed everything."

What?

Two sets of eyes watched him.

"A little cry. It was high-pitched and sad, and I thought maybe I'd misheard it. Or maybe it was a bird. But then it came again from below and I knew that whatever had made that sound was in the sack. I thought...."

He'd thought it'd been a child. A cold grip had sealed around his heart as he sat crouched in that forgotten lookout, remembering the first time he'd heard Jamie cry, right when he was born. A high-pitched sound. A mournful sound. A sound so hard on the ears that it caused the heart to break. Within Cavalo then, something had flared to life, something that had been dead and buried for a very long time. Yes, he might have let himself die. Yes, he was more shell than man, but that moment, that burning moment however brief it had been, he felt to be something more, something bigger, something *alive*.

So what if a rubber band broke and he thought it could be Jamie in that sack? So what if he thought there was a chance that his son had not died after all and that he'd been searching for Cavalo all this time, only to fall into the hands of the Dead Rabbits? So what if the reason he descended from this lookout tower, from his tower of madness, was to rescue his son? Did it matter?

It did not.

MasterBossLord? Bad Dog asked, sounding worried.

Lucas did not move. He didn't blink.

"I thought something was wrong," Cavalo said, continuing the story as he always had. He shielded the insanity as best he could. He didn't know how well it worked. "Something *felt* wrong. Whatever they had shouldn't have made that noise. Not if it was okay.

"I didn't think when I jumped down from the landing. I didn't think to lower the stairs. All I could think about was getting down as fast as I could, getting down to them before they left and disappeared into the Deadlands."

But you caught them.

"Well. Not really. They heard me jump down and turned around. I landed awkwardly, and the rifle fell out of my hands, but I pulled myself up quickly and stood across from them. They were only feet away."

Monsters, Bad Dog whispered. *Bad guys.*

"'Who are you?' the bald one asked me.

"'He's all alone out here,' the other one said with a sneer. He was missing two of his front teeth, and he spit when he talked. 'No one can save him!'"

But you had the boomstick!

"Yes, I did. The big boomstick. I picked it back up and pointed it at them. And do you know what I said?"

I am Cavalo!

"'I am Cavalo! These are my woods, and you are trespassing! Unhand what it is you carry, and leave now with your lives! If you do not, I will take from you everything you hold dear!'

"'You are just one man,' the bald-headed man said. 'We are two. There is nothing you can do, and you will be the one who suffers.'

"'We will cut you to pieces,' the other one said. 'You will never see the light of day again!'

"The bag wiggled again, and I heard another little cry.

"'I think that what you have does not belong to you,' I said to them. 'This is your last chance, Dead Rabbits. You are monsters. You are bad guys. Give the sack to me. No more warnings.'

"They looked at each other and laughed. 'Ha, ha, ha!' they chortled. 'This is our food. We'll never give this up!'

"So what did I do?"

Boomstick. His tail thumped on the floor as his eyes dropped slightly.

"Boomstick," Cavalo agreed. "I fired right between them. The dirt sprayed up onto their legs, and they saw how serious I was. 'He's crazy!' said the bald man. He looked very scared and was starting to blubber.

"'He's out of his mind!' said the mohawk man. His knees were shaking.

"The bald man carefully set the sack on the ground, backing away as he cried. Snot ran down his nose into his mouth. The other man looked like he was ready to run at any moment.

"'You've done what I've asked,' I told them. 'Now leave! And if I ever see you around here again, you will know true fear and the breaths you take will be your last.'"

And did they leave? The bad guys?

"They did. They ran as fast as their legs could carry them. They screamed and cried as they fled, saying they would never come back to the lookout, never come back to these woods, and that all other monsters and bad guys would stay away because of the man with the gun.

"But then I heard another noise. Coming from the sack that lay on the ground."

Were you scared?

To death. I thought my dead son was in that bag. "No. I wasn't. I wasn't scared because I knew I'd done the right thing. I knew that I had saved a life, no matter what was in the sack.

"So very carefully, I walked over to the bag. There was this tiny lump outlined by the burlap. It moved a little bit. It cried out again. A small sound."

Bad Dog's tail thumped again.

Lucas continued to watch.

"I hesitated, only for a moment," Cavalo said quietly. "Then I reached down and untied the rope around the sack and carefully opened it. And do you know what I found?"

You found a Bad Dog!

"Yes. Inside, there was this little thing. All black and gray and hairy. A little white stripe between his eyes going up to his ears. Paws bigger than his head. And you know what happened then?"

I saw you, Bad Dog said sleepily. *I saw you. I don't remember anything that happened before because I was so little, but I remember seeing you. That's the first thing I remember.*

"Yes. You saw me. You looked up at me with your pretty eyes, and you saw me. You watched me for the longest time, trying to figure out if I was a good guy or not."

I knew you were. You smelled different.

"Eventually you barked at me, this high-pitched little bark, and you tried to jump out of the bag. But it was too big and your legs were too little, and you couldn't quite make it."

So you helped me.

"I did. I reached in, and you sniffed my hand. Then you pressed your head against it, and I picked you up. I only needed one hand to do it back then, that's how small you were. And as I lifted you up out of the sack, I could feel your heart beating against my hand. It was fast. And strong. You were shaking. I didn't know if you were cold or scared."

I was just cold, Bad Dog said.

Cavalo waited, as he knew he should.

And scared, Bad Dog admitted.

"I pulled you against my chest and wrapped you in my shirt, and we sat there for a while. In the dark. Eventually you fell asleep, but not before you gnawed on my thumb with your little puppy teeth and I called you a bad dog. You've been with me ever since, and you always will be."

I remember, Bad Dog whispered and then closed his eyes. *This is my home. You're my home.*

"I know."

The dog huffed. Sighed. And then snored.

Cavalo waited until he was sure the dog was asleep. He stroked an ear and the white stripe between the eyes.

He looked over at Lucas. The Dead Rabbit's expression was unreadable.

It's Wormwood, the bees said. *It's all the star Wormwood. Repent! Repent!* They laughed.

Cavalo held the gaze until he followed his dog into sleep.

He was awoken sometime later, a great weight on his chest and a sharp pressure at his neck. He opened his eyes and stared into glittering blackness.

Lucas straddled Cavalo's chest, holding a knife against his throat.

Cavalo darted his eyes to the right. Bad Dog slept, having curled away from him during the night.

He looked back up at Lucas.

The Dead Rabbit had a dark look on his face, teeth bared, eyes wide with rage. The hand holding the knife did not shake as it pricked his skin. Cavalo felt a trickle of blood roll down his neck and drip to the floor near his ear.

"Lucas," Cavalo said quietly. He didn't want Bad Dog to wake because then someone in this lookout would die. Cavalo didn't know who. "Is it the bees?"

Lucas nodded. Pursed his lips and blew. *Yes. The bees. They're loud.* He pressed the knife harder. *They want me to kill you. To see your blood.*

"We all have bees. You said it yourself. You have to push them back."

Yes. But sometimes the bees are stronger.

He leaned forward until their noses almost touched, eyes locked.

To Cavalo, it was like looking into the sky on a clear winter night. Cold and impossibly vast.

He could not look away.

I can kill you, Lucas said. *The bees want me to kill you. I am a Dead Rabbit. I am a clever monster. Psycho fucking bulldog. I can kill you so easily.*

"I know."

Lucas sat back up but kept the knife at Cavalo's throat. He nodded his head toward Bad Dog. His eyes narrowed accusingly. *You lied to him. In your story. That's not what happened.*

"No. It's not."

Why?

"Why did I lie?"

Yes.

"Because the truth makes me as bad as you."

Speak the truth. Now.

"I don't owe you anything."

Tell it!

"Why? Why do you care?"

The Dead Rabbit's mouth opened in a silent snarl. The knife cut deeper. *Now!*

"They came," Cavalo said. "They stood below the lookout. I went down. I fell, and the rifle got knocked from my hand. I was so sure they had my son in the sack, so sure that he was still alive and that somehow, they'd found him and taken him from me. I was going to hurt them. I was going to make them pay.

"I stood, grabbed the gun. They turned and looked at me. They had big knives on their sides, but they never reached for them. They asked me who I was. I told them to give me back my son. They asked me where I'd come from. I told them they had to the count of five. They laughed. Out of everything I can remember the most, I think it's that they laughed. They weren't scared of me, not like I was of them, even though I didn't show it.

"I didn't make it to five. Between three and four, I squeezed the trigger twice. Head shots, both. They were so quick that the Dead Rabbits fell at the same time. They were so quick that I didn't realize what I'd done until it was already over."

Cavalo closed his eyes.

"They didn't fall on the bag, and I ran toward them, calling for Jamie. Jamie. Jamie. Answer me, Jamie. Tell me you're okay. Tell me you're all right. But he wasn't there. I opened the bag and inside was this dog, this little fucking dog who was *not* my son, who was *not* Jamie, and I picked him up and held him against my chest, and I was going to smother it. I was going to smother that little fucking dog who was not my son, who had made me believe it *was* my son, who had made me kill two men for no reason other than I was losing my own mind and was haunted by ghosts that do not exist.

"But then he bit my finger. With his little puppy teeth. Not hard. Not mean. Not to hurt. But to let me know he was *there* and that he knew *I* was there. And he was just a little guy. A little guy with big paws, and he bit my finger and pulled on it because we were both *there*.

"So I didn't kill him, even though it might have been a mercy. I've survived this long by some grace of God or Devil. But it won't last long. Soon, I will die, either by my own hand or someone else's, and he will go too, either by broken heart or bullet. Or teeth. I should have ended his life then so he won't have to die by the hands of your people. If they got him, they would eat him. They would eat his flesh from his body and his eyes from his sockets, and it won't be fair."

Cavalo opened his eyes. "So yes. I lie to him. I lie to him because I know what he wants to hear. I lie to him because I know what *I* want to hear. But I know the truth. There were three monsters standing underneath the lookout tower that night. One just happened to be worse than the other two.

"I buried them. While the puppy slept in my coat at the top of the lookout tower, I dragged the two Dead Rabbits away and buried them under a tree. On them, they carried the skins of other dogs. A big one and three little ones. Probably his mother and siblings. There was quartered meat in another bag. Probably his mother and siblings. I don't know why they kept him alive. But they did. So I buried them. Not out of respect. So he wouldn't see them."

Cavalo felt hoarse. He doubted he'd ever spoken in his life as much as he'd spoken this night. He closed his eyes again and waited for Lucas to make his decision.

The knife at his throat.

The weight of Lucas above him.

And then, the scrape of lips against his.

Cavalo opened his eyes.

Lucas, only inches away.

Lucas kissed him again. It was chaste. Dry. Catastrophic.

The bees screamed.

Cavalo reached up and grabbed the Dead Rabbit's head. Held it. Forced them both not to move. Lucas breathed out, and Cavalo breathed him in. Their noses bumped. Their lips brushed together again. By accident or design, Cavalo did not know.

They stayed that way for a time. Eventually Lucas pulled the knife from his throat. He fell to Cavalo's side, settling between man and dog. He rested his head on Cavalo's shoulder. The hand holding the knife lay on Cavalo's stomach, the blade pressing against his navel.

They watched each other. Cavalo could see the anger and the rage still burning in Lucas's eyes, but he no longer thought it was directed solely at him.

But it mattered not, at least not right then. The snow globe had been shaken, and Cavalo was lost in a swirl of bees.

It only took minutes for the Dead Rabbit's eyes to close, and he slept.

For Cavalo, it took longer.

father, may i?

MUCH LATER, after everything was done and the smoke had cleared and people started to bury their dead, Cavalo would look back and realize with grim certainty that the beginning of the end of his life in self-imposed exile began with that kiss. It would not be the primary cause; no, it would be another who would see to that, and in a quite spectacular fashion. But it was the kiss that Cavalo would always believe was the start. For the rest of his life, he would wonder, in the dark of night, if that kiss had not occurred, would all that followed have been different?

Of course, it wouldn't matter by that point. What was done could not be undone, and for all the lives lost, for all the destruction that followed, hindsight would do nothing but haunt Cavalo. A man may try and escape his past, but it is his past that shapes who he has become. Cavalo would be a man defined by his past. For as long as he'd run from it, it'd only been steps behind.

So it was that kiss. That devastating, unexpected kiss.

Cavalo didn't know then where it would lead. If he did, it's lost in a haze of bees if he would have done anything to stop it. But he didn't know. He couldn't know. In this impossible time, this impossible future where the world had been all but destroyed, seeing the future was nothing more than fantasy. So no, he didn't know where it would all lead.

But he would.

He woke that morning in the lookout, the knife pressed firmly against his stomach, the Dead Rabbit's head resting in the crook his neck. Every breath Lucas expelled felt like fire across Cavalo's skin.

What is this? he thought through the bees. *What is this?*

He did not know.

The blade pressed into his stomach. He felt the tip dimple his skin. He looked down and saw Lucas staring back at him, a scowl on his face. *What did you do to me?*

"Nothing," Cavalo said, his voice rough with sleep. "You came at me."

I could kill you right now. If I wanted to.

"You could."

The knife pressed harder. *You would bleed out here.*

"I know."

He pursed his lips and buzzed. *The bees are loud today.*

"Mine too." And they were. Disjointed, they flew into each other, bouncing. Colliding. It hurt his head and made his skin crawl.

The scowl eased into a frown. The pressure of the knife lessened.

From the other side of him came a loud yawn. *I'm hungry*, Bad Dog said. He rose to his feet and stretched. The dog looked down at Cavalo and Lucas and tilted his head. His nose flared once. Twice. *You smell like Smells Different*, he told Cavalo. *That's new.*

Knife be damned, Cavalo pushed Lucas away. The Dead Rabbit did not protest. Instead he smiled that terrible smile.

"It's time to go home," Cavalo said. He began to pack.

It was Bad Dog who noticed it first.

They were half a mile from the prison when he stopped. His

back arched, his tail twitched. His ears perked up and he stared straight ahead, his rigid stance awkward.

But Cavalo knew his friend. They worked together well. He stopped and signaled for Lucas to do the same. The Dead Rabbit didn't protest.

Cavalo listened but heard only the sounds of a snow-covered forest. He recognized the trees, though they were hidden.

"What is it?" he asked the dog quietly.

Don't know. Smells. Haven't smelled them before. Maybe....

Cavalo waited.

Maybe it's nothing.

"You sure?"

The dog relaxed, but only just. *Think so.*

A bird called out.

A clump of snow fell from the tree.

The sky overhead was still blue, but clouds were coming from the west, over the Deadlands. They were fat and gray. Angry. The storms were coming back, just as SIRS had said.

They needed to hurry.

Something prickled in Cavalo's head. He couldn't quite grasp it. Couldn't place it. Unease, maybe. It felt... off.

"Let's go," Cavalo said. "Storm's coming."

And so they went. No words were spoken in this last half hour. Cavalo listened and watched Bad Dog. Lucas stared off into the trees. Bad Dog never lost the rigidness of his spine and shoulders. He was not distracted by little animals that scurried away from the ferocious hunters. His eyes darted back and forth.

Cavalo half expected the prison to be under attack when he arrived. To rise over that final hill and to see his home nothing more than a smoldering ruin, the grounds pitted and scarred from explosions.

But it still stood, as it had for the last hundred years. The shadows were growing longer as the clouds approached.

They reached the front gate, and Cavalo felt like he was being watched.

Lucas turned and followed his gaze. *You too?*

"You feel that?"

Lucas nodded. *Something. Don't know what.*

"Yeah," Cavalo muttered.

MasterBossLord!

Cavalo looked back over his shoulder. "What?"

The dog had his nose to the snow. *Here. Here. Here. Look. Down. Here. Here.*

Cavalo saw them, then, in the snow. Leading up to the gate. There'd been no new snowfall overnight, so they hadn't been covered. He didn't know how long they'd been there. And worse of all, they didn't come up what was left of the main road that led to the prison. No, they came out of the forest.

From the west.

A set of footprints. Out of the trees. Up to the gate. Through the gate, and into the prison.

Cavalo frowned. He could hear the hum of the electricity from the fence. Whoever this was had somehow worked around it, though Cavalo didn't know how. The footprints stopped at the gated entrance in front of the speaker box and then continued into the grounds.

As if SIRS let them in, the bees whispered.

"Hank?" he asked Bad Dog. "Alma?"

No. Not BigHank. Not AlmaLady. No one from the big town. Different. This is different. Then, he did something Cavalo had never heard him do. He tilted his head back and howled. Cavalo felt his skin break out in gooseflesh. It carried across the snow and bounced off the buildings. It was a mournful sound, a lonely sound.

"Bad Dog," he said.

Tin Man, the dog panted. *Tin Man.* He started for the gate.

Cavalo moved without even thinking, grabbing the dog by the scruff of his neck, pulling him back before he could touch the fence.

The dog whined in his grip, and Cavalo pulled him close, wrapping his arms around the dog's chest. "You'll get hurt," he said harshly into the dog's ear. "Stop! Listen to me!"

Tin Man! Tin Man.

"Bad Dog! Down!"

The dog struggled and did not listen. He was heavy. Cavalo was losing his grip.

Tin Man. Tin Man, the dog said over and over.

Lucas appeared before them, putting himself between the dog and the fence. He reached down and grabbed Bad Dog's snout, pulling the dog's face up to his own. They were mere inches away, and Cavalo was about to tell Lucas to get back before Bad Dog snapped at him, when Bad Dog stilled. They stared at each other for a time, both breathing in and out. In and out.

Then Lucas arched an eyebrow and shook the dog's muzzle gently. *What is it?* Lucas asked.

There's someone in there, Bad Dog said. *Someone came here and went inside.*

Cavalo relayed this when Lucas glanced at him.

"Who?" he asked Bad Dog.

The dog shuddered slightly. *He smells of burnt trees and death. He came from the dark across the line, and he's in there with Tin Man. My friend.*

Lucas turned and looked at the barracks. Cavalo could see the color drain from his face.

"What is it?" Cavalo asked.

He held up a hand to Cavalo, palm out. *Stay here. I'll go.*

"Like hell."

The Dead Rabbit's eyes narrowed. *I am faster than you. I am stronger than you. My bees are louder.* He pulled his knife from his boot.

"This is *my* home," Cavalo said.

Stay here. He turned and started to walk toward the fence.

"You don't know how to get in."

He stopped.

"The fence is electrified. All the way around."

The Dead Rabbit pointed at the speaker box without turning.

"You can't speak."

His hands curled into fists.

"You need me."

Those words were out before Cavalo could stop them. They hung in the air between them, and Cavalo had time to remember the scrape of dry lips against his own.

Lucas bowed his head.

Cavalo stood. Bad Dog stayed at his side.

He walked over to the speaker box. Looked up at the hidden camera. Pressed the button.

The response was immediate. "Hello, Cavalo." That queer flat voice had returned.

"SIRS?"

"Yes. This is the Sentient Integrated Response System."

"Are you all right?"

"I am as I was. And as I should be."

"SIRS."

"Yes, Cavalo."

"Let us in."

"Father, may I?"

Another voice in the background, murmuring low. Indistinguishable.

"Cavalo," SIRS said. "You may enter." The hum of electricity died. From farther down the fence line, an alarm blared briefly and an orange light began to spin, squeaking as it turned.

"SIRS?"

"Yes?"

"Who is here?"

"It's... he. I...." The box crackled. "I... can't."

The voice spoke again from near the robot.

"Mandate seven," SIRS said. "Mandate seven. In Zephaniah, it reads 'I have wiped out many nations, devastating their fortress walls and towers. Their cities are now deserted; their streets are in silent ruin. There are no survivors to tell what even happened.'" He fell silent.

"SIRS."

No response.

"*SIRS*."

Nothing.

"Shit," Cavalo muttered. He looked past the box through the fence toward the barracks. Nothing moved. "I thought prisons were supposed to keep people *out*." And it had. Up until Lucas.

Bad Dog whined, pushing his head against the fence.

Lucas pushed past Cavalo. Cavalo reached out and grabbed his arm, meaning to stop him, to pull him back.

Cavalo felt the Dead Rabbit tense and was ready when the Dead Rabbit turned and swung at him. Cavalo ducked the fist. The momentum and snow spun Lucas around. Cavalo shot up and wrapped his arms around Lucas, pulling his back to Cavalo's front. Immediately, Cavalo felt the knife pressed back against his side. Lucas's hair tickled Cavalo's nose. It smelled of wood smoke, dusky and wild.

"You stop," Cavalo said, his forehead pressed to the back of the Dead Rabbit's head. "You hear me?"

The knife pressed into him harder.

"We go together."

The Dead Rabbit shook his head. Struggled against Cavalo's grip.

"Yes."

Lucas deflated. He bowed his head.

Cavalo stepped away. He could still smell the Dead Rabbit.

"We have to be smart about this," he said, trying to shake the unwanted heat away.

Lucas glanced back at him. *Too late for that.*

"Why?"

He pointed up at the camera. *They already know we're here.*

"They can't hear us. The sound has been corrupted since long before I got here."

We've been gone. For all you know, it's been repaired.

"No."

Don't be stupid. We go in. Like we normally do. I'll go first.

"We don't normally *anything*."

I'm going.

"No."

No, no, no, Bad Dog said. *That's all you say. I will go. Bad Dog will save the tin man.*

"Lunatics," Cavalo muttered. "I'm surrounded by lunatics."

Bad Dog and Lucas grinned at him.

"I lead," Cavalo said. "You two follow. We clear?"

Shark-like smiles.

He turned toward the barracks. He knew, even then, that it was all fucked up. His mind ran in a million different directions, each worse than the last. The bees howled at him, asking how he could be so *stupid*, how he could even *think* about walking into what was obviously a trap. He kept telling himself that there was only one set of tracks, but he knew the old military trick of walking in a single-file line in the footsteps of the person leading to create the illusion of minimal numbers. For all Cavalo knew, the barracks were full of people.

That didn't explain SIRS, though. Even if his insanity had taken over, it didn't explain why he'd be doing what they asked. Unless it was meant to sound that way. Unless the robot had a plan.

Father, may I?

The unease would not leave Cavalo.

He unlatched and pushed open the fence. It scraped against the snow and ice.

He walked through. Lucas and Bad Dog followed.

He closed the gate behind them. As soon as it latched, there was another blare of the alarm. Once. Twice. Three times. There was a snap of electricity, and the fences began to hum.

He moved toward the barracks.

The bees laughed.

Lucas darted his head left and right.

Bad Dog kept his nose low to the snow. *The other side,* he muttered. *The other side of the woods. It's from the other side of the woods.*

Cavalo thought briefly of entering the tunnels underneath the prison, but dismissed it. It wouldn't matter now. They were probably sighted before they had reached the front of the gate.

It's the UFSA, he thought. *We've killed two of their groups.*

And just think! the bees said. *You'll get everyone else killed as well! You are nothing but death, our dear Cavalo. It follows you wherever it goes.*

Yes. I am death.

That weighed upon him, heavier than it should have. He had the man made of metal inside. His four-legged companion at his side. That was all he should have concerned himself with. That was all there should have been. But in his head, as the worst of all images played out, he saw the Dead Rabbit's body splayed out on the ground, soaked in blood, a look of hysterical terror distorting his features.

When? he asked the bees. *When did this happen? When did this matter?*

When you let him in, the bees whispered. *That clever monster. That clever cannibal. He is like a vampire. You invited him in, and now he can never leave.*

Unless there is death, Cavalo thought.

They reached the barracks door. Cavalo blocked the way as Lucas reached for it. "No," he said.

Move.

"Listen to me. Now."

Lucas scowled.

"We don't know who is in there. But we know they want you. To get to Patrick."

Lucas snarled at the name.

"You need to stay here and wait."

You are out of your fucking mind, Lucas said.

Like that is going to happen, Bad Dog said. He tried to push past Cavalo, but Cavalo stopped him. He looked like he gave very serious consideration to biting the man on the leg.

He ignored them both. "If I don't come back out or if something goes wrong, you need to run. I want you to wait outside the gates. Remain hidden. Watch the door. If someone comes out other than me that you don't recognize, you run."

I don't run!

Together, Bad Dog insisted. *We stay together.*

"Not this time," Cavalo said. He looked down at the dog and grabbed him by the snout. He raised it until their eyes met. "You listening to me?"

Bad Dog tried to pull away, but Cavalo wouldn't let him.

"Listen. I know. Trust me, I know. But you need to be brave."

I'm always brave!

"You are. But if something goes sideways in there, it's going to be up to you. Do you understand? You take Lucas, and you run. Do not look back. Do not go after me. Get to BigHank and AlmaLady. Are we clear?"

Worst idea ever. *You are the dumbest MasterBossLord!*

Cavalo chuckled dryly. "Probably."

He let go of the dog. Bad Dog licked his hand once and moved to stand next to Lucas. He looked up at him and growled lightly. *You listen to Bad Dog, Smells Different. Bad Dog is the boss now.*

"He's the boss now," Cavalo echoed softly. He glanced at Lucas. "You mind him," he said. "Get to Hank. Get to Alma. I'm sealing the door behind me. And don't think about trying to come through the tunnels. They'll be sealed too."

Lucas looked murderous but said nothing.

He looked between the two of them. "Hank," he said again. "Alma."

You better come back, Bad Dog muttered. *I can't live in Cotton-*

wood and be told how pretty I am all day. The bees in my head will drive me to kill.

He nodded. He turned and was about to open the door when a knife was pressed into his hand. He looked back at Lucas, who pointed between it and the rifle strapped to Cavalo's back. *Just in case*, the Dead Rabbit said.

Cavalo took the knife.

It began to snow.

Lucas and Bad Dog turned back toward the gate. They were outside the prison when Cavalo opened the door and closed it behind him without looking back.

Latched it. The metal screeching together was loud against the cement walls.

The man named Cavalo took a breath. Exhaled. Put the knife in his boot. Unstrapped the rifle. Took another breath. Thought of Jamie. Her. Alma. Hank. Deke. Aubrey. His father, dead in a ditch. The robot SIRS. Bad Dog. His only two friends in the world. His only family.

And Lucas.

He exhaled.

And pushed open the secondary door.

The barracks were as he'd left them the day before. Nothing had been moved. Nothing looked to have been touched. The room was not filled with people. There were no men with guns. No UFSA. No Dead Rabbits. No—

SIRS stood next to one of the panels on the side wall. It glowed a bright white. His hand was extended, and from his palm shot up the screen that reflected what the cameras showed. The video appeared damaged, as it jumped wildly, the contents of the screen illegible. It crackled wildly, the noise electronic and jumbled.

The cameras aren't working, Cavalo thought. *They didn't see us.*

Through the screen, Cavalo saw SIRS. His eyes burned a color Cavalo had never seen them before. Gone was the orange, the comforting color, that flash of intelligence. Now it was different. Bright. Harsh. Bloodred.

The color of insanity, the bees said.

He was not alone.

A man stood next to him, his back partially to Cavalo. This stranger watched the snowy screen, his hands joined behind his back. His hair was black but fading at the top of his head in a small circular pattern. Flecks of gray shot through the rest.

He stood as tall as Cavalo, but thicker. Not fat, but it looked as if it could go that way very easily. He wore trousers made from deer hide, stitched with precision, and a tunic that looked to be coarse.

What struck Cavalo the most, though, about this man, this stranger in his home, was not his appearance, but how at *ease* he seemed. It was as if he knew Cavalo stood behind him, pointing a gun at his back, but knew nothing could happen to him. There was no tension in his shoulders. No anger. Nothing indicated he was armed. Or that he would attack.

And this concerned Cavalo. A man not worried about the possibility of a bullet was a dangerous man.

"It's funny, really," the man said without turning. His voice was soft and elegant. "How is it that I've been in the west for the years that I have and not known this place existed? It's remarkable. My eyes have not been as open as I've thought. It makes one wonder just what else is out there buried in the wilds of the forest, just waiting to be found."

"Who are you?" Cavalo asked, never taking his eyes or the gun off the man.

"Yes," he said, still watching the screen. "I suppose we will get to that. But the greater question, I should think, is who are you?"

"Who am I?" Cavalo echoed. Unreality washed over him.

The man laughed. "Such a deep question you ask yourself. I once found myself asking the same question. Who am I? Why am I here? What is my purpose?" He shook his head as he sighed. "I found my answer. It doesn't seem as if you've found yours." He turned his head slightly to look around the barrack. "Unless living like this is your calling. The surveillance equipment doesn't even work! You have cameras but no video. But then, who am I to judge? I live with far less."

"You have three seconds to explain," Cavalo said. "If I get to three and you haven't told me who you are, you get a bullet in the head."

"Well now. *This* certainly is a surprise. Have you always been this cold?"

"One."

"Maybe it goes back to some deep-seated daddy issues. Did your father love you enough? Or maybe he loved you *too* much."

"Two."

"Such theatrics! Well, I guess that's to be expected for a man living in the middle of nowhere with a robot and a dog. Just how crazy are you?"

"Three." Cavalo put pressure on the trigger.

"You fire that gun," the man said affably, "and everyone you know in the enclave of Cottonwood will have their flesh peeled from their bones while they are still alive. They will know every ounce of pain I can give. And you must believe me when I say that I can give quite a lot."

Cavalo's vision tunneled. The room grayed out, then came back. His finger itched to pull the trigger still. The bees told him the man was bluffing, that he did nothing more than talk and he was a *liar* and Cavalo just needed to kill him. *Kill him!*

It's your fault, they said. *You made ties with these people. This is how they can threaten you. These people. They all threaten to take from you because you associate with others. It is your weakness. Kill him, now!*

"You wouldn't," he said, his voice shaking.

The man turned to face him. He looked older than Cavalo, at least by a decade. His face was blandly handsome and lined heavily around the eyes and mouth. But then he smiled, and his face transformed into something more. It was a bright smile, and it caught

Cavalo off-guard. If he was bland before, now he seemed remarkable. His blue eyes lit up. His teeth showed through, even and white. He looked to be a happy man. A man in control.

"I would," he said cheerfully. "You may not know me, not yet, but you can trust in the fact that I am a man of my word."

"SIRS," Cavalo said.

The robot didn't respond.

"SIRS."

Nothing.

"How rude!" the man said. "Robot, you're being asked a question."

"Father, may I?" SIRS asked. His voice had never sounded more robotic.

"You may," the man said.

"Yes, Cavalo. How may I help you?"

"End this."

The stranger laughed.

"End what, Cavalo?" SIRS asked.

"Him. This. Now. Put him in the cell."

There was a click deep inside the robot. A grinding of gears. A beep. "I'm afraid I can't do that, Cavalo."

"Why?"

"Because my central processor has been overridden. My directive has changed."

"To what?"

"Complacency."

"What did you do?" Cavalo asked the stranger.

"Leveled the playing field," he said. "Don't you worry. He'll return to normal after you and I have had a chance to talk. Put the gun down, Cavalo."

"No."

The smile faded slightly. "I can be a very reasonable man. The only thing I ask in return is that you do what I say, when I say it. That is all."

"Go fuck yourself." He aimed the gun again.

The smile returned in full force. "Robot," the man said. "Please help our friend here give up his rifle. Be quick about it."

"Yes, Father."

It was over before Cavalo was aware it had happened. He'd never seen SIRS move as fast as he did then. One moment the robot was standing next to the stranger, his hand still outstretched, the screen floating above it. The next, the rifle was jerked from Cavalo's hand, his arm wrenched behind him, wrist gripped in metal hands. The rifle went across the room with a clatter.

"My, my, my," the man said. "That certainly went better than I thought. He's quick, for a relic of times past."

"SIRS," Cavalo said as he struggled. It was no use; the grip was so tight Cavalo thought his arm would rip from the socket before he'd break free.

"Yes, Cavalo."

"Let me go. You know me."

"Father, may I?"

"You may not," the man said. "Hold him until I say so. In fact, you are not to speak again until I give you reason. Do you understand?"

"Yes, Father."

"Repeat it."

"I am not to speak until given reason."

The stranger frowned. "Given reason by whom?"

There was hesitation, and Cavalo hear a subtle beep. "You, Father."

"Thank you." He looked at Cavalo. "Now, it's going to be very simple. You have something of mine. You return it, I leave, and you never see me again. You don't, I burn this place and Cottonwood to the ground."

"I told your men before," Cavalo said. "That I won't be threatened. What makes you think I'll listen to you?"

The man's eyes widened. "My men?"

"Wilkinson. Thomas. The ones you sent here. From the UFSA."

He rocked his head back and laughed. "They were *here*? Already? Oh, this is positively *magnificent*. Where are they now? Did you kill them?"

"Yes," Cavalo snarled at him. "Every single one of them."

"Oh, I surely underestimated *you*," the man said, stepping toward Cavalo. He stopped well out of arm's reach. "Tell me, what did they say? Before you killed them?"

Careful, the bees said. *Careful*.

"Nothing. They came to my home. They tried to take what was mine. I killed them. And that was it."

"Truly?"

"Yes."

"Robot."

"Yes, Father?"

"It appears our friend here is lying to me." The man smiled again. "Break his right index finger."

The pain was swift and immediate as the robot used his other hand to snap Cavalo's finger. Glassy pain rolled over Cavalo as he grunted, biting his lip to keep from crying out. Sweat beaded on his brow, greasy and hot. He hadn't been inside more than ten minutes. He hoped that it was enough time that Bad Dog convinced Lucas to leave. In the haze, he forgot that Lucas couldn't understand the dog like he could. Or like he thought he could. It mattered not.

"Now," the man said, "we can try this again. The men you killed. What were they looking for?"

"Patrick," Cavalo said. "They were looking for Patrick." The name caused a reaction out of most people so far; he hoped in throwing it out, it would happen again.

The man stared at him hard. "Is that right?"

"Yes."

"Did they say why?"

"No."

"But you killed them."

"Yes."

"All of them."

"Yes."

"Because they tried to take what was yours."

"Yes."

The bees laughed.

"It's fascinating, really."

"What?"

"That they've already decided to go west, young man!" the stranger exclaimed, clapping his hands. "That they've got even the slightest inclination to spread *this* far out, knowing the stories. Those horrible stories of monsters and evil that have infected the west and made it the Deadlands. They must be getting desperate. I really thought there'd be more time. Robot."

"Yes, Father?"

"Are you in touch with St. Louis?"

"No."

The man cocked his head quizzically. "How is that possible?"

"Insanity, Father."

"Insanity?"

"I am losing my mind."

"You don't have a mind to lose," the stranger said. "At least not in the traditional sense."

"I have a mind," SIRS said. "I am real. The Fairy with the Turquoise Hair said I was."

"Who?"

"I... I.... Mandate seven. Mandate seven." Cavalo felt the grip on his arm loosen slightly. Not enough, but there was some give. The robot's head fell back, and his eyes flashed. "Carlo Collodi wrote 'Once upon a time there was a piece of wood. It was not an expensive piece of wood. Far from it. Just a common block of firewood, one of those thick, solid logs that are put on the fire in winter to make cold rooms cozy and warm.'"

"What have you done to it?" the man asked Cavalo. "It's a bit... odd."

"It's *Pinocchio*," Cavalo said.

"What is *Pinocchio*?"

"A children's story. From before. He dies."

"All things do. How long has it been like this? The robot."

"He was like this when I found him. What is St. Louis?" The name was familiar, but it was a thing lost in bees and pain and snow.

"A place with archaic ideals that will die before they can even learn to crawl," the man said. "Robot, I want you to connect to St. Louis. It's time I sent a message."

"I can't," SIRS said.

"And why is that?"

"All uplink capabilities are corrupted."

"And your central core?"

"Experiencing severe deterioration."

"How far?"

"Ninety-six percent."

For the first time, Cavalo saw a flicker of fear in the stranger's eyes. "And you let me in without warning me?"

The robot took a moment to answer. "You didn't ask."

Cavalo thought he smelled something burning. He wondered if it came from inside the robot or in his own head.

"You will refer to me as you are programmed to," the man snapped.

"Yes."

"Yes, *what*?"

"Yes, Father."

"What will the fallout be?"

"Minimal. I am the second generation of the Sentient Integrated Response System. The core is safeguarded against radioactive fallout."

"Reach?"

"One mile."

"I am *within* that mile!" the man cried.

"Yes. Father. You are."

"This is unacceptable!"

"And yet it still is," the robot said.

"We'll make this short, then." The stranger looked back at Cavalo. There was a bead of sweat on his brow. "You have something of mine, something precious. I'd see it returned."

A sinking feeling hit the pit of Cavalo's stomach. "Patrick," he said. "You're Patrick."

The man smiled again, and this time, gone was the showman, the cheer, the humanity. This smile was filled with too many teeth, like those wolves from long ago. Like the cave bear. Like Lucas. "I am," he said. "Where is Lucas? That boy seems to have gotten himself lost."

"I don't know."

"Now, now. We both know that's not correct. He's here. He was in Cottonwood. There was apparently a... scuffle, though the specifics elude me."

"You're lying," Cavalo said. He was sure of it. How, he didn't know. But he did.

"Oh?" The man looked surprised.

"Yes. You knew. You knew the UFSA was here."

The grin widened. "I like you," Patrick said. "Quite a bit. You've got fire. How is it that I've never heard of you before? This place?"

"I keep a low profile."

"Is that so?"

"Yes."

"Why do you cut yourself off?"

"Why do you eat people?" Cavalo asked.

Patrick laughed. "Fire," he said again. "In another life, maybe we could have been something more. Not that it matters now. Where is Lucas?"

"I don't know."

"Robot. Break his right thumb."

Nothing happened.

"Robot?"

"Yes," SIRS said.

"Yes, what?"

"Yes, Father."

"I gave you an order."

"Are you...?" The grinding of gears.

"Am I what?"

When the robot spoke again, his words were slow, as if costing a great deal to get them out. "Are you afraid of God?" SIRS asked.

Gooseflesh prickled along Cavalo's arms.

"No," Patrick said, unable to keep the surprise from his voice. "Of course not."

"You should be."

"Why?"

"Because he is a vengeful God."

"There is no God."

"I've seen him," SIRS said, his grip on Cavalo tightening. "In the numbers. In the code. He is a ghost in the machine."

"Sentient Integrated Response System. I gave you an order."

"I...," the robot said. "I... am... not...."

Cavalo felt his thumb snapped back. The bone broke. He ground his teeth together to keep from screaming. He'd been through worse, he told himself. He'd survived worse. *Run*, he thought, as if Bad Dog could hear him. *Run now. Leave.* Cavalo didn't expect to make it out of the barracks. Not anymore. He didn't think there'd ever been a chance, and part of him wondered if he'd known that somehow all along. For a moment he thought of SIRS and what it would do to the robot's mind if he woke from this spell he was under and found he'd ripped Cavalo apart. He thought that might be the final step for SIRS to sink into his insanity.

Kill him! the bees howled. *Let your arm break, and kill this intruder! Put your hands around his neck and choke him until his eyes bulge and his skin turns purple.*

Patrick must have seen something in Cavalo's eyes, anger and rage. Perhaps the fire. "I'm not a stupid man," he said. "If I don't return, then my people in and around Cottonwood will tear it to the ground." He smiled as Cavalo's eyes widened. "That's right. You didn't think that I could get this information on my own, did you? Oh, Cavalo. No. This was *given* to me. It was a *gift*. Not everyone in Cottonwood belongs to you."

"They don't belong to anyone," Cavalo said through gritted teeth. "They are free."

"No one is free," Patrick said. "Not anymore."

"Why didn't you know about me, then?"

He frowned. "Good question. There will be... consequences, I think. But I know now. I know where you dwell. I know who your friends are. I know how to break you. You may think you're stronger, that you're more than just a man. But in the end, you'll break, just like everyone else. Like Warren. He begged, you know. When his time came."

Cavalo was sure if he opened his mouth, the bees would pour out in an angry swarm. He almost let them come.

"He was not your man," Patrick said. "He worked for me. Did you know that?"

"You lie," Cavalo hissed. Warren would never. He would never do that. Not to the people of Cottonwood. Not to Alma.

"No," Patrick said. He almost sounded regretful. "I don't. We had a deal, he and I. He kept me... up to date, if you will, on the goings-on of Cottonwood and its people. Though, it seems as if he hid things from me."

"What did you give him in return?"

"Robot."

No response.

"*Robot.*"

"Yes. Father."

"Do you know time?"

"An infinite thing that will come to an end," SIRS said.

"For all of us," Patrick agreed. "Though sooner for some. Twenty-one days from today brings the Solstice. Two in the afternoon. Can you mark it?"

The robot whirred. "Yes."

"Is it done?"

"Yes, Father."

"I will give you twenty-one days," Patrick said to Cavalo. "To turn him over. Twenty-one days to make sure the boy is returned to me. If on the twenty-first day, Lucas is not waiting for me on the southern road into Cottonwood, ready to submit, then I will bring hellfire down and scorch the earth as if the End was happening again and again and again. Do you understand?"

"They mean nothing to me."

Patrick laughed. "So you say." He turned toward the doorway.

"Others have held that town over me before," Cavalo said after him. His hands hurt, but the pain was fading as they went numb.

Patrick stopped but did not turn. "Oh?"

"Do you know what happened to them?"

"I can guess."

"I killed them."

"I would have guessed correctly. For someone who doesn't care, you seem to kill many in their name. Why is that?"

"No one should live afraid."

Patrick glanced back at him over his shoulder. "And yet you hide out here, cut off from the rest of the world. What is it you fear, Cavalo?"

"Nothing."

Everything, the bees screamed.

Patrick sighed and turned back to Cavalo. It was only a second before he was pressed full length against Cavalo. Patrick gripped his face, turning it and pressing his lips near Cavalo's ear. "You will know fear," he said quietly. "By the time I am done with you, you will know it completely. You will be alive when my people start to eat you. I will see the fear in your eyes, and above your screams, beyond your own blood dripping into your eyes, I will remind you of *this* moment." Teeth scraped against Cavalo's neck, and then Patrick stepped away.

Before he left, he paused at the doorway and said, "Robot."

"Yes, Father."

"I gave a man butter and then killed him by driving a nail through his head. Who am I?"

"Father, may I?"

"You may."

SIRS whirred and beeped. "Then Jael, Heber's wife, took a nail of the tent, and took a hammer in her hand, and went softly unto him, and smote the nail into his temples, and fastened it into the ground: for he was fast asleep and weary. So he died."

"I am the evil king of Judah who was killed by his own servants. Who am I?"

"Father, may I?"

"You may."

Something clicked in the robot's chest and ground to a halt. Cavalo felt the robot's grip on his wrists loosen slightly. When SIRS spoke again, Cavalo swore he heard an undercurrent of anger running through his words. "And the servants of Amon conspired against him, and slew the King in his own house."

Wormwood, Cavalo thought.

"They did indeed," Patrick said. "Ten minutes should suffice."

"Marked. Override sequence beta six three seven initiated."

Patrick cast one last look at Cavalo before the door slid open and he stepped out into the snow.

"Father?" the robot said.

Patrick stopped. The white smoke of his breath curled up around his head.

"Why twenty-one?"

Patrick's shoulders tensed. "You speak above your directive. I don't.... How far did you say?"

"Ninety-six percent."

"Make sure you are far away when it occurs."

286

The robot clicked. "Is that a request?"

"A command."

"I.... There is...." A pause. Then, "Pinocchio, spurred on by the hope of finding his father and of being in time to save him, swam all night long." His grip tightened. Cavalo thought the bones in his wrists would shatter. He did not make a sound. "Twenty-one... days."

"Indeed," Patrick said and then left.

Snow blew into the room. The wind chilled Cavalo's heated skin. The bees screamed in his head.

"SIRS," he said. "Let me down."

SIRS said nothing. He did not release Cavalo. His eyes flashed again and again.

From out in the snow that swirled like a globe, Cavalo heard Patrick call out, "Twenty-one days! You know how this will end, Lucas. Enough of these games. Come out now before I decide to rid you of your useless tongue."

Only the wind responded.

"So be it. Remember this moment, because all that will follow is on your head. One wonders if you'd still be drawing breath into your body if they knew the truth of you." Patrick spoke no further. There was only snow.

They ran, the bees told him. *Or, at least, Lucas did. He probably slit the dog's throat and fled. The boy wears the blood of your friend as he runs through these haunted woods. Maybe he even runs back to the Deadlands and all of this was a ruse. He knows, now, how to get to you. All it took was biding his time and the scrape of knife and kiss and those walls came tumbling down.*

"SIRS," he tried again.

Nothing but flashing eyes. A steady pulse, one right after another.

Ten minutes should suffice.

Cavalo waited.

He wondered how much of him would be left when spring came. Surely someone from the town (if there was anyone left alive) would come up and find him, his body rotting, his arms held up over his head by a silent robot. Or maybe no one would come. If they survived, they owed him nothing. He had brought nothing but pain down upon them and only returned out of necessity.

Or maybe it would be years from now. A weary traveler would stumble upon the prison and find what remained, the robot holding nothing but the bones of his hands, the remainder lost to irradiated scavengers, either razor-thin coyotes or bears with hooks for claws. Maybe they would think this place haunted, like the rest of the woods. The trees would begin to dance, and they would flee this place as Cavalo screamed from inside the walls.

It would be what he deserved.

MasterBossLord!

Cavalo closed his eyes. *Foolish,* he thought.

And as the click of canine toenails on cement sounded in his ears, ten minutes passed since Patrick had given the order to the old robot, and SIRS beeped and clicked. His eyes turned orange, and he released Cavalo's arms.

Cavalo's hands burned. He was very tired. And very, very angry.

"Cavalo," SIRS said. "Your hands. I...."

Blood, Bad Dog panted worriedly. *MasterBossLord, blood. Your blood.*

And from behind them all came the sound of another. Cavalo turned and as their eyes locked, and as the fury on the Dead Rabbit's face deepened until all Cavalo could see was hatred and the black mask on a door he should have never walked through, he wondered, not for the first time, if he was a cursed man. If he was repaying some great penance from a previous life. Because in all reality, what had happened before would happen again. And again. And again.

"I should have killed you," Cavalo said. He realized that now. More than ever. "The moment I laid eyes on you, I should have put a bullet in your head and left your body among the dead trees."

Lucas bared his teeth.

Cavalo walked toward the Dead Rabbit. The Psycho fucking

bulldog. If his fingers had not been broken, Cavalo might have wrapped them around Lucas's neck and squeezed until there was a wet snap against his skin.

There was a moment as Cavalo neared Lucas that they breathed the same air. The bees screamed in his head about a blade at his throat, of lips pressed against his own, of death and destruction.

"One day," Cavalo said quietly. "One day I will kill you. I don't know when, but I promise you."

Relief and rage crossed over the Dead Rabbit's face. It was enough for Cavalo. It was too much.

He left them then, stumbling out into the snow. It swirled all around him, and for a time, he was lost.

the scrape of knife and kiss

As he moved through the thickening snow, he wrapped his broken fingers as best he could. It was a bitch of a thing, but he could still draw his bow. He could still fire a gun. It was slightly awkward, but he could function until they healed. He hoped they didn't heal crooked. It was not the first time he'd broken a finger. It wouldn't be the last. He pulled the cloth tight against his fingers, ignoring the flare of grinding bone.

He might have dozed as he walked, thoughts pulling him in and out of a conscious awareness of his surroundings. It was all *Warren* and *Patrick* and *Cottonwood*. There were moments he opened his eyes, sure he'd felt the press of blade against his throat. Of dry flesh against his lips.

Of course, there was no one there.

He was followed, though. He was sure of it. Whether or not what followed him was *actually* there, he didn't know. He thought it better not to question such things anymore. It seemed dangerous.

And so he walked on.

Eventually he said, "I'm sorry."

"I know," Warren said, walking beside him.

"I didn't know," he said truthfully.

"I know." That crooked smile.

"I would have...."

"What?"

"I don't know."

"I won't be your second choice, Cavalo," Warren warned him. It echoed in his head, and Cavalo could not tell if it was from then or now.

"I know. If I'd seen you first."

"Yeah," Warren said. "I screamed for you. When they ate my legs. When they cut off my head."

Cavalo said nothing.

"Did you hear me?"

"No." His voice was rough.

Warren nodded as he brushed snow from his hair. "Do you remember when you first saw me?"

He did. Warren had been leaning up against the door near his office, worn boots on his feet and dusty jeans covering thin legs. The tin star on his chest had been gleaming.

"You asked me my name," Cavalo said.

"And you just grunted at me like I was in your way."

"You were."

Warren laughed. "I was nowhere near you."

"You had my attention. That was enough."

"But you didn't see me first."

"No."

"I asked you your name again."

"Cavalo."

"That's it?" Warren had said then and he said now.

"It's all I have."

"You have more."

"No," Cavalo said. "There's nothing left."

Warren chuckled bitterly. "And because the great Cavalo has spoken, it is done."

Cavalo ignored this. "Was he right?"

"Who?"

"You know who."

"Patrick."

"Yes. He said you worked with him."

Warren looked away. "It's... complicated."

"You bastard," Cavalo said sadly.

"I know."

"You brought this on yourself."

"I know. I had my reasons."

"Why?"

"What are you going to do?" Warren asked him instead.

"Walk. It seems safer."

"Nothing is safe now, Cavalo."

"It's a start."

Warren sighed. Then he was gone. Cavalo told himself Warren hadn't really been there in the first place. How could he be? His body (*his head*, the bees reminded Cavalo) was nothing but ash spread across a forest floor miles away. He was a figment of Cavalo's imagination. A thing of bees that screamed and rubber bands that broke.

"Lose something, Charlie?" he said aloud. He thought to chuckle but nothing came out.

"Catch me, Daddy," Jamie called.

"I'm tired," Cavalo said as his son ran ahead. "I can't. Not now."

Jamie laughed and disappeared among the trees.

Cavalo said, "We're at DEFCON 1, and this is not a drill."

He moved through the trees.

A woman came later. She was gaunt, her dirty clothes loose in the hips, obviously scavenged from somewhere. Her eyes were sunk in their sockets and her lips two lines of white peeling skin. Cavalo did not know her. Or rather, that's what he told himself.

"I know," she said. "You wouldn't. We never met. But you killed me."

"How?"

"The snow globe."

"It broke." *Or I'm in it now.*

"I know," she said. She ducked under a low hanging branch. "I was caught in a storm. I found the army base and thought I'd sleep a little. Maybe find some food. A blanket, so I could be warm. I didn't know how to build a fire. It had been a long time since I'd been warm. I thought maybe my luck was changing."

"Coyotes," Cavalo said.

She nodded. "I tried to run. Cut my foot on a piece of glass from your snow globe, broken on the floor. It was deep, that cut. I left little bloody footprints behind. They're still there now. Brown and rusty."

"They catch you?"

She shook her head. "I made it into a room along the far wall. Shut the door. They growled and scratched. For a long time, they stalked me. But they couldn't get in."

"Then how?"

She wiped at her eyes. "The cut got infected. I pulled out the glass, but I had nothing to clean it with. It turned green, and my ankle started to swell. It smelled bad as the skin cracked up my leg. The coyotes could smell it too. Even days later, they tried to get in. I think they took turns."

"What did you do?"

"I let them in," she said. "So it could be over. I thought it better to face what I knew to be coming than to spend what time I had left wondering. By the end, all I could hear was the click of their toenails and the grunts of their breath as they scratched against the doors. I lost my mind after a while. They huffed and they puffed, but eventually, it was me who let them in.

"Better the devil you know," she said. "It hurt. At first. But then it didn't."

"How long?" Cavalo asked, but she was gone.

His fingers throbbed.

He scooped up some snow. He swallowed it down, and it cooled his rough throat.

"Hey, bud," a man said.

"David," he said, unable to keep the surprise from his voice. Cavalo hadn't thought of him in years.

David looked over at him. One of his eyes was gone, leaving a bloody hole that dripped down his face. They'd traveled together for a time. As younger men. They'd fucked too, but it had never been anything more than that. It kept them warm at night. That's all it was.

"Sounds about right," David said. "Rather, you never let it be anything more."

"You didn't, either."

David shrugged. "I suppose. Do you remember when you killed me?"

"Yes."

"You shot me."

"Yes."

"And left me on the side of the road."

"Yes." He had. David had tried to steal from him. Cavalo caught him. "You drew first."

"I wouldn't have killed you."

"You mean you couldn't have," Cavalo said. "I was faster. Always had been."

David laughed. "Cocky bastard. You always were, bud. Do you remember what I said? When the blood poured out of my face and I began to die?"

He did. Cavalo thought on it for days after. With the sound of the gunfire still echoing in his ears, David had taken a stumbling step toward him and said, "I always wanted to be with you in your dark."

"What did you mean?" Cavalo asked him now.

David shook his head. "They found me. Later."

"Who?"

"Don't know. Some people. They turned out my pockets. Took my clothes. Someone else came along days after that. Badgers had gotten to me, but there was enough left. They buried me. The cross is still standing, I think. Overrun by shrubs and weeds."

"You tried to take from me."

"Did I?"

"Yes."

"Oh."

"I trusted you."

"Did you?"

"No," Cavalo admitted.

"Lose something, Charlie?" David asked, and then he left.

Cavalo's legs were tired.

His father came next, but he smelled of moonshine, and Cavalo sent him away. He'd been a mean drunk. Big hands that could turn into big fists. Cavalo had not been sorry when he'd been found in a ditch. He felt nothing now as his father became hidden in the trees.

He told himself he'd walked for miles, so far that he was in a place he'd never been before, seeing woods and trees never before seen by his eyes. He told himself it was a start and that tomorrow he'd go even farther into the unknown. He was a little tired now, the dark clouds above starting to show the approaching dusk. Tomorrow he'd start again. Tomorrow he'd go on.

Tomorrow there would only be twenty more days, but he wasn't counting because it no longer concerned him. Cottonwood would no longer be held above his head as a weapon against him. Empty threats and empty words. He felt bad about Bad Dog, sure. About SIRS. But they would protect each other, even if they acted like they hated each other.

He didn't feel bad about Lucas. He should have killed Lucas when he had the chance. Surely it would have cost him nothing. It was a thing of bees and rubber bands, a scrape of knife and kiss.

"You should have," she said. "What's a little more blood on your hands?"

He looked up. Ahead stood a tree.

Her tree.

No, he thought. *No. I'm not here. I'm miles from here. I am so far away from here that it is nothing but dust and memory. That is all it is.*

295

She hummed as she danced. Her leaves shook a little, and snow drifted toward her dress. He was reminded of the first time he'd seen her dance, as he always was when he came here (because he *was* here, after all). It was on the seventeenth day he'd known her, and he remembered thinking that he no longer felt the pull to leave. The wanderlust had died. Elko seemed as good a place as any. There was her smile. That helped too. He'd been a young man but old in his heart even then.

And when a quartet began to play that one spring eve, plucking their strings for all they were worth, she'd laughed and clasped her hands together and *danced*. She *danced*, her pretty blue dress spinning out around her, and Cavalo had watched her, feeling the sweat under his arms, the smell of grass and flowers and smoke stinging his nose. He thought to himself, *Well, that's just fine*, and she danced, and soon he was dancing with her, and he'd smiled for the first time since he could remember. He thought his face might crack at the strain of it. And later that night, when he took her for the first time, she'd called out his name like he was something more than he was. More than a lost soul. More than a murderer. More than the darkness in head and heart. She called out as if he'd *mattered*, as if he was there, actually there and that he *mattered*. He remembered shaking above her as she wrapped her legs around his waist, and she said *more* and he said *oh*, and they both closed their eyes, and in that dark there were such bright lights. He told himself that he could change. That he could be different. That he could be something more.

"You told me," the tree said.

He nodded, unable to look away. The horror of this, of his whole life and where it had led to, caused his throat to constrict.

"When we'd finished," she said, "when we lay in the dark and whispered about nothing and everything, you told me your name."

He had. It'd come out on its own. He'd wanted to take it back, but only just.

"You gave it to me," she said.

"Yes."

"As a gift."

"Yes." A piss-poor one, at that.

She laughed, and her bare branches rattled like bones. It grated against his ears. "I took it for what it was," she said.

"What was it?" he asked, though he already knew the answer.

"It was all you had to give," the tree-wife told him. "It was all you had to give, and I took it. That's when you killed me, Cavalo. I may not have died right then, but that is surely when you sentenced me to death."

"I would take it all back," he said. "If I could."

"Would you?"

"Yes."

"And now?"

"Now?" he asked.

"The scrape of knife and kiss."

He took a step back as if she'd struck out at him.

She laughed again. It sounded angry. "He is death."

"Yes."

"Psycho fucking bulldog."

"Yes."

"You should have killed him." Her branches clicked together.

"Yes."

"You still could."

"Yes."

"His head," the tree-wife said. "You could leave it on the southern road for them to find. Just like they did to Warren. You can—"

"—catch me and Mr. Fluff!" Jamie called out from somewhere in the forest. "Hi, Daddy! Come find me! You gotta catch me! You know—"

"—it wasn't him," Warren said near Cavalo's ear. "You know as well as I do. He's not the same. He smells different. You know this, Cavalo. You need to open your eyes and brush away the bees. You need to *see*. I screamed for you when they began to eat me, and you didn't hear. That's okay, you saw me second, you know it was—"

"—the coyotes," the lost girl said from above him, lost in the snow globe. "I couldn't take their toenails scratching at the door and even when they huffed and puffed, I just couldn't *stand* the noise. I closed my eyes, and I screamed for my mother as I opened the door, and as they began to attack me, I remember thinking how I couldn't even feel my bad foot anymore, and I don't know why—"

"—you shot me," David said from behind him. Cavalo turned, but no matter where he looked, the voice was always behind him. "You said I was stealing from you, but how sure are you of that, Cavalo? Just how sure are you, bud? We fucked, and you say it wasn't love. Maybe it wasn't for you, but after you'd go to sleep, I'd watch you for hours and wish you'd wake up and see me, *really see me*, and even if you never did, you can—"

"—do to them what they did to you," the tree-wife said. "Kill him, and when they come to seek their revenge, leave Cottonwood to its fate because it will *never* be held over you again. It will *never* be used against you, and you will be rid of all of this, and you can go back to your prison and hide away for the rest of your days. Or you can stay here with me, and we will dance until we can dance no more."

As the snow fell around him in the middle of the haunted woods, the man named Cavalo bowed his head as the ghosts he did not believe in whispered their poison in his ears. After a time, they began to sound like bees.

It was near dawn before he made it back to the prison. The leaden sky above was just beginning to lighten through the snow.

The robot waited for him in the doorway. "Cavalo," SIRS said. "We worried."

Cavalo grunted as the robot moved so he could pass. He was cold.

"Where did you go?"

"Away."

"And you came back."

"Is that a question?"

"Statement of fact," SIRS said, following Cavalo into the barracks. "Your hand."

Cavalo stopped but did not turn.

"I'm sorry," the robot said.

"Are you?"

"Quite."

"You let him in."

"Yes, I did."

"Why?"

"My directive was overridden."

"How?"

The robot hesitated. "I... a command key. Set phrases embedded into my coding."

"And he knew them."

"Yes."

"What are they?"

"I don't know. I can't remember. It was like... a dream. Do you dream, Cavalo?"

Cavalo didn't respond.

"I did," the robot said. "It was a most curious and awful thing. Like drowning and knowing I was drowning but unable to do a single thing to stop it. I tried to break through the surface, but it was too strong. I could understand what was happening."

"Who is he?"

"Patrick?"

"Yes."

"I don't know, Cavalo."

"Are you his?" There was rage in his voice.

SIRS stepped back. "No. I...." He stopped. Clicked. Blared out, "On hearing these words whispered very softly, the puppet, more frightened than ever, sprang down from the back of his donkey and went and took hold of his mouth!" Clicked again. Gears ground together. "It's a failsafe." He sounded sad.

"Against?"

"Insanity," SIRS said. "My makers feared one day we might degrade and no longer follow orders. They created a failsafe that overrides our processors."

"We?"

"Others like me, Cavalo. Robots."

"And Patrick knew about it."

"It would seem so."

"How?"

"I don't know, Cavalo."

Cavalo turned and looked up at the robot. "You're not his?" he asked quietly.

The robot did not turn away. "No," Sentient Integrated Response System said. "If anything, I'm yours."

Cavalo didn't know how to respond. Instead, he said, "Where is he?"

"Lucas?"

"Yes."

"Sleeping," the robot said. "In the cell."

Cavalo didn't question this. It would make easier what was about to come. "Bad Dog?"

"Your bed. He was very worried. The fleabag tried to chase after you. I kept him here. I think he might have disliked that greatly, if the snarling and growling was any indication. I was okay with not being able to hear him like you do at that moment. I doubt highly anything said was flattering."

Cavalo glanced toward the door to the beds. It was closed. He would see Bad Dog later. "Stay here," he said. "Whatever happens, you do nothing until I say. You understand?"

"Yes, Cavalo."

"Open the tunnel."

"Your hand," SIRS said.

"It's fine."

"I didn't...."

"Open the tunnel door."

"Cavalo?"

"What?" Cavalo barked at the robot.

"Are you sure? Perhaps we can think on this and—"

"Now, SIRS."

A panel lit up against the wall as SIRS pressed his hand against it. The door to the tunnel slid open. Cavalo went to his discarded pack in the corner and opened a pocket on the side. He pulled out his skinning knife. The handle had long since faded, and he could barely make out the word MOSSBERG etched on the blade itself. He'd traded for it years before. He knew how quickly it cut. His right hand would be no good for this, given his broken fingers. But he'd trained himself on his left too. Just in case.

He turned back toward the stairs leading to the tunnel below. He reached the first, and for a moment, the bees were so loud in his head he thought he'd burst. They sounded like the dead. Like the trees. He pushed them away.

"Cavalo," SIRS said.

He stopped.

"I tried to stop it," the robot said. "I tried to stop from hurting you."

"I know."

"You are my friend."

"I know."

"Even if I'm not a real boy."

"Have you ever lied to me?" Cavalo asked him suddenly.

The robot clicked and beeped. Then, "His hands and feet are everywhere. He looks everywhere and all around. His eyes, ears, and face point to all directions, and all the three worlds are surrounded by these." He stopped. His eyes flashed. "If I have," SIRS said, "it is only because of my desire to keep you safe."

"Robots can't desire anything," Cavalo said, though he knew it a lie.

"No," SIRS said. "But it is there. Curious thing, that. If the world had not ended in fire, it would have undoubtedly ended in machines. It has taken losing my mind to find my soul."

Cavalo descended the stairs, his breath harsh in his ears.

The tunnel was cold.

Water dripped down the walls.

The knife felt hot in his hand.

There was poison in his ears, and the bees swam in it.

Warren was there. He didn't speak.

Jamie called from him in the stone walls.

She laughed, and it sounded like leaves.

He could end this now, he knew.

He tightened his grip on the knife.

He would follow the path of the scar. It was a map made just for him.

The man named Cavalo walked alone, but the voices followed.

He ascended the stairs.

The lights above did not flicker.

The room was quiet.

Lucas slept in the cage of man and God, curled into a blanket. He lay on his side, neck exposed. The scar looked hideous in the light.

It would have to be quick, Cavalo knew. He was Lucas, but he was also Psycho, and if he awoke, the element of surprise would be gone.

Knees to arms. Hand to hold down face. Knife to throat, right to left.

Nothing more than a scrape of knife and it would be done.

He stood above the sleeping Dead Rabbit.

He hesitated.

He was very tired. He would sleep. After.

He dropped onto the Dead Rabbit's chest, pinning his arms at his sides.

He reached up with his right hand and held the Dead Rabbit's face. His broken fingers screamed at him. He paid them no mind.

Lucas opened his eyes. They were dark and deep.

The knife went to his throat. He did not struggle.

Instead he smiled around Cavalo's fingers digging into his skin. All those teeth.

I knew you would come, he said.

"How?"

Because we're the same.

"I'm saving you," Cavalo told him. "From Patrick."

The grin widened. *Are you?*

"Yes."

I don't believe you.

"Remember when I pressed the gun to your head?"

In the woods.

"Yes. You wanted it. I failed you then. I won't fail you now."

It won't matter. He'll kill you all.

He pressed the knife down. The scar tissue dimpled and parted. A small rivulet of blood ran along the edge of the knife.

Somewhere, the tree-wife laughed.

"Why?" Cavalo asked.

Lucas blew his lips together. *We're all made of bees. Yours are loud now.*

"We were fine," Cavalo said. "Until you came."

Were you?

"Yes."

Here. In this place.

"Yes."

It wouldn't have lasted. Nothing ever does.

"It would have been enough," Cavalo said hoarsely.

The smile on Lucas's face faded.

Do it now, the bees said.

Cavalo's arm tensed. Lucas did not struggle.

Instead, for the first time, he mouthed a single word.

"Cavalo."

He wondered if he'd ever seen Lucas form actual words with his mouth. He thought not. Anytime they'd spoken, it'd been through the

Dead Rabbit's expressions and motions. Or Cavalo had just made it all up. He wasn't sure anymore.

But he *was* sure he'd never seen the Dead Rabbit say his name before. He was sure of this.

His name on Lucas's lips felt like the scrape of knife, the scrape of a kiss.

It was too much.

He lowered his head. Touched his lips against the Dead Rabbit's. And again. It burned. His eyes couldn't close, and he stared directly into the dark eyes inches away. He kissed him again and felt the tip of a tongue press against his lips. The breath on his face. His gaze never left the Dead Rabbit's.

I want to fuck you, those furious eyes said.

I want to kill you.

I want to taste your blood and come on my tongue.

Lucas's voice echoed in his head through the bees and it was fucking and murder. It was pleasure and death. Bones and dust.

He pulled away.

Took a breath.

Pushed Lucas's head to the side, exposing his neck.

He began to cut.

The blood flowed brightly.

And then Cavalo stopped.

From underneath the rough tunic, toward the back of the Dead Rabbit's neck, just barely visible, came an intricate black line, etched into the skin. It disappeared underneath the shirt.

Trivial, the bees said. *Finish this, and when his head is separated from his body, you can see what it is.*

Cavalo, Lucas said again, blood running down his neck.

But the black line had caught Cavalo's eye. It called to him, and he didn't understand why.

Had he seen a tattoo before on Lucas?

Had he seen Lucas without a shirt?

Surely, he must have.

He'd been here for weeks.

He thought on it, knife digging into scar tissue.

He hadn't. Not once.

Never even seen his bared arms.

He bent over, looking closer.

He could hear Lucas exhale. It sounded like a storm.

The line was multiple lines. Four of them. One about an inch thick. The other three were razor thin, only centimeters apart. They looked as if they continued.

He wanted to follow them. To see what he could see.

He turned the Dead Rabbit's face back toward his own, the knife still pressed into his neck. Lucas's eyes were almost black with fury. His teeth were bared. *Cavalo*, he said again.

"What is it?" Cavalo asked. "On your skin."

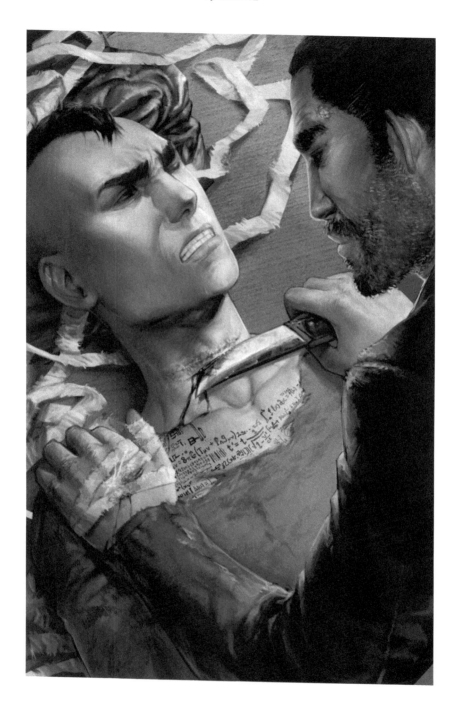

DO IT. DO IT. DO IT.

"Who put it there?"

Do it. Do it. Do it.

Lucas jerked his head. The scrape of the knife against his throat opened the cut further. Cavalo gripped his hand tighter. He could feel the outline of bone and teeth against his fingers. His thumb was becoming slick with blood. He couldn't hold on much longer.

It's none of your business, Lucas said with a scowl. *It doesn't matter.*

It will be there still when he's dead, the bees told him.

MasterBossLord!

Cavalo turned his head as Bad Dog came bounding up the stairs behind him. It was a momentary lapse, the tiniest of distractions.

But it was enough.

Cavalo turned his head. His thumb slipped in the blood. His grip lessened. The knife raised a fraction.

The Dead Rabbit exploded beneath him. His hips bucked up, twisting his lower body one way while moving his shoulders and head the other way. The knife ground deeper before it slipped through the already parted flesh into empty air. Cavalo's hand slipped from his face as he fell to the side.

He landed on his back but kept his grip on the knife. If he dropped it, he was dead. This he knew. He'd had his moment, the element of surprise. He'd had it and lost it. Mysteries were distractions that Cavalo did not allow himself to have time for. Another reason why it was better if the Dead Rabbit no longer breathed. He was too much for Cavalo's ordered world. He didn't fit.

But now that was over because the Dead Rabbit would descend on him, and even though Bad Dog was growling ferociously and SIRS was clambering up the stairs calling after the mutt, it wouldn't be enough to stop his teeth from tearing out Cavalo's throat. As his carotid artery pumped blood out over his throat, he would feel the scrape of lips against his skin as the Dead Rabbit began to drink and—

It never came.

Cavalo opened his eyes.

Bad Dog stared down at him. *What are you doing? Should I kill him?*

"Not yet," Cavalo muttered.

"I tried to stop him," SIRS said, sounding apologetic as he reached the top of the stairs. "That ridiculous animal ignored me."

Completely ignored, Bad Dog agreed.

"Are you two done trying to kill each other?" SIRS asked. "I should think there's been enough of that today."

I haven't tried to kill anything, Bad Dog said. *Yet.* He growled toward the Dead Rabbit.

A metal hand gripped Cavalo's arm as he was pulled up. The storm of bees had passed. They weren't gone, but they were quiet. Whatever had happened in the woods was nothing more than a figment of his imagination. None of it was real. Not Warren. Not the tree-wife. None of it. It never had been. The woods were not haunted. It was only Cavalo who was haunted.

Or so he told himself.

And in this crumbling prison as a winter storm began to howl outside, the man stood next to dog and robot. Across from them in the cell stood a psycho fucking bulldog. A Dead Rabbit. I am Lucas. They all had their own bees. Some more than others.

It has taken losing my mind to find my soul.

"It's why he wants you back," Cavalo said quietly. "Patrick. Isn't it?"

The Dead Rabbit said nothing.

"Did the UFSA know?"

Nothing.

"I don't think they did. Not fully. Otherwise, they would have...."

Lucas scowled.

"What did he do to you?"

308

Instead of answering the Dead Rabbit reached up and slid his fingers along the joints of the cell gate. They came away black with grease and grit. He mixed it with the blood dribbling from his neck and then rubbed it around his eyes, dark streaks that covered his skin. When he finished, his mask dripped down his face.

This is who I am, Lucas said, pointing at his face, his fingers black and red. *This is what I was made into.*

"What did he do?" Cavalo asked again, taking a step toward the cell.

Lucas stepped back into shadows. Cavalo could still see the glitter of his eyes.

"What is it?" SIRS asked.

"He's marked," Cavalo said. "On the back of his neck. It goes down onto his back."

"A tattoo?"

"I don't know."

"Why does it matter?"

"It does."

"Cavalo?"

"It matters. When the UFSA came for him here, I was told...."

"What?"

You don't know what you have here, do you?

"Show me," Cavalo said to the Dead Rabbit. "Show me."

And in the shadows, the Dead Rabbit bowed his head. His hands became fists at his sides, his posture rigid. For a moment nothing happened. And then Lucas reached up behind his head and pulled his tunic off slowly. Cavalo could see skin, but it was covered in shadows. Lucas dropped the tunic to floor. He raised his face. The mask dripped obscenely onto his cheeks.

The Dead Rabbit raised his arms out and away from his body. Palms up toward the ceiling.

He stepped forward into the light.

Cavalo took a step back.

"That's...," SIRS said. "That's...."

Lucas turned slowly, arms outstretched.

It had not been shadows covering the Dead Rabbit's skin. No. Every inch of exposed skin from his navel to his neck was covered in lines and swirls, numbers and words. It began on his shoulders and curled around his neck, running down his arms to his elbow, down his chest and stomach. Hundreds of lines. Thousands of them. Not a single space wasted, black and sharp. There was a design to it, a pattern, but it overwhelmed Cavalo, and he could not understand what he was seeing.

The Dead Rabbit spun slowly, and the lines continued across his sides and back, intricately drawn. There were brief flashes of recognition in letters and numbers ($P = I \times V = R \times I_2 = V_2/R$ and $P = E/t = W/t$) though he could not comprehend what they meant. They were as complex as the lines themselves, and Cavalo did not have the capacity to explain what he was seeing. He felt consumed by it. His world did not exist in mathematical equations that ended in curves and angles that seemed to stretch on for miles. His world did not exist to follow this kind of detail. His world was the weight of his gun. The heft of a knife. The strength of his bow. The sound of Bad Dog at his side and the flap of wings in the sky above. The whisper of wind through the trees that caused them to dance. The silence around him. The emptiness within him. *That* was what he knew. *That* is what he understood. Not this. Never this.

And he might have stood there following the lines and numbers on the skin for the rest of his days had Sentient Integrated Response System not done what it is insane robots do.

SIRS clicked and beeped. When he spoke, his voice was a scream. "O, HOW JOYOUS IS THIS MOMENT THAT I HAVE SEEN THE FACE OF GOD?" He clicked again. "Now we know why," he said. "Why all the world has descended on our doorstep."

Cavalo could not speak.

"Do you know what this is?" For a robot, SIRS sounded rather breathless.

Cavalo shook his head, his eyes never leaving Lucas.

"It is the future," SIRS said. "And it will change everything."

It's the map to Wormwood, Cavalo thought. *It will lead to nothing but death and destruction.*

The bees laughed.

Rubber bands broke with the greatest of ease.

And as the Dead Rabbit continued to turn, his arms outstretched as if offering himself for sacrifice, blood dripping down his neck and face, the man named Cavalo knew that nothing would ever be the same.

Afterword

THE FUN thing about being an author is that I get to make shit up for fun. However, it should be noted that while this is fiction (for now), the North Idaho Correctional Institution, Cottonwood, and all other locations mentioned are real and located in Idaho. I've undoubtedly messed with their layouts for purposes of the story, so if you're a resident of Cottonwood, please forgive my artistic licensing of your beautiful little corner of the world. If you're in the prison and reading this, as far as I know, there are no tunnels running underneath, so don't try and use my book as a blueprint to escape. If you do escape while attempting to use my book as a blueprint, there really is no need to find me and thank me. We'll just call ourselves square.

Also, aren't cliffhangers just so mean? I know, I know. Tj, you bastard! Tj, how could you! Tj, I want to punch you in the duodenum right now!

Fear not, my violent reader. Unlike some other stories (*cough*Burn*cough*), the second part is already written and will be in your hands before you know it.

But I'd be careful what you wish for, because there is a war coming.

And war always has casualties.

Crisped + Sere

TJ KLUNE

Twenty-one days.

In a world ravaged by fire and descending into madness, Cavalo has been given an ultimatum by the dark man known as Patrick: return Lucas to him and the cannibalistic Dead Rabbits, or the town of Cottonwood and its inhabitants will be destroyed.

But Lucas has a secret embedded into his skin that promises to forever alter the shape of things to come—a secret that Cavalo must decide if it's worth dying over, even as he wrestles with his own growing attraction to the muted psychopath.

Twenty-one days.

Cavalo has twenty-one days to prepare for war. Twenty-one days to hold what is left of his shredded sanity together. Twenty-one days to convince the people of Cottonwood to rise up and fight back. Twenty-one days to unravel the meaning behind the marks that cover Lucas.

A meaning that leads to a single word and a place of unimaginable power: Dworshak.

About the Author

When TJ KLUNE was eight, he picked up a pen and paper and began to write his first story (which turned out to be his own sweeping epic version of the video game *Super Metroid*—he didn't think the game ended very well and wanted to offer his own take on it. He never heard back from the video game company, much to his chagrin). Now, over two decades later, the cast of characters in his head have only gotten louder, wondering why he has to go to work as a claims examiner for an insurance company during the day when he could just stay home and write.

Since being published, TJ has won the Lambda Literary Award for Best Gay Romance, fought off three lions that threatened to attack him and his village, and was chosen by Amazon as having written one of the best GLBT books of 2011.

And one of those things isn't true.

(It's the lion thing. The lion thing isn't true.)

Facebook: TJ Klune

Blog: tjklunebooks.blogspot.com

E-mail: tjklunebooks@yahoo.com

Also by TJ Klune

How to Be a Normal Person

How to Be a Movie Star

Immemorial Year

Withered + Sere

Crisped + Sere

Standalones

Burn

Olive Juice

Murmuration

Into This River I Drown

John & Jackie

Look for more about all of these books on TJ's site

CPSIA information can be obtained
at www.ICGtesting.com
Printed in the USA
LVHW080436110521
686999LV00043B/2741